CHRIS RYAN

ULTIMATE WEAPON

arrow books

Published in the United Kingdom by Arrow Books in 2007

11

First published in the United Kingdom in 2006 by Century
First published in paperback in 2007 by Arrow Books

Arrow Books
The Random House Group Limited
20 Vauxhall Bridge Road, London, SW1V 2SA

Addresses for companies within The Random House Group Limited
can be found at: www.randomhouse.co.uk/offices.htm

The Random House Group Limited Reg. No. 954009

A CIP catalogue record for this book
is available from the British Library

ISBN 978 0 09 949214 6

The Random House Group Limited supports The Forest Stewardship
Council (FSC), the leading international forest certification organisation. All
our titles that are printed on Greenpeace approved FSC certified paper carry
the FSC logo. Our paper procurement policy can be found at:
www.rbooks.co.uk/environment

Typeset by Palimpsest Book Production Limited, Grangemouth, Stirlingshire
Printed in the UK by CPI Bookmarque, Croydon, CR0 4TD

Acknowledgements

To my agent Barbara Levy, editor Mark Booth, Charlotte Haycock, Charlotte Bush and all the rest of the team at Century.

PROLOGUE

16 November 1994.

Nick Scott walked in silence. He could feel the cold air blowing down from the side of the mountain, brushing across his raw skin. A thin sweater was all that was covering his chest, and a light dusting of snow was filling the morning air. It made no difference, thought Nick sullenly. A man who has lost his wife doesn't feel the cold. He doesn't feel heat, pain or pleasure, or any other sensation. Just a frozen emptiness inside.

Particularly when the man knows he has only himself to blame.

He glanced up towards the mountains. The heights of Les Houches, the smaller of the two mountains that dominated the Chamonix valley, were right ahead of him. A shaft of sunlight suddenly broke through the clouds, illuminating its lustrous white surface, while on the other side of the ravine the larger Mont Blanc was still shrouded in mist and cloud. It was a week now since Mary had died. Three days since they had buried her, here among the mountains she loved, and where they had hoped to make their new life together. A life that didn't involve war, fighting, endurance or survival.

A life that had nothing to do with the Regiment. Just the two of them, their ski school and their daughter. A small, happy family, just the way it always should have been.

And now it's gone, buried along with Mary, and every other dream I've ever had.

'You OK?' he said, looking towards Sarah.

'I'm scared,' she replied flatly.

She was walking at his side, the buttons of her ski jacket done up tight against her thin neck. Just fifteen, thought Nick. Christ, she was young. Sometimes he had to pinch himself to remind himself that although she was starting to look like a woman she was still just a kid. Ever since she was born, she'd constantly surprised him with how fast she'd developed. Sarah was always ahead of the other kids, able to talk at two, count at three and read before she was four: it was as if she was rushing through life, getting her childhood out of the way, crashing forwards towards a rendezvous with her own destiny. When your dad's as rubbish as I am, maybe you have to grow up fast, he reflected bitterly. *With no one to look after you, you learn to look after yourself.*

'I'm scared of what's going to become of us now that Mum's not around any more.'

She stopped in the snow, and turned to face him. Her expression was worried, frightened. Sarah had long brown hair, and blue eyes that shone out of her thin, freckled face like the headlamps on a car. Her features were delicate, finely painted like her mother's, but in her forehead and across her cheekbones there were traces of her father's brute, ox-like strength. 'You can say what you like, but I just know,' she continued. 'We're not going to be OK.'

'Of course we are,' snapped Nick. 'I'll look after you.'

'What happened to you in Iraq, Dad?'

The words struck Nick harder than any of the bullets he had ever taken. A bullet was just a lump of cold steel. It could tear through your flesh, and fracture your bones, but so long as you were still alive it left your spirit intact. This was worse. This hurt in a way that no bullet ever could.

'I'm all right,' he said quickly.

She walked two paces ahead of him, twisting into one of the pathways that started to lead up the side of the mountain. They had lived here for just over a year now, but she had adjusted to the place much better than he had. Sarah spoke French like a local, and had adapted to the school. As for me, thought Nick, I have hardly got to know a soul. I came here to escape. *But you can't escape from yourself.*

'I'm fifteen,' she said, not turning to look at him. 'I can handle the truth.'

The truth, thought Nick. Maybe she can handle it, and maybe I can't. The bald outlines of the story were clear enough. He was a Regiment man, had been for a decade. He'd just missed the Falklands War but had been involved in every action the SAS had fought in since then, and fought with distinction as well. He had the medals and the scars to prove he was as good as any man in the Regiment. Then, in the lead-up to the Iraq

War, he'd been dropped into enemy country. First into Kurdistan, then travelling south in a small unit of four men until they hit Baghdad. Two of his mates had been killed on the way. Two of them had been captured. What happened to Ken, Nick had no idea. The last memory he had of him was the grimace of defiance on his face as the Iraqi soldiers smashed the butts of the rifles into his ribs as they led him away. Probably rotting in a shallow, unmarked grave by now. Nick had been taken into the prison cells below Saddam's Republican Palace, and tortured. What the hell they'd been trying to get out of him, he never knew. Perhaps it was just sadism. Their army was getting whipped, and they needed someone to take it out on. He just happened to be there. It was nothing personal. It just felt like that when they were plugging electrodes into your balls.

It was only after the war had ended, as part of the ceasefire agreement, that Nick had been released. He had had no idea the war had even ended, and when they came to haul him out of the dark, dank cell in which he had been living for the past few weeks, he'd assumed it was a firing squad he was about to meet, not a helicopter to ferry him home. It had taken two months in hospital to patch up his wounds, but the mental damage had been far worse than the physical impact. After he returned to the Regiment, it was impossible to get back to soldiering again. The orders didn't make any sense. The training had no purpose. The missions seemed stupid. After a year, he quit, disgusted with both himself and the army.

'Nothing happened in Iraq, silver girl,' he said, slipping into the nickname he'd had for Sarah since she was a toddler.

He put his arm across her shoulder, but she shook it away.

'Then why are we here?'

The move had been made just a few months after Nick had left the army. Nick and Mary had talked about opening a ski school for years. Both of them loved the mountains, and they had met on the French Alps twenty years earlier when he was doing his army ski training and Mary had been waitressing in one of the tourist bars. They'd taken Sarah from the moment she was born: she could practically ski before she could walk. They'd leased a small office, hired Heinz, a young German skier, to help out, and Nick had done most of the teaching while Mary took the bookings and looked after the accounts. But nothing had gone the way Nick had planned it. The first season was tough, and the clients were all idiots. Rich bankers from London who could barely stand up, let alone ski, and who thought it was Nick's fault. They spoke to you like you were dirt. A couple of times he'd lost it, shouting at them. Couldn't help myself, they were spastics, he said later. But word soon got around that he was difficult. Mary was furious with him, and the bookings were starting to dry up. They'd sunk all their savings into this school. They were arguing all the time.

We argued the night she died . . .

'To do something different with our lives,' said Nick.

'I don't want to,' said Sarah, her voice suddenly icy with controlled anger. 'I don't want to be here.' Tears were starting to stream down her face. 'I just want my mum back.'

'It's going to be OK,' said Nick, reaching out for her.

'No, it's not,' screamed Sarah. 'Nothing's going to be OK, not now, not ever.'

She was running away from him now, her legs skidding across the frozen surface of the track. Her hair had come loose, and was now streaming in the wind behind her. Not ever, heard Nick, the words bouncing off the side of the mountain, and bouncing back towards him. Nothing's going to be OK, not ever.

And the worst of it is, maybe she's right.

Nick caught up with her, reaching out with his arms, hugging her tight to his body. Her breath was short, gasping. 'I just want to hide from the world,' said Sarah, wiping the tears away from her eyes.

Nick glanced up towards the brooding slopes of Les Houches. There was a dip on the left-hand side of the mountain, where the rock seemed to fade into the cloud to create a shape like a crescent. 'You see that mountain,' he said, cradling Sarah in his arms. 'I hid in a mountain just like that when I was dropped into Kurdistan. Hiding isn't as simple as you think it is when you're fifteen. It's hard, lonely work that cuts into a man's soul. Hide for long enough and you forget who you even are.'

Sarah turned to look at him, her eyes fierce with anger. 'Well, you should know, Dad. You've been hiding ever since you came back from that stupid war.'

ONE

10 February 2003.

Jed Bradley could feel the muscles in his neck tightening. His throat was dry, and the knuckles on his broad, strong fists were tapping against the surface of the wooden table. I don't mind being dropped from a helicopter, he told himself. I don't mind sleeping rough, tabbing fifty miles with a pack on my back, or escaping through hostile territory. I don't even mind being shot at.

But I don't like being sneered at by morons. *That's not what I joined the Regiment for.*

'I said it's fucking bollocks,' snapped Jim Muir. 'We need proof. Proper proof. Not this fucking, poxy, vomit-inducing bollocks.'

Jed shot him a glance. Muir was a short man, with thinning brown hair, a pallid complexion, and a thick, glowing nose so red it could have won a prize in a tomato-growing competition. A former tabloid reporter, he'd joined the Prime Minister's press office two years earlier, and had already earned himself a reputation as a bruiser. Should have stuck to the Page Three girls, mate, thought Jed.

'Maybe *you'd* like to go into Iraq next time,' said Jed.

His tone was polite, restrained. But the anger was still evident in the expression on his face.

'None of your bloody lip, solider boy,' spat Muir. 'I thought the SAS was supposed to be tough.' A mean cackle started to rise up from his chest. 'Not just a bunch of bloody, bed-wetting pansy boys.'

Jed leant forward on the table, and was about to speak, when the woman sitting next to him put her fingers on his arm. 'Let's all calm down,' Laura Strangar said, 'and try to examine what we have.'

They were sitting in the Vauxhall headquarters of the Firm, just next to the Thames. For the last three years, all the important meetings had taken place in one of the secure rooms. There were no windows a terrorist could launch a missile through. You needed the highest possible security clearance to be allowed through the door, and even then you were searched and put through a metal detector. It was the safest place in London.

There were seven people sitting round the table. Muir was directly opposite Jed. At his side was Mike Weston, the government's chief weapons scientist, plus his younger deputy, Miles Frith. On the other side sat David Wragg, the deputy director of the Firm, and the man feeding intelligence on Iraq into the system. There was an American intelligence officer who never gave his name, and never spoke; he just sat there, making notes on his Blackberry. And next to him, Laura Strangar, the intelligence officer assigned to directing Jed's work. Plus me, thought Jed. *The only one of these intelligence experts who might actually have set foot in the country they're supposed to be experts on.*

Strangar intrigued Jed. He had first met her two weeks ago at his briefing for the mission. She was no more than thirty-five, he guessed, but like many young London career women, it was hard to tell her exact age. They spent so much time in the gym, and were so careful about their diets, the years never seemed to clock up on them in the usual way. Her muscles were toned like a man's, and yet her skin was soft and white. Her elegant features were highlighted by a dusting of face powder, and the natural redness of her lips was enhanced by a thin film of lipstick.

Jed's mission had been the most perilous he had undertaken in the four years since he had passed selection into the Regiment from the Paras. He'd been made to grow a beard, and kitted out with some old Arab clothes – one of the reasons he'd been chosen was because he had brown eyes that would help him to blend in with the locals. A chopper had dropped him into Iraq, into a patch of scrubland six miles to the west of Baghdad: the British and the Americans had total control of the skies, even though there was no war yet, but there were still only a few places a special forces soldier could land safely.

Next, he'd made his way by foot around the perimeter of the city, until he hit one of the roads running into its north-west corner. The suspected weapons laboratory was two miles from the dropping-off point, located at the centre of an industrial suburb.

It was a drab, prefabricated block that could have passed for an out-of-town retail shed back in Britain. The one advantage of Baghdad, Jed had reflected on the journey, was that the whole population was so terrified, nobody ever came out at night. It also reminded Jed of some of the care homes he'd spent the better part of his childhood in while his dad made regular trips to the local nick. *Once you got out, you didn't ever want to go back in again.*

The mission had sounded straightforward enough. Go in close to the lab, and lie up somewhere you can't be seen. Then, using a high-powered digital camera, take as many pictures as you can of the facility. 'Just make sure they're nice and clear,' Laura had told him as he'd left for Kuwait.

Easy for you to say, Jed could recall thinking as he lay behind a low wall, looking across at the facility through his night-vision goggles. A lot harder to do when you're here. Maybe they'd like me to get a couple of palm trees and a nice sunset into the snaps as well. *Make it look like the Baghdad tourist brochure.*

He took a series of pictures of the perimeter of the facility, but that told you nothing. A grey concrete wall, that's all. Above it there were several towers, something like a chemical plant, but even though Jed had studied engineering at Cambridge before joining the Paras, he couldn't recognise them. Not at this distance, anyway. He took some more pictures, then tried to get closer. The gates were to his left. He inched forward, taking up a position in the doorway of a boarded-up shop about thirty yards from the entrance. It was two in the morning, and the city was asleep. He could see a thin whisper of smoke escaping from one of the high chimneys, but that aside, the plant looked dead. The gates were secured with thick steel locks, and there were no guards on duty: Jed could only assume there were plenty inside, and he wasn't about to risk finding out. *Not on a solo mission.*

By the time dawn rolled around, his legs were stiff and freezing: in February, the night-time temperatures in Baghdad dropped to zero. As the first light of morning started to break over the distant horizon, a truck pulled up at the entrance. It was a battered old Toyota, its back covered with thick black plastic sheeting. The gates swung open. Inside, Jed could see six guards hurrying forward, ushering the truck into the compound, then swinging the doors firmly shut after the truck drove inside. He managed to take a series of snaps with the digital camera, a dozen in total. By then the street had fallen quiet again, and a boy was looking at him. He was twenty yards away. Jed was dressed in a grubby white tunic and blue trousers. His skin was tanned, and with black hair there was nothing to distinguish him from an Iraqi. Still, the boy was staring right at him. He was no more than six, with huge brown eyes and a hungry look to him. There was no sign of his mother.

Jed scowled, then looked away. He could see the boy from the corner of his eye. Then he started walking towards him. He was saying something in Arabic, but Jed couldn't understand it: back in Hereford they'd been running elementary Arabic classes – with an Iraqi instructor giving them the right dialect – for the last six months, but most of the lads hadn't signed up for them. The only Arabic I need to understand is the rattle of an AK-47, as one of his mates had put it. It's not as if we're planning on talking to the buggers. Jed paused, wishing he understood the language. Then he waved at the boy with his arms. Go, he mouthed silently. *Bloody well piss off.*

The boy pointed at Jed's camera. He was just a dozen yards from him now. Jed was thinking fast. Any closer, the kid was going to realise he was a foreigner. Any kind of commotion right now and half the Republican Guard was going to be steaming towards him. His orders were ringing in his ears. 'Any trouble, get the hell out of there. The last thing we need is for an SAS guy to get picked up in Baghdad while we're still trying to get the bloody surrender monkeys at the UN to sign up to the war.'

In the end, there had been no choice but to evacuate. He had fifty snaps of the plant already on the compact digital camera, and that meant the mission was complete. Retracing his steps through the dark, quiet city, within an hour he'd been back at the drop-off point, collected by a chopper and back in Kuwait. In less than twelve hours, he was on home soil again. The pictures didn't show much, but they were all he could get in the circumstances. *If they didn't like them, they'd just have to go and get their own.*

'Can you tell us exactly what you saw, Jed?' said David Wragg. He coughed nervously. 'As you know, we have to examine every piece of evidence coming out of Iraq with minute care. It would be bloody embarrassing if we ended up invading the place, and then found out they didn't have anything more dangerous than a couple of pea-shooters in their locker room.'

He was a thin man, with greying hair and green eyes that bore down into you as you spoke, like a drill cutting into rock. He was smartly but casually dressed: he wore chinos and an open-necked shirt, but still had cufflinks and black lace-up brogues. The Firm was edging its way into the dress-down era, noted Jed, but none of the senior guys looked really comfortable with it. Give them a chance, and they'd be back in their three-pieces and bowler hats.

'It's all in the pictures,' said Jed.

'Yes,' said Wragg carefully. 'The trouble is, the pictures don't tell us that much.'

Muir leant forwards on the table. 'We're looking for what our friends in the porno business call a come shot, laddie,' he said. 'A nice big picture of Saddam cuddling up to a missile with the word anthrax written on the side.'

Jed noticed Wragg leaning into Muir's ear, and whispering something. Cool it, maybe. If so, it was good advice. Any more lip from the Scotsman and he was going to get that bright red nose smacked.

'Well, this is all we have. Like it or lump it.'

Laura smiled at him icily. 'We all have to understand that there is a lot of pressure to come up with some convincing intelligence about Iraq's WMD and come

13

up with it quickly. All our sources tell us that this is a very important facility. Whatever is going on in that lab, it matters a lot to the Iraqis. That's why we sent you there.'

'I got the best pictures I could, short of risking capture,' said Jed coldly. 'If you wanted me to go in, those should have been my orders.'

'We appreciate that,' said Wragg quickly. 'And we appreciate your bravery. We just want to get a fuller description, that's all.'

From the corner of his eye, Jed noticed that Muir was doodling a picture of a naked woman, with outsized breasts and a tiny miniskirt. Christ, he thought, when did they put this psycho in charge of the country?

'What did the building look like?' pressed Wragg.

'Nothing special,' answered Jed. 'A carpet factory. Could be making rugs from the looks of the place.'

'And special defences?'

'Just a high perimeter fence, and thick steel gates.'

'No guards?'

Jed shook his head. 'Only on the inside.'

'Searchlights?' asked Laura.

'Two on either side of the compound,' said Jed. 'But fixed. They weren't scanning the area. They might have been built to, but they weren't that night.'

'Electronic surveillance?'

'Not that I could see.'

'What did it smell like?' said Weston.

Jed paused. That was a good question. It smelt like fear, if he was being honest. His own terror sweating

14

off him as he stood next to the plant, wondering if he was about to spend the next few months being tortured to death by the Iraqis. 'Just dust, really,' he replied. 'Concrete, tarmac. Tossed-out rubbish and dog piss. The same sort of smell you might get on any industrial estate in this country on a hot day.'

'No fruity smells?' said Weston.

'Like what?'

'Burnt almonds, dried oranges, anything like that,' said Weston. 'Just any kind of memorable smell.'

Jed shook his head. Weston was a short, plump man, with a greying beard that looked like it could use a trim. He'd be more at home at a real-ale convention than the offices of the Firm. Still, he knew more about chemical and biological weapons than any man in the country. If it could come out of a test tube and kill you, then Weston was the man to spot it.

'Nothing like that.'

'How about lights?' said Miles Frith. 'What kind of light was it giving off?'

'It was dark.'

'I know,' said Frith. 'But any kind of glow.'

Jed shook his head.

'Pipes?'

'What do you mean?'

'Any kind of thick pipe running into the place?'

Frith was younger than the other men, no more than thirty, Jed thought. He wore half-moon glasses that made him look older, and a short-sleeved blue shirt. His voice was thin and whiny, like a cat being prodded with a hot

15

stick, but his manner was firm and decisive. Weston took him along to every meeting he attended, but no one else could understand why he was there.

Jed closed his eyes. In his mind, he recalled images of the pictures he'd taken. He'd looked at the building for hours, committing it to his memory, the way a photograph is committed to a roll of film. He could see the drab concrete wall that surrounded the place, and the cylinders poking above them. And then to the right he could see a pipe.

'On the right of the plant,' he replied.

'How thick?'

'Maybe a foot in diameter.'

'Oil?'

Jed shook his head. Oil pipes usually came in a standard size, and they were smaller than that. And industrial plants didn't need raw crude. 'Water,' he said. 'I think it was a water pipe.'

'Just into the plant.'

Jed nodded. 'There were no pipes running off it, so yes. The plant must have had its own water supply.'

Weston looked suddenly interested. 'What about the road leading into the place? Was it reinforced in any way?'

Jed nodded again. 'There was thick tarmac on the road leading up into it. A lot thicker than any of the surrounding roads.'

Weston looked up at the picture Jed had taken of the building. He was scrutinising it, the way an angler would scrutinise the fish on the end of his rod, looking at it from every angle to judge whether he'd landed a prize catch. From the look on his face, Jed judged this one wasn't about to be tossed back into the water.

'So what have we got here, ladies?' snapped Muir. 'I can't piss around all day talking to you fucking pansy boys. Is it WMD or not? Have we got the evidence?'

Weston stood up. After a brief moment of hesitation, Frith stood up as well. 'What we are looking at here, I believe, is not WMD. At least not in the conventional sense.' He turned and walked out of the room. Frith followed, shutting the door softly behind him.

'I think that brings the meeting to a close,' said Wragg quickly. 'Thank you, gentlemen.'

Muir snorted, collecting his pad from the desk. 'Next time, try to get us the come shot, boy,' he said, looking menacingly across at Jed. 'Missiles, that's what we want. Vats of fucking rat poison, marked "For Delivery to London". Not this overgrown Meccano bollocks.'

He leant over, so that Jed could smell the stale after-shave on his skin. 'And you should shave that stupid beard off, sonny,' he sneered. 'You look like a bloody tramp.'

Jed was about to speak, but once again he could feel Laura's hand on his wrist, restraining him. There was something about the touch of her skin on his that he liked: smooth, reassuring and firm. The words stalled in his throat. Just as well, he reflected, as he stood up and started to walk across the room. Even a couple of years in a social services care home, then a couple more as a squaddie, didn't prepare you for a swearing contest with that tosser.

'What the hell was that all about?' said Jed, turning round to look at Laura as they left the room.

They were standing in the corridor on the second floor of the Firm's headquarters. A couple of men scurried past, holding bottles of mineral water and thick-looking bundles of paper. Jed could feel the tension in the air: it was the same mixture of anticipation, tension and excitement you got at the Regiment the night before a big scrap was about to blow up.

Laura looked at him, a dazzling smile suddenly flashing across her full red lips. Her left hand reached up to play with the single pearl earring.

'That was something that could make my career,' she replied.

TWO

Nick Scott glanced left and right as he walked through the green channel on his way out of Heathrow Terminal 3. A couple of customs officers looked at him, and Nick could tell they were weighing up the hassle of stopping and searching him. A tall, tanned man, with weather-beaten skin and a black rucksack slung over his shoulder, recently arrived from North Africa, I probably fit all the profiles for a search, he thought. But it's almost lunchtime. *They can't be arsed*.

His flight from Algeria had touched down an hour earlier, but it had taken almost forty minutes for the baggage to turn up on the carousel. It was already ten past one. Nick walked across the crowded terminal, sat down at the coffee bar, and ordered himself a tall latte and a cheese-and-ham sandwich. He stared into the busy mass of people, already wondering how he was going to fill the rest of the month until his next shift on the rigs started up again. *I get back to Britain every other month, with my salary – about eight grand – sitting in my bank account, and I still don't know what the hell to do with myself.*

He fished his Nokia from his pocket, and glanced at the screen. No messages. No texts. *Nothing*.

He took a bite on the sandwich, relieved to have some decent food again. For the last five years, he'd been working as a security consultant on the oil rigs off the Algerian coast. Four weeks on, then four weeks off, with your flights and all your meals paid for. It was OK work for a man who had just turned fifty, and he knew he was lucky to have it: there were plenty of former Regiment blokes having to run much greater risks for a lot less money. He liked the sea, and the shifting crew of Egyptians, Moroccans, Somalis and Algerians who manned the rigs made OK company so long as you didn't mind the constant smoking, the smell of couscous, or their insatiable demand for porno DVDs featuring German blondes. Being at sea meant you couldn't spend any cash, and it kept you away from the bottle: most of the rig workers were Muslims and didn't drink. But it was hot, dull work, and by the last week of every tour, he was just counting the days until he could get back to Britain again.

Until he could see Sarah.

Every man needs something to live for, he'd reflected as the plane had touched down on the runway. Something to pull him through the days. A wife. A job. A dream. For me it's my daughter. *The only thing I ever got right*.

He glanced at the Nokia again. He'd sent her a text yesterday afternoon, but they often took a long time to get through – the Algerian landlines hardly worked at all, and the mobiles weren't much better. Still, the routine was well established. Every time he got back from the rigs, usually with a few grand in his pocket, he'd get the train straight up to Cambridge to see her. They'd go out and have dinner, and share a bottle of wine or two. These days, Nick only allowed himself a drink every couple of months. Any more than that, he knew he'd be in trouble again. *And then who would look after Sarah?*

The screen was blank.

Funny, thought Nick.

Like most twenty-somethings, Sarah was a text addict. Send her a message, and you'd usually get a reply within minutes. He jabbed at the tiny keyboard, and double-checked the inbox. Nothing. Next he looked up 'Missed Calls'. Nothing. *Christ, I'm a miserable bastard. A month out of the country, and in all that time I haven't had a single call.*

There were only three numbers stored on the phone. His own, the company that supplied the muscle to the rigs and Sarah's. He flicked on to Sarah's number, then pressed the green dial button. It was picked up immediately. 'Hi, this is Sarah,' said the familiar voice. 'I can't take the call right now, but leave a message and I'll get back to you.'

'It's Dad,' he said gruffly. 'I'm at Heathrow. Give me a ring when you get the message.'

Nick folded the phone back into his pocket. He took another bite of the sandwich, but his appetite seemed to have deserted him. Slinging his rucksack over his back, he started walking towards the tube. He stopped to buy a paper, glancing down at the headline as he queued to pay. WAR WITH IRAQ DRAWS CLOSER ran the headline. Nick put the paper back, and grabbed one of the motoring magazines instead. They can go to bloody war with the Iraqis again, if they want to, he thought. But I don't want any part of it. *Don't even want to read about it in the paper.*

The Heathrow Express into central London took just fifteen minutes. Along the way, Nick had some time to think. Sarah had been living in Cambridge for six years now. After Mary died, he'd fallen apart faster than a self-assembly bookshelf. The drink had turned him into a shambles. The ski school had only lasted another few months before they ran out of money: nobody wanted an instructor who swayed down the side of the mountain reeking of bourbon and gin. Back home in Hereford, there had been no work, and no prospects. It was a miracle Sarah managed to look after herself, but after one of her teachers became suspicious, and called in the social services, she was taken into care for a while. After three weeks of heavy drinking, Nick had realised that unless he straightened up his life, he was never going to get his daughter back. Get close to them when they're young, he could remember someone once telling him. That's the only time they really need you.

Social services returned her after six months, and Nick had straightened himself out. He got a job, first bodyguarding, then on the rigs. They muddled through, although the damage was plain to see. Sarah was always brilliant academically – top As at schools, then a first in natural sciences at Cambridge – but emotionally she was wild. As a teenager, she disappeared on weekend raves. Nick was certain she slept with too many boys, and took too many drugs, but she'd never talk to him about it. When she got home, she'd always go straight back to her studies. Intense work, followed by intense R&R, Nick sometimes reflected. *She'd have fitted right into the Regiment.*

He climbed down on to the platform at Paddington Station. As he stood next to the train, he checked his mobile again. Nothing. He pressed dial on the phone. 'Hi, this is Sarah,' repeated the familiar voice. 'I can't take the call right now, but leave a message and I'll get back to you.'

Where has she got to, he wondered.

Nick looked at all the people bustling through the station. Places to go to, he reflected. Offices and homes waiting for them. The only appointment I've got is a plane back to Algeria in a month's time. He shifted his rucksack on his back and started walking towards the Bakerloo Line. He could take that to Oxford Circus, switch on to the Central, then get a train to Cambridge from Liverpool Street. A poster for the *Evening Standard* caught his eyes. SADDAM'S MISSILES 45 MINUTES FROM LONDON, it said in thick black letters. Bollocks, thought Nick. I've been there. It takes those jokers forty-five minutes to tie their shoelaces in the morning.

With his rucksack still over his shoulder, Nick pushed his way through the barrier, and down on to the platform. Sarah's bound to turn up soon, he decided. When she does, I'll be waiting for her. Go out and have some good food. And a drink.

Lana was wearing just a simple white T-shirt and a pair of baggy jeans when she opened the door. Her blonde hair was tied up behind her head. Nick had met her several times before: she'd been sharing a flat with Sarah for the past three years while they both completed their doctorates. She treated him with the polite indifference that the young have for their friends' parents. Nick had got used to it as soon as Sarah hit her teens. You were just part of the grey mass of boring old people in the background.

'Is Sarah around?'

Lana shook her head. At a moment like this, Nick was suddenly conscious of his appearance. He was still wearing his jeans and a black sweatshirt, and with his rucksack and tanned skin he looked like an itinerant building worker. Most of the other students at Cambridge had dads with skins that were pale white from sitting in an air-conditioned office all day, who arrived in brand new Land Rovers, and who had plenty of contacts to fix up their kids with work experience that would sparkle on the CVs. And me, thought Nick. If you want to know how to shoot a man between the eyes at a hundred yards so that he never gets up again, I might be able to help you. *Apart from that, I'm useless.*

'Not for the last few days.'

Nick stepped into the flat. It looked like student digs anywhere. A sofa, a TV, a hi-fi with an iPod plugged into it, and that musty smell you get when you stub cigarettes out in beer cans. There were two bedrooms, a sitting room, kitchen and bathroom. 'How long exactly?' said Nick, looking back at Lana.

She shrugged. 'Almost a week.'

'A week,' snapped Nick. 'What the hell is she doing disappearing for a week?'

'I'm her flatmate, not her mum,' said Lana crossly.

'Her mum's . . .'

Nick was about to say the word dead, but he stopped himself just in time. Lana knew, of course. She was Sarah's best friend. But it never did any good to mention it. People just squirmed with embarrassment. 'A bender?'

Lana reached across the table, and poured herself a glass of apple juice from an open carton. 'I guess so.'

'How long since the last one?'

Lana sat down. Nick could see the strain in her eyes. Like most students, she liked to act cool, and nonchalant and tough, but you could see the anxiety just below the surface of the skin. 'Almost two months, I reckon.'

'Has she been drinking much?'

'Only at parties,' said Lana. 'A few cocktails, some gin. Nothing much.'

'She seem OK in herself?'

Lana smiled. 'The same old Sarah,' she said softly. 'Brilliant, but impetuous.'

'Nothing different?'

'She's been working incredibly hard, that's all,' said Lana. 'Spending whole nights down at the lab. I think she's getting close to finishing her thesis. Last time I saw her, she wouldn't tell me anything about it, but I could see she was excited.'

Nick was glancing around the sitting room. On the CD rack, he could see a few of Sarah's favourites, and on the bookshelf there was a picture of her with Mary. He remembered the picture, although it was more than a decade since he had taken it. They were standing on one of the ledges that jutted out of the side of the trails leading up Mont Blanc. It must have been just after six in the evening, and they were all tired after a long Sunday afternoon walk. The sun was just starting to set, and the light was fading into the white snow to fill the valley below with a glowing orange light, like the embers burning away as a fire extinguishes itself. Mary was holding Sarah tight to her chest, and both of them were smiling. That was two days before she died, thought Nick. The last sunset she ever saw.

'She's been gone a week, you reckon?' he said, looking back at Lana.

'I don't know exactly,' said Lana quickly. 'I was down at Mum and Dad's for the weekend. When I came back on Tuesday, she wasn't here.'

'And you last saw her when?'

'Friday.'

It was Thursday today. That meant she could have been gone a week. Or maybe just three days. Sarah went on occasional drinking binges, and had done ever since she was fifteen. She just took off, stayed in some town somewhere by herself, drank in the local bars, or just in a hotel room. Nick didn't know that much about it.

She wouldn't tell him, and quite possibly couldn't quite remember herself. He'd been on a few week-long drinking sessions himself before he kicked the bottle, and he knew how hard it could be to remember. Usually she came back after three days, and by the time she sobered up she was fine again. It was almost as if it was something she just had to get out of her system.

'A note?'

Lana shook her head. 'When she takes off, she never says anything.'

He walked through to the bedroom. The duvet was drawn up, and a couple of cushions arranged perfectly next to the pillow. Sarah never bothered with decorating any of her rooms. Even as a child, she never had a special toy, or posters on the wall. She travelled light through life. Another reason, Nick reflected, why she might have made a good soldier.

'Has she packed a bag?'

'Not that I can see,' said Lana. 'But you know what she's like. A pair of jeans and a sweatshirt, and she's happy.'

Nick wrote his mobile number down on a piece of paper, and put it down in front of Lana. He could see the first drop of a tear starting to form in her eye, but decided to ignore it. He had never been any good at comforting women. *My talent is for making them feel worse, not better.*

'If you hear from her, give me a call,' he said, his tone harsh. 'Right away.'

★   ★   ★

One of these decades, I'm going to buy myself a suit, thought Nick as he stood at the customer service desk of the bank. Start looking like a businessman. Maybe that way I'd start getting better service in these places.

'The name and account number,' said the girl at the desk, who according to her lapel badge was called Sandrine.

'Nick Scott and Sarah Scott,' said Nick. 'It's a joint account. The number is 62115073.'

'I'll check.'

Nick had spent the night at a bed and breakfast on the outskirts of the city. He liked Cambridge, had done ever since Sarah got her place at King's College six years ago. Maybe it was the pride, he sometimes reflected to himself. No one from his family had ever been to university, never mind Cambridge. Mary's family had all the brains: her grandfather had been a professor of biology at Manchester University, and her father a doctor. As he walked around the city, he'd always taken pleasure from its ancient courtyards, and the views of the river as you stepped away from the colleges.

Not this night, however. After leaving the flat he'd checked his kit into the B&B, then walked down to the local pub to get some food and a drink. He allowed himself one pint of lager and a double Irish whiskey to chase down the burger he ordered from the bar. The drink tasted good. Too good, he reminded himself as he finished the whiskey. Something is wrong, he kept telling himself. I know Sarah's disappeared plenty of times, so maybe I shouldn't worry, *but this just feels bloody crooked.*

Chris Ryan

'Letter two and six from the password,' said Sandrine, returning to the desk.

'L and H,' answered Nick.

He'd set up the joint account when Sarah started university. Her fees were paid for, but Nick hadn't wanted her to take out a student loan to live on: he'd signed up for the army at eighteen, and the only loan he'd ever taken in his life was to start the ski school. He hadn't needed to borrow money so he didn't see why she should either. From his wages on the rigs, he paid a thousand every month into the account he'd opened in both their names, but it was her money: Nick never touched it. This month, he'd decided to check the account, just to see if it gave any clues as to where she might have got to. Most bank statements these days gave you the location of any cash machine you used. If she'd taken out any money in the past couple of days, he'd find out where she had gone drinking. Maybe even find her, and get her sobered up.

Sandrine looked down. Her expression changed subtly. Nick could hear a slight intake of breath, then a measure of curiosity as she looked back up at him. 'You have a hundred thousand pounds,' she said. 'Plus seven hundred and thirty-two.'

Nick leant across at the neatly printed-out piece of paper on her desk. 'There's some mistake,' he said.

'Would you like me to check?'

He looked straight at her, and he could tell from her eyes that she was already suspicious. Men who look like me don't usually have a hundred grand of loose change

29

in their account, he thought. *And if they do, they certainly know where the hell it's come from.*

'Just give me a copy,' snapped Nick.

He took the sheet of paper and walked swiftly away from the bank. As he hit the street, he turned left. He had no idea where he was going, or why. He just needed to feel the ground beneath his feet, and let the cold morning air fill his lungs. Anything to try and calm himself down.

A small thunderstorm of connections and conjectures had already exploded within his mind.

Sarah has disappeared.

There's a hundred grand in the account.

Something has happened to her.

THREE

Jed looked around the apartment. There was a view out across the Thames, and in the distance he could just make out the top of Big Ben. The block was one of the modern apartment buildings that had sprung up on the south side of the river in the past few years: huge, luxury towers where the flats started at half a million, and the penthouses set you back three or four times that amount. The walls were painted off-white, and the furniture was minimal and modern, but there were two nineteenth-century oil paintings dominating the main walls. Both military pictures, Jed noticed. Scenes from the Battle of Waterloo, unless his history was rustier than he thought.

'Nice place,' he said.

'Convenient for work anyway,' answered Laura from the kitchen.

Jed poured himself a glass of Chablis from the bottle open on the dining table. A Diana Krall CD was playing on the hi-fi – the kind of sultry modern jazz that girls liked to go with their pasta, salad and white wine. It tasted cold and dry: Jed would have preferred a beer, but at least there was a kick to the alcohol. There were

31

moments, sitting in a place like this, when he wondered whether he'd made the right choices in life. Four years ago, he'd graduated from Cambridge with a 2:1 in engineering. With that qualification, he could have walked into a job in one of the City banks, and might well be pulling down a hundred thousand a year by now. A lot of his mates were. Instead, he'd signed up for the army. They had been recruiting hard around the universities in the past few years. The days of the tough, brave squaddie were over, the Rupert signing him up had argued. There was so much kit to operate these days, the army needed men with a first-class technical education. Jed enjoyed the work, no question about that. Like all soldiers, he got a kick from testing himself against the most extreme conditions imaginable. You climbed a wall of fear every day. There was nothing to beat the feeling as you made it to the other side.

Still, when he saw a flat like this, he wondered. The pay was crap, and the risks terrible. He knew why he'd really joined the army. It was just that he didn't like to admit it to himself.

'You've already got a drink, I see,' said Laura, stepping out of the kitchen. 'The food will be ready in five minutes.'

Jed was surprised by how good she looked. It was a different Laura from the one he'd met at the offices of the Firm. Her blonde hair had been let down, and curled around the delicately sculpted features of her skin. A dusting of make-up had freshened up her face, and her lips were glossed until they shone. When she'd called to ask him over to dinner, he'd guessed it was some kind of come-on, but he couldn't be certain. *Now I'm pretty sure.*

'What have you been doing with yourself?' she asked, pouring herself a glass of the Australian white and raising it to her lips.

Jed laughed. 'A squaddie with a few days' leave in the big city,' he said. 'What do we usually do with ourselves?'

Laura smiled. 'Get rat-arsed, and go on the pull.'

'Well, I tried to persuade a couple of the lads we should take in a poetry reading, then catch a string quartet at the Wigmore Hall. But I got outvoted. So, yeah, we got tanked up, and went looking for slappers instead.'

Jed grinned, but actually it wasn't quite true. After the meeting at the Firm, he'd been told to stay in London for a few days in case they needed to speak to him again. He was allocated a room at the Chelsea barracks, but there was nothing for him to do, so he'd filled up the day watching reruns of the football on Sky, and trying to get hold of Sarah. She wasn't answering her mobile, and there was no reply from the flat either. Last time they'd met, she'd insisted they were on one of their breaks, but she did that all the time, and he'd learnt not to take much notice. Now she'd vanished from the face of the earth, the way she did sometimes. A girlfriend was around to take your calls, when you had some un-expected time off. Was that too much for a guy to ask for, he'd asked himself bitterly as he ate some miser-able mess grub and watched Andy Gray on Sky Sports overhype yet another match between two teams who weren't going to win anything in a million years.

'I'm sure the slappers couldn't believe their luck when you boys came in,' said Laura. 'You're in better shape than most of the brickies and insurance salesmen they usually get off with.'

Jed smiled, following Laura into the kitchen as she took the pasta out of the pan, mixed in the seafood sauce, and tossed the dressing on to the salad. It was an age since he'd had a woman cook for him: Sarah wasn't much of a hand in the kitchen, and although there had been other girlfriends during the many breaks in their relationship, none of them had known any more about cooking than he did. Maybe I don't attract that kind of girl, he thought. The homemakers see me, and they run a mile. And, frankly, I'm not sure I blame them.

Laura was wearing a crisp white blouse, through which he could clearly see the outline of a black bra that held her small yet rounded breasts in place. Her tan leather skirt revealed a pair of legs that were perfectly toned, and the smell of the food mixed with her musty perfume to create a scent that was delicate, feminine yet strong all at the same time.

'What's a smart guy like you doing in the Regiment?'

'Who says I'm smart?'

Laura took a sip of her wine. 'I took a good look at your CV before choosing you for this mission,' she said. 'A degree from Cambridge. Not many Regiment guys have one of those.'

'More than there used to be.'

Laura nodded. 'The world is changing. The battles we're fighting now are more about brains than brawn. The old Regiment guys don't really understand that.'

Jed laughed. 'I remember one of the old guys explaining their SOP to me.'

'And . . .'

'Standard operating procedure for this Regiment, boy: Bang, bang, then run like fuck.'

'Maximum speed and maximum aggression, that was always the old motto,' said Laura. 'Now maximum intelligence has been added to the list. The only trouble is, some of the older hands haven't quite caught up with what century we're living in.'

'And that's why you wanted me to go into Iraq?'

Laura nodded. 'We need people who can recognise what they're looking at.'

Jed served himself another helping of the seafood pasta: the dish was a mixture of fresh prawns, squid and clams, drenched in oil, garlic and basil, and made a change from the sausages, chips and beans that made up a typical menu in the mess. He could eat his way through her whole larder right now. 'I *didn't* recognise it, though.'

'You did enough.'

Jed shook his head. 'I could feel it during that meeting. Everyone was pissed off with me for not getting closer to that lab.'

'We're under a lot of pressure,' said Laura. 'I've been at the Firm for thirteen years now, ever since I got out of university. I've never known anything like it. The place is buzzing, but it's also getting a bit weird. We have

35

to come up with the goods on Iraq, no matter what. And it doesn't matter how we get them.'

'Or else that dickhead Muir bites your arse.'

Laura laughed. 'You saw the bugger in a good mood. You should catch him on an off day.'

'So what did I see in there?' said Jed, looking straight into Laura's eyes.

She glanced towards the window. 'We're still waiting for a full analysis –'

'But you've got an idea,' interrupted Jed.

'There are theories all over the place about what's happening in Iraq,' said Laura. 'It's impossible to keep track of them all.'

'Try,' said Jed firmly. 'If I get confused, we'll draw a diagram.'

She leant closer to him, and he could feel her hand brushing against the inside of his jeans. 'I like you, Jed,' she whispered, moving on to his lap. Before he realised what was happening, he was kissing her. Her mouth was full, and her lips hard, like rubber. He could taste the pasta on her breath, and the seafood on her tongue. The kiss tasted salty and acid, yet supple and exciting all the same. For a brief moment, Jed hesitated, wondering if he was doing the right thing: he'd seen the kind of trouble some men had got into by sleeping with their colleagues, and although he and Sarah might be going through one of their breaks, she was still just about his girlfriend. But the doubts drained out of him as he could feel Laura's hot breath against the skin of his chest, and feel her hands roaming down the muscles on his back. I've never been

36

able to think straight with a woman in my arms, he reminded himself. *No point trying to learn now.*

He wrapped his arms tight around her back squeezing her close to him. They were still sitting on the chair, but it was rocking backwards, and in seconds they had fallen down on to the carpet, both of them laughing. Jed was lying on top of her, his lips running down the side of her body. Her skin was smooth, with just a pale tan, and her muscles were toned and hard. He pushed her bra up over her neck, running his tongue around her nipples, then slipped his hand down between her legs. She groaned softly, a small, throaty noise somewhere between a cough and a sigh. 'Keep going,' she muttered. 'Keep going.'

Jed didn't need any encouragement; he guessed she was trying to avoid answering his question, but that could wait. Her hands were already reaching up for the buckle on his belt. Her legs parted, wrapping themselves up around his back, and she pushed herself upwards towards him. 'Take me,' she said. 'Take me right now.'

Twenty minutes later, she lay sweaty and calm in his arms, her blonde hair draped across his chest, silent and exhausted. Jed could feel the carpet against the skin on his back. There was a graze down his left ribcage where she had scratched him while they were making love. Beats another evening in the mess, he thought to himself. *And it beats sending text messages to Sarah that she never replies to.*

'I'd better go,' said Jed, looking around for where she had tossed his clothes.

'Stay,' said Laura.

Jed paused. He hadn't taken her for the romantic type. It was hard to imagine she wanted him cluttering up the bathroom in the morning. 'It's OK,' he repeated. 'I've got a place at the barracks. I can kip there.'

'Stay,' she repeated.

'I'm not on leave.'

'Stay,' said Laura, a firmer tone to her voice this time. 'I might want to fuck you again.'

He looked across at her and smiled. 'So answer my question,' he said. 'What the hell was I taking pictures of in Baghdad?'

'I already told you,' said Laura, her tone suddenly hardening. 'You'll find out later.'

Laura looked straight through him as Jed stepped into the room. She was still wearing the same clothes he had seen her put on that morning – black skirt, white blouse, a string of pearls, two diamond earrings, and black lace underwear he could still feel the taste of in his mouth – but her expression had changed completely. From flirty and fun, she had become stern and businesslike: her face, he was starting to realise, was a mask she could change as easily as other women changed their perfume.

'Not this bed-wetter again,' snapped Muir. 'Hasn't the Regiment got any decent blokes in it? I thought they were meant to be tough.'

'They are,' said Wragg sharply.

'Well, we haven't got the shit to put in our next dossier, have we?' snarled Muir. 'And that's because the bloody pansy boys haven't been able to go in and get it yet.'

Jed took a deep breath and composed himself. The call had come through on his mobile an hour ago from Laura. He was needed back at the Firm. When he'd asked what it was about, she'd clammed right up. Just get in a cab, she'd told him. Be here in an hour.

One of these days, mate, thought Jed, glancing fiercely at Muir, *I'll show you some real violence to put in your dodgy dossiers.*

He looked around the room. Wragg was sitting next to Laura, with Mike Weston on his other side. Next to him sat the silent American, his mouth still shut, but with his Blackberry switched on. There was no sign of Miles Frith. At home with his mum, perhaps, wondered Jed. They were all looking straight towards him.

'We've analysed the information you brought back from Iraq,' said Weston. 'And it was important. Very important.' He paused, scratching a finger through his grey beard. 'But we need more data to be sure of what exactly the Iraqis are doing in there.'

Wragg looked at Jed. 'We need a small group of men to go inside and find out what's happening in those labs.'

Jed shrugged. 'That's what the Regiment is there for,' he said flatly. 'Tell them what you want, and they'll pick the men for the mission.' He smiled thinly. 'We're all on the payroll.'

'There's a twist,' said Laura.

'It's got to be off the fucking books,' snapped Muir.

'Off the books?'

'That's right, laddie,' said Muir. 'We've got a vote in Parliament on whether to go to war with Iraq in less than a month's time. We need to know what's in the lab before then. And we need to make sure that no one could possibly think the British government is taking a peek.' A sour chuckle started in his throat. 'After all, people might think we'd already decided to go to war with Iraq and were just looking around for an excuse.'

Jed could see Wragg casting a distasteful look at Muir. The golden rule of the Firm − that you never said what you really meant − had just been broken. *There would be payback for that one day.*

'We need you to lead a group of four men to go into that lab,' said Laura. 'You'll have full backup and support from the Regiment. But officially you'll be on leave, freelancing. Anything goes wrong, and we won't be able to help you.'

Jed looked at her closely. Maybe that's why she fucked me last night. *Just so I'd know what it felt like when she did it again the next day.*

'If I'm freelancing, then I guess I have some choice in the matter,' said Jed. 'I can decide whether I take the mission or not.'

'Christ, we don't need any of this barrack-room shop-steward bollocks,' snapped Muir. 'You'll be showing us your union card soon.'

'I thought you were a member of the Labour Party,' said Jed. 'Or are they not interested in the workers any more?'

40

Muir doodled another pair of breasts on his notepad, but remained silent.

'Do you have a problem with the mission?' said Wragg.

'I'm a soldier,' said Jed. 'I signed up to fight for my country, and I don't mind laying down my life for it, although I'd rather not if I can help it. But I'm not the Whips Office of the sodding Labour Party. If they've got problems justifying this war to their backbenchers, that's their problem.'

A silence fell over the room. The air was cold with anger. Jed could feel the raw fury in the five pairs of eyes trained upon him. They were shocked but also contemptuous. Well, it's your own fault, he thought. You wanted to recruit smarter guys into the Regiment. *No point in being surprised if they turn out to be able to think for themselves.*

'Obviously it's up to you whether you take the mission or not,' said Wragg coldly. 'Because it's off the books, we can't force you. Still, if you choose not to, I'll have no choice but to recommend you be RTU'd.'

There was no need for him to spell out the acronym. Jed knew what it meant. RTU stood for 'returned to unit': it meant being sent back to the unit you'd left to join the SAS. Within the Regiment, there was no more punishing disgrace. It stripped you of every last shred of dignity and self-respect. The verdict it delivered on your abilities could be summed up in four brutal, unforgiving words. *You weren't good enough.*

'Maybe I couldn't give a toss,' snapped Jed.

Mike Weston looked at him. 'I hear what you saying,' he said softly. 'But whatever you might think of the way this war is being presented, what's going on in that lab is important.'

'Then tell me what it is.'

'No,' he said. 'You go in there, and tell *me* what it is.'

Jed slammed his fist on the table. 'And how the hell can I look for it when you won't even tell me what the fuck it is.'

'You don't need to know,' said Muir, glaring straight at him. 'That kind of information is above your pay grade.'

'If you don't trust the men on the ground, then the whole operation is fucked from day one,' said Jed, glaring back.

'There's only one person who's fucked in this room, laddie,' said Muir. 'And it's the bloody pansy boy with the beard.'

Jed remained silent. They couldn't make him go, he knew that. But they could humiliate him if he didn't. Maybe Weston was right. Maybe there really was something important inside that lab. *But they wouldn't know unless somebody went and took a look.*

'The mission will be ready to start in three days, Jed,' said Laura. 'I've already talked to Hereford, and your leave is extended until then. I'll expect to see you there in sixty-four hours. If you're not there, well, that's your choice.'

Jed stood up, nodded at Wragg and walked towards the door. The meeting room was on the first floor, and he walked quickly down the single flight of stairs. He stepped from the building and straight out into the south London scuzz of Vauxhall. It was a miserable morning. Rain was beating down on the streets, and a cold wind was blowing in off the Thames. Hell, I might as well be in Iraq, he reflected bitterly. *At least I could work on my tan.*

He looked at the headline screaming from the *Standard* billboards: LABOUR REBELS STAND FIRM OVER IRAQ. Jesus, muttered Jed. It's tearing the country apart. *Maybe the sooner we get on with the shooting the better. Get it finished and move on.*

He walked over the bridge, then turned right and started heading along the Embankment. His mind was buzzing. He knew it had been dicey questioning whether he should take the mission. Still, it was his choice. Once you went off the books, the risks quadrupled. You couldn't call on any backup. You couldn't expect any help if you were in a jam. *And if anything went wrong you'd be thrown out like yesterday's garbage.*

He fished out his Motorola V20 from his pocket, and pressed Sarah's number.

Where the hell are you? *It's been nearly four days now since I've heard from you.*

Lana was wearing just her nightie when she opened the door. Jed could hear Dido playing on the hi-fi, and he could smell cocoa on the cooker. A girl's night in with the telly, he thought. She's probably got a tub of Häagen-Dazs already open.

'I was just wondering if Sarah was around?' said Jed apologetically.

'Christ,' said Lana, 'it's after eleven at night.'

Jed stepped into the flat. He was wearing jeans and a suede bomber jacket, and had a black kitbag slung on his shoulder. He'd had two beers on the train up to Cambridge, and plenty of time to think. He'd probably take the mission. He had no choice really. But he wanted to speak to Sarah first. *To hear what she thought.*

'I haven't been able to get hold of Sarah,' he said. 'I wanted to see if she was OK.'

She was watching *Ally McBeal* on one of the satellite rerun channels, but the volume was so low it was impossible to hear much of what was being said. Ally seemed to be worrying about her job. I know how you feel, thought Jed. Add in a few Ruperts and some semi-automatic machine guns, and we'd be in the same boat.

'Her dad's already been here today,' said Lana.

'Nick? Jesus, what's he doing here?'

'Same as you,' said Lana. 'Looking for Sarah.'

Jed sighed. 'He's not still here, is he?'

Lana smiled and shook her head. She knew all about the argument that had rumbled through years between Nick and Jed. Jed and Sarah had started dating when they were both fifteen: they'd been in the same care home for three months after her mother died, and after Jed's own father had been sent to jail for the sixth and, as it turned out, final time. They only lived twenty miles apart, in villages on either side of Hereford, and they kept up the relationship in the on-and-off way teenagers do. The same at Cambridge during the three years Jed had been doing his degree. But he'd always kept as far away from Nick as possible. The guy had never liked him, not from the first moment he laid eyes on him. Maybe that was why I joined the Regiment, Jed sometimes reflected. To try and impress the old bugger, make him see I was a man to be reckoned with. *Well, it sure as hell never worked.*

'I don't suppose he asked if she was with me,' said Jed.

'Funnily enough, no,' said Lana.

'What's happened to her?'

Lana shrugged. 'I've no idea.'

'Has she been drinking?'

'No worse than usual.'

Jed walked through to the bedroom. He could smell her the instant he opened the door. It was not just her perfume, but her clothes, her books and the scented candles she liked to keep beside her bed. 'You might as well kip here for the night,' said Lana. 'It's not as if Sarah would mind you being in her bed.'

Jed sat down on the edge of the bed. From the sitting room, he could hear the sound of *Ally McBeal* being turned up. More boyfriend problems. He got up and put his kitbag down in the corner, closing the door behind him. He glanced down at the desk, but could see nothing of interest. Sarah travelled light through life: unlike just about every other woman he had ever known, she had none of the clutter that most girls carted around with them. There were no chequebook stubs to look at. No bank statements, or maps. If she had planned where she was going, she hadn't left any traces behind.

This doesn't feel right, he told himself, as he took off his sweatshirt and lay back on the familiar white sheets.

Where the hell is she?

FOUR

Lana paused as she opened the door. In the background, there was a smell of fresh coffee, and the sound of music playing on the hi-fi. 'Any word from her?' said Nick.

It was just after nine in the morning. Nick had been up since seven, and had already taken himself for a run along the river: as his feet smashed into the pristine grass along the banks, he had been trying to make sense of what he'd learnt about Sarah in the past twenty-four hours. He knew nine o'clock was early to be calling on a student, but sod it, he had told himself just before knocking. *I need to find out what might have happened to her.*

'No,' said Lana, still holding the door no more than ajar.

Nick was about to step inside, but she seemed to be barring his way. 'I thought I'd check her room,' he said. 'See if there are any clues.'

'Maybe later,' said Lana defensively.

Nick was still thinking about the hundred thousand pounds he'd seen in their joint bank account. He knew there were lots of different ways a person could make that kind of money quickly. The trouble was, almost none of them were legal. The sooner he found her the better. *There might not be much time.*

'You don't understand,' said Nick gruffly. 'I need to check it right now.'

He stepped forward. Nick was a big man, with an imposing physical presence. His hair was turning grey but there was still plenty of it. He measured six foot two, and his chest was fifty inches, thick and strong like a barrel. His arms were solid as oak trees, and rippled with muscles, and there was not so much as an ounce of fat on him. Lana was a slim girl, only about five foot four, and as he moved forward he just brushed her aside like a feather floating past him.

'You should . . .'

She was speaking, but Nick wasn't listening. He turned the knob on the door to Sarah's room, pushing it open. Then he paused. There was a man lying on her bed. For a brief second, he wondered if he might have come into the wrong room. Maybe this was Lana's boyfriend. Then he noticed Sarah's stuff – there was even a picture of him tucked into the mirror on the desk. And he recognised Jed. Even lying down, with his back to him. *I've known and hated that boy for a decade. I'd spot his ugly hide anywhere.*

'What the fuck are you doing here?' he shouted.

Jed snapped awake. He swung over and looked up suddenly, as if he'd just heard the sound of gunfire. Regiment training, thought Nick. A man had to be awake, alert and ready for battle within just a fraction of a second. *Sometimes his life would depend on it.*

Chris Ryan

'Fuck, it's you,' he muttered.

'I want to know what the hell you're doing in my daughter's bed,' snarled Nick.

'Trying to get some kip,' snapped Jed. 'I'm alone, in case you hadn't noticed.'

'Good to see everyone's getting along so well,' said Lana. 'How about a nice cup of coffee? Maybe then we can all calm down.'

Nick followed her to the kitchen. He took the cup from her, stirred in two sugars and drank half of it in one gulp. From the shower, he could hear a blast of noise as Jed washed. 'He's not so bad, you know,' said Lana, looking up at Nick. 'He really cares about Sarah. I keep trying to tell her how much that should mean to her, but I think she's so used to it, she just treats it like the weather, something that is always there.'

'He's a soldier,' said Nick firmly. 'Army life isn't right for Sarah.'

Jed walked into the room. He took the coffee Lana offered him, cradling it between his two thick, strong palms. 'So what exactly are you doing here?' said Nick sourly.

'Same as you, apparently: looking for Sarah.'

'Why aren't you with your unit? Or has it all got a bit hot for you now that there might be an actual war.'

He knows I fought in Bosnia, and I've been under-cover in Kurdistan, and Indonesia, thought Jed. Why does he needle me all the time? 'Let's just try to talk about what might have happened to Sarah.'

Nick took a step forward. There was an unmistakable

air of menace to his stance, like a brawler coming out of the pub on a Saturday night. 'It's got nothing to do with you.'

'Bugger it, Nick. I'm her boyfriend.'

Nick shook his head. 'You mean nothing to her. Got that? Bloody nothing.'

'Then why the hell has she been going out with me for the last ten years.'

'She hasn't,' snapped Nick. 'Last time I saw her, she said there was nothing going on between you any more. She was talking about one of the guys in the labs. She was talking about her work. Talking about anything except *you*.'

'And when was the last time you saw her exactly?' said Jed.

Nick paused. 'Almost two months ago.' His tone was quieter.

'Great bloody dad you turned out to be then. Too busy fighting and drinking and working to take care of your own daughter.'

Nick took another step forward. He might be fifty, reckoned Jed, but there was an air of calculated menace to his stance: the position taken by a man who knows his own strength, and the fear that it can generate in an opponent. Not to me, he thought. *You don't scare me at all.*

'Back off,' growled Jed.

Nick took another pace. He grabbed the collar of Jed's polo shirt, and twisted it between his fingers. 'A bastard like you knows nothing about being a father,' he said. 'Your old man spent half his life in the fucking nick, and that's probably where you'll end up as well. So don't give me any lectures on bloody fatherhood.'

Jed wiped the spit from his cheek. He could smell the sweet, sugary coffee on the man's breath, and feel the heat and anger in his eyes. He was aware of the damage a fight between two strong men would do to the kitchen: the unit and half the furniture would be smashed to pieces. 'Let's finish this outside, grandad,' he snarled.

Nick slammed his cup down on the table. It cracked, sending slithers of china crashing to the floor. The remains of the coffee splashed on to the table. 'I'm sorry,' said Nick towards Lana.

'Just go and fight outside if you have to,' shouted Lana. 'And maybe when you've stopped acting like a pair of bloody toddlers, you can start worrying about what's happened to Sarah.'

All three of them fell silent. Jed reached for a brush, and started to sweep up the remains of the cup. Nick knelt down to push a piece of broken china into a rubbish bag. He looked up at Jed, immediately feeling sorry for the way he'd reacted. These days his temper was usually under control. But seeing Jed was like sparking up the blue touchpaper on a firework: it always made him explode. 'We can finish this later,' he said. 'In the meantime, I have to try and find out where Sarah is.'

'I'm coming with you,' said Jed firmly.

'Don't push your luck.'

'And don't push yours, grandad.'

Both men were kneeling on the floor, the broken china between them, facing each other off like a pair of angry bulls again. 'I'm going to look for Sarah as well,' growled Jed. 'We can do it together, or we can do it separately. It's your choice.'

A slow smile started to spread across Nick's lips, but there was not a hint of humour or warmth in it. 'OK,' he replied. 'But just so I can keep an eye on your thick skull.'

'Jesus, just so long as you both get out of my kitchen,' said Lana, her tone exasperated. 'I'll be relieved when Sarah gets back. She's the only person who can knock any sense into either of you.'

The lab was a grey Victorian building, on one of the side streets leading away from the Milton Road. Nick had only visited the Cambridge Institute of Advanced Physics once before, picking Sarah up before one of their regular dinners. It looked like a miserable place to work. A series of gloomy corridors, punctuated by small offices, overflowing with books and papers, and five big laboratories bristling with more pipes, tubes and measuring devices than the inside of an aircraft carrier. 'I'm looking for Professor David Wilmington,' said Nick to the man at the front desk.

'And you are?'

'Nick Scott,' said Nick. 'Sarah Scott's father.'

Jed was standing at his side. From the flat, they had walked straight here. Most of Sarah's time was spent at the laboratory. If anyone was likely to know where she had got to, it was her professor. Who knows, Jed had remarked as they stepped inside, maybe they just sent her to a conference. She might have forgotten to tell anyone.

'He's busy,' said the receptionist. He was a man in his fifties, with balding grey hair, a cheap black suit, and a white shirt open at the collar. From his manner, Nick guessed he was just punching the clock until he collected his pension. No point expecting him to help. 'It's urgent,' he said flatly.

'The professor said he was busy all —'

'Listen,' interrupted Jed, leaning forward on the desk, 'tell him we just need a few minutes.'

The expression on the man's face suggested even speaking was too much trouble. He sighed, picked up the phone, then whispered into it. 'His meeting is important,' he said, looking back up at Jed. 'You'll have to make an appointment for next week.'

Nick slammed his fist down. 'Listen, mate —'

'Easy,' said Jed, grabbing Nick by the arm.

The man looked shocked. 'We'll arrange another time,' said Jed quickly.

He walked from the building, steering Nick out of the door. Somehow the old man was going to have to learn to control his temper, thought Jed. But not from me. *I'm hardly the guy to start delivering tutorials in anger management.*

'There'll be another way in,' said Jed as they stood on the pavement. 'This place is about as secure as Hyde Park on a Sunday afternoon.'

They started walking around the perimeter of the lab. There was a bicycle stand at its front, with around thirty bikes chained up to it. Around the back, there was a small car park with a collection of Hondas, Renaults and Volkswagens. A back door led into what looked like a canteen. Jed pushed the door open and stepped inside. The smell of the food hit him in the face: a mixture of overboiled potatoes, fried onions and stewed beef. Jesus, he thought. *The grub in this place must be even worse than in the army*.

Apart from two people sharing a coffee, the canteen was empty at this time of the morning. It was just after eleven, and most of the scientists were working in their labs. Jed paused to ask for directions, and was told to take the second corridor on the left. He'd find Professor Wilmington's office there. Jed and Nick walked quickly through the building. They passed two people on the way, but nobody paid any attention to them. Jed hesitated for just a second outside the door, then knocked twice. Without waiting for a reply, he turned the handle. Seize the moment, he reminded himself. *It might not come again*.

'It won't matter soon . . .'

Jed caught just the tail end of the sentence of the shorter of the two men standing in front of him. This must be Wilmington, he decided. The professor was a slender man of fifty or so. His dark hair was combed back, and his glasses were perched on the end of his long, raking nose. His skin was tanned, but his face was pitted with pockmarks, and his eyes were capped by a pair of thick eyebrows that crawled out over his fore-head like ivy crawling across a building. Next to him stood a taller, younger man. An Arab, Jed judged, but it was impossible to tell from a brief glance which country he might come from. He was about six foot, with a thin, wiry face, but strong shoulders and a thick neck. His hair looked like it could use a trim, and he had a thick black moustache.

'Who are you?' said the Professor.

'My name is Nick Scott,' said Nick firmly. 'And this is Jed Bradley. We're sorry for bursting in on you like this, but we need to speak to you right away.'

'I told reception –'

The second man tapped him on the arm. 'Let them speak,' he said softly.

'It will just take a few minutes,' said Jed.

Wilmington nodded. 'OK,' he said cautiously. 'I guess you're Sarah's father.' He looked from Nick to Jed. 'But who are you?'

'I'm a friend of Sarah's.' He glanced at the taller man. 'And you are . . . ?'

Jed could feel the hostility in the man's eyes as the question was posed. It was like having a snake looking straight at you, deciding whether to shoot its venom into your veins. 'My name is Salek al-Fayadh. I'm a scientist, from the Lebanon.'

'So, since you're here,' said the professor, 'what do you want?'

Nick glanced edgily at Salek. 'We should speak to you alone.'

'There's nothing that you can't say in front of Salek,' replied Wilmington. 'He's an old friend.'

Salek moved closer to Nick. The room measured fifteen feet by ten, with a window that looked out on to the street. A light drizzle was falling outside. Three of the walls were covered with bookshelves, each bulging with thick-looking scientific works. A stack of papers was balanced in one corner. On the far wall there was a desk, with a computer on it. Next to that a blackboard, with a set of equations drawn on it. Jed knew enough physics to know they related to nuclear reactions of some sort, but he couldn't identify which kind. The professor was probably just preparing for a tutorial.

'Are you soldiers?' said Salek, looking at both Nick and Jed.

'What makes you say that?' said Nick.

Salek smiled, his moustache creasing up as he did so. 'I've been around military men, I recognise their manner,' he replied. 'Which regiment?'

'It doesn't matter,' said Nick.

'So you are soldiers, then . . .'

There was a slight chuckle in his voice that grated on Jed's nerves as if he was laughing at them.

'I told you, it doesn't matter,' snapped Nick. He looked back at Wilmington. 'Sarah's gone missing,' he said. 'We're both worried about her. Very worried. I wanted to check when she was last in the lab?'

Wilmington rubbed his hand against his cheek. 'I might have spoken to her last Friday,' he said. 'But I'm not here every day myself, so I can't be certain.'

'Do you know if she's contacted anyone here in the past couple of days?' said Jed.

'Not that I know of,' he said, 'but I can put out a general email. One of her colleagues might have spoken to her.'

'There's been no sign of her for at least four days,' said Nick. 'Do you have any idea where she might be?'

Wilmington shook his head.

'Maybe she had to go to a conference?' said Jed.

The professor shrugged. 'Not that I know of.'

'Nothing to do with her work that could take her out of Cambridge?'

Again, Wilmington shook his head. 'Sarah is a very brilliant young woman,' he said. 'Quite possibly the most brilliant young physicist in Cambridge, which means she is probably the best in Europe. You should be very proud of her.' He smiled at Nick, then turned round, walking towards the window. The rain was starting to fall more heavily now, splattering up against the glass. 'But she is erratic. She is unstable. That's true of many great scientists, although in Sarah's case she's had incidents in her past that may have made her prone to mild depression, and perhaps even schizophrenia.' He turned back to Nick, his expression accusing. 'I suppose you know all about that. She regularly disappears for several days at a time. But she has always turned up again in the past, and I suppose she will again.'

He stepped away from the window, standing right in front of Nick and Jed. 'So I'm sorry not to be more helpful, and I understand your concern,' he said, 'but

I'm sure she's fine. Now, I'm afraid, I have a tutorial to give.'

'She's never disappeared for this long before,' snapped Nick, his tone exasperated.

'There's a first time for everything,' said Wilmington.

'What kind of work was she doing recently?' asked Jed.

Wilmington shrugged. 'Nuclear physics,' he said. 'Even I had trouble understanding some of the concepts she was exploring. I imagine they'd be way beyond you.'

Nick ignored the insult. 'Anything to do with weapons research?'

'A soldier's natural question,' said Salek.

'Well, what's the answer?' said Nick, ignoring Salek.

The professor chuckled. 'When you say nuclear physics, the average person always thinks it's something to do with weapons. But of course, just about all physics is nuclear physics, since our work revolves around what laws govern the subatomic world. Nothing that Sarah is working on is ever likely to make a big bang, of that much I'm certain. We don't do that kind of work here.'

'Can you be sure of that?' said Jed. 'You saw her work?'

'I can be quite sure,' said Wilmington. 'There's actually very little interesting theoretical work being done in nuclear weaponry any more. It's just engineering and computing. All the conceptual work was done fifty years ago.' He looked hard at Nick and Jed. 'Now, much as I'm enjoying this conversation, that tutorial is going to start in one minute. So you really must excuse me.'

Salek smiled at Jed. 'I hope we meet again one day,' he said, with exaggerated courtesy.

Jed nodded but remained silent.

'In fact, I feel sure we will . . .'

Jed walked briskly along the road, his jacket pulled up high around his neck to protect himself from the rain. 'Maybe the professor is right,' he said. 'Maybe Sarah is just on another of her benders. It's happened often enough in the past.'

'This time is different,' said Nick

'I don't know,' said Jed. 'You're always away, so you don't see as much of her as I do. Or the people in the lab.'

'I'm her father,' snarled Nick. 'I know her better than anyone.

'Fathers always think that.'

'What the hell does that mean?'

'It doesn't matter,' said Jed, turning away.

Nick looked at him. He was thinking about the money deposited in the joint account. It didn't matter what anyone said: nobody made a hundred grand without doing anything. If they disappeared right afterwards, it meant something had happened to them. And he would find out what. Just him. *Nobody else.*

'This is my business, you hear,' he said. His voice was raised, and a woman walking down the street with a baby in a buggy started to cross the road to get away from them. 'So you just keep out of it.'

'Right, because you've made such a great job of

looking after her in the past,' said Jed. 'Maybe that's why she goes on drinking benders all the time. Maybe that's why she pops pills, and doesn't believe she can ever commit to another man.'

'You know bloody nothing about it,' said Nick.

Jed could see the fury in his eyes. The pupils were glinting with anger, and there was a bead of sweat running down the side of his face. Jed had been in enough fights in his life to know when a punch was about to be thrown: there was a moment between two men when a point could only be settled with fists, not words, and they had reached that point now. 'Just give it to me, grandad,' he snapped. 'Let's see how tough you really are.'

Nick took a step forward. His shoulder muscles were tensed, and his arm was starting to draw backwards. Jed steadied himself, ready to use his arms to deflect the force of the first blow.

'Never talk about Sarah like that again,' growled Nick.

The mobile in Jed's pocket was ringing. He was about to ignore it, then he wondered if it might be Sarah answering one of the many messages he had left for her. 'Yes,' he said into the receiver.

He listened for a minute, then snapped the phone shut. He looked back at Nick. The man was standing right next to him, his legs apart, his fist ready: the stance of a trained fighter. 'I've been recalled to base,' said Jed. 'Immediately.'

Jed turned round and started walking towards the station. It didn't matter where you were or what you were doing. When the Regiment said it needed you,

you did as you were told. Those were the rules, and they were unbreakable. 'We'll fight another day,' he said, looking back at Nick.

'Trust me, we will,' said Nick. 'And next time, there will be nothing to save you.'

FIVE

Daniel Sutton looked at Jed coldly. He was only a couple of years older than him, and hadn't been to such a good university, but he'd been to the right school, and had the right accent, so that made him a Rupert. 'I hear there was a bit of a dust-up down in London,' he said.

Jed nodded. 'I voiced some reservations about whether I wanted to take the mission,' he said. 'It's off the books, so I have a choice.'

They were sitting in a bare concrete briefing room. There was one simple wooden table, with Sutton behind it, and Jed opposite him. In the corner, there was a single lamp bulb, spreading a pale light up into the room. 'Technically, you have a choice,' said Sutton. 'Just like technically you can appeal against a parking ticket. But it won't do you any good, because no one gives a sod. You can refuse the mission if you want to, but the Regiment has no place for men who refuse to do what their country needs. That understood?'

'How long do I have to make up my mind?'

'About five minutes.'

There was a silence. A minute went by without either

man speaking. If you've got five minutes, you might as well use it, Jed decided. He knew the risks of going into Iraq. He'd been there only two weeks ago. The whole country was wound up like a crowd of football fans minutes before a Cup Final kicked off: it was tense with anticipation, trigger-happy, and looking for a fight. That made it dangerous. Without backup, they'd be exposed to dangers that he probably couldn't even imagine.

But that wasn't it. If he wasn't able to handle danger he wouldn't have joined the Regiment in the first place. The real reason he wanted to turn down the mission was because he wanted to stay here. *To find Sarah.*

Three minutes ticked by on his watch. Jed was still thinking.

'Listen,' said Sutton, his expression softening. 'You're a good man, Jed. You've got a great future in this outfit. With your academic qualifications and your skills in the field, you could go all the way. I don't know what's bothering you, but let me tell you this, if you blow out of the Regiment now, you'll regret it for the rest of your life.'

Jed looked back at him. He thought about the way he'd felt when he'd walked back into the regimental headquarters a few minutes ago after getting back from Cambridge. He thought about the trophies on the wall of the mess, marking the different battles the Regiment had fought throughout the world. He thought about the mates he had made since he signed up: men who would lay down their lives for him, and for whom he would gladly do the same. I belong here, he told himself. *I sure as hell don't belong anywhere else. Never did.*

'When do we start?' he said.

Laura was standing at the front of the room. She glanced down at Jed, and a brief smile flickered across her lips. Obvious enough that I will know what she means, he thought to himself. But subtle enough so that no one else will.

'Here,' she said, pointing a finger at the map. 'The target is right here.'

Jed looked around the room. He'd been introduced to the rest of the team ten minutes ago. Steve was a twenty-six-year-old Londoner, with two years in the Regiment behind him. Jed had worked with him once before and rated him as a tough, efficient operator. Rob was from Nottingham, and at thirty was the oldest of the unit. Married with one kid, he was a quiet and serious man. Jed had not worked with him before, but he'd heard good things about him. Matt was the final member of the four-man team, a loud Geordie, with an obsessive interest in football and women, who was usually found at the bar late at night with a beer in his hand, slagging off Sven-Göran Eriksson for not picking more Newcastle players for the England team. They were all good men, Jed decided. They probably deserved better than what they were about to get.

'The drop-off will be three miles from the site,' continued Laura.

From the black-and-white satellite map it looked

more like Birmingham than Baghdad. A set of grey warehouses, surrounded by factories, and a huge great concrete road slung across another, smaller road with little thought for the local people.

She pointed to the compound, and even from a shot taken a couple of miles up in the sky, Jed could tell it was more heavily guarded than when he had taken pictures of it a couple of weeks ago: somebody had taken the trouble to build up its fortifications, and that was suspicious in itself. There was a thick set of concrete walls, topped off by barbed wire, with machine-gun turrets stationed every fifty yards. Inside the perimeter wall, there was what looked like a deep ditch or a moat: it was impossible from the satellite to tell which. *Whatever the Iraqis were keeping in there, they certainly didn't want anyone stumbling across it.*

'You'll start out in Kuwait, then a Black Hawk will take you up to Baghdad,' said Laura. 'You shouldn't have any trouble on that bit of the journey. The Iraqis have given up contesting control of the air and are letting us do pretty much what we like up there. We'll be using electronics to jam their radar systems in the vicinity, so hopefully they won't even know there's a chopper coming in. But, as you know, none of those systems are fail-safe, so you'll have to be prepared to fight your way out of trouble if you need to. If it gets too hot on landing, the Black Hawk will abort and try to find another setting-down point. But once you're down, that's it. The chopper won't be coming back. You'll be on your own.

'Jed has already been into the territory, so he'll be leading the way. You'll skirt around the edge of Baghdad for two miles, then strike into the centre of the city. You'll have detailed maps so you won't have to stop and ask for directions.' Laura glanced around her audience, but quickly realised no one was smiling. 'Once you get there, you'll need to lay up and survey the scene. We'll sort you out with plenty of dollars and some gold coins, so if you get the chance, bribe one of the locals to help you out. But remember, the most important thing is not to get caught.'

A second image flashed up on the screen. It showed the compound in greater detail. Jed recognised some of the details from his last visit: it had pipes running into it, and chimneys arranged around its core. 'The mission is to get inside, and get pictures of what they are doing in there,' Laura continued, tapping her finger impatiently against the satellite image. 'If you can, get samples as well. You'll all be issued with biological protection suits, because we have to assume there is some kind of chemical weapon inside this facility. If it gets too dangerous, evacuate, but make sure you've planned a way to get back in.' She paused, her eyes resting on each man in turn. 'This mission is critical. We have to find out what's happening in there. If you don't get it first go, you just have to keep trying.'

'How are we supposed to fight with the bio suits on?' said Matt.

Laura looked at him. 'We have thirty-six hours until drop-down. I suggest you practise as hard as you can.'

'But if we get faced with a choice, what's the operating procedure?' said Rob. 'Abandon the suits and keep fighting, or retreat. What's the intel? How great is the risk of contamination?'

'Keep fighting,' said Laura, with a hint of steel in her voice. 'Before you go, one of the scientists is going to come from London to give you a basic briefing on what a biological weapons lab is going to look like. He'll tell you what kind of kit to look for, the test tubes and testing facilities, and what it should be safe to touch. But you have to understand, we have limited intel on this plant. The only thing we know for certain is that it is very important. We haven't much idea what's in there. That's why we must get you in.'

'And how do we get out again?' said Jed.

Her eyes latched on to his. 'On your own,' she replied.

'All the way out of the country?'

'We'll give you maps, but you'll have to make your own way down south to Basra. Once you hit the coast, radio in, and a navy boat will come and pick you up. You can call us on the satellite phone and tell us your position. If it is possible, we'll send a chopper in to come and lift you out. But we can't guarantee that. The war might have turned hot by then, and kit could be in short supply. So you have to be prepared to make your own way south. Laura paused. 'Remember, the thing the Iraqis want most over the next couple of weeks is to capture some British or American special forces operating inside the country. It would be a huge coup for them. So unless you all want to be saying hello to your mums live on al-Jazeera, I suggest you lie low, and get down to Basra as fast as you can.'

Jed was about to speak, but Sutton had already stepped forward to close the briefing down. 'We've got thirty-six hours,' he said. 'I suggest you get plenty of kip, and all the last-minute training you can.'

Andy Tullow had a craggy, tanned face, and an open, engaging manner. He was in his mid-forties, and most of the men knew who he was even before he'd been introduced. They'd seen him on TV when he was captured on a scud-busting mission last time around, his face broadcast around the world when Saddam Hussein took him hostage. 'If I can help you I will,' he said, looking around at Jed, Rob, Matt and Steve. 'But once you hit the ground, then it's up to you.'

In the last six months, the Regiment had been calling in some of the older guys who had fought in Gulf 1 to brief everyone on what it was like to fight on the ground in Iraq. Nobody was listening to the debate in the news about whether Saddam would comply with UN resolutions, or whether Parliament would vote for the war. The shooting was going to start soon. Everyone knew that. *And it would be their fingers on the trigger.*

'Don't ever underestimate the average fighting Iraqi man,' said Tullow. 'And don't overestimate his kit. That's the main thing I'd say to you. When we went in we had all this bollocks from the Ruperts about how the Iraqi Army had top-grade Russian weapons, but the men didn't want to fight. All crap. None of their kit worked.

The Russian guns were more of a threat to the blokes firing them than they were to us. It was even worse than the rubbish they gave us. But the blokes were happy enough to get into a scrap. They may not have liked Saddam that much, probably still don't, but they don't like a bunch of Brits running around their country with guns either. So watch them. If you get into a scrap, they'll be bloody vicious.'

The talk lasted for half an hour or so. Steve and Matt were asking most of the questions. How was the weather? Did it get cold at night? What was the layout of the houses like? Where would snipers take up their positions? Where could you expect to lay up and get cover? Could you drop into a sewer if the fighting got rough? They were all good, smart questions, and Tullow answered them all straight. You could never know too much about the territory you were about to wage war in. One stray scrap of information might save your life. Jed knew that. But he was only half listening: his mind was still focused on what might have happened to Sarah.

When Tullow's session was over, they had a talk from a Mossad guy, who would download everything the Israeli intelligence agency had learnt about Iraq in the last few years. The SAS and Mossad had maintained close links ever since the Israelis had helped out with tracking down the arms shipments the Libyans gave to the IRA through the 1980s, and in return the Regiment had provided training and assistance for its boys. It was an informal arrangement that had worked well over the years – certainly Mossad would have no objections to seeing Saddam taking another beating. As the rest of the unit got up to leave, Jed paused by the door. He wanted to speak to Tullow before he left. Alone.

'What was it like?' he said, checking that the other three had already left the room. 'Being captured?'

Tullow hesitated for a moment. 'Worse than you can ever imagine.'

'You know a guy called Nick Scott?'

'Nick? Hell, yes. What's happened to the bugger? I heard things got pretty rough for him. Bailed out of the Regiment, then his wife died. Is he OK?'

Jed nodded. 'He's getting by,' he said. 'He went through a spell with the bottle, but he's mostly sober now. Works in security.'

'Well, I'm pleased,' said Tullow carefully. 'He was a good man once, you know. That's what being captured does to a guy. It breaks them.'

'What happened to him in there?'

Tullow looked straight at Jed, and for a brief moment the younger man could sense real anger in his eyes. 'You never ask a man that,' he snapped. 'Whatever happens, never ask a man who's been captured what went on while he was a prisoner. That's a conversation he has with himself, and no one else.'

Jed could smell the perfume on his skin: a faint, musty smell, as if a sprinkling of fresh flowers had been tossed across the bed. Her face was lying next to his, and her hair was lying across his chest. According to the clock on the wall, it was just after one thirty in the morning.

Laura had arrived in his barracks room about half an hour ago, sneaking in like a schoolgirl breaking into the boys' dorm. He'd taken her in his arms, and made love to her without really thinking about it: her body was flawless, perfect and toned, but there was something mechanical about having sex with her, as if she were just using him for her own pleasure. Hell, he'd thought, as he felt her legs curling around his back. When a man's about to go on a mission from which the chances of returning alive are no more than fifty-fifty, he should grab every last morsel of pleasure he can extract from life.

When they were finished, he reached for the side of his bed, checking his mobile phone: still no message from Sarah. *Not even a text.*

'What's your bird like, then?' said Laura.

Jed paused, taken aback by the question. He hadn't imagined that Laura knew about Sarah. She certainly didn't act like the possessive type. *Christ, maybe she was about to start getting out Ikea catalogues, and talking about seating plans for the wedding.*

'Which bird is that, then?'

Laura ran her fingers through the hairs on his chest. 'There is always a girl somewhere.'

Jed shook his head. 'No one special.'

'I've seen the files, Jed,' said Laura sternly. 'What's her name again? Sarah? The daughter of a Regiment guy, right.'

Jed shrugged. 'We might be on a break right now, I'm not really sure.'

He could hear Laura trying to stifle a laugh. 'Guys always say that when they're shagging someone else. Does she *know* about this *break*?'

'It was her idea.'

'So what's she like?'

Jed rolled over, so that his body was lying right next to her. He could feel the friction of her skin against his. 'First you tell me why we're really going to Iraq.'

'We told you, to find out what's in that plant.'

'Bollocks,' said Jed. 'There are easier ways of doing that than sending an SAS team into the place.'

Laura arched up, stretching out her lips so they met his. 'You just do the shooting,' she said. 'Leave the thinking to us.'

SIX

Nick took the pizza from the oven, opened a bottle of water and started eating. There was always pizza in the freezer, and it always tasted the same. Sometimes he wondered why he bothered taking them out of the box: the pizza tasted of cardboard, so he might as well eat the whole thing.

On the hi-fi, he was playing Simon & Garfunkel's 'Bridge Over Troubled Water', a song that had been among his and Mary's favourites. They'd played it at their wedding, and he'd played it to Sarah when she was a baby: there was something about the harmonies that seemed to help to get her to sleep. 'Silver girl,' he thought to himself as he listened to the final verse of the song. It was where his nickname for her had come from. '*Sail on silver girl, sail on by,*' crooned Art Garfunkel. '*Your time has come to shine / All your dreams are on their way.*'

He glanced through the two-bedroomed cottage. He'd bought it with Mary, but she'd died before they had time to decorate it. He'd thrown some magnolia paint on the walls, and in the study he'd kept a few mementos of his time in the Regiment, but otherwise it could have been a rented cottage. Tonight it looks even emptier than usual, Nick thought. It was missing something. Sarah. She wasn't here very often, but there was always the sense that she might come home for a visit. Just the fact that she had a room made a difference, even if it was empty most of the time.

Right now, it doesn't look like she's coming back anytime soon.

He'd checked the phone as soon as he stepped through the door. Nothing. He'd checked the mail, but there was nothing apart from the usual bills, credit-card offers and a letter from the agency confirming his next shift on the rigs.

Finishing the pizza, he walked up to Sarah's room. It was next to his own bedroom, and he'd left it almost exactly as it was when she was a teenager: there were some posters of Blur and Pulp on the wall, an easel where she liked to paint, and bookshelves crammed with all the books she'd needed for her A levels. Nothing else. Just like her room in Cambridge, Sarah left little of herself in any of the places she stayed. She took everything with her.

Her diary, thought Nick. It must be around here somewhere.

He found it in the drawer of her desk. He skipped past the writing – she'd only kept it for about six months when she was seventeen – towards the phone numbers. There was a list of about twenty of them, all written in her neat, black lettering – Sarah updated it occasionally when she came to stay so she could call her friends locally, but she hadn't touched it for at least two years now. It was a long shot, he knew. Sarah wasn't necessarily in contact with any of these people now. *But when somebody vanishes off the face of the earth, where else do you start?*

'Is that Louise?' he said into the phone as soon as it was answered.

'Yes.'

The woman sounded tired and stressed. Somewhere in the background, he could hear a baby screaming. 'It's Nick Scott, Sarah's dad.'

There was a pause while she tried to place them. 'OK,' she said.

'I was just wondering if you had heard from Sarah at all?'

'Is she OK?'

'I don't know,' said Nick. 'No one has heard from her for a week or so. I was just wondering if she might be with one of her old friends.'

'I haven't seen her for almost two years,' said Louise.

'Sorry to trouble you.'

'Jesus, I hope she's OK.'

'So do I.'

Nick put the phone down and glanced out of the window. It was a cold but clear night. The cottage was halfway up a hill, with a view on to the Black Mountains beyond. A three-quarter moon was hanging in the sky, sending pale shafts of silvery light into the grey-green hillside. Somewhere in the distance, he could hear a car, but it was half a mile to the next house, and tonight, like every night, the hills were cloaked in silence. Nick tried the next number on his list. Emma had been Sarah's best friend at school, the pair of them inseparable from the ages of fifteen to seventeen, although her mother, keen for her daughter to climb the heights of Herefordshire society, hadn't liked Sarah much, and approved of Nick even less. Last he'd heard, Emma was working in London on a women's magazine. He tried her on the mobile number. No, she told him. She hadn't heard anything of Sarah. In fact, she hadn't spoken to her for six months. Emma had called her asking if she could be a case study for a magazine feature about how brains stopped a girl from getting a proper boyfriend, and, to use Emma's phrase, 'she seemed a bit miffed about it'. So, no, she hadn't heard from Sarah recently. Nick put the phone down, and looked out of the window again. He felt desperate for a drink, and was thankful that there was nothing in the cottage: if he'd been in town, nothing would have stopped him nipping out to the off-licence. He tried another number: James, a guy Sarah had dated when she stopped seeing Jed for about a year in her early twenties. No luck there. He'd changed address, and the person answering the phone didn't know where he'd moved to. Bugger it, thought Nick. *A brick wall would be more help than this.*

Again he looked out of the window. Something was moving. A shadow maybe. Nick looked closer. He could hear a rustling, but that might just have been the wind blowing through trees. No, he decided. Tonight was just like every other night on the edge of the Black Mountains. Empty. Still. *Abandoned.*

He tried another number. Gill was one of Sarah's friends from university: she was now working in Manchester as a doctor. Nick knew that she sometimes went up to stay with her for the weekend. They'd spend twenty-four hours getting wasted on the clubbing scene. Maybe she was just crashing there for a few days. Perhaps she'd just forgotten to take her mobile charger with her. It was easy enough to do. Nick sometimes forgot to charge up his mobile before leaving for the rigs.

No, said Gill. She'd been up for the weekend about a month ago. She seemed her usual self: strung out like a wire, babbling about work, drinking too much, always looking for the next party, the same old Sarah. There had been a text a couple of weeks ago, but since then Gill had heard nothing. 'I'm sorry,' she said. 'Let me know if there's anything I can do.'

With a sinking feeling, Nick put the phone down. He was running out of options. None of her friends knew where the hell she was. Her professor was acting evasively. She had a hundred grand in her bank account. *What the hell has happened to her?*

Suddenly, Nick could feel how cold the cottage was. It was a few weeks since he'd been here, and a cold snap meant its old stone walls had frozen solid: they were like ice cubes, freezing everything around them. He'd put the heating on but it would take a couple of days for the place to thaw out again. He looked out of the window again, trying to remember if the BP station on the road into Hereford sold beer or wine, and whether it might be open at this time of night. Just one

77

drink, he thought to himself. *To get me through the next few days.*

Another movement. Something was out there. *Somebody. He was certain of it.*

Nick remained still. The expression on his face was relaxed, impassive, as if he was just admiring the shapes the moon and the clouds were creating on the hills. But inside his mind was working furiously. Someone is out there, he told himself. *Somebody is watching me.*

He started moving away from the window. Whoever they were, he didn't want them to know they'd been spotted. Just act casual, like you have no idea they're out there.

Flicking on the TV, he caught the closing headlines on the ITV news. Blair was talking some rubbish about the threat of Saddam Hussein supplying biological weapons to terrorists. Nick turned the sound down. If anyone was watching the house right now, they'd think he was just slumped in front of the box. No threat to anyone.

Quietly, he slipped away to the phone. He picked up the receiver, and started to dial, but used only eight digits instead of nine. The phone just made a rapid bleeping sound. That was fine. Nick didn't want to speak to anyone right now. Still holding the phone to his lips, he turned his back to the window. Kneeling down, he started to unscrew the back of the phone. It was a cheap receiver he'd bought in Argos for a tenner: the back came away simply enough. Inside, he could see a small black chip measuring one centimetre lengthwise and half a centimetre across. Nick recognised it at once.

A bug.

Someone was listening to his calls.

He screwed the receiver back into place, then dialled Sarah's mobile number again, just for a number to ring. Whoever was listening into the calls, he didn't want them to know they'd been rumbled. Not yet. 'Hiya, silver girl, it's me,' he said when he got the voicemail message that was now tediously familiar. 'Give us a ring when you can.'

Slowly he moved back towards the TV. A Clint Eastwood film was just starting. Perhaps he'd watch it. After all, there wasn't much chance of sleeping tonight; maybe just crash out in front of the box. *Let them think I haven't seen them.*

The listening device was familiar to Nick. One of the first things you learnt on the security circuit was how to sweep a room for bugs. This was nothing special: a simple plug-in device you could buy from a couple of dozen firms that sold them over the Internet. It took the phone call and transmitted it over a short-wave radio signal to a listening post nearby. Its range was about half a mile, depending on the terrain. In these hills, maybe less. That meant they were close by.

Glancing up at the silent screen, Nick could see Clint pulling his Magnum from its holster. *Somebody is watching me. And my phone is tapped.* Nick repeated the same two phrases to himself sombrely.

Well, mate, all I know is this. You picked on the wrong fight this time. *You've got a hell of beating coming to you.*

★   ★   ★

The sky was darker tonight, Nick noted. A thick layer of clouds had settled into the valley early in the day and showed no signs of moving. The moon was hidden, and none of the stars was visible. Perfect, he told himself. *For this evening's work, I need all the darkness I can get.*

Once or twice he'd glanced towards the spot where he'd seen the movements, but he hadn't looked at it for more than a fraction of a second. That would create suspicion. He had no idea who might be watching him, or why, but he assumed they'd been properly trained. That meant one of the first things they'd be looking for was a sign that they'd been rumbled. Any hint of that, and they'd evacuate the place on the spot. The first rule of surveillance was always the same, whoever you were working for: *Don't get bloody caught.*

Nick picked up the phone. There had been almost twenty-four hours now since he'd realised he was being watched. Enough time to plan his response down to the last detail. He called Sarah's mobile again, waiting for the voicemail to click on. 'It's me again, love,' he said. 'I'm going to be in all evening, so give me a ring.' Next, he called Ken's Pizza Delivery in Hereford. 'One large pepperoni, and a beer,' he said, then gave the address. 'For about ten, please.'

That should convince whoever is listening I'm staying in for the evening.

For a few minutes that morning, Nick had wondered if he should call Jed and get his help. He could stay in the house, while Jed could stalk the men in the bushes. He'd decided against it. *I can handle this by* myself. *I don't need that arrogant little tosser buggering things up.*

Nick flicked the TV on. It was already pitch black outside. He glanced out of the window but could see nothing, only darkness. He pulled the curtains together, then bolted the front door. Taking off his shoes to stay as quiet as possible, he walked upstairs to his bedroom. The cottage only had one entrance, at its front. The back door that led into the kitchen had been bricked up years ago. His bedroom looked out on to the side of the house, and was protected by a large oak tree which, even in winter with its leaves down, effectively camouflaged the window. Stopping by the cupboard, he pulled out a tin of boot polish, and started to smear some across his cheeks and forehead. He was wearing black jeans and a black sweat-shirt. Catching a glimpse of himself in the mirror, Nick flashed a menacing, malevolent smile: the smile of a man intent on beating his way to the truth. It feels good to be back in action, he told himself. *This is who you are.*

Swinging open the window, Nick climbed gently on to the ledge. He'd owned this house for more than a decade, but until this evening he'd never thought how to turn it into a fortress. A gutter ran down the side of the house, a yard from the window. Nick reached over, gripping the pipe tightly into the palm of his fist, then started to lever himself across the side of the house. The stone from which the cottage was built was pitted with crevices, perfect for climbing. In a few seconds, he'd secured his grip, and slid effortlessly down the drain-pipe on to the grass below.

Keeping low to ground, with his back bent double, he moved across the stretch of lawn towards the adjoining field. There was a gap in the hedge through which some sheep sometimes broke and ate whatever few flowers Nick had bothered to plant in the garden. He pulled himself through, and started to walk across the field, keeping himself close to the hedge. Glancing up at the sky, he could see it was still pitch black; the cloud cover was heavy, and a few light drops of rain were starting to fall. A biting wind was blowing through the mountains. Perfect, Nick thought. The worse the weather is, the harder it will be to spot a man coming towards them.

He reckoned the observing post was where he'd spotted the movement last night. It would be nothing special – if they had any brains, they'd keep themselves as mobile as possible. A sheet of green tarpaulin to cover themselves, and a pair of binoculars, plus whatever kit they needed for listening to the bugged phone calls. So long as their clothes were camouflaged as well, that should be enough to stop them being spotted. Nick's plan was to skirt around the front of the house through the fields, then crawl up on them from behind. Keep it simple, he could remember one of his instructors yelling at him during his training courses for the Regiment. *If you can stab the fuckers in the back, that's as good a place as any.*

Nick paused. He'd moved about three hundred yards now: two hundred yards up from the front of the house, and a hundred yards across the field, so that he was looking straight down at the cottage. He could see the light seeping out from behind the curtains, and underneath the front door. The light above the porch cast a few pale shadows across the path that led to the road, and just about touched the bonnet of his six-year-old Rover parked a few yards from the door. Otherwise, the hillside was shrouded in darkness.

The rain was starting to gather strength. Nick could feel it starting to beat on to him. Water was curling around his hair, and dropping down over his face. The blacking on his face was starting to smudge. He looked down towards the house, his eyes scanning the surface of the ground. They'll be somewhere, he told himself. And they'll be looking in the wrong direction.

Nothing. He scanned the field that lay directly in front of the cottage, and where he had seen the movement last night, but it was completely still. The rain and the darkness made it hard to get an accurate picture, but two men even lying flat under a green sheet should be visible from here. He started to inch closer. Maybe I just need to get nearer, he thought.

Nick advanced ten, then twenty yards. Somewhere to the left he felt certain he heard a noise. He paused, listening harder. A creak. He glanced nervously in the direction the sound had come from. A tree was starting to sway as the wind and the rain battered against it. Nick pressed forward. He was seventy yards from the front of the house now, in the centre of the field looking down on it. No sign of them. Maybe the buggers decided to knock off for the night. Maybe they don't like getting their hair wet.

He started to move to the left, heading towards the next field. He squatted down close to the hedge and came to a gap. The ground was chewed up by the cattle that sometimes grazed there, and the rain had filled it with puddles that mixed the mud with cow dung to create a foul-smelling pond. Nick held his breath, and crawled through the gap. The dung was soaking into his body. Too risky to stand up, he warned himself. If they're here, they'll see me.

A gust of wind whipped up through the field. Fifty or sixty yards in front of him, Nick felt certain he saw something. It was just a shape. The field was rough, sloping down towards the side of the cottage, but the hump was a distinct mark. It rose up out of the ground by a foot or so, and it was looking straight down at the cottage. Nick crawled forward. He was forty yards from the lump now. And the conviction was growing within him: he'd found them.

He steered himself further along the field, then looked straight down. He was twenty yards back from their position. Nick sometimes wished he'd kept a gun in the house, but with his reputation for drinking, the local police would never have given him a licence. Instead, he'd armed himself with a thick, two-foot length of lead pipe, and a sharp, six-inch steel kitchen knife. That should be enough, he told himself. You don't need guns to take vengeance on a man. *Just muscles, determination and the will to fight*.

Suddenly, he heard a voice: it was just a whisper, but carried on the wind it managed to travel to where Nick was squatting as vividly as if the man was lying right next to him. 'Shit, this rain.'

You've got worse things to worry about than the rain, pal, Nick thought grimly.

Nick pulled himself forward. He could feel his body rustling in the long grass, but in the wind and rain the noise of his approach was smothered. His skin was soaked already, and the mud made progress slow. He could smell the cow dung reeking off his body. Ten yards. He hesitated, and took a closer look. The sheet measured six foot by five, and was spread flat over the ground so it blended into the ground. Nick could just about see the soles of four boots sticking out of it. Two men. Lying flat on their stomachs, with binoculars trained on the house. They probably did shifts of four or five hours, so there must be some backup not far away. I'll have to deal with them fast, before the help arrives.

He took two more lunges forward. The mud was spitting up into his eyes and his face. Five yards. He took the kitchen knife from his pocket, and held it tight in the fist of his right hand. He could see the boots wriggle as the rain lashed into them, and he could hear one of the men speaking.

'I think the old bugger's fallen asleep in front of the telly again,' the man said, in what sounded like an Irish accent.

'Looks like another cold, boring night,' replied his mate, in what sounded to Nick like a German accent.

Nick plunged the knife into the first foot he could see before him. The thin blade sliced though the leather then cut through the sock and into the skin below. A blood-curdling scream howled up from the man's lips. Nick swiftly withdrew the blade: he'd have liked to have searched around for a vein to cut, but the edge of his blade risked getting caught in the leather of the boot. He stood up swiftly, holding on to his lead pipe, swinging it forward. Both men were scrambling to their feet. The metal collided with the jaw of one of them, smashing into the bone and breaking the skin, so that a small trickle of blood started to dribble on to his neck.

Nick stood straight up. He had the pipe in one hand, the knife in the other. Even through the murky darkness, he could make out the faces of the two men. The guy with the Irish accent was the taller of the two. He had longish brown hair, and a short, close-cropped beard, and eyes that seemed to sparkle in the rain. He had taken a bad blow to the side of his face from the pipe: it looked as if at least one tooth had been knocked out, and there was blood on his tongue. The smaller man, with the German accent, had dirty blond hair, cropped, and a thick, bull-like face that was pitted with spots. He'd taken a nasty slice to his foot, but was standing firm on the ground. He knows how to take a cut, Nick thought. *And he probably knows how to deliver one as well.*

'Who the fuck are you?' shouted Nick.

His face was red with fury. Rainwater was pouring down the side of his blackened face, and the blood was still dripping from the lead pipe in his hand. 'Who the fuck sent you to watch me?'

He was standing three yards from both men. The

shorter man was inching towards him. He had no weapons in his hand, but Nick could see he didn't need them. He held the knife out in front of him. 'Where the fuck is my daughter?'

The man swung a fist. Nick slashed at him with the knife, but missed. He was just cutting the air. A blow landed on the side of his face. Instinctively, Nick thrust his arm up to parry it. He could feel the bone stinging where the fist had landed. A kick landed on his shins, briefly destabilising him, but he managed to hold his balance. He swung the pipe round, hitting the German in the stomach. 'Fuck you,' spat the German. 'Fucking bastard.'

'Leave it the fuck alone, Kurt,' shouted the Irishman. 'We're not here to fight.'

Nick slipped as Kurt had raised his fist, and Nick could see that it was about to crash into his skull. 'Who in the name of hell are you?' Nick shouted again, louder this time.

The German's fist was about to crash into him, when his mate rushed forward and got hold of him, pulling him back. Nick reached out, grabbing at the Irishman's hair, but he ripped himself away, leaving just a few strands in Nick's fist. 'We've no reason to fight, old man,' snarled the Irishman. 'And we certainly don't want you dead, you're no use to us like that.'

The German broke free. He smashed another blow into Nick's stomach, doubling him up in pain. The pipe dropped from his hand. The German picked it up, and crashed it into Nick's ribcage. He could feel at least one bone quiver, then snap. The pain was shooting up through his spine and exploding inside his head. Still bent over double, he smashed his head into the man's groin, but his muscle was like rock, and Nick could feel a bruise on his skull start to swell.

'Leave him alone, you bloody idiot,' shouted the Irishman.

'I can finish him,' shrieked the German, his voice turning ugly.

'We're not meant to kill the old fucker.'

The German wasn't listening. He lunged forward with the pipe in his hand. Swinging around, he smashed it towards Nick's chest, aiming for the broken rib. Nick swerved. Next, the man was flinging a punch with his left fist. It collided with the side of Nick's jaw, impacting against his skin with the force of a mallet. A dull ache started to spread down his neck into his spine. He thrust the knife towards the man's stomach, but he saw it coming, and put his arm out to deflect the weapon. The knife ripped into the waxed surface of his jacket, tearing the cloth. As it snagged in the material, Nick lost his grip on the blade and, within a second, the German had whipped it free. He pointed it towards Nick, then thrust the blade at him. Nick jumped backwards. The German advanced, oblivious to the wound in his foot. The knife was stabbing in the air. It slashed into Nick's arm, cutting the fabric of his sweatshirt. Nick slammed his fist into the side of the man's arm, planning to knock the blade out of his fist. The German's grip flinched as the blow struck him, but his muscles were like iron, and the knife stayed steady in his hand. He flicked it upwards, this time cutting into Nick's skin. He could feel its cold blade slicing into his flesh, and a cry of pain erupted from his lips. Another strike. This time the blade sunk deep into his arm. He screamed, louder this time. Blood was starting to flow from the wound, mixing with the rain that was lashing into his side, and running down into a muddy, crimson pool beside him. He steadied himself, but the German was advancing towards him once again. There was a look in his eye that Nick recognised from the battlefields he'd fought on: a steely mask of concentration that descended on a man's face in the moment before he was about to kill someone.

'Leave it, you fucking idiot,' shouted the Irishman.

He rushed forward, holding tight on to the German. At first the man shrugged him aside, using all the strength in his shoulders to break himself free. Then the anger within him started to subside. Grabbing the German, the Irishman started to run down the hillside towards the path. Nick was running after them, but they were younger and fitter than he was, and even with the wounds they had taken, they were more agile across the muddy ground. Nick pushed himself forward, running through the field. The rain was beating into him. He tripped, falling face down in to the mud. He could feel the wind wrapping around him, and the flow of blood was starting to increase from the wounds on his arm. His head was splitting from the blow he had taken. He could feel the strength start to drain out of him. Ahead he could see the two men running on to the path, disappearing into the darkness.

Shit, he muttered to himself. If I die here tonight, I don't much care. But who will help Sarah?

Without me, she had no one.

SEVEN

Jed knelt down in the mud. The rain was lashing into him, and the wind blowing hard down off the side of the mountains. The night was still pitch black. Pure luck, thought Jed. If my torch hadn't chanced to shine in this direction I wouldn't have noticed you. *On a night like this, you might have died.*

Nick's eyes had closed, and there was a thick pool of blood at his side. Jed tore a strip from Nick's sweatshirt, and ripped it into a long thin bandage. Taking it between his hands, he twisted it around the top of Nick's arm, putting all his strength into tying the knot. That should staunch the bleeding, he told himself. Until I get the old bugger to a doctor.

He put his arms around his waist and hoisted Nick into the air. He must have weighed just over two hundred pounds, and the load was a heavy one even for a strong, fit man. He'd parked the Ford Probe he'd borrowed from one of the other guys in the Regiment at the bottom of the drive, where it hit the road. Another five hundred yards, he reckoned. He needs some medical treatment as soon as possible.

He pushed on to the bottom of the field, then used

one hand to lever open the gate while holding Nick on his back. The weight was crushing. What the hell happened to him? Jed wondered. How did he get to be lying unconscious in a field?

First Sarah vanishes. Then this. *Nothing makes any sense right now.*

He walked as swiftly as he could to the car, then flung open the door, bundling Nick on to the back seat. Suddenly his eyes flashed open. He lay still for a moment, then groaned loudly and looked up.

'What the fuck are you doing here?' said Nick, looking straight at Jed.

'Saving your bloody skin,' snapped Jed.

He could see the damage in Nick's eyes. They were bloodshot, and beaten: the eyes of a man who'd stumbled into a fight, and hadn't been able to handle it.

'What happened to you?' said Jed.

'I . . . I . . .'

Nick was struggling for the words. His breath was short, and his body lacked the strength even to sit up. Jed got into the front seat, and turned the key in the ignition. The sooner he got the old guy to a doctor the better. He'd lost more blood than he probably realised: at least a couple of pints judging by the pool next to him, and after losing that amount of juice, a man usually didn't even know his own name any more.

'Hey, Nick,' said Jed, trying to smile. 'Try not to bleed all over the bloody car, will you? I borrowed it from a mate.'

He looked round, as the car's headlamps cut a beam

of light through the darkness of the narrow country lane, but Nick had already lost consciousness again.

Jed pushed aside the thin curtain, and looked down at the man lying stretched out on the grey, functional army bed. 'I would have got you some flowers,' he said. 'But I wasn't sure if you preferred carnations or lilies.'

Nick looked back up at him, without a hint of amusement on his face. 'I'm OK,' he said sullenly. 'I'll be on my way in a day or two.'

'You don't look OK,' said Jed.

'I'll be fine,' said Nick fiercely.

They were in Jed's room at the base. Every guy in the Regiment got his own room, even if he lived off base with his wife. It was nothing more than a ten-foot by six-foot box, with a metal bed, a desk, a basin and a place to stash your kit. When Jed had arrived back at the base late last night, he carried Nick straight through to his room. The Regiment kept medical staff on call twenty-four hours a day, and he begged one of the doctors to come and take a look as a personal favour. He'd been chippy at first, complaining that this was the army, not the NHS: there was an A&E department in Hereford for dealing with the public. Sod that, Jed had told him angrily, the guy is ex-Regiment, and he's hurt, so you can treat him now. The doctor – a young guy called Ed Merrill – had agreed, but warned Jed he was going to take a bollocking if anyone found out. Nick had taken a series of bad cuts to the arm and a nasty blow to the head, and had lost enough blood for him to pass out. They popped another pint into him – the Regiment always had plenty in stock, since it seemed to be remarkably careless with the stuff, the doctor had joked – and patched up his wounds. He'll be OK in twenty-four hours, the doctor had said. We'll keep him here until then, and let him get some rest.

Jed had returned to see him just after lunch. His morning had been taken up with final briefings for the mission. The squad was due to fly out to Kuwait at dawn tomorrow, and their time was taken up with last-minute preparations. He could only spare a few minutes to see what was happening to Nick.

'What the hell happened last night, then?' he said.

Nick was lying on the army bed. The Regiment only had doctors. There were no nurses running around to get you some fruit juice. But the medical care was first-rate. The one thing they did for you was patch up your wounds, Jed reflected. *So you could get out there and get some more.*

'I fell over,' said Nick.

'And ended up with knife wounds in your arm?'

Nick shrugged. 'I got into a dust-up with the farmer about his sheep crossing into my garden.' He tried to smile, but the pain in his jaw was making it hard for him to move his lips. 'Country life is pretty rough, you know.'

'Why don't you tell me what *really* happened?'

'What were *you* doing there, anyway?'

'Christ, you're even more of an ungrateful old bastard than I realised,' said Jed angrily. 'I know you and I have never got along, but I'm bloody worried about Sarah, just the way you are. I tried to call you last night to see if you'd heard anything from her, since I know you wouldn't have the sodding decency to call me if you did hear from her. I couldn't get hold of you, so I borrowed a mate's car to come and see you. When you weren't answering the door, but your car was there, I figured something up. I found you in the field, knocked out. And it's lucky for you I did, otherwise you'd have bled to death.'

'I'm strong enough,' snapped Nick. 'I'd have been OK.'

'Right,' said Jed. 'But you'd be in the A&E in Hereford, with the local coppers asking you questions about what fight you'd been in.'

'I'd have sorted them out,' said Nick. 'Now, piss off and let me get on with my life.'

Jed gripped on to the side of the bed. Whoever it was who'd stuck that knife into him last night, he was starting to know how they felt. 'I love her as well,' he said, a hint of steel in his tone. 'And I want to find out what's happened to her.'

'You don't love her, you're just a bloody soldier,' said Nick. 'I know your kind, and you're not good enough for her.'

'You're a soldier as well,' said Jed angrily.

'That's different,' growled Nick. 'I'm good enough for her.'

'And I'm good enough to save your sodding life,' snapped Jed. 'I'm beginning to wish I'd left you in that fucking field to die . . . it's what you deserve.'

Nick paused for a moment. Jed could see the flash of anger in his eyes start to fade away, replaced by a look of sorrow. *If the old bastard wasn't so annoying, I might even feel sorry for him.*

'Yeah, well,' he said, his voice turning down to just a whisper. 'Maybe I wasn't good enough for her.' He sat himself up in the bed, and took a sip of water. 'I was a soldier, you see, and soldiering and parenting don't mix. Different trades. I was away fighting all the time, for this bloody Regiment. Her mum was worried sick. It was rough, you know, over the water, then out in the Gulf. Guys' cards were getting punched all the time. One or two wives would be getting the knock on the door around here every month. It used to do Mary's head in. She was on the point of a nervous breakdown a lot of the time, and that was no good for Sarah either. Then when I came back from Iraq I was a wreck. I was nervous, exhausted, I was drinking, I didn't know how to cope any more. Then after Mary died, we fell apart, and Sarah was taken into care.'

He looked at Jed. 'So, you see, I was a crap dad, and a crap husband,' he said. 'And so will you be. All us soldier boys are. I don't want that for Sarah. She's had enough of that to last her a couple of lifetimes already.'

Jed nodded. 'Just let me help find her, OK,' he said. 'We can sort the rest of it out later. I'm off to Iraq myself. Tomorrow morning. And I want to help as much as I can before then.'

For a moment, the two men remained silent. The

clock on the wall was ticking closer to two o'clock. Nick took another sip of the water, wishing it was something stronger, then looked back at Jed. 'There was money in our joint account.'

'How much?'

'A hundred grand.'

Jed whistled. 'Jesus, where did that come from?'

Nick shrugged. 'I have no idea.' He hesitated before continuing. 'Then these two blokes were watching my house. I saw them. That's what I was doing. I went out to confront them, and see what the hell they were doing.'

'And took a beating.'

'I gave a good account of myself, thanks,' growled Nick sourly. 'They went home with a few bruises.'

'How long were they there?'

Nick shook his head. 'Not long,' he said. 'They tapped my phone as well. I don't think they are interested in me. Christ, there's nothing about my life you'd want to watch, so it must be something to do with Sarah.'

'Someone's kidnapped her?'

'Maybe,' said Nick.

'I don't get it,' said Jed. 'Sarah's just a postgrad, why the hell would anyone give her that kind of money? Why would they be looking for her?'

Nick eased himself out of the bed. There was a thick layer of bandages around his head and arm. He walked unsteadily, and lifted his jeans from the hook, and dug into the pocket. Handing a few strands of hair across to Jed, he sat back down on the bed. 'This is from one of the blokes that was watching me,' he said. 'You're

Regiment. You've got access to the police labs to run a DNA test on it. Find out who it belongs to. Then we'll know who's looking for Sarah and why.'

EIGHT

Laura switched her laptop to screensaver as soon as Jed stepped into the room. She was sitting in one of the small offices the Firm had taken over at the Hereford base six months earlier: a series of rooms, each one painted regulation grey, where the spies had been directing operations. First sending guys into Afghanistan, now into Iraq, the Firm and the politicians were treating the Regiment like their own private army. Even the Ruperts were starting to get pissed off.

'I need something,' said Jed, looking across at her.

She stood up from behind the wooden desk. She was wearing black trousers and a cream blouse, with a single string of pearls slung around her neck. He could smell a dab of perfume on her skin.

'I thought I took care of that last night,' she said.

Jed grinned. If I have to flirt with her, that's OK with me, he told himself. *Just so long as it helps me find out what's happened to Sarah.*

'A DNA test,' he said.

'We're not planning to have children, Jed,' answered Laura with a light giggle.

'It's for a friend. A bloke attacked him. I've got a

piece of his hair. I want to run it through the labs, and see if we can get a fix on who the guy is.'

Laura shook her head. 'Jed, we've got an important mission into Iraq to organise. We can't run around doing errands for our friends.'

'Listen,' said Jed, his tone turning harder. 'This is bloody important. I want it done.'

Laura seemed taken aback by the harshness of his expression. She could see the anger in his eyes and hear the strength in his voice. 'We've got a few hours down-time before we have to assemble the guys,' said Jed, trying to soften his tone. 'That's all it will take.'

'Just some hairs?' said Laura.

'About three or four strands.'

'There's no time,' said Laura sharply.

'The plane doesn't leave until dawn,' snapped Jed.

Laura was already walking back to her desk. The mobile sitting next to the computer was ringing but she ignored it. 'The Firm's DNA labs are all in London,' she said stiffly. 'We can't make it there and back by tonight.'

'There's a police lab in Cardiff that you can get access to. We can be there and back in three hours.'

'I've said there isn't time.'

Jed took a pace forward. 'Then make time.'

Laura was glancing towards the small window. It was a cold, cloudy day, and some drizzle was spitting against the glass. 'I've told you already,' she said, a hint of exasperation in her voice. 'I can't become involved in anyone's personal issues.'

'Then I'm not going on the mission to Iraq,' said

Jed. He was looking straight at her, his eyes filled with determination.

'It's an order,' said Laura. 'Remember.'

'No it bloody isn't,' snapped Jed. 'This one's off the books, so you can deny I was ever born if I get into trouble. I can go or not go. It's my choice.'

'If you change your mind now, it's career suicide, Jed.'

Jed shrugged. 'And if you don't get me into Iraq to find out what's in that compound, then I reckon your career's toast as well.'

'What does that mean?' she said.

'Just help take these hairs to the lab,' said Jed, 'and you won't have to find out.'

The lab was spotlessly clean. A series of wooden benches filled one side of the room, and some sunlight was drifting in from the sides of the tall windows. From one of them, Jed could see the pillars of Cardiff's Millennium Stadium rising into the sky. 'Here,' he said to the technician who had introduced himself simply as Dr Jones. 'Two strands of hair. Fresh. Just came off the guy's head yesterday.'

Dr Jones nodded. He was a thin man, no more than thirty, with curly brown hair, and a pair of thick glasses. 'It doesn't make any difference whether it's fresh or not,' he said. 'We can accurately test the DNA of a dinosaur.'

'Just make it quick,' said Laura. 'We haven't got much time.'

They had driven at breakneck speed. Jed took his mate's Ford Probe. Stupid name for a car, he thought every time he got into it. They might as well have called it the Ford Shag. Still, like most Fords, it was a nicely built car, and if you knew how to work the gears, it could cruise comfortably at over a hundred. Jed drove it hard, steering wildly into the corners on the road that twisted down along the Wye Valley towards Chepstow, then on to the motorway to Cardiff, but he was a good driver. Laura sat in silence for most of the journey: she didn't want to come, and she didn't mind if he knew it.

Like most women I've met, thought Jed, she doesn't need any lessons in sulking. *They must teach it to them when they play with their Barbie dolls.*

Jed followed Jones towards the bench. He was working with nimble, practised fingers, but the expression on his face suggested that having done a thousand DNA tests, they no longer carried much interest for him. He gave a brief explanation of how the DNA was first extracted from the root of the hair, then analysed. The original strand of hair is dissolved into a chemical dish, to break it down into its component parts. The fragments are then transferred to a nylon membrane soaked with a radioactive solution. The radioactive chemicals bind with the DNA to produce an image which can then be captured on a computer, he explained. 'What you end up with,' said Jones, 'is an image that looks pretty much like the bar codes that they put on stuff in the supermarket. That's what we use to identify people.'

Jed looked at the computer screen. A series of black lines, some thin, some fat. 'That's him?' said Jed.

Jones nodded. 'The DNA has come out well,' he replied. 'You'll be able to identify him from this easily enough.'

'How?'

'We just input it into the computer, then it compares the codes,' said Jones. 'Like I said, it's just like a bar code in the supermarket. The computer can read it, and compare it to the millions of other people on its database. Then it tells you who it is.'

Behind him, he could smell Laura's perfume. She was leaning into his back, looking at the image on the screen. 'Run it,' she said coldly.

'You have authorisation?'

Laura took a card from her wallet, and put it down on the desk. She had already used her ID pass from the Firm to get them access to the South Wales Police Headquarters, and to demand that they be shown straight to the DNA lab. The pass she had just produced told Jones she was senior enough to have access to the entire police and intelligence services network. Jones looked at it and nodded. 'OK,' he said, visibly impressed by her level of seniority. 'I'll run it on the big one.'

He started to tap a series of commands into the computer, looking at the screen pensively as it responded to the request.

'What's the big one?' said Jed.

Laura smiled, but there was little warmth in her expression. 'Officially, the police are only supposed to collect and record the DNA data on people who've been arrested. That's not much use to us most of the time. We're not interested in the drunks and the burglars who get nicked by the local coppers. The people we want to find are too clever to get picked up for shoplifting. So the NHS have been helping us out. Every person who goes to the doctor for any kind of test, even when they give a urine sample to register with a GP, gets a DNA sample taken from them, and it gets stored on this network. The ordinary police don't have access to it. But Special Branch do, so do the murder squad boys. And, of course, us. We've got about 70 per cent of the population on it, and it's going up all the time. Pretty soon we'll have the whole country.'

'Here,' interrupted Jones, his finger pointing at the screen. 'Your man.'

Jed leant forward. He could feel his pulse racing as he did so.

'Keith Merton,' said Jones, reading the words from the screen. 'Male. Caucasian. Thirty-seven. Sample taken at the A&E department, Cheltenham, three years ago.'

Jed toyed with the name. Keith Merton. Common enough name, he thought. There could be dozens of them out there. *I've certainly never heard of him.*

'Irish, by any chance?' he said.

He remembered Nick telling him that one of the men had an Irish accent, the other a German one.

'The database just gives names, not nationalities or ethnic groups.'

'Does it mean anything to you?' he said, turning to Laura.

She shrugged, then sat down at the computer next

to Jones's. Her fingers moved swiftly across the keyboard, playing it the way a pianist might play her instrument. Jed could see that she was tapping into some kind of database, but over her shoulder he couldn't see what it was.

'Who's your friend?' she said, suddenly turning away from the computer and looking straight at Jed.

He could feel the coldness in her eyes.

'Just a mate who got into a fight.'

'I asked you a question,' she snapped, shutting down the database. 'Who's your friend? Where'd you get this DNA?'

'That's my bloody business,' said Jed, his voice rising. 'Who the hell is he?'

'I've no fucking idea,' said Laura. 'There's no record of the man on our files.'

'You know.'

Laura folded her arms.

'You know,' repeated Jed, trying to suppress the anger in his voice. 'I could see it. The database found the guy's name.'

'Who's your friend who gave you those hairs?' repeated Laura.

From the corner of his eye, Jed could see Jones anxiously backing away.

'Just tell me who Keith Merton is,' said Jed, taking a step closer.

Laura started walking towards the door. 'There's nothing on the database,' she said. 'We have to get back to Hereford. There's a mission to run.'

Jed had already walked past her, and was jangling the keys to the Ford in his hand. 'Find your own way back,' he said.

NINE

Nick was standing by the bed when Jed stepped into the room. He was wearing the jeans and black sweatshirt he'd had on when Jed found him. 'I'm out of here,' he said, looking across at Jed.

Merrill was standing next to him, with the stern, long-suffering expression doctors adopt when patients aren't behaving themselves. 'I can't recommend it,' he said.

'He'll be OK,' said Jed. 'He's as tough as old boots.'

'You lost blood, and you've taken a series of nasty cuts,' said Merrill. 'You need antibiotics and you need rest.'

'I'll be fine,' growled Nick.

'Are you going to vouch for him?' said Merrill, looking at Jed. 'You checked him in here.'

Jed nodded.

'Then you're both a pair of idiots, with a death wish,' said Merrill turning around, and walking back towards his own office. 'You fit right into this place.'

Nick laughed, and started walking towards the door, but Jed could see that the guy was struggling. Blood loss weakened a man, particularly by the time he got to fifty. You had to be young to make a swift recovery from combat. As he stepped outside, Nick noticed how much the Regiment had changed since he'd left. The new Credon Hill base looked more like a modern university campus than a military base: it consisted of drab concrete office blocks, interrupted by the odd hangar. Some things never changed, however. There was a smell of war about the place today, he noted: the atmosphere of sweaty, adrenalin-fuelled fear and anticipation you found in any military encampment in the days before a battle started.

'Let's get out of here,' said Jed. 'I'll run you home.'

They checked out of the barracks. Jed was still on leave, officially, until midnight tonight. It was six now. There wasn't much time, and there was a lot to get sorted before they left for Iraq. Who knows, he reflected grimly, *I might not be coming back.*

In the Ford Probe, it took just fifteen minutes to speed through the countryside towards the cottage. It was dark already, and the first signs of a wintry frost could be seen crawling down the side of the Black Mountains. As they approached the house, Jed slowed the car down. He put the full beams on and steered the car carefully along the path. 'Think the bastards might still be here?' he said.

Nick was looking into the darkness. 'They'll be out there somewhere,' he said. 'They didn't look like they were about to give up.'

They climbed out of the car. Jed walked over to the field where he'd found Nick the previous night but it was empty. He checked the next one, then the next one. Nothing. Maybe they realised there was nothing worth watching.

By the time he got back to the cottage, Nick had already brewed up two mugs of tea. One of the light bulbs in the kitchen had blown, and the room was only half lit. Nick looked at Jed through the murky light. 'The place has been searched,' he said sourly.

Jed could see the anger written into his face. His brow was furrowed, and his eyes intense. It was one thing to be watched. It was another to have your house searched. *It was a violation of a man's territory.*

'You sure?'

Nick nodded. 'I put a single hair between the door and the frame, fixed in with superglue,' he replied. 'It's been broken.' He gripped his mug of tea between both hands, and Jed could see the steam rising up on to a face already flushed red with anger. 'The bastards.'

'They're looking for Sarah,' said Jed. 'They must be.'

'You have any luck with that hair I took from the bugger in the field?'

Jed sat down at the table, sipping on his own mug of tea. 'The guy's name is Keith Merton.'

'Any idea who he is?'

Jed shook his head. 'Means nothing to me. How about you?'

'Never heard of the sod.'

'The Firm know him,' said Jed. His tone was soft and controlled. 'The woman who's organising my mission took me down to Cardiff to get the DNA tested. She

109

put the name into their database, and then she clammed up.'

'She recognised the name . . . ?'

'I'm certain of it. It's just that the bitch didn't want to tell me anything.'

Nick ground his fists together. 'I'd have forced it out of her.'

'Right, I'm going to start slapping around an officer from the Firm in police headquarters.' Jed laughed. 'Even I'm not that stupid.'

Nick took a sip of his tea. He was glancing towards the window as if he might see something outside. The rain was starting to fall harder, beating against the window. 'If the Firm know who he is, then he must be on the circuit, a villain, something like that,' said Nick. 'If they can find him, then so can I.'

Jed stood up. It was already almost seven. He had a final briefing at nine, and then a chopper would take him down to RAF Brize Norton where the plane for Kuwait was due to leave at dawn. This time tomorrow, he'd be inside Iraq. 'You find him, Nick,' he said. 'And you make sure he tells us where the hell Sarah is.'

It was only when he spoke the words that Jed realised how desperate he was to see her again. He glanced at the staircase. When they first started knocking around together, they'd come to this cottage when Nick was away, and make out on the sofa, or go up to her bedroom and crawl under the duvet together. Sarah wasn't the first girl Jed had slept with, but she was the first one he'd cared about. What the hell am I doing flying off to Iraq to fight for my country? he thought. *I should be fighting for her.*

'I'll find her,' said Nick looking back up at Jed.

'I wish I could stay to help.'

'You're a soldier,' said Nick gruffly. 'You don't quit on the eve of a battle.'

'Let me know if you find out anything about Sarah.'

'Right, I'll just patch a call through to the Baghdad exchange and ask to be put through to the SAS blokes. That should work.'

Both men laughed.

Nick reached out and patted Jed on the shoulder. 'You look after yourself out there,' he said, his expression turning serious. 'Don't let the buggers capture you. You'd be better off dead.'

Jed paused. 'I'm scared,' he said finally. 'I wouldn't admit it to anyone else, but you've been there so you know what it's like. One slip, and you're done for.'

'All soldiers are scared,' said Nick. 'The good ones anyway. The one's who aren't scared are just nutters and you're better off without them.'

'What happened to you out there?' said Jed.

He was looking straight at Nick. The light was murky, and the rain was beating against the glass of the window behind them. He could see the man's brow furrow, as if he was still wrestling with his own memories. 'There were four of us,' he said slowly. 'It was dark and cold. Really bloody cold, as bad as these mountains out here. You don't expect that in the desert. We were out tracking Scuds, although it was a sodding thankless task. The head shed didn't have a clue where the buggers were, and neither did we. Our patrol was hunkered down in a wadi for the night, and we'd brewed up some tea. Ed heard a noise coming from the main road, and went out for a recce. Andy and I stayed behind in the bunker. The next thing, we heard a shot. Ed had gone down on the tarmac. I looked up from our OP, and I could see the poor sod rolling around on the ground. He'd taken a couple of bullets straight into the spine, and the pain was driving him crazy. There was no sign of the guys who'd shot him. We could hear him screaming. After a couple of minutes, Andy and I couldn't take it any more. We had to try and get him to safety. We figured maybe it was just an Iraqi patrol who'd taken a shot at him, then moved swiftly on. The Iraqis did that all the time. Most of them were too scared to do any proper fighting. Andy and I rushed out. I put Ed over my shoulder, while Andy covered us. There was blood pouring out of the bugger, down on to my shoulders and shirt. Next thing, we were surrounded. Must have been thirty of them, rising up out of the desert like bloody sandworms. They told me to put Ed back down. As soon as I did, their commanding officer stepped up, and shot the guy in the head. Next thing we know, Andy and I have been stripped bare bloody naked, our weapons taken off us, and we're thrown into the back of their truck. They knocked me out with a rifle butt. When I woke up, I was in the dungeons of the Republican Palace. Forget the Bangkok Hilton, we called this place the Baghdad Ritz. Nastiest fucking place you could ever imagine.'

'They tortured you, didn't they?'

Jed could see Nick's eyes glinting in the darkness. 'The bastards torture everyone, it's a local speciality,' he said, steel entering his voice. 'That's the fucking Iraqis for you. They can't cook, can't build stuff, and some of them don't even know how to crap. But they know how to inflict pain.'

'You survived it.'

'Maybe . . .'

'How?'

'Everybody deals with torture in their own way,' said Nick slowly. 'They think they can teach you about it, but they can't. You're on your own, just you and the bugger plugging your balls into the wall sockets.'

'But you must have learnt something . . .'

'Just take one lesson,' said Nick, suddenly turning round and staring out of the window. His back was to Jed, and his voice had turned cold. 'Looking back, after that Iraqi bastard gave Ed the double tap, I wish I'd fought him. They'd have killed me, but I could have taken down four or five of them. Anything's better than being captured alive. Even if you get out, it's a living death. You'd rather you hadn't.'

Daniel Sutton, the Rupert in charge of inserting the unit into Iraq, was standing near the door to the room. There was a map on the wall, portraying a shape that was already imprinted on Jed's mind: the square, blocked outline of Iraq. 'Thanks for joining us, Mr Bradley,' said Sutton. 'Next time we'll ask Mr Saddam to hold up the whole bloody war, shall we? Just so you can get a bit more kip.'

Jed remained silent, taking his seat next to Steve, Rob and Matt. He could feel their hostility as he sat down. He should have been here ten minutes ago, but he had been so transfixed by Nick's story he'd lost track of time. In the Regiment, there were few worse sins than late-ness: when a time was set for a rendezvous, the life of your mates could depend on it being met.

'The drop will be right here,' continued Sutton, pointing at the map. 'You'll fly to Kuwait at dawn, so try and get some kip if you can. It's going to be a tough few days. When you get there, you'll pick up your gear, then we'll have a Black Hawk to take you into Iraq. We've managed to arrange for one of the locals to meet you, and take you close to the centre of the city where the target is. He's an agent who is used by both the British and the Americans. After the last dust-up in Iraq, the CIA took his family out of Iraq, and we've been using him on and off ever since. The guy is getting paid, and paid well, but he's also taking a big risk, so try to keep him out of harm's way. We might want to use him again, so let's keep him alive if we can.'

Sutton tapped a finger against the map. 'As you already know, you're going into some kind of research lab. We don't really know what the Iraqis are cooking up in there, but the chances are it's bloody nasty. That's why you're going to have a look. The Americans are lending us some of their JSLIST suits – or MOPP suits as the soldiers usually call them. That stands for mission-orientated protective posture. You get charcoal-lined trousers – pants as our allies insist on calling them – a charcoal-lined jacket, two pairs of gloves – one cloth and one rubber – and some thick rubber boots. The whole kit comes with clasps so it's airtight, Make sure you fix those on securely. Lastly, you get a rubber face mask.'

'How do we know when it's safe to breathe?' asked Rob.

Sutton coughed. 'Not very technical, I'm afraid. You take the mask off and give the air a bit of a sniff. At each stage of the operation, you have to nominate someone who is "least mission critical".'

'And he tests the air . . .' said Rob.

'You just nominated yourself,' said Steve. 'Thanks, mate.'

Sutton ignored the remark, and tapped the map again. 'We're putting you in two miles to the east of the perimeter of Baghdad. Mr Bradley knows the place, so if you can get him to stay awake, he might be able to help you find your way into the city.'

Steve, Rob and Matt laughed, and Jed smiled weakly. You had to get used to the Ruperts trying to rile you up. It came with the territory.

Jed glanced up. Laura was standing at the entrance to the room. She looked towards him, but there was nothing he could read into her expression.

'Good luck,' said Sutton. 'If you can come back with the pictures we need of some real WMD, then you'll probably all get a personal phone call from Tony Blair. Get as much information on the place as you can.

Pictures, files, anything. When you've finished, blow it up.'

'What happens if the war starts when we're there?' said Steve.

Sutton shook his head. 'It's not going to,' he replied. 'The Americans tell us it is going to be at least another three weeks until they've got enough troops in the area for the fun and games to begin. And they're still trying to persuade the Turks to let them come in from the north. So don't worry. You'll be well out of the place before the starting gun gets fired.'

'Is there an evacuation procedure if we get compromised?' said Steve.

'No, if that happens you're buggered,' said Sutton. 'You have to fight your way out the best you can. It's 120 miles down to the Kuwaiti border, and our boys should be punching their way upcountry pretty quick once the kick-off starts, so your best bet is to head south and hope to break through to our lines.'

'Are there any Iraqis we can turn to for assistance?' persisted Steve.

'Apart from the guy who is going to meet you off the Black Hawk, you're on your own.'

'I thought the British and Americans had people on the ground working for us.'

'They might do,' said Sutton. 'But we can't risk compromising any of them by letting you boys get in touch with them.'

Laura stepped into the room. 'I know this isn't the most popular mission you've been asked to undertake,' she said. 'It probably isn't the most popular war either. Never will be. But we've got a job to do. And, trust me, there are dangerous weapons in that country. If you can get in there and get the evidence, you'll be doing a great service for your country. Probably greater than you can imagine.'

Matt sat back in his chair. 'Why are we getting pictures?' he said. 'If we know it's WMD, why can't we just blow the place? It would be a lot easier.'

'Because that's the mission,' growled Sutton.

'The point of this Regiment is that the mission is meant to make sense,' said Matt. 'We're special forces, not robots.'

'We need the pictures because we're in the bloody spin business now,' said Sutton. 'We all are. Get used to it.'

TEN

The office was in one of the tangle of side streets that ran behind St Pancras Station up towards Camden. It was on the first floor: there was a bookmaker below, and a legal aid solicitor above. Perfect, thought Nick. Somewhere to waste your money after you had made it. And a guy to help you out with whatever trouble you got into after blowing your wad. The army guys who come here looking for work will have everything they need.

He knocked twice on the door. BTM Security was one of hundreds of little outfits that made up the circuit – the network of former Regiment men who rented out their lives by the hour or the day. The name came from the initials of its three founders: Barry Teal, Tim Ruff and Mark Seal. Seal had long since retired to the Costa del Sol – according to the gossip he'd helped out some gangsters with a job, and was putting his feet up on the rewards. Tim, who Nick had served with in the Regiment, had never taken to desk work, spending most of his time out in the field. So it was Barry, the smartest of the three of them, who actually ran the business. Nick had done a couple of jobs for him after he gave up the ski school, but BTM specialised in the sharp end of the trade – kidnappings, insurgencies and counterterrorism – and Nick soon found he wasn't cut out for that any more. He preferred quieter protection work on the rigs. Still, they'd always got along fine. It wasn't the best outfit in the business, Nick thought, but it was the best connected. If anything was going on, Barry would be sure to know about it.

'You keeping well?' said Teal, stepping forward to shake his hand. 'How are the rigs?'

Nick nodded. 'Not bad,' he said. 'The food is pretty miserable, but the pay is OK.'

'And nothing ever happens, does it?' said Teal. 'The Algerians always think that someone is going to have a pop at their oil installations but nobody ever does. I don't think any of those al-Qaeda nutters or the rest of the ragheads even know where the bloody place is.'

'Quiet, and that's the way we like it,' said Nick.

He had travelled down to London that morning on the early-morning train. From Paddington, he'd taken the tube to King's Cross St Pancras. After spending the night in the cottage, he felt certain that it wasn't being watched any more, but he couldn't be certain: when a professional was tracking you, they did their best to make sure the target was not aware of them. He'd searched the field at dawn, but found nothing. As he drove towards Hereford to pick up the train, he'd seen nobody on the road. Even so, in London he switched tube trains four times, tracking back on himself, to see if there was anyone on his trail.

But he'd seen nothing.

That doesn't mean anything, he reminded himself. *Just because you couldn't see them, it doesn't mean they weren't there.*

'I'm looking for someone,' said Nick. 'A bloke who might be on the circuit.'

His reasoning was simple enough. He had the guy's name, Keith Merton, but he had no idea who he was, or who he might be working for. Chances were he was a circuit guy, however. He had the bearing, manner and discipline of a solider: he knew when to fight, and when to run, the first distinction they taught you on any kind of military training. If he had been hired out of the army, then someone in the network of private contactors would know who he was. And who he was working for.

'His name's Keith Merton,' said Nick. 'Irish guy. Big.'

Teal looked at him closely. There was a mass of papers on his desk, left in random piles. Next to it was a pair of coffee cups and a half-eaten bacon sandwich. How the guy had survived military cleanliness and order, Nick couldn't imagine.

'It's not a grudge, is it, Nick?' said Teal.

Nick knew at once what he was driving at. The circuit was a small and often vicious world. The men on it were constantly clashing with one another. The missions were often dangerous, and usually badly led. There were plenty of incidents of guys coming back with scores to settle with the men they'd been fighting with just a few weeks earlier: those debts were invariably settled with violence.

'Family business,' said Nick flatly. 'I've nothing against

the guy, I just want to get hold of him.' He looked straight at Teal. Whether he believed him or not he neither knew nor cared. *Just give me the lead . . .*

Teal was tapping the keyboard of the computer on his desk. 'There's a couple of Keith Mertons on the list,' he said. 'How old is this bloke?'

'Maybe forty,' said Nick. 'Could be a bit younger.'

Teal nodded. 'He's done work for an outfit called Energy Protection down in Chatham,' he said.

Nick rested his arms on the desk. He could feel the sweat on his palms. 'That rings a bell,' he said.

'It should, with all the time you spend on oil rigs,' said Teal. 'Not a bad little outfit, but very rough. They specialise in working for the big oil companies. All the nasty little jobs that have to get done but you wouldn't want put in the annual report.'

'Protecting rigs, that kind of thing?'

Teal shook his head. 'More upmarket than that. Toppling regimes in Africa, rescuing hostages, and a bit of industrial espionage as well from what I hear. Small scale and very expensive.'

'Who runs it?'

'Bloke called Danny Stonehill.'

'Regiment?'

Teal shook his head again. 'Irish Guards, a colonel. There was some kind of scandal, and he bailed out about five years ago and set up this business. Cruel bastard by reputation.'

'Thanks, I owe you one,' said Nick as he stood up and headed for the door.

Teal laughed. 'Don't worry, I'll collect,' he said. 'I always do.'

The building was smarter than Nick had expected. Most of the security firms he'd dealt with over the years spent about as much on their offices as they did on their mother-in-laws' Christmas presents. The guys who organised his work on the Algerian rigs had a couple of rooms above a kebab shop in Kilburn. 'Good to have your own canteen,' Dave who ran the accounts would always say on the rare occasions Nick went into the place.

Energy Protection was different. It was sited above a smart-looking dental surgery on the London Road in Chatham. The nameplate was picked out in brass, and looked as if it was polished once a week. Nick rang the bell. 'I'm here to see Danny Stonehill,' he said, and the buzzer was pressed.

There was just one guy inside when Nick pushed open the door that led into the office. He was wearing brown cords and a yellow and brown checked shirt, open at the neck. His hair was sandy blond, with flecks of grey around the edges, but he looked in good shape. 'Can I help you?' he said.

'Are you Danny Stonehill?'

The man nodded.

Nick paused. He'd thought about how he would question Stonehill. All the private firms on the circuit were fiercely protective of their clients. There weren't many rules in the industry, but the one everyone stuck to was this: Don't stitch up the guys who are paying the bills. If Merton was working for Energy Protection, then Stonehill wouldn't want to tell Nick about it. *At least not willingly.*

'I'm looking for a man called Keith Merton. I heard he works for you sometimes.'

Stonehill shrugged, glancing at the door. Nick could see straight away what he was thinking. It was written into every muscle on his face. *How little can I get away with telling this guy?*

'And you are . . . ?'

'It doesn't matter,' said Nick. 'Just some guy who wants to find Merton.'

No good telling him who I am, thought Nick. If he set Merton on to me, then as soon as he knows who I am, he's going to clam up completely.

'Have I seen you before somewhere?' said Stonehill.

He took a step forward, examining Nick the way he probably used to examine men on the parade ground. 'I was in the army,' said Nick. 'From '75 to '95. Same years you served.'

'Which regiment?'

'There only is one.'

Stonehill nodded. An army man himself, thought Nick, he would know precisely how tough you had to be to get into the SAS, and how hard it was to survive there. He wouldn't underestimate his strength, or challenge it lightly.

'And who says I know who Merton is?'

Nick glanced around the office. The room they were

standing in was a reception area, but it didn't look like it was ever staffed. There was a desk and a chair, but no computer or phone. Behind it were two offices, one with the door opened. Nick stepped towards it.

'Where the hell are you going?' snapped Stonehill.

'We need to talk in private.'

It was Stonehill's office, Nick could tell that instantly. It had 'the boss' stamped all over it. There was an antique desk, with an Apple laptop resting on it. Next to that a landline phone, and two mobiles. Clearly a man who likes to have lots of different conversations at once, thought Nick. On the floor was a Persian rug, and there was a fine piece of African wood-carving in one corner. Up on the walls were two paintings, both of hunts, and one photograph: a stylish brunette, and two boys, aged around two and three. The family, thought Nick. *Every man's weak point.*

Nick stood with his back to the desk. 'I'll give you a chance to deal with me straight before this turns nasty,' he said, his tone hard and edgy. 'Two guys have been following me and my phone has been tapped. I got into a scrap with them a couple of nights ago. I don't know why they were following me, but my daughter has disappeared, and I've got a pretty good idea they've got something to do with it.' He looked straight at Stonehill, clenching his fists as he did so. 'One of them was Keith Merton. The guy works for you. Now, save yourself a lot of trouble and tell me who hired Merton, and what the hell he was doing following me.'

'Get the fuck out of my office,' spat Stonehill.

He was leaning against the edge of the door frame. Nick edged forward. Stonehill was a big man, over six foot two, and weighing around two hundred pounds. He may look in good shape, but he was management now, decided Nick, sitting around on his arse all day making phone calls and playing with his spreadsheets. In a scrap, a man who still worked with his muscles was always going to have the edge: he was fitter, sharper, and he knew how to take a punch as well as dish one out. 'I've given you a fair warning,' he growled.

'And I've given you a fair warning as well,' barked Stonehill. 'Now get the fuck out of my sight.'

Nick slammed a fist into the man's stomach. He took the blow hard in the ribs, and Nick could feel his muscles absorbing the blow. He swung his right fist hard up towards the side of Nick's jaw, but Nick had readied himself for a predictable response, and had already ducked. The blow landed in the air, temporarily loosening his balance. Nick slammed up his right knee, crunching it into Stonehill's balls. Should have worn iron underpants, mate, thought Nick grimly. *It's going to be a couple of weeks before you're bothering the tasty-looking brunette in the picture.*

Stonehill was staggering back clutching his groin. 'You fucking bastard, I'll bloody throttle you.'

Mistake, pal, thought Nick. This is not a moment for conversation. Talking saps your strength, and weakens your concentration. With his head still down, he slammed his skull straight into Stonehill's stomach. The air emptied out of his gut, and he started choking. His body collided hard with the wall, and one of the pictures crashed to the floor, sending shards of glass across its surface.

Nick straightened himself up, and then slammed his fist hard into the side of Stonehill's face. He could feel his knuckles digging into the jawbone, sending ripples of pain up through his arm. He smiled. It was the kind of pain that told a fighter he'd landed a telling blow.

Time to finish you off, pal.

He slammed his fist hard down again, this time aiming for the nose. But Stonehill showed an unexpected turn of agility. His face ducked out of the blow, letting Nick's fist crash into the plaster of the wall.

Stonehill jerked his right knee upwards, catching Nick in the third rib. It was a powerful blow, expertly struck, and Nick reeled backwards. His chest was shuddering under its impact. Another knee flew up, this time catching Nick on the chin, jerking his jaw hard upwards. He could feel the muscles in his neck stretching, and he was struggling to breathe. Stonehill was already scrambling to his feet, and Nick was struggling to match his agility. Suddenly he was above him. Both his fists were clasped together, and in the next instant they smashed down like a hammer into the back of Nick's neck. He grunted, then fell to the floor. It felt as if an axe had just been thrust into him. He was lying face down, his mouth barely an inch from the carpet. If this is the way you want to play it, pal, that's your choice, he thought. *Let's make it interesting.*

He rolled on his side, and kept rolling until he'd put five yards between himself and Stonehill. He leapt to his feet. His back was still aching, and the throbbing from his ribcage was starting to spread out across his chest. Ignore the pain, he told himself. *You can deal with that later.*

'Now get the fuck out of my office,' shouted Stonehill.

Nick looked at the man. Sweat was pouring off his face, and there was a trickle of blood down the side of his mouth. But his eyes were still strong, and his expression determined. There's plenty of fight left in the bugger yet, thought Nick.

'I'll die here if I have to,' said Nick. 'My daughter's bloody vanished, and you know something about it.'

He rushed forward, his body fuelled by an angry mixture of adrenalin and fear. He was about to bring Stonehill down to the ground, but his opponent was prepared for him, and a glancing blow smashed into the side of Nick's face, followed by a foot crashing into his stomach. He was hurled backwards, colliding with the desk, taking a nasty hit to the spine, then falling to the floor.

'If you're not out of here in one minute, by God I'll fucking kill you,' said Stonehill.

Nick reached across the floor. A shard of glass from the picture was lying close by. He picked it up, and gripped it tight into his palm. He could feel it cutting into his skin but ignored the pain. Advancing slowly, he could see Stonehill edging away from him. With one swift lunge, he threw himself forward, stabbing at Stonehill's shoulder with the glass. The shard cut through his shirt, then sunk into his flesh, cutting it deep. A spurt of blood shot out, and a howl of agony erupted from the man's lips. Nick let go of the glass, then took a step back. Blood was dripping from his own hand. He curled it into a tight ball, slamming it into the side of Stonehill's face. He staggered sideways. Another blow, then another, both of them to the jaw. Stonehill fell to the ground, his face and shoulder a messy pulp of blood and sweat. Nick crashed his foot down into his chest, then pinned his arms down to the floor. He leant his face downwards, so close that Stonehill could feel the fury on his lips.

'If you don't start talking to me this minute, I'm going to fucking kill you, then I'm going to go round to your house and kill your wife and kids,' he said.

There was a silence for a moment. Nick could feel the man's breath, and he could see his eyes darting from side to side. Blood was still seeping from his shoulder, and although the wound wasn't serious, if it wasn't bandaged soon, he was going to lose a lot of blood – and that could be serious. He can't hang around, thought Nick. He knows what's going to happen to him. *If he doesn't talk to me soon, he's going to die.*

'Keith Merton was on our payroll,' said Stonehill.

The words were hardly more than a whisper.

'Following me?'

Stonehill nodded.

'Who's paying?'

Stonehill took a deep breath. 'Let me bind up the wound, then I'll tell you.'

Nick pressed hard into his chest. 'Talk to me first,' he spat. 'Who hired you to follow me?'

'An outfit called the Lubbock Group.'

'Who the fuck are they?'

'It's an informal grouping of all the big oil companies,' said Stonehill. 'They meet in Lubbock, Texas, once
a year. It's very secret, because those boys aren't meant
to be forming cartels. They discuss issues that affect them
all – technology, security, the works. And they pay a few
guys a lot of money to look after their interests. That's
who the job was for.'

'So why they hell are they interested in me?'

'They're not.' Stonehill paused. 'They're looking for
your daughter, Sarah.'

'They kidnapped her,' shouted Nick. His fist was
hovering just inches from Stonehill's face, and he could
see the man start to grit his teeth in anticipation of the
blow. 'If they lifted her, I'm going to kill the buggers.
By hand. One by one.'

'They haven't kidnapped her. They're looking for her
as well,' said Stonehill.

Nick stayed his hand. 'Why the hell would a bunch
of oil industry guys be interested in Sarah?'

'Her work,' said Stonehill quickly. 'She was working
on something in Cambridge. Some science to do with
energy. One of the things they pay us to do is to keep
tabs on a few scientists whose work might be interesting
to them. Tap their phones, keep an eye on the emails,
that kind of stuff. They were interested in Sarah all of
a sudden.'

'Why "all of a sudden"?' said Nick.

'I don't bloody know,' snapped Stonehill. 'I know fuck

all about the science. They just give us the names, and we keep an eye on them.'

'So where the hell is she?'

'We don't know,' said Stonehill. 'She vanished over a week ago. You know that already. We reported that back to the Lubbock Group, and they went apeshit. I've never seen them get themselves in such a state. They told us we had to find her. Money no object.'

Blood was still trickling down the side of his mouth, and Stonehill paused to spit it away from his lips. 'So we followed you. It was about the only lead we could think of. If she re-emerged, or got in contact with anyone, then it would be you. When that happened, we wanted to know about it.'

Nick relaxed his grip on Stonehill's chest. He'd seen men lie under torture before, and he'd seen them tell the truth as well, and he reckoned he'd learnt to tell the difference: you could sense when the fear had got to them, when they knew there was no point in hiding anything, and you could hear an edge of pleading in their voice. Stonehill was telling the truth, he felt sure of it. *If he was lying, he'd come up with a better story than that.*

'So I'm looking for you because you might tell me where she is, and you're watching me because you think I might know where she is,' said Nick. He grinned, but there was no warmth in the smile. 'We're going round in bloody circles. We could have saved you a cleaning bill if we'd figured that out at the start.'

He unpinned Stonehill's hands and stood up. His jaw

and ribs were aching, and there was a smattering of blood down the front of his blue denim shirt. Stonehill got uneasily to his feet.

'Maybe we should work together.'

Nick stared at him. 'I'm not working with you tossers. You've no business following my daughter, and you've no business tapping my phone and sending a couple of clowns to watch my house. So stay the fuck out of my way.'

'We've a lot of resources at our disposal,' said Stonehill. He was wiping some blood from his cheek, and clutching on to his jaw as if he had lost a tooth. 'We might be more effective together.'

'I work alone,' snapped Nick, heading for the door. 'It's the only way I know.'

ELEVEN

The noise of the chopper, flying in at no more than thirty feet from the ground, was brutal. Jed sat close to the doorway, letting the cold night air rush over his face. He'd been keeping his eyes peeled to the ground during the one hour they had been flying upcountry from Kuwait, but now they were approaching Baghdad there was a sprinkling of lights. Once the war kicked off, they'd impose a blackout, but right now it was lit up like Oxford Street.

Five minutes, he thought. *Then we get a chance to kick off this war single-handed.*

At his side were Matt, Steve and Rob. From Brize they'd flown straight to Kuwait where the Regiment had established a makeshift base about a hundred miles back from the border: choppers were ferrying the troops up from Kuwait airport to the base. It had supplies in place, some QMs handing out kit, an armoury, a barracks, ammo pallets and a cookhouse. As Jed set eyes on the place, he remembered how he'd seen Tony Blair on TV as they left talking about the 'last chance for peace'. As you looked at the Regiment's base, it was clear that chance had long since passed, and he must have known it.

When they checked into the base, they had a few hours to eat, prepare their kit and pick up on the local intelligence: Iraq was in turmoil, according to the steady stream of defectors making their way across the border, with the army concentrating on how to minimise its casualties in the upcoming war, and the people already braced for the plotting that would start after Saddam's inevitable defeat.

For the mission ahead, none of them were taking any more than essential supplies. They were wearing plain clothes to stop them from drawing attention to themselves: black cheap slacks and boots, made in Syria, and loose nylon sweaters underneath which they had fitted lightweight Kevlar bulletproof jackets. Inside their packs were the MOPP suits to put on before they went inside the compound. They were carrying black-market AK-47s with two hundred rounds of ammunition each, plus six hand grenades, the same number of stun grenades, five pounds of Semtex and two detonators. For hand-guns they had brought Browning BDA 380s with silencers: they were small reliable pistols, with wooden handles, and a semi-automatic firing mechanism that could store twelve 9mm or thirteen 7.65mm rounds. They were carrying popular mass-produced weapons that were available anywhere, so that if they were captured, they could try to pass themselves off as free-lance mercenaries. Their orders were to deny they were working for the British government no matter what happened.

For food, they had a supply of camping meals, and,

most importantly of all, they had five hundred dollars in ten-dollar bills to bribe any locals, plus sixteen ounces of gold in unmarked coins. Dollars and gold were the universal currency inside Iraq. With that kind of money, you could buy yourself out of most forms of trouble.

'Get ready to land,' shouted the pilot into the radio, his words instantly transmitted into the helmets of the four men sitting behind him.

The Black Hawk was flown by experienced US Air Force pilots, experts at special forces insertions. It came in low, to make it impossible for the Iraqi radar to lock on to them. That made for a choppy ride, as the machine soared above electricity pylons, then dropped down to hug the surface of the terrain again. Talking was banned inside the Black Hawk: there was too much risk of the Iraqis picking up the signals.

Jed braced himself. He'd been in combat before, and had learnt to recognise the mixture of excitement, fear and anticipation that overtook him every time a battle started. It was OK once you were in there. The action overwhelmed your senses, and the will to stay alive kicked in, making it impossible to think about anything else. It was the moments beforehand that made Jed uneasy: it was then that the doubts started to creep in, when you started to wonder whether you were going to live through the next few days. Forget it, Jed told himself. Just get the job done, then get home and find out what's happened to Sarah.

The Black Hawk flew fast into Baghdad and Jed could see the lights of the city spreading out ahead of him.

The slums to the east and the west of the city generated almost no lights at all: most of the people were too poor to keep the electricity running through the night, and after a decade of economic sanctions half the power stations didn't work properly anyway. The centre of the city was brightly lit: you could make out the big blocks of the main government buildings. Over to the north, he could see the runway of Saddam Hussein airport.

The pilot was lowering the Black Hawk on to the ground. This was the most dangerous moment of the mission. Drop-down. Flying up from Kuwait, they hadn't been troubled by any Iraqi aircraft: the few planes that had survived the last Gulf War had all been grounded, and most of them were so old they were probably more threatening to their pilots than to the enemy. It was radar they had to worry about, not the Iraqi Air Force. They still had the capability to check incoming flights, and if they'd spotted the Black Hawk coming in, despite it flying low, there could well be a battalion waiting to meet them. It wasn't hard to put an RPG into a descending chopper. Just point and press the trigger, thought Jed. *Then sit back and enjoy the fireworks.*

With a twisting motion that was making Jed's stomach heave, the Black Hawk dropped clean downwards. They were heading for a strip of scrubland, just alongside Highway 5, five miles outside the city. The pilot had no lights on, to make sure the helicopter didn't draw attention to itself. The drill was to bring the Black Hawk down hard if the ground looked clear. You kept the throttle open all the time, so the chopper could be pulled up again rapidly if it faced any incoming fire. It made for a nasty bump when you landed. But it was better than getting hit by a missile.

'Clear,' snapped the pilot over the intercom. 'Get ready.'

Jed held on to the metal frame of the chopper. The blood rushed to his head as the Black Hawk descended the last few feet. Just before landing it suddenly jerked upwards, like a yo-yo being snapped back. This was the most dangerous moment of all. Only last week, an American special forces team going in by chopper had been blown apart by a single sniper lying on the ground waiting for them. All it took was one bullet into the fuel tank. All five guys on that mission had died in an instant.

With a thud, the chopper came to rest on the muddy surface of the ground. The pilot had counted down the time until landing, and on one, Jed pulled the headset away, casting it to the floor. Jed rushed forward to the open door, hurling himself to the ground. Around him, he could here Matt, Steve and Rob do the same, while behind him he heard the Black Hawk's huge steel propeller roar into overdrive as it revved up the power to lift the machine into the sky. It had only been on the ground for five seconds. As it rose back up towards the sky, its propellers sucked up a storm of sand, rising in vertical columns into the air, then exploding against the night sky as if fireworks had been set alight. All right for you, mate, thought Jed, as the Black Hawk disappeared behind the clouds. You'll be sleeping in a nice warm bed tonight, watching the hotties on MTV. Not camping out in this hellhole.

'Clear the area,' he hissed.

The Iraqis could be on the way to meet them right now. Lying flat on the ground, Jed glanced at his watch. For the next ten minutes, he would just lie there, completely silent, waiting to see if their position had been spotted. Slowly he started to recover his senses from the noise and the heat of the chopper. The stretch of scrubland covered about four hundred square metres. Straight ahead of them was a ridge of mud, and behind that some rusting cars and decaying industrial machinery. As the time elapsed, Jed picked himself up and ran towards it, keeping his head down. He scrambled up over the ridge, then waited, recovering his breath. Steve, Matt and Rob were at his side. 'Everyone OK?' he asked.

The three men nodded in turn. A silence had descended upon the wasteland. Jed took a deep breath. This was the second time he had had Iraqi air in his lungs, and it was starting to taste familiar: even in winter there was a heat and tension to the oxygen that was nothing like anything Jed had ever tasted before. You could feel the violence in it. He looked around him, peering into the darkness. 'British, British,' hissed a voice. Jed looked straight ahead. He could see nothing, but he could hear the voice clearly. Then a pair of eyes crept out from behind an abandoned truck, as vivid and bright as a cat's. Jed whistled once, then twice. The man stepped out of the shadows and into enough light for Jed to get a clear look at him. He was medium build, maybe five

137

nine, with a thin, muscular body, and the expression of a born huckster. In some more normal country, he'd be selling apartments for an estate agency or trading currencies at a brokerage, thought Jed. In this nuthouse, he was selling out his country to the new rulers. And who could blame the bastard? Everyone knew who was going to win the war. It was just a matter of making sure you got on the right side at the right time. The Iraqis have been around for thousands of years, Jed reminded himself. *They know all about survival.*

'British, British,' the man repeated.

Jed had checked on his GPS to make sure that they had come in at the right location. He was holding the AK-47 to his chest, his finger on the trigger, poised to fire if necessary. There was a preset code, and it had to be followed to the letter.

'How far to Tipperary?' he hissed.

'Five miles,' the man hissed back.

OK, thought Jed. That's our bloke. The man took a step nearer. 'Radhi al-Shaalan,' he said, in voice that sounded as if he'd learnt English from listening to the World Service. 'At your service.'

Jed nodded and turned round to give the thumbs up to the other three. 'We need to get out of here,' he said quietly.

Al-Shaalan signalled over to the scrubland. 'I have a car,' he said.

Jed followed closely in his tracks, as he started picking his way through the debris and broken machinery. Matt, Steve and Rob were right behind him. When they saw it, Jed wasn't sure you could readily tell the difference between the car and the rubbish that filled up the site. A Datsun 100 dating from sometime in the mid-1970s, he could remember seeing one on the street where he grew up, but the wheels had been taken off and it was slowly falling to bits. He'd never seen one actually start. 'I need the gold,' said al-Shaalan, as he opened the door.

Jed took two one-ounce coins from his kitbag. Al-Shaalan rubbed them briefly with his thumb: like most Iraqi traders, he could tell gold just by touching it. He smiled, tucking the coins into a purse on the inside of the belt. 'Get in,' he whispered.

It was a tight squeeze. Jed got in the front, with Matt, Steve and Rob on the back seat. 'Fuck it,' muttered Ron, as he slammed the door. 'Next time we're going to Hertz, and hiring a minivan.'

With a turn of the key, the Datsun fired into life. Al-Shaalan pressed his foot on to the accelerator, and the engine screeched like a cat with its tail stuck in the door. Slowly, it started moving up towards the road, its headlights still switched off. The weight of its load was a strain for the 1.3 litre engine, and it refused to move any faster than twenty miles an hour. At the end of the dump, there was a dirt track, and the car moved steadily across it. 'Ever thought of going into the minicabbing business, mate?' said Steve. 'With this motor, you'd be a natural.'

'How far?' said Jed, glancing across at al-Shaalan.

'Five miles to the outskirts of the city, and then another one mile to your target,' replied al-Shaalan. 'We have a safe house organised where you can stay for the night.'

Jed could hear the nerves in the man's voice, and his eyes had the wild, beaten look of a man who knows he could be in more trouble than he could handle. 'Don't flap, mate,' hissed Jed. 'We know what we're doing.'

After a few hundred yards, they hit a stretch of road. The car turned on to it, and after half a mile they hit a slip road that took them up on to Highway 5. Jed was struck by how clean and modern it looked: it could be any big motorway anywhere in Europe. It had three lanes, with a tarmac surface, a hard shoulder, and big green-and-white signs written in English and Arabic. There were plenty of old wrecks like the Datsun chugging along in the slow lane, but also a steady stream of Mercedes, Land Rovers and Lexuses racing past them. It's a first-world country that's about to be bombed back into the Stone Age, Jed thought. Hide those fancy motors, mates. They aren't going to survive the next few weeks.

The Datsun creaked as al-Shaalan pulled it down into a slip road. Jed had studied a street map before his last trip to Baghdad, and had a pretty good idea of the geography of the city in his head, but this looked unfamiliar. There were two blocks of prosperous-looking suburban houses, probably with pools in the back gardens, and air-conditioning units pumping processed air into the night sky. Just like Sevenoaks, thought Jed. The smart houses faded after half a mile, replaced by rows of poorly built concrete blocks, the dust rising up from the sand behind them, and with every doorway filled with men standing around, smoking and drinking tea. 'Quiet,' said al-Shaalan.

Jed looked straight ahead. 'Shit,' he muttered under his breath. 'Stay still, guys.'

The police checkpoint was manned by just two officers. They were both dressed in the dark blue uniforms of the Iraqi police, not the baggy, black overalls of the Fedayeen, the fanatical secret police that owed its loyalty only to Saddam Hussein, and which had terrorised the local population for the last two decades. 'Let me handle this,' said al-Shaalan.

Jed could see the fear written into the sweat already starting to trickle down the side of his cheek. The police looked as if they were checking every fifth car. They were stationed at the side of the road, just as the residential area gave way to an industrial estate. 'How much further to the safe house?' hissed Jed.

'A mile,' said al-Shaalan.

'We could get out here and walk it,' said Jed.

Al-Shaalan shook his head. 'They are watching for people trying to avoid them. They can see us from here. We'll just try and drive through.'

The Datsun slowed down as it approached the road-block. Jed glanced once at the two policemen, then looked away. He didn't want them looking too closely at his eyes. In the dark, in the right clothes, you might not notice he was European; if you stared into his eyes, you'd see it right away. One car was flagged past, then another. Stop the guy in front of us, thought Jed. Then you won't have time for us.

'*Waqf*,' shouted the policeman as they drew level.

Jed slipped his hand into his pocket, and gripped tight on to the handle of his Browning BDA 380 pistol. He didn't know much Arabic, but he knew the word 'stop'. And he knew that meant they were about to get into a fight.

The policemen leant into the window, on the driver's side of the car. He was looking at al-Shaalan, then past him towards Jed and the three men in the back. All of them were sitting perfectly still. Jed could see the truncheon on the man's belt, and the Russian-built AK-47 assault rifle slung over his back. There was probably a pistol in there as well. It was dark in the car. There were lights beaming back from the street, but they were weak and the visibility was poor. Doesn't matter, thought Jed, keeping a tight grip on the Browning. *You don't have to be Sherlock Holmes to know there's something suspicious about us.*

The policeman snapped something at al-Shaalan. Jed couldn't make out the words. He was taking a flashlight from his pocket, flicking the switch. He shone it directly into Jed's face: all he could see was the bulb of the torch, blocking out the rest of his vision. With one swift movement, he jerked the Browning upwards. No time to aim properly, and no vision either. He pointed the gun eight inches above the flashlight: on a normally built man, that should take the bullet straight into the heart. He squeezed the trigger, once, then again. As the bullet smashed into the man's chest, the torch dropped out of his hand, and suddenly the car was dark again. Jed pushed open the door, and rolled out on to the ground. It felt dusty and dry as he hit the side of the road. The second policeman had already pulled his gun from his holster, and was pointing it straight at al-Shaalan. He was shouting at him, his voice ragged and scared. Maybe twenty-three, twenty-four, decided Jed, looking straight at the man, and raising the Browning so that the sights on the pistol were level with his eyes. Sorry about this, pal. You just happened to be at the wrong roadblock on the wrong day. That's all.

He squeezed the trigger. The bullet ripped straight through the centre of the man's forehead, slicing into his brain. He muttered something under his breath, spat out a mouthful of blood, then started to crumple to the ground. Jed fired again, this time putting the bullet straight into his windpipe. No real need for a double tap, he told himself. The bastard was already dead. But you stick to the routine, no matter what. The rule book said that you always put two bullets into every target. One to kill him, and the second to kill him again. Better that than having the bastard crawling towards you with vengeance on his mind.

Jed looked back to the first policeman. Matt was already standing over him, a whisper of smoke curling away from the muzzle of his own Browning: Jed's bullet had wounded him but Matt had had to finish the job. Next to him al-Shaalan was lying on the ground, badly wounded. The policeman must have shot him before Matt had a chance to put a bullet into him. He was clutching on to his chest, but the blood was seeping

143

from his side, and it was clear he wouldn't hang on much longer. Looking over at Matt, he held up a piece of paper. 'Meet my cousin in this café,' he said. 'He'll be able to help you.'

In the next moment, his head fell to the side. His eyes closed. *Dead*.

Kneeling down, Matt put one of the policemen's guns in his hand. With any luck, the local coppers would assume it was just a gangland killing when they found the bodies. They didn't want anything to alert them to the fact that there were special forces soldiers dropping into the city. Jed glanced down the street. They were about half a mile from the last apartment building, but he could hear shouting. The gunfire must have been audible to the other cars that had already passed through the checkpoint. He couldn't hear any sirens, but he didn't even know if they had sirens on Baghdad police cars. Shit, he thought. We're on our own in the most hostile, dangerous city on earth.

Matt stepped across him, getting into the driving seat of the car. The engine was still running. Jed climbed into the passenger seat and slammed the door.

'Find us a bar, cabbie,' said Rob, his face breaking into a rough grin.

'Then a lap-dancing club,' said Steve. 'See what the local talent look like when it gets its burka off.'

Jed laughed. 'Let's make a weekend of it.'

Matt's foot was pressing hard on the accelerator, squeezing all the life it could from the Datsun's engine. The car was wheezing and shuddering: at moments, the speedometer would flicker up to twenty-five miles an hour as they hit a downward slope, then it would fall back. Bloody useless. They were driving away from the murder scene in a car that was capable of little more than a gentle jog. As soon as somebody found those bodies, they were dead.

'Get off the road,' said Jed.

Matt nodded. There was no need to discuss it. They all knew they couldn't stay where they were. The road was twisting through an empty industrial estate, and had come out into another stretch of wasteland. About a mile ahead, Jed could see another highway. 'Here,' he hissed.

Matt steered the car off the road, into the mud and weeds that ran along its edge. There was no track, just a couple of miles of empty land, its surface rough and pitted, broken up by the occasional palm tree. 'Head towards the inner city,' said Jed, pointing towards the light sparkling from central Baghdad. 'We'll get lost in there. It's our best chance.'

His body jerked forward as the Datsun hit a rock. The suspension creaked and groaned, and somewhere inside the vehicle Jed was certain he could hear something snapping.

'We'd be better off with a sodding camel,' said Matt.

He was twisting the car through the rough ground, trying to avoid the dips, but the Datsun was hardly up to driving on a proper road. Steam was coming from the engine, and it was over-revving furiously each time Matt tapped the accelerator. Another mile, thought Jed.

Hold out that long, then at least we're clear of the scene.

The ditch took him by surprise. The Datsun dipped, and Jed could feel his head crashing into the steel roof as his body was thrown upwards. Matt tried to get the car back on track, but the engine was just revving. Nothing was happening to the wheels. 'Bugger it,' said Matt. 'We're fucked.'

Jed opened the door and climbed out of the Datsun. The trench measured fifty feet across by ten wide, and was at least five feet deep. It looked man-made. There had been at least two occasions in the last fifteen years when Baghdad had built up its perimeter defences: at the height of the Iran-Iraq War, when the Iranians briefly broke through the lines, and looked like threatening the capital; and after Gulf 1, when the allies could easily have kept marching north until they hit Baghdad. Must have been dug for one of them, thought Jed. *And finally, the bloody thing has actually stopped some attackers*.

'I think we'd better do the rest of the trip on foot, guys,' said Jed.

Matt, Steve and Rob had already climbed out of the car. The machine had died on them, and it didn't look as if much would bring it back to life. Rob was the best mechanic among them. 'What d'you think, Rob? Any chance of fixing it?' said Jed.

Rob opened up the bonnet, then shook his head. 'It would take a couple of hours, and then the bloody thing would just break apart again on this ground,' he said.

146

'Unless we can get our hands on an SUV, we're better off on foot.'

'Fuck it,' snapped Steve. 'We've only been in the sodding country an hour, and the whole thing's gone tits up already.'

'We'll be OK,' said Jed.

They were equipped with rough maps of the city. Using the satphone, Jed checked in with Laura back at the Firm's headquarters in Vauxhall. She told him they just had to press on. The mission was too critical to be abandoned. They worked out their position from their drop-off point: they had travelled around its outskirts, and were now heading towards the Ad Dawrah region to its north, but they were still at least five miles from the target. They would have to get across the Tigris. That would be when they were at their most vulnerable. Through the streets of any city, even Baghdad, you could pass unnoticed so long as you didn't draw attention to yourself. But before they crossed any bridges, they would have to make sure there weren't any roadblocks.

Jed started walking, heading due north. From the map, he reckoned they had about two miles of scrubland before they hit streets again. Ad Dawrah was a cheap factory workers' district, close to a big oil refinery. Once they crossed the river, they were into Baghdad proper. *That's when this gig would start to get interesting.*

They walked at a steady, measured pace. The unit lined up in a regular formation: one man went a few paces in front, to scout the area, while another man hung back a few paces to keep an eye on the rear; the other two guys stayed in the middle, one looking left, the other right. They never drifted more than five yards apart from one another: if they came under attack, they would need to fall back into a unit to defend themselves.

They covered the ground in silence. The air was quiet and still out here, and any voices would travel an unexpected distance. Somewhere, Jed could hear a desert dog howling. Huge animals, like Alsatians on steroids, they roamed the outskirts of the city, and could take a chunk out of a man's limb with a single bite. If you came across one, the only option was to shoot it on sight.

An hour had passed by the time the bridge loomed up before them. Two miles of the trek towards the target had now been completed. They had passed through the scrubland, and made their way through the backstreets of the Al-Dawrah district. It was an area of heavy industry, served by the big boats that made their way up the Tigris from Basra. As well as the refining plant, there was a cement factory, a series of workshops, and a huge chicken farm, which, according to some of the intelligence reports Jed had seen, might also have been used to breed biological weapons: chickens could incubate all kinds of viruses. 'We'll give the chickens a miss,' whispered Jed to the others, as he consulted his map to steer the unit towards the bridge.

'Right,' said Matt. 'We're only the fucking SAS. We wouldn't want to get mixed up with a bunch of hens in a bad mood. They might think we're stealing their eggs.'

Jed checked his watch. It was just past three in the morning. The still of the night was all around them. There were apartment blocks housing the workers for the factories, and cafés, shops and petrol stations dotted through the district, but everyone was sleeping. This was the second time Jed had walked through Baghdad at night, and he'd noticed it was a timid city: there were only a few nightclubs, and they were in the smart hotels in the centre of the city. Otherwise, everyone went to bed early. Luton on a wet Tuesday evening was more fun. This was a place where you kept your head down, got on with your job and tried not to attract any attention. They'd seen a couple of police patrols but since you could hear the cars approaching, the unit had enough time to duck into a doorway and let them pass – they could walk around without anyone seeing them.

But that was about to change. From about four onwards, the city would suddenly spark to life. Jed reckoned the factories would start up at six, just as the dawn was breaking. The trucks would start delivering supplies. The cafés would open. Suddenly they would be surrounded by people. Yes, they could lose themselves easily enough in a crowd, but it would always be risky. One false move and they would be exposed.

'Hold it,' whispered Jed, raising an arm. They were standing by the banks of the river, looking up. The Fourteenth of July Bridge ran straight up from the southern side of the city into the Republican Palace complex where all the most important government buildings were located. From there they could skirt to

149

the east of the city to hit the compound. The bridge was named for the day in 1958 when the Baath Party overthrew Iraq's last monarch, King Faisal II: it was the country's first suspension bridge, and still one of its most impressive.

That means it's even harder to get across, thought Jed.

The roadblock was clearly visible. Two barriers were slung across the road, and there were at least five armed policemen stopping the few vehicles making the crossing. Most likely, they'd already found the two guys they'd shot earlier. Even if they assumed it was Iraqi gangsters, they would be looking for their killers.

'Want to chance it?' whispered Rob. 'We might be able to bluff our way through. And if we don't we've got the ammo to take them out.'

Jed shook his head. He glanced at the river. The Tigris was a thick, fast-running stretch of water, muddy and dirty, with scum foaming on its surface from the raw sewage and industrial waste that was pumped into it every day. 'Too risky,' he muttered. 'They'll have backup they can call on. Get into a shoot-out on a bridge, and you've got no space. Better to try and swim it.'

'I can see a boat,' said Steve.

He led the way. The jetty was about three hundred yards back along the river, a decent enough distance from the bridge. Jed, Matt and Rob followed, keeping their bodies low to avoid attracting attention. It was a simple wooden rowing boat, measuring eight feet, tied up to the side of the wooden jetty. There didn't seem to be any alarms. Steve knelt down, using his knife to cut through the ropes, then climbed on. Jed, Matt and Rob followed, Rob kicking the boat out into the river. Steve grabbed the oars, and started steering them to the other bank. The river was about two hundred yards across, but the current was thick, swirling around them. Jed cast a quick glance up towards the bridge. There was no question they would be visible to the guards. It was just a question of whether anyone looked.

The oars were slicing into the water. Steve was a big man, over six three, and with the muscles that came from working out for an hour every day in the gym. He was pulling hard, pushing the boat through the vicious current. Matt and Rob sat at the back of the boat, while Jed was at the front to try and balance their weight through the tiny vessel. Their kitbags were slung on its floor. He glanced down into the water. It was thick and brown, the colour and texture of dried blood, reflecting back nothing but its own brute strength. *A river that could wash away an army*, thought Jed.

A light. His head spun round, looking up towards the bridge. A searchlight had flashed down from the police checkpoint. It was skimming across the water, its beams catching in the flowing currents and spinning out across the surface. Bugger it, he muttered under his breath. The rest of the unit had noticed it as well. Matt and Rob were hunkering down at the back of the boat. Steve was pulling furiously on the oars, dragging them faster towards the opposite shore. They were still forty, maybe fifty yards, from the bank, and the current was taking them away from the bridge. Jed's mind was racing. Stay moving, and it made them easier to spot. Stop moving, and it made them easier to capture if they were spotted. In an instant, the decision was made. *Get the hell out of here as fast as possible.*

'Keep going,' he hissed to Steve. 'Fast as you bloody can.'

The light was spinning closer towards them. Jed glanced back towards the bridge. The searchlight was revolving in a circle, spreading a beam about ten metres in circumference. It was panning up and down the river. Looking for something. *Us.*

'Fuck it,' he muttered. 'Can't we go any faster?'

'You try it,' hissed Steve.

The boat was picking up speed but it was hard going. As they drew to within forty yards of the shore, the current seemed to gather strength. There were specks of foam and dirt swirling on the surface of the river, and the water was crashing into the side of the boat, pushing it further and further downstream. The searchlight danced just a few feet away from them. Jed held his breath, watching as the light illuminated the water, changing its colour from murky brown to a slimy, stewed green. He looked at the shore. Thirty yards, nothing more. The light turned, and suddenly he could see it heading straight for them. It was skimming across the river, travelling at a dozen feet a second. 'Left, left,' he said to Steve, wondering if they could spin out of its path. Steve was tugging on the oar, and Jed could feel the boat turning beneath him.

Collision. The beam hit the boat, and Jed could suddenly feel its full force. The light flooded the boat, its heat pricking Jed's skin. He could see the faces of his unit: fear mixed with determination, the usual expression of soldiers who knew they were going into combat. The beam skimmed across, and for a moment Jed wondered if the policemen might have missed them. It flicked past, paused on an empty stretch of water, then inched back towards them as the man controlling it slowly adjusted its direction. Then the light was fully on them, covering the entire boat in a neatly illuminated circle. Just like a target, thought Jed. *With us in the bloody middle of it.*

He could hear the sound of gunfire before he could feel it. The slow rattle of a machine gun revving up to life. The bullets splattered into the water, breaking up its surface like tiny pebbles. Steve was yanking furiously on the oars, sweat dripping from his face, as he stabbed the wood into the water and dragged it back furiously towards him. Behind him, Matt and Rob were hunkering down in the back of the boat, retrieving their kitbags and slinging them on to their backs.

A splintering sound. A couple of bullets had ripped into the bottom of the boat, ripping up the wood, then slicing through into the water below. They had passed just inches from Jed's legs. Already water was starting to seep up through the holes the bullets had created.

Then a scream. Jed looked up. Rob had taken a shot. The machine-gun fire had raked past him. The Kevlar jacket underneath his shirt had protected his chest, but one bullet had taken a chunk of flesh clean out of his shoulder, and another had hit him in the neck. Blood was pouring down his front. In his eyes there was the stunned, disbelieving look of a soldier who knows he had just been hit. Badly.

Jed tried to get past Steve. The machine-gunner had raked his bullets past the boat, and was now firing aimlessly into the water. Its surface was breaking up under the fire. Then it changed direction. It was drawing closer to the boat again. 'Into the fucking water,' shouted Steve. 'We're fucking corpses in this bloody thing.'

With a single swift movement, Jed threw his kitbag onto his back and tossed himself into the water. He didn't need to think twice. Under fire, your best bet was to get as deep down into the water as you could. The gunmen couldn't see you. And the water between you and the surface offered some measure of protection: it could deflect the path of a bullet enough to save your life. Taking a lungful of air, he sunk below the surface. In the next three seconds, he sunk six feet, before kicking his legs to stabilise himself. The water felt cold and slimy, clinging on to his skin, and he could feel the strength of the current knocking into him. Jed opened his eyes, trying to adjust to the water, but it was almost impossible to see anything. The water was too thick with dirt, and there was too little light on its surface. He could just about see Steve, then Matt holding on to Rob. They were still fifteen yards from the shore. Blood was streaming from Rob's neck, mixing with the water. One or two bullets were still spitting onto the surface, ripping through the water towards the bottom of the river. Jed swam forward, grabbing hold of Rob's arm, and together with Matt they started pulling him. The current was taking them downstream, and they were both kicking furiously with their legs to propel themselves towards the riverbank. He could see that Rob's mouth was open. The man's lungs were filling with water. Jed kicked harder. Another ten yards. If there was to be any chance of saving him, they had to move fast. Right now, it was a question of whether he bled to death or drowned first.

Ahead, Jed could see the ground sloping upwards. The bank was drawing closer. His lungs were already bursting for air: he could feel the oxygen draining out of him as he used his one free arm to propel himself forwards. Suddenly, he could feel ground beneath his feet. He stood up, and started to wade towards the shore, Matt at his side, helping him to push Rob up. His head broke through the water, and he looked up at the bridge. The searchlight was still revolving in a round arc, skipping across the water, but so far as he could tell they couldn't be seen. Glancing back he could see that the boat was shot to pieces, its frame splintered and shattered by the bullets.

He pulled Rob up from the surface of the water and dragged him towards the shore. He had lost consciousness, and the blood was still draining out of the wounds he had taken to his neck and shoulder. Some of the slime and foam from the river was sticking to the raw flesh torn open by the bullets.

Jed pulled hard, getting him clear of the water. The

tide was half out, and there was a stretch of thick mud that ran up to a walled embankment. Above, there was a road running alongside the river, but at this time of night there didn't seem to be any cars on it. The search-light was still scanning the river, but the gunfire had stopped. Jed could hear voices carried down from the bridge on the wind. Perhaps they thought they'd shot whoever was in the boat, sending them down to the riverbed to meet the hundreds of corpses that must be tossed into the Tigris every year. But Jed couldn't be certain of that. They might be sending a search party along the banks of the river right now. They were only five hundred yards down from the bridge. *They had to move fast.*

Jed knelt down. Rob still had a pulse on him but he was fading fast. His mouth was choking with the blood running through from his neck. At his side, Matt had pulled out a stretch of cloth from the medical bag in his rucksack, and was busy tying it round the neck wound. The bleeding was starting to slow, but it was impossible to say how much blood he'd lost under the water. Two, maybe three pints. The skin around the two wounds was covered with mud: any diseases in the water – and it looked like there were plenty – and they would have infected him by now. The guy needs a hospital, thought Jed. And probably for a few weeks at least.

He glanced anxiously up and down the riverbank, then up towards the bridge. The light was still hovering over the boat, but hadn't been flicked across to the shore. Jed listened hard. He could hear the lapping of the water a few feet away from him. And somewhere in the distance he could hear the rumbling motor of a truck.

'We've got to move,' he hissed to Steve and Matt.

'You grab his arms, I'll get his shoulders,' said Matt.

Jed paused. There were just fractions of a second to finalise the decision. 'We can't take him,' he said flatly.

'Bollocks,' hissed Matt. 'He's our mate. Now grab his legs.'

Jed stood up. He could see the anger in Matt's eyes. 'Half the sodding Republican Guard could be here in a minute,' he said. 'If we don't move now, we're fucking dead.'

Steve was looking from one man to the next. Jed could tell he was weighing the argument. He knew the drill book, Jed was aware of that. Standard operating procedure said that when a man was down, you gave him first aid, then moved on. You couldn't jeopardise the mission to save one man. No special forces unit could work like that, it would never achieve anything. Yet the drill book didn't always matter. When one of your mates was shot up, and needed help, it was hard to leave him behind. Most soldiers cared a lot more about the men in their unit than they did about the mission. *And those that didn't were the psychos, thought Jed.*

'We're not leaving him,' said Matt, his voice rising above a whisper for the first time. 'The fucking ragheads will torture the sod. Now let's get the bugger to safety.'

'It's no fucking use,' said Jed. 'He needs a hospital. What are you going to do, check him into the Baghdad

Central A&E? If we don't leave him, we'll be bloody captured.'

'He's my mate. Now lift his legs,' said Matt.

'You're jeopardising the mission.'

'Sod the mission,' snapped Matt. 'You're just a fucking wannabe Rupert, Jed. We don't need any bloody grad-uates slumming it with the proper soldiers. Just fuck off, and let us look after our mate.'

Jed looked at Rob. Putting his finger to his wrist, he could tell the pulse had stopped. He'd lost too much blood, and it was still draining out of him. 'It doesn't make any difference,' he said quietly. 'The poor sod is dead.'

There was silence. Without a word, Steve helped Jed lift up the body, and started to carry it towards the rushes by the side of the river. Pushing the corpse down into the weeds, they covered it as best they could. Taking out his GPS reader, Jed measured his precise position. 'When this war is over, we'll be back to get you,' he said. 'Make sure you get a proper burial.'

For a moment, Jed could see the hatred in Matt's eyes. His pupils were like bullets, loaded up and ready to fire. Then it subsided, replaced by a look of sadness that rode across his face like a wave. 'Let's bloody go then,' he muttered.

I've been in the army for four years, and this is the first time I've seen a man I know go down, thought Jed as he walked away. *Let's hope to God it's the last.*

TWELVE

Nick took the cup of tea Lana had just made him. She had always been thin, but today she looked like she'd lost weight. The redness in her eyes suggested she hadn't been sleeping well. *It's getting to her*, he thought. *Just the way it is getting to all of us.*

'So no word at all?' he said, taking a sip on the tea.

Lana shook her head. 'Nothing,' she replied.

'You've asked around?'

Lana nodded. 'It's ten days now since anybody heard from her. No text messages, no phone calls, no emails. Nothing.'

Nick nodded. The young stayed in touch in ways that hadn't been possible when he was in his early twenties. He could remember when he was first in the army; he'd been gone a month before getting in touch with his mum or any of his mates. She must have been worried sick, he realised now, and he regretted not having done more to let her know he was OK. 'Seen any guys hanging around the flat?'

Suddenly Lana looked worried. She was a frail girl, Nick noted, but not timid: she had a purpose and strength to her that suggested she wouldn't back down easily in any confrontation. Nick hadn't told her anything about the money that had been paid into Sarah's account. Nor had he said anything about the men following him, or the investigators hired by the oil industry. But she wasn't stupid. She must suspect that something bad had happened to Sarah.

'Guys? What the hell do you mean?'

Nick shrugged. 'People watching the flat, following you, anything like that. Just anything suspicious, that's all.'

Lana gripped her mug tighter. 'No,' she said anxiously. 'I mean, I haven't noticed, but I haven't been looking either. What should I look for?'

'Maybe a couple of guys just sitting in a car out in the street, the same face looking at you as you walk to your college, anything like that,' said Nick.

'Christ, no.'

Nick walked over to the window. The flat was on the first floor of a Victorian terraced block. He looked down into the street. He could see a row of parked cars, mostly cheap run-arounds that parents had bought for their student offspring. None of them were occupied. He looked at the houses opposite. Maybe they've taken a bedsit in the street so they can keep an eye on the place. He scanned the windows, but could see nothing except drawn curtains or empty rooms. They must be here, he thought. *Somewhere.*

Lana joined him at the window. Raindrops were spitting down on to the glass. 'What's happened to her, Nick?'

'I don't know.'

'But you're suspicious? You don't just think she's gone on a drinking bender?'

'For ten days?' Nick shrugged his shoulders. 'Even for a girl who can drink like Sarah can, that doesn't sound very likely.'

'Then what?'

'It might be something to do with her work,' said Nick.

'She's just a student,' said Lana.

'Doesn't matter,' snapped Nick. 'I need to know what she was doing in those labs.'

Lana paused for a moment. She was sipping on her tea. 'Then speak to a guy called Sam Beston.'

'Who's he?'

'A colleague at the lab. Sarah never speaks to me about her work because I don't suppose I would understand it. But she talks to Sam about it. He's the guy she's closest to. I think he's a little bit in love with her, but she wouldn't go for him. He's the thoughtful, scientific type, and she always has this whole macho thing going.'

'Where will I find him?'

'I don't know where he lives, but Cambridge is a small place. If you don't find him at the lab, try the Three Crowns. That's where all the scientists go drinking.'

Nick nodded. 'I'm trying the professor again,' he said. 'If there's no luck there, I'll track down Sam.'

Lana reached out to touch the side of his arm, but Nick instinctively pulled it away. He regretted it instantly, but since Mary's death, he hadn't liked to have other people touch him. Only Sarah. 'You should go to the police,' she said.

'And tell them what, exactly?' said Nick. 'That a student hasn't called her dad for ten days? That'll give them a bloody good laugh.'

He headed for the door, then paused, looking back towards Lana. He could tell how frightened she was. 'I'll find her,' he said firmly. 'And I'll do it by myself.'

With his head down, Nick walked out into the street. The rain was starting to fall heavily, and the water was already flowing fast into the gutters. Nick pulled up the collar of his leather jacket, but ignored the rain lashing his hair. I wasn't able to rescue her mother, he thought. *But I can sure as hell rescue Sarah. Or die trying.*

Nick looked at the computer screen. He was sitting in one of the Internet cafés in Cambridge, and he'd just done a Google search on the Lubbock Group. From the information he'd managed to beat out of Stonehill, he didn't reckon they were his best lead. If they were tracking me, he thought, it follows that they didn't know where Sarah was. But they might be part of the conspiracy all the same.

The search turned up a couple of dozen entries. They were mostly fringe websites, some of them compiled by left-wing organisations, others by survivalists and environmentalists. The sites described it as a group of the leading players in the oil industry – the big oil companies, OPEC, the British and American producers, and more recently the Russians – who gathered together once a year at a secret location. According to a couple of the sites, they were very close to the Bush family – one described both Bush presidents as nothing more than frontmen for the Lubbock Group. They were ascribed the power to start wars, change governments, direct the global economy – to do whatever was necessary to keep the oil barons in dollars. Why would they be interested in Sarah, wondered Nick. What had she been working on?

There was one six-year-old story from *Business Week*, which discussed the rumours about the Group, but dismissed them as probably untrue. That was the only reference Nick could find in the mainstream press. Wrong, mate, thought Nick, as he finished the article. They're real. And the Lubbock Group is looking for Sarah, just like me.

Professor Wilmington, thought Nick, getting up and walking out of the café. That bastard knows where Sarah is. And he knows why the Lubbock guys are looking for her.

Professor Wilmington looked up from his computer when Nick walked into the room. 'What the hell are you doing in my office?' he snapped. Nick could see him calling up the screensaver before he stood up and walked towards the doorway.

'Looking for my daughter,' said Nick firmly.

It had been a half-hour walk from Sarah's apartment to the labs, and Nick's hair was wet and matted to his head. Glancing round the room, he could see that the professor was alone.

'Well, as her father, I'd have thought you were the man responsible for her welfare, not me,' said Wilmington.

The equations had been wiped clean from the blackboard but Nick could still see traces of the chalk left behind. There was a faint smell of cigarette smoke in the air, although he couldn't see any sign of an ashtray. 'I need to know what she was working on.'

'I already explained to you,' said Wilmington. 'I don't follow the work of all my students that closely.'

There was a note of exasperation in his voice that was starting to annoy Nick. Whatever it was that the professor cared about it clearly wasn't his students.

'Something to do with energy, maybe,' said Nick.

A thin smile spread across Wilmington's lips. 'Well, I think you'll find that most of advanced physics relates to energy in one way or another. Or maybe you're not familiar with Einstein's work.'

'It doesn't matter what I'm familiar with,' said Nick. 'I need to know whether Sarah was doing anything that might get her into trouble.'

Wilmington stepped closer to Nick. The two men were just inches apart: so close that Nick could smell the thick, cloying aftershave on his chin. 'I really don't appreciate the way you keep barging into my office like this,' he said. His voice was low, but there was a thread of real anger running through it. Wilmington was not a big man, nor did he look in great physical shape. Nick knew that he could snap him like a match-

stick if he needed to. But there was a physical presence to him all the same: his eyes were focused and
intense. 'Now, I really must ask you to leave. I have
work to attend to.'

'Something to do with the oil industry?' persisted
Nick.

'This is ridiculous,' snapped Wilmington. 'We don't
do industrial research here.'

'Then what kind of research was she doing?'

'Pure science,' he said. 'Now, if you don't leave this
minute, I'll have to call security.'

Like most soldiers, Nick knew how to adopt an air
of menace, and didn't mind using it when necessary. He
was used to intimidating people. Yet so far as he could
tell, the professor was not in the least bit afraid of him.
'I want to see her papers.'

'We don't keep papers here.'

'Her computer, then.'

'I'm afraid that's not possible either,' said Wilmington.
'All the students use their own laptops, and the lab's
mainframe can't be accessed by outsiders.'

'You won't bloody lift a finger, will you?' said Nick
angrily. 'It doesn't matter what I ask you, you'll just say
no.'

'Quite so,' said Wilmington. 'For the third and, I hope,
final time, please leave my room.'

'It's my daughter we're talking about,' said Nick. 'How
would you feel if your family was under threat?'

'I know all about that,' said Wilmington coldly.

For the first time, Nick felt he could see a flicker of

concern flash across the man's face. Maybe he has a daughter of his own, he thought. Maybe that's the way to get through to him.

'If I don't get any answers from you, I'm going to bloody lose it,' he said.

Wilmington looked towards the door. Nick could hear a movement. The door was opening. As he turned round, he saw the man he'd seen here last time. The Arab.

Salek.

He was stepping into the room, walking briskly towards the professor. 'Is this man bothering you?' he asked.

Wilmington glanced at him, but who was controlling whom he couldn't tell. 'He's just about to leave.'

'Not until I get some answers.'

'There are no answers here,' said Salek patiently. 'The professor is concerned about Sarah's well-being, as is everyone in the laboratory. But he sees nothing to worry about yet, and certainly doesn't believe it relates to her work here. This is a purely academic establishment.'

'Who are you?' said Nick.

'A friend.'

Nick just rolled his eyes.

Salek took a step forward. He was dressed in a white cotton shirt and black tousers, and his brown eyes were looking straight at Nick. With one sudden movement, his right hand flashed up, grabbing Nick's left wrist and tugging it into the air. Nick could feel the nerves being stretched, and a burst of pain rattled up through his arm.

For a moment, Nick was paralysed by the attack. His chest and neck were seizing up. He looked into Salek's eyes, and could see the contempt in his expression slowly replaced by amusement.

Christ, he thought. This man is at least a decade younger than me. A decade quicker and a decade stronger. He must have had some kind of military training to know those kinds of moves. So why is he hanging out in Wilmington's office all the time?

Nick struggled to regain his composure. His left wrist was being twisted tighter and tighter: Salek was turning it like a screw, scrunching the nerves and the arteries. The pain was blinding. Steeling himself, Nick rolled his right fist into a ball, focused his eyes, then slammed his fist down hard into Salek's right hand. There was a momentary pause. Nick could feel the impact of the blow travel down from his right hand, into Salek's fist, then down into his own left hand. He cursed, trying to control the pain. Then his eyes flickered up. Salek had loosened his grip. Nick snatched away his fist, cradling it next to his chest.

'You're a strong man, Mr Scott,' said Salek. 'At least, for a man of your age.'

'You'll find out how strong soon,' snapped Nick, 'if I don't get some bloody answers.'

'That would be a pleasure,' said Salek. 'But you must realise you aren't going to get anything here today. Your threats and intimidations are no good here. You're not my equal in strength, and if anyone hears a fight, there will be a couple of security guards here in a minute, with the police backing them up a few minutes later.' He looked at Nick and smiled. 'So fuck off.'

Nick's fist was still clenched. The pain was rippling through his left arm and into his neck, making it hard for him to concentrate. 'Who the hell are you working for?'

Salek's hand flashed out towards Nick's wrist but missed. 'There are a dozen different way to inflict pain on you, old man,' he said. 'Like I just said, fuck off.'

Nick turned round. This was useless. Whether he could beat the man in a fight, he didn't know. He *did* know he had the guile of a snake. It would be a tough battle. Nick wasn't afraid of the man, but what would be the point? The noise of the fight would bring the police down on them in seconds, and he'd end up spending the night in the cells. It wasn't going to help anyway. He'd learnt a long time ago that you had to know when to march to war and when to retreat, and he wasn't about to forget the lesson now. 'This isn't finished,' he said, heading for the door. 'And if I ever discover that either of you had anything to do with Sarah's disappearance, I'll rip both of you apart limb by bloody limb.'

Behind him, he could hear Salek laughing. 'You know what your daughter needs?' said Salek, as Nick strode out of the room. 'A stronger and better father. It doesn't matter what the fight is, you're always going to lose.'

THIRTEEN

The air was dark and thick with tension. Jed walked slowly through the empty side street. He could see the garbage filling the huge black metal bins, and he could hear Steve and Matt close behind him. Each step was taking them deeper into enemy territory. Take a single wrong turning, and they'd find themselves in Saddam's bedroom.

'Which way?' hissed Steve.

'Keep bearing left,' said Matt. 'We'll hit the industrial area eventually.'

They had left Rob's corpse by the river, and scrambled up the banks that led to an avenue running alongside the Tigris. It was lined with palm trees and, on the opposite side of the road, the big apartment blocks used by the Baath Party officials and senior army commanders. Up ahead, they could see the lights of the Republican Palace, a high, gaudy building, flanked by vaulting columns and two huge statues of Saddam cast in bronze. They were skirting the heart of the Iraqi government machine, Jed reminded himself. It was like a group of Germans walking down Whitehall in 1940. We're as close to the edge as a soldier can get. *And as close to death as well.*

It was just after five in the morning, and they had to get to the target as fast as possible to remain undetected: they wouldn't go in until tonight, but it would be harder to travel around the city during the day. There were still three miles to cover. According to the intelligence briefings he'd sat through, Baghdad's security was entrusted to three different groups. The Special Republican Guard were the elite unit of the army, and the most fiercely loyal to Saddam. It was commanded by Saddam's son Qusai. The Fedayeen, the internal security apparatus, was commanded by another son, Udai. They were the specialists in torture and interrogation – if they were about to capture you, you were better off dead. And then there were the foreign fighters. Mostly Syrians, but also Lebanese, Egyptians and Moroccan mercenaries, Saddam had hired thousands of them to help defend the city, mostly because he no longer trusted his own army to fight for him. Intelligence reported that the three groups hardly spoke to each other. There was no coordination between them, and just because the Republican Guards were searching for you, it didn't mean the Fedayeen or the mercenaries would help them.

Bugger intelligence, thought Jed. We keep our eyes open and rely on our own wits. If there was one thing he'd learnt in the last couple of months, it was that all the intelligence on Iraq was crap. Nobody knew anything about what was happening inside this country. *And the more they claimed to know, the less they really did.*

Dawn was breaking. Up ahead, Jed could see a dust cart driving down the street, two men on the back, stopping at every apartment and office block to pick up the night's rubbish. He walked in a straight line, not stopping, not looking at the men. We're just three Iraqis on the way to work, he thought. We all have black hair, beards, brown eyes, and the sun has tanned and dried out our skins. *We blend in as well as any foreigner can be expected to.*

They kept walking. By six in the morning you could feel the city coming to life all around you, Jed noticed. The cars were growling along the streets, and the cafés and shops were opening for business. You could smell sweet Arabic coffee in the air: a thick, nutty aroma that gave you a shot of energy as you walked past a café.

They had skirted north of the Republican Palace, tracking the river as it rolled through the city. A few clouds were smudged across the sky, but it looked like a fine day. As he crossed a road junction, Jed watched a couple of kids dragged by their mothers towards the gates of their school. Poor sods, thought Jed. *They have no idea what's about to hit them.*

'How far, you reckon?' said Steve.

He was speaking in hushed tones, making sure no one could hear him before he opened his mouth. If anyone heard them speaking English, the alarm would be raised. That couldn't be risked.

'About a mile,' said Jed. 'That will take us into the industrial centre on this side of the river. Then we have to lie up until darkness, and plan our entry.'

Steve nodded. They crossed the road, skirted past the school, then took a side street that led away from the river and headed north. By the river, Jed could see some men digging trenches. They were hoisting out the earth and putting down sandbags; next to them, you could see the machine-gun turrets being assembled. The war is coming, Jed thought. They realise it. We realise it. *And whatever anyone says there is going to be some bloody hard fighting before we take this city.*

He looked first towards Steve, then Matt. As he did so, Matt turned away. Leaving Rob behind was still hurting, Jed could see that in the man's expression. He was a good soldier, but emotionally volatile. Losing one of his mates mattered to him. Not my fault, thought Jed. But that doesn't mean he doesn't blame me for it. But we have to work together. *Otherwise we're done for.*

A roadblock. Jed glanced ahead, trying to get a good look at the soldiers. They were right at the end of the street, fifty yards away. A Toyota SUV had been parked across the road, and the soldiers were stopping people at random, checking their papers and asking them questions. They were wearing the drab, olive-green uniforms of the Republican Guard. Not for them the purple insignia of the SRG, nor the black, baggy pyjama-style uniform worn by the Fedayeen. The weakest link in Baghdad defences, decided Jed. The regular Republican Guard were just ordinary guys who'd been drafted and couldn't wait to get home to their families. *But that didn't mean their bullets wouldn't bite.*

'Seen them,' hissed Steve.

Jed dropped back a pace, so that he was walking level with Steve and Matt. It was important not to slow down when you saw a roadblock. Don't break stride, Jed told himself. And don't turn round. The soldiers were taught to look for anyone who didn't want to be stopped. Draw attention to yourself, and you were already dead.

'Just keep walking,' said Jed. 'Act like we're on our way to work.'

'I say we turn round, skirt past them on the next street,' said Matt.

His voice was low, nothing more than a whisper. The street led towards one of the big ministry buildings, and beyond that the factory district. There were no small side streets. Plenty of people were coming this way to work. Most of them were tired, and nearly all of them were nervous. Everyone minded their own business.

'We walk past them,' hissed Steve. 'Turn round now, and they'll spot us.'

'It was your fucking idea to get the boat across the river,' said Matt. 'And now Rob's dead.'

'Shut it,' hissed Jed. 'You turn round if you want to, but we're walking straight through.'

He kept his head down, and walked steadily on. The guards weren't stopping everyone. There were too many people on the streets at this time of the day. As he drew closer, Jed could see them more closely. Three boys, around eighteen or nineteen, with AK-47s slung around their shoulders and knives stuck into their leather belts. All of them had green tunics on, but two of them had black trousers. The Iraqi Army was so poorly equipped, many of the men didn't even have proper uniforms. He looked up, but avoided their eyes. He was level with

173

them now, with Steve and Matt both silent at his side. He took a step, then another. His breath was practically silent. Inside his chest, he could feel his heart skipping a beat as one of the soldiers glanced towards him. He could feel the man's eyes resting on his skin, examining him. Then, in the same instant, he lost interest, his eyes flicking on to the next man walking past.

Without varying his pace, Jed walked on. The temptation was to quicken the pace, to break into a run. But he knew that was a mistake. 'Thank fuck for that,' he muttered when they were fifty yards clear of the roadblock.

'Close one,' said Steve. 'Too bloody close for my liking. We've got to find ourselves some cover.'

Jed glanced at Matt, but the man was silent, and his expression angry. Does he want to get caught? Jed wondered. Matt's not handling the pressure. *We need to watch him.*

The ministries and apartment blocks fell away after half a mile, replaced by the dustier roads of the industrial district. It was approaching eight thirty now. The kids were all in school, and the workers in their offices and factories. The streets were emptier, and Jed was conscious that three men walking through the roads were more conspicuous. Twice more they saw trenches being dug and machine-gun turrets being put up. Yet all around the preparations for war, people were getting on with their normal lives: shopping, cleaning, working. What else can the poor sods do, Jed thought. They didn't ask for this fight. *It's just bad luck the battle is going to rage through their homes.*

Up ahead, Jed recognised a tower. It was just six storeys of dusty concrete, with air conditioners sticking out of every window, but to Jed it was familiar. 'We're getting close,' he whispered to Matt and Steve.

The street gave way to a square. Another three hundred yards on the left, and there was a road that took you down to the facility. Their target. Jed could feel the tiredness in his limbs. It was twenty-four hours now since they had slept. They needed to rest before they attempted the recce. And they needed to wait for darkness.

A truck pulled up alongside them. Jed could smell the fumes pumping out of its exhaust. He watched the trucker walk across to a café, then sit down outside with a coffee and a roll. 'There,' hissed Jed. 'That's the place.'

He'd checked the piece of paper a couple of times already: this was the café that al-Shaalan had told them to meet his cousin at. He walked slowly towards the café. There were trucks all around the square, most of them old, and all of them belching diesel fumes. The smell of chemicals, concrete and deep-fried food hung over the place, and the voices he could hear around him came from right across the regions: Syrians, Moroccans, Indians, even some Filipinos. If we can't blend in here, Jed told himself, we can't blend in anywhere.

He put his kitbag on the ground, then waved at the waiter. A man in his late forties, wearing a stained white apron, he paid little attention to Jed's accent as he ordered. '*Kahwa*,' he said, holding up three fingers, and slurring the word so that the waiter wouldn't notice how terrible his accent was. A minute later he put three tiny cups of sweet coffee down on the table. Jed drank it in two sips. He could feel the jolt of concentrated caffeine hitting his bloodstream, yet the energy only made him more aware of the danger they were in.

'Jesus, this tastes like crap,' muttered Matt.

'Quiet,' hissed Steve.

Jed could see a couple of men looking at them, then look away. There were no women in the café, just guys aged between twenty and forty, most of them with thick, black moustaches, and sweaty, grease-stained T-shirts. At the next table there were two men, one about forty, the other around thirty. Right-looking table, reckoned Jed. He coughed and caught the man's eyes. He looked straight at him, as if sizing him up.

'How far to Tipperary?' said Jed.

'Five miles,' replied the man.

Jed nodded. Contact. This was their guy.

From his pocket, he pulled out a roll of Iraqi dinars. The notes were brightly coloured, with big pictures of Saddam on them, but ever since the last Gulf War a shortage of printing equipment meant Iraqi money had no watermarks or metal strips, making it dead easy to forge. These were real ones, Jed reflected, as he peeled out twenty thousand, supplied by deserters who shipped up in Kuwait and were only too happy to trade their dinars for dollars supplied to them at the American army camps. He caught the eye of the man at the table next to him, then pushed the notes across the table. 'We need somewhere to stay,' he muttered in a low voice. 'Just for a day. We can pay in gold.'

He paused, scrutinising the man's face. Twenty thousand dinars translated to about ten dollars at the black-market exchange rate. Peanuts, but this was a country where men sold their lives for practically nothing. There was no point showing them too much money. In a place like this, if they thought you were rich, your throat would be cut in an instant. The only way they'd help was if they thought it was less trouble, and more profitable, than killing you.

'Where's my cousin?' asked the older man.

'Hiding,' said Jed.

There was no point in telling these guys al-Shaalan was dead. It would only antagonise them.

There was a brief burst of conversation from the men. Jed tried to follow it, but it was impossible. Finally, the older man looked at him. 'The back of my truck is empty,' he said. 'You can sleep there for twelve hours. For two ounces. Solid gold.'

Jed shook his head. 'One ounce is all I have,' he said. 'One ounce, plus one hundred thousand dinars.'

The man nodded. 'Payment up front.'

'OK,' said Jed.

'Tell him we want some grub,' hissed Matt.

'Some food,' said Jed. 'Can you bring us some food?'

The man laughed. 'You want girls as well?' he said. 'For more gold, maybe I can arrange something.'

Jed smiled. 'Just somewhere to sleep, my friend.'

He stood up. The older man was walking from the

café, surveying the area. There were plenty of people about, but no soldiers. 'This way,' he muttered.

Jed followed a couple of paces behind, with Steve and Matt at his side. The square was bustling with traffic, but the streets leading away from it were much quieter: just warehouses, factories and small workshops. Their workers were all inside at this time of the morning, and most of the deliveries had already been made. The street they were walking down was empty. *A good place to cut a man's throat.*

'Here,' said the man.

The truck was a Mercedes, but it must have been at least twenty years old. Jed didn't recognise the number plate – not Iraqi anyway, he was sure of that. It was about sixty feet long, with a white body that was covered in dust and scratches. 'You give me the money now,' said the man, unhinging the back door.

Jed peeled out some notes and one gold coin. 'Bring us some food,' he said. 'Anything you can find. And some bottled water.'

'A kebab,' said Matt. 'I could murder a kebab.'

The man looked at him closely. 'What happened to al-Shaalan?' he repeated.

Bloody idiot, thought Jed. Don't push him. We're about to go to war with this country, and he knows it. *If they find us, they'll kill him, then torture his whole family to death.*

'Hiding, like I said,' said Jed.

He could see the calculations running though the man's head. He was afraid, but he wanted the money as

178

well. Fear or greed? It was just an issue of which emotion was the strongest.

'Two ounces,' said the man.

His younger friend was stepping up to his side. He kept his mouth shut, but his eyes were angry, looking for a fight. We could break you like a matchstick, thought Jed. But that would put us in deeper trouble.

'That's robbery,' said Jed.

'Then find another truck,' sneered the man.

Jed pulled one more coin from his kitbag, and handed it across. 'That's all we've got,' he muttered.

The man took the coin, scratching at its surface with a dirty finger. A drop of nitric acid was the only way to tell for certain there wasn't bronze or copper underneath a thin plating of gold, but a fingernail was almost as good: plated coins would scratch, and would weigh differently in the palm of your hand. The man nodded, satisfied with his money, and tucked it into his pocket. He opened the doors of the truck, and motioned the three men inside.

It was dark in the back of the truck. As he climbed inside, Jed could smell goats and mechanical grease. There were some old papers lying on the floor, and in one corner some empty crates, but otherwise the truck was empty. Jed heard the doors closing behind him. 'We'll be back later with some food,' said the man.

Jed peered into the darkness. He scrunched some of the newspapers together to make a bed. Tossing his kitbag down, he lay back, putting his head on the bag. 'Better get some kip, lads,' he said. 'Who wants first watch?'

'I'll do it,' said Matt. 'Don't think I'd want to trust either of you to watch my back. You'd probably leave me to die – just the way you left Rob.'

'Drop it,' snapped Steve. 'There was nothing we could do about it.'

Matt looked at him menacingly. He was sitting on his haunches, watching the door, but his blue eyes glowed in the darkness like the eyes of a cat.

'Let's get some sodding kip,' said Jed, rolling over. 'Then maybe we can get this job done, and then get home again.'

Jed walked slowly down the street. It was just after ten, but although the factories and the workshops had shut up for the night, the place was still full of life. The cafés were full of men drinking coffee and talking, but the atmosphere was brittle.

He'd slept for almost ten hours. It was one of the first lessons he'd learnt on joining the army: sleep and eat as much as you can when you can, because you never know when you'll see a decent plate of grub or have a chance to put your head down again. After two hours' sleep, the men had returned with the food: several packs of soft pitta bread, some dried fish and beef, sunflower seeds and a couple of melons. Jed had wolfed it down: they had some ready-to-eat camp meals in their kitbags, but they'd save those for the retreat. They tasted like microwaved dog crap anyway. After eating, Jed had taken the watch for a couple of hours, then they'd switched around. By nightfall, he was feeling rested and fed. And ready for the fight.

He could see the facility about two hundred yards ahead of him. He recognised the network of streets from the last time he'd been here: off to the right he could see the spot where the small boy had been hassling him. This time at least the little bugger should be asleep, thought Jed. And if he isn't, he's in trouble.

Of the three of them, he thought he should be the one to recce the area. He knew the layout of the streets best, and someone has to put his neck on the line, he told himself. It might as well be me.

He paused. He could see a truck pulling up. It was right outside the facility. Eight men climbed out, opening up the gates to the plant and walking inside. They were wearing olive-green uniforms, carried AK-47s and shoulder pistols, and on the right-hand side of their tunics, purple insignia. Special Republican Guard, thought Jed. They've beefed up the security on this place since I was last here.

He walked on a few more yards, keeping his pace steady so as not to draw any attention to himself. There were maybe a dozen other people on the street, but nobody gave the soldiers a second glance. They were so used to the military in this city, they no longer paid them any attention. *It was just something that happened in the background, like the weather.*

The truck was pulling away from the plant, and the soldiers were shutting the thick metal gates that blocked its entrance: it looked like a change of shift, and from the numbers of guys getting out, Jed reckoned there were twenty men protecting the plant. He took a few more paces. The facility was a square courtyard, each side about 150 yards long. The gate was the only way in. There were four watchtowers, and machine-gun placements every fifty yards, but only two of them appeared to be illuminated tonight. From street level, you could see the pipes sticking up into the air: thick smoke was billowing from one of them. There were no high buildings overlooking the plant. If you wanted to get in, there were only two options. You could walk up and ring the bell. Or you could try and get in over the wall.

He turned round and walked back to the truck. 'Here,' he hissed, as he tapped on the steel door of the Mercedes. Steve opened it, and Jed scrambled inside. Matt was sitting on the floor, chewing sunflower seeds and spitting the husks out on the floor. 'How's it looking?' he said.

'Like crap,' said Jed. He knelt down, grabbing a hunk of pitta and chewing on it. 'I just saw the SRG going into the place.'

'How many?' said Steve.

'Eight,' said Jed. 'And there are two watchtowers.'

'So how are we going in?' said Matt.

'We have to go over the wall. There isn't any other choice.'

'We can't go through the door?' asked Steve.

'No way. That'll be where they've got the heavy-duty kit.'

'It's bloody suicide,' said Steve.

Jed shrugged. 'I guess that's what we're paid for.'

FOURTEEN

The plan had been agreed back in the truck. They would wait until three in the morning, the moment when the guards inside were most likely to be asleep. Two of the watchtowers were manned, with lights beaming on to the courtyard, but there was a patch of about ten yards where the lights didn't overlap. Two of them would scale the wall, while the third man would wait outside to provide covering fire if anything went wrong. Once inside, the two men would scout the place out, grab as much information as possible, then get out quickly.

The plan was nasty, ugly and violent. *I guess that's why they picked us, thought Jed.*

The wall was eight feet high, and made from solid concrete. Jed leant against it, running his hands along the side. It was as smooth as skin, with almost nothing to grip on to. There was only one way over. A leg-up, and then lie flat and hope to hell no one sees you.

The MOPP suits felt heavy and cumbersome. Jed had strapped the charcoal-lined jacket around himself and pulled on the trousers. Everything had to be sealed up with lightweight plastic clasps so that not a single inch of skin would be exposed to the atmosphere. On his hands there were rubber gloves, and at his side he had a rubber face mask to pull on at the last minute. He'd taken just a pistol and an AK-47 to keep himself light, and his grenades were packed tight to his waist. The MOPP wasn't a bad bit of kit, he thought. They'd made it as light as they could, but it was still hard to move quickly. They had talked through what kind of chemical weapons might be in the plant – anthrax, mustard gas, or something the British didn't even know about – and Jed didn't mind admitting the thought of them turned his blood cold. Still, the suit should offer some protection. *I feel like a bloody turkey about to be put into the oven*, thought Jed. *And maybe that's what I am.*

'You ready?' he said, looking across at Steve.

Steve nodded. 'Let's go,' he said tersely.

Matt was kneeling down, with his hands clasped together. Jed put his right foot into Matt's hands, and within one second he was being lifted clean into the air. Thrusting his arms forward, he grabbed hold of the rim of the wall, then levered himself up. Rolling his body forward, he pulled his legs up behind him, so he was lying flat on the surface.

A pause. There was a soft hum coming from some of the kit inside the plant. He glanced up at the two watchtowers, but the lights weren't moving. His patch of wall was shrouded in darkness. Looking down, he nodded to Steve. Matt hoisted him into the air, and within a second he was lying flat on the wall next to Jed. Another pause. Jed glanced again at the lights. Nothing. He looked down. The inner courtyard was just a dusty concrete surface, with truck marks smeared across it. On one side, he could see a single-storey admin block that looked like it was put together in a hurry. On the other side, he could see the plant. It consisted of a tangled mess of tubes and wires. At its centre, there was a metal ovoid, like a giant egg, with a series of pipes running into it, and with two chimneys stretching fifty feet into the air. Some white gas was escaping from one of them. From his time as an engineer, Jed could guess that it was some kind of experimental chemical or nuclear facility. But what they were cooking up in there it was impossible to say.

That's why we have to get inside. This might be the actual evidence of WMD everyone had been talking about for the past few months.

'Over there,' whispered Jed, pointing to a hut next to the main metal gates that led into the compound.

Steve's eyes flashed towards it. The hut had been placed right next to the metal gates. From the back you could see a man's foot quite clearly sticking out. The night guard.

Jed pointed to his own chest. He didn't need to say anything. Steve could understand what he was saying perfectly well. *I'll take the bugger.*

Jed looked down. It was eight feet to the ground. He rolled his body into position, then gripped on to the side of the wall with his fingertips. Carefully he lowered his body down so that he was hanging flat next to the inside of the wall. He paused, checking that he couldn't hear any movement, then let go.

Impact. He landed on the ground, letting his knees buckle as he did so, to absorb the force of the landing, and to minimise the noise. He glanced back up at Steve, and gave him the thumbs up. He could see Steve unstrapping his AK-47 and putting the gun into position. If anything went wrong, he would be ready to lay down some covering fire.

Jed glanced ahead. It was forty yards across open courtyard to the hut. He looked behind him to the admin block. There was just a chance they could get inside without being detected. No, he told himself. Better to finish the guards off one by one.

From inside his jacket, he took out an eight-inch steel-plated hunting knife. He'd practised running in the MOPP back in Hereford, and he knew that although it weighed him down, once you got used to it, you could still move at a fair clip. The ground was covered within a few seconds, but it was impossible to run without creating any noise, and as he moved across the open concrete, he could see the feet sticking out from the hut whip away. He kept moving, his legs pounding against the concrete. As he approached the hut, he could see the soldier start to move. Jed threw himself up against its wooden back. He waited, holding his breath, not making a sound. Then footsteps. One, two, then three. He could see the side of the man. With one sudden movement, he lunged forwards, grabbing the guy by the neck with his left hand. His right hand jerked up, then slashed into the side of the man's throat. The muscle was tough, resisting the cold steel of the blade for a second. Then it slid neatly into the windpipe, like a gear slotting into place. Jed twisted it around, severing the muscle and cutting off the supply of oxygen to the heart. He could feel blood foaming up from the man's mouth, dribbling down on to his arm. The guard was starting to jerk. He was kicking out with his legs, trying desperately to get some traction on his assailant. He was strong enough, thought Jed, but badly trained: he had no idea what muscles would still be working as his neck was being sliced to pieces. It was like pulling a fish out of the water. *He could thrash around, but he didn't know how to save himself.*

One cut, then another. The knife was as sharp and deadly as a surgeon's scalpel and was taking its prey apart just as effectively. The breath was dying on the man's lips. Jed took out the knife, and let him fall helplessly to the ground. Within seconds, the rest of the life had drained out of him. Jed looked down into the face of the corpse. He couldn't have been more than twenty-one or twenty-two, with shallow brown eyes and spots on his skin. His uniform fitted him poorly, and the safety catch hadn't been released from his gun. He had the surprised, hurt expression familiar to a solider who has seen men fall on the battlefield. Those eyes will be staring back at me for the rest of my life, Jed thought bitterly.

He ran back to the wall. Until the alarm was raised, they had a fair amount of time: once it was, they would have no more than a few minutes to complete the job. Steve had lowered himself to the ground. Jed gave him the thumbs up, and together the two men ran towards the admin block. They were keeping a close eye on the two watchtowers, but so far as Jed could tell, although the lights were on, nobody was watching. He knelt down in front of the door. The mission was to get inside and get as much evidence as possible of what was happening.

Jed took out his pistol, holding his finger on the trigger ready to fire. At his side, Steve was stabbing at the door with his knife. He'd been trained to break locks, but there was no time for anything fancy now. He was just cutting it away with the blade. Within seconds his work was done. The wood had loosened, and two hard heaves from his shoulders finished the job. The door was open, and they went inside.

Dim light was coming from some of the rooms, but the corridor was dark. Jed could see there were turnings to both the left and the right. His AK-47 was stretched out in front of him, and he had unclipped a stun grenade from his pack. If he saw anyone, he wasn't planning to hesitate.

He paused, waiting to see if there was anyone coming. Breaking the door had made more than enough noise to alert a guard. Nothing. The corridor was completely silent. 'Which way?' hissed Steve.

'Let's start left,' said Jed.

He walked along the corridor. The first office had just a series of white boards with some equations written on them. Jed glanced at them, but they didn't mean much. He was an engineer, not a physicist. He took out a digital camera, flashing a dozen snaps in quick succession. Maybe they'll mean something to the boffins back at the Firm, he thought. They sure as hell mean nothing to me.

By the time he'd finished, Steve had already checked the next room. There were just some files arranged over a desk, all of them written in Arabic. Steve had taken a series of pictures. Jed strode through the corridor, opening another office door. A desk, a computer and a couple of chairs. He looked at the board. Nothing. We're finding sod all, he thought. One of us has already died, and we've nothing to show for the mission.

'Next corridor,' hissed Steve as Jed stepped out of the office.

He followed him down the length of the corridor that snaked along the side of the building. Through the doors, Jed could see an array of scientific equipment. A couple of neon strips ran down the centre of the room, casting a pale light across the workbenches. There were some computers, some stools, but it was mostly measuring equipment: microscopes and sensors, used to detect subatomic particles. First, Jed approached one of the computers, and slotted a flash memory key into its USB port – the Firm had kitted them out with these sticks that could instantly download and store all the information on the hard disk of a computer. Next, he took out his camera, taking another series of pictures. The camera was designed to take snaps in poor light, but the flash was still popping every time he hit the shutter. Like sending out a bloody beacon, he thought to himself. *We might as well be waving flags around saying come and get us.*

Jed paused, stuffing the camera into his pocket and sniffing the air. A slight smell of dried apples was mixed with the singed metal and rubber of the scientific equipment. A perfume, maybe. Light Blue by Dolce & Gabbana. The same perfume that Sarah always wore.

'Where next?' said Steve.

'The plant,' said Jed. 'We need some close-up pictures of that.'

Jed moved swiftly. Sweat was already pouring off him. The MOPP suit turned into a furnace when you ran, and because it didn't let any air through, your skin couldn't breathe. He could feel the liquid running down his neck and along his back. 'Cover me,' he hissed to Steve.

Steve knelt down, next to the admin block, his AK-47 held out in front of him. Jed started to run across the courtyard towards the spherical chemical plant, rubber soles kicking up dust. He looked anxiously at the watchtowers. Nothing. He checked his watch. Ten past three. They'd been in this place for ten minutes already, and so far their luck had held. But it couldn't last much longer.

It was twenty yards across to the plant. Grabbing the digital camera from his pocket, he fired off another series of snaps. The camera had been fitted with a high-density memory card, enabling it to take twelve-million-pixel snaps, and store up to five hundred of them. After taking a dozen, Jed started to crawl around the base of the plant, taking more pictures as he did so. He could feel the heat radiating out of the orb at its centre, pulsing waves of hot air that seemed to be vibrating out of the thing as if it had a heart of its own. Christ, I hope it's not nuclear, thought Jed. Radiation sickness meant a slow, lingering death that could take a decade or more. *Better to get shot here than to go through that.*

At the back of the plant there was a hatch. It was made of galvanised steel, with some rubber sheeting placed across it. Jed took some more pictures. Next to the hatch, there were two thick water pipes. Jed got in as close as he could to get detailed images on to the camera. They had to find out exactly what this piece of kit was making and how. Steve was still kneeling on the ground, his AK-47 straight out in front of him. A noise. Jed was convinced he could hear something. Inside the pipes, there was a rush of water, and the machinery inside the plant growled and groaned. But this sounded like footsteps. And a cough.

Jed stopped. A rattle of gunfire was breaking out over the courtyard.

'Run, Jed, run,' he could hear Steve shouting. 'Run like fuck.'

He looked round. Steve was holding out his gun, firing in rapid bursts towards the main entrance to the compound.

Jed took the pistol strapped across his belt, slamming it into his fists. He unclamped its safety catch. He could see the burning red of tracer fire bursting out of Steve's gun. He was firing into the darkness, but his position was horribly exposed: he had nothing he could hide behind. Jed's head swivelled round, trying to get a lock on where the fire was coming from. Jed glanced towards the watchtower closest to the entrance. He could see a guy up there, turning the light towards where Steve was. Jed pointed the pistol straight ahead of him, letting off a burst of fire. The man screamed as the bullets tore through him, then fell to the ground. One down, thought Jed. Make that two, counting the guy next to the gate. *But how many of the buggers are there?*

More fire was starting up. Jed was hiding next to the back of the plant, taking shelter, but he could hear the bullets pinging off its metal skin like raindrops hitting a tin roof. He could feel the blood rushing to his head, as the adrenalin of the fight took hold of him. 'You there?' shouted Steve, across the courtyard.

There was no point in worrying about chemicals now. They were about to die anyway. The air rushed into his lungs, hot and humid: he could taste the gunpowder and oil in it, and it made his stomach wrench. 'Here,' shouted Jed.

'Get towards the back wall, I'll cover you,' shouted Steve.

Jed glanced around the side of the plant. He could see that Steve had run away from the entrance to the admin block, and was crouching close to the entrance to the plant. There were two dead bodies at his side. One man was up in the watchtower, and at least a dozen more were firing from the broken windows of the admin block. But with enough fire laid down to keep their attacks at bay, there was just a chance Jed could get across the courtyard, and on to the wall where Matt would be waiting for them. 'What about you?' shouted Jed.

'I'll be OK, man. Now just fucking run. I can't hold these fuckers much longer.'

Bugger it, Jed thought. I can't leave Steve there. We've already lost one man on this bloody mission. *We're not going to lose another.*

He took out a grenade, pulled the pin and started running. With one swift movement, he lobbed the grenade towards the admin block. It crashed against the side of the building, exploding in a haze of smoke. The rate of firing increased, but it was wild and inaccurate. The enclosed courtyard was starting to fill up with smoke and bullets, a nasty fog of death. Jed tore into the darkness, steering himself towards Steve by memory. 'Here, man, here,' he was shouting, his voice ragged, his lungs filling up with the smoke from the grenades. 'We're clearing out together.'

He grabbed hold of Steve's arm, the two of them starting to run together. It was forty yards back to the wall where they had come over. Matt had thrown down a rope and an AK-47, and was lying flat on the top of the wall, his own AK-47 pivoted towards the admin block, laying down rapid bursts of fire. The rate of fire was increasing. Jed pulled the pin on another stun grenade, tossing it towards the admin building and waiting to hear the sound of the explosion before running on.

Steve stumbled, and a low scream started to rise up from his lips. 'Move. Fuck it, move,' shouted Jed. He dragged at his arm, but could feel the weight of the man pulling him back. Bullets were smashing into the ground all around him, kicking up dust and blowing tiny chunks of brittle concrete up into the air. The MOPP suit was filling up with sweat and dirt, making Jed's whole body feel as if it was being licked by flames. He tugged hard. Then he turned round. Steve's foot was dragging behind him, his face twisted with pain. Jed could see the fear and despair that was starting to take a grip on the man. 'It's my foot,' said Steve. 'The bullet's gone into my fucking foot.'

'You'll be all right,' shouted Jed. 'Just hold on to my arm.'

He started to drag him. Steve was trying to bury the pain as the wounded foot scraped through the dust. Jed looked forward. Another twenty yards to the wall. He could see the rope, twisting down, and he could see Matt laying down fire towards the admin block. One scream, then another. The Iraqis were taking a beating, but they weren't about to give up. They knew they had the edge, in numbers. *With enough time, they can just outgun us.*

Another bullet ricocheted off the wall, then slammed itself into Steve's chest. The Kevlar underneath his T-shirt deflected the tiny lump of metal, but the blow still struck him like a hammer. He stumbled and fell, crashing to the ground. The smoke from the grenades was filling the courtyard with ugly, thick plumes of dust, and they were still ten yards from the wall. Matt was laying down some fire in the direction of the admin block, but the

Iraqis weren't taking any punishment. They couldn't see well enough to aim, but that wasn't stopping them firing aimlessly into the courtyard. This is a slaughterhouse, Jed thought grimly. *And I'm in the middle of it.*

Another bullet smashed into Steve's thigh. The wound was a bad one, and blood was starting to gush from it. Steve rolled over, his fist clenched together in agony. 'Just bugger off,' he muttered. 'I'm done for. Just leave me.'

Jed knelt down. He could hear the bullets stinging the ground all around him. The noise was battering his ears, and the smoke and debris of shattered concrete was filling his lungs. He gripped Steve's leg, and started trying to push his hand down on to the bleeding wound to staunch the blood loss. 'Grab it, you fucker,' he shouted down into Steve's face.

'I'm not going to bloody make it,' said Steve. 'And if you don't run now, neither are you.'

Jed was suddenly reminded of what Nick had told him. He wished he'd fought the Iraqis and helped his mate. It might mean death. *But it was better than being taken alive.*

'Just keep bloody quiet,' he snapped. 'You're losing enough strength as it is.'

Jed grabbed Steve around the chest, and with one heave lifted the man clean off the ground. He grunted, then hoisted him up over his shoulder. Steve was a heavy man, weighing in at almost two hundred pounds, and his kit made the load even heavier. Ignore it, Jed told himself. Ten yards. That's all.

He staggered forward. One step, then another. Blood was flowing freely from the wound, mixing with the sweat and dirt that had already filled Jed's suit, creating a pungent, sticky, crimson mess.

A bullet. It hit Jed hard in the chest, just below the heart. The impact was like a crane smashing into your side. He could feel the square lump of steel thump him, and pain started to ripple out into every muscle. The Kevlar deflected the path, and within an instant Jed knew that it had saved him. But the bullet had unsteadied his balance. He was wobbling, finding it hard to keep a grip on the ground. He staggered one more step, then another, fighting his way though the fog and noise. Another bullet had ripped into Steve's side, lodging itself in the man's stomach. The blood was falling from two wounds now, emptying itself out of his body like the liquid from a broken bottle. He had lost consciousness. And within a few seconds, Jed realised, probably his life as well.

He staggered forwards, pushing himself to cover the last few yards. His breath was ragged, and his heart thumping in his chest. He'd seen combat before, but he'd had the right kit then, and enough force. This was something different. This was a beating. *And the way it looked right now, they were all going to die.*

'Blow the fuckers up,' Jed screamed at Matt.

He put Steve down, relieved to get the weight from his shoulders. It only took one look into his eyes to see that he was dead: the glazy, watery, despairing look of the corpse had already taken hold of him. The rope was dangling against the wall. Jed gripped hold of it. One bullet smashed into the wall, then another. Bits of concrete were chewed out of its surface, spitting up into the air. The fog from the grenades was starting to clear, and the Iraqi fire was becoming more accurate. In a few seconds, they'd be able to see him clearly. *Then I'll be dead for sure.*

'Get Steve,' said Matt.

'He's bloody dead,' snapped Jed.

'Bring him up,' yelled Matt.

'I told you, he's bloody dead,' shouted Jed. 'Now blow the fuckers.'

Matt's eyes furrowed together. A look of blind fury contorted his face, twisting his mouth and cheeks into an ugly grimace. He took a series of grenades from his belt, and started tossing them into the centre of the compound. He could hear a series of screams as the explosions took down three, maybe four of the Iraqi soldiers. Great clouds of smoke and dust were billowing out of the courtyard as the grenades detonated, each explosion amplifying the last one.

Jed grabbed hold of the rope, hauling himself up the wall. He could see Matt turning his fire towards the door of the admin block, laying it into the area around the door, to keep the Iraqis pinned back. There were cries of pain and shock as men's bodies were caught up in the explosion, then more cries and barked commands as they tried to make sense of the situation.

Havoc and destruction, thought Jed, as he cowered from the rising blast. *What this Regiment has always done best.*

Matt looked at him, his eyes blazing with fury. 'You fucking killed him, you tosser,' he shouted. 'That's two of us you've done for now.'

'Don't be bloody stupid,' snapped Jed. 'It's a sodding slaughterhouse down there.'

Down by the admin block, Jed could see that two of the Iraqis had caught fire, their bodies burning on the edge of the courtyard. The sickening smell of singed flesh was filling the air, mixing with the burning wood and plasterboard. One soldier had run forward to try and put out the flames licking across his mate, but Matt had already turned his pistol on him, spraying him with a sprinkling of bullets that ripped through his chest and lungs. The guy fell to the ground. Jed could see flames racing across the courtyard spitting upwards into the night sky. Whatever the hell it was they were making in there, thought Jed, it was certainly flammable.

He rolled off the wall, hitting the ground with a thump, then tore off his MOPP suit. 'Move, you fucker,' he shouted up at Matt.

He looked around. The street leading away from the plant was already starting to fill with people. Some were leaning out of windows, trying to see what was happening. A few – the smarter ones, thought Jed – were evacuating the area. They were running out of their houses, some of them getting into their cars. He could already hear the wails of police and army sirens, but they were some way off. A mile maybe. Enough, he decided. In the crowd, we can still escape.

'I said, bloody move,' he shouted at Matt again.

Behind him, he could hear the first muffled sounds of an explosion. 'Let's go,' said Matt, landing with a thump at his side.

Jed had cast aside his MOPP suit, and stuffed it in his kitbag. Sprinting away, the two men plunged into the crowd. People were thronging on to the street now, many of them still in their nightclothes. A smell of fear was filling the streets, and the noise of men and women shouting was deafening. Flames were still rising up from the plant, as fire started by the grenades started to spread, along with an odour of tar and burnt paint.

'Just lose ourselves, but keep tight to me,' hissed Jed.

He could feel a mass of panic-filled people all around him. One guy was elbowing him, trying to make some space for his family. A woman was wailing, looking around desperately for one of her kids. Jed fingered the digital camera in his pocket. Two good men have died already for these pictures, he thought bitterly. *For what?*

FIFTEEN

The pub smelt of cold lager and lukewarm chips. A typical student hang-out, thought Nick, as he sat himself down at the bar. Scruffy, cheap, and not too bothered about how drunk you got.

'Diet Coke,' he told the barman.

I'll save the drinking for later. For when I really need it.

He looked around the main room. A group of young guys had sat themselves down at one table, starting an animated debate about last night's football. Nick checked his watch. It was just after six. Lana had said Sam Beston always came into the Three Crowns around that time for a beer. About six foot, she'd said, with lanky brown hair, and usually wearing baggy jeans and a sweatshirt, often with his iPod plugged into his ears. Useful, thought Nick. Most of the guys in here look just like that.

She'd given him a mobile number, but he hadn't wanted to ring it. After his confrontation with Wilmington, he'd been more certain than ever that whatever had happened to Sarah, it had something to do with her work in the Cambridge labs. If I get in touch with the kid, then he might disappear as well.

Who's to say they're not listening to his mobile calls, the same way they followed me and tapped my phone?

Whoever the hell *they* are.

Two guys were standing next to the bar, both ordering pints of bitter. Both tall, both with brown hair, but one of them was wearing jeans, the other chinos. Nick looked across. 'I'm looking for a guy called Sam Beston,' he said.

The taller of the two students glanced at him. There wasn't even a trace of suspicion in his eyes, Nick noted. 'That's me,' he replied.

'I need to speak to you.'

Beston paused for a moment. Nick was suddenly aware of how young he looked. His skin was fresh and unlined, and his eyes clear. Same as Sarah, he thought to himself in a flash. She's too young to be out there by herself. She needs looking after.

'I'm Sarah's dad,' he continued.

'Nick?'

He nodded. 'She's mentioned me, then.'

Beston took a step closer. His friend nodded to them both, then walked away to join another group of young guys who had just walked into the pub. Whatever was happening here, it wasn't any of his business. 'What's happened?'

Nick looked at the barman, then back at Beston. 'What makes you think something's happened to her?'

Beston shrugged. 'She hasn't been into the lab for a couple of weeks,' he replied. 'That's not like her.'

Nick nodded. Most of his life he'd worked on instinct,

and had learnt to trust it over the years. His instincts told him that Beston was young and naive and probably telling the truth. As Lana said, he probably had a bit of a crush on Sarah, but he wasn't her type: she liked the action man, butch hero, just like Jed, rather than the slightly dweeby type like the boy standing next to him. None of that mattered. He cared about Sarah, and he could trust him. *More than I can trust anyone else she works with in that lab, anyway.*

'I'm trying to find her,' said Nick.

'Shit,' said Beston. Suddenly he looked worried. 'I mean, I thought she was at home or something. I did text her last week, though, and didn't hear back from her. That was pretty weird. Sarah always texts you straight back.'

The words tumbled out of him, as if a tap had just been turned on. Nerves, thought Nick. They make some people talk too much. 'I need to find out what she was working on in the lab,' said Nick.

Beston took a gulp on his beer. 'You really think something's happened to her, don't you? Christ, it couldn't be anything to do with her work, could it?'

'I'm just trying to find out, that's all,' Nick said. 'I need to know everything she was up to in the last few weeks. It doesn't matter how small or insignificant it is. I just need to build up a picture of what she was doing.'

Beston laughed, but the sound was hollow and dry. 'Just working,' he said. 'Working really hard.'

'On what?'

'Do you know much about the labs?'

202

Nick shook his head. 'I spent most of my life in the army. I'm not a scientist.'

'We all work pretty much by ourselves,' said Beston. 'Most of us are doing our doctorates, a few have junior lectureships. The professors and the more senior fellows all have their own areas of interest. So it's not like we're all working together in a team or anything. Still, most of us have some idea of what the others are working on. We talk about things we've wrestled with, swap ideas around, share different skills. It's helpful.'

'And Sarah?'

Beston shook his head. 'Not her,' he said. 'Sarah didn't like to discuss her work with anyone. Said it ruined her concentration. She kept it all to herself. The only person she talked to about it was the professor.'

'Wilmington?'

Beston nodded. 'He was always fussing over her. Taking her aside, spending time going through her equations.'

Right, thought Nick. *And the bastard told me he didn't know what she was working on.*

'More than the other students?'

'Much more,' said Beston. 'Some of the guys reckoned he fancied her, but not me.' He paused, looking straight at Nick. 'Sarah's bloody clever, you know. I mean, we're all clever down in the labs. We've all got firsts in physics, and Cambridge isn't exactly a crap university. But Sarah is really the dog's bollocks. Much smarter than the rest of us. That's why the professor's always fussing over her. He knows she's smart. If anyone's going to come up with anything really startling then it's going to be her.'

Nick drained the rest of his Diet Coke and ordered another for himself and a pint for Beston. He was gasping for a drink himself, but knew he couldn't. He had to concentrate. And once he had a drink inside him, he was useless to everyone.

'She must have given you some clues as to what she was working on.'

'Only once.'

Nick pushed the pint across the bar. 'Tell me about it.'

'It's funny, we were in this very pub,' said Beston. 'About a month ago. We were all just standing around at about six in the evening, talking about what was happening at the weekend, that kind of thing. And Sarah was about to get a round in, and everyone was complaining about the cost, and she suddenly said: "I'll buy this pub soon. Then maybe I'll make it a free bar."'

Nick thought for a moment. A month ago. That could have been just before the hundred grand arrived in her account. *She knew it was coming.*

'Go on,' he said softly.

'We all laughed, and one of the guys was ribbing her, but Sarah said: "I'll buy it with the money from my Nobel Prize." And the way she said it, I wasn't sure she was joking.' Beston paused, taking a gulp of his drink. 'Well, we all laughed. Guys in the labs are always saying stuff like that. Nobel this, Nobel that. Most of them don't even know how to change a light bulb. It's just students bragging. But Sarah wasn't like that. She never even talked about her work, let alone bragged about it.'

'You think she meant it?' asked Nick.

'I followed her to the bar, and started helping her get the drinks in. She looked at me with those big eyes of hers, and pushed her hair out of her face, and said. "Unlimited clean energy. That would be worth a prize or two, wouldn't it?"'

Beston put his pint down on the bar. He pulled up a stool that had just come free, and propped himself against it. 'Sarah didn't kid around, not about her science. "Cold fusion," I said to her. "If you think you've cracked that, forget it. It's just a pipe dream." And all she would say was "Wait and see". I asked her to tell me some more, but she just said we had to get the drinks back to the rest of the guys.'

Nick looked at Beston. 'I don't even know what the hell cold fusion is?'

'Only the holy grail of applied nuclear physics,' said Beston. 'It's a nuclear reaction, but one where atoms are fused together rather than split up. So, just as in a conventional nuclear reaction, tremendous quantities of energy are released, but it is completely safe. A single cup of water could be used to power the whole of Britain for a year.'

'Christ,' said Nick.

'Well, it's great in theory,' said Beston. 'But nobody has ever been able to make it work in practice. Every few years someone comes along and says they've cracked it, but it always turns out to be a hoax. The technology is just about impossible to construct. So most people reckon that although the theory is fine, nobody will ever be able to make a reactor that actually works.'

Nick leant forward, propping his elbows up on the bar. A couple of guys were within earshot, but seemed engrossed in their own conversation. 'But if they could, what then?'

'Unlimited clean energy, at virtually no cost,' said Beston. He paused, taking another swig of his beer. 'I don't know where you would start. It would finish off the oil and gas industries for a start. That would wipe out at least a dozen of the world's biggest companies. Most of the countries in the Middle East would be buggered, and so would the Russians. The economics of the Third World would be transformed. I guess most of the existing power structures in the world would be overturned.' He smiled to himself. 'But like I said, it's just a pipe dream. It's not really going to happen.'

The oil industry would be wiped out, thought Nick. He turned the phrase over in his mind, once, then twice. The Lubbock Group – whoever the hell they *really* were – were following Sarah's work. Beston is wrong. It is really happening. And Sarah was on to it.

That's why they wanted her.

'And she didn't tell you anything else?'

Beston shook his head. 'Like I said, she didn't like to talk about her work. She'd only discuss it with Wilmington, and I'm not certain she even told him everything.'

He finished the drink and looked at Nick. 'Do you really think something has happened to her?'

'It's probably nothing, said Nick. 'I'm her dad, so I'm worried about her, that's all.'

He pushed a mobile number across the bar. 'You hear anything, you give me a call, OK?'

Beston nodded. Nick shook his hand, and started to walk away. From the corner of his eye, he could see Beston returning to talk to his pals. He looked nervous. And so you should be, thought Nick. You don't know much, but you know something. *And my gut is telling me that anyone who knows anything at all about what was going on in that lab is in trouble.*

He stepped into the street. The rain had stopped, but the wind had picked up force. He pulled up the collar of his leather jacket to protect himself from the weather. Cold fusion, thought Nick. If it really worked, and if it really had the power to wipe out the oil and gas industries and redraw the political map of the world, then it was just the kind of science that would attract Sarah. And it was just the kind of science that some big and powerful people would do whatever was necessary to stop from ever coming out of the laboratory and into the real world. Fortunes and nations were at stake here.

That was Sarah, thought Nick as he walked round the corner, heading back to the B&B where he was staying for the night. Just like me, she was always fighting for something. And just like me, she ended up paying the price for it.

SIXTEEN

The corpse was starting to rot. Jed glanced nervously up and down the river, checking that no one could see them. It was four in the morning, and although there were some lights shining down on them from the bridge five hundred yards away, he felt certain they couldn't be seen. Rob's corpse was among the rushes where they had left it last night, yet the water had filled his lungs, and his skin was already starting to peel away from his body. A stench of soggy flesh was drifting up from him: if anyone happened to be standing by the riverbank they'd probably find the poor sod just from the smell.

'Is it there?' hissed Matt.

Jed nodded. 'It's here,' he said.

After escaping from the plant, they had moved as quickly as they could through the bodies fleeing the scene. There were people screaming and running, but within minutes the Republican Guard had arrived in force. Jed had seen five trucks pull up, with heavily armed Iraqis pouring out of them. They were beating men and women with their rifle butts to restore order, and Jed saw at least one man get shot in the head for daring to question his orders. He and Matt stayed right in the

208

centre of the crowd. That was always going to be the best place to lose yourself. There were several hundred people thronging the tiny streets: it was easy enough for a man dressed in civilian clothes to vanish into the crowds.

As the streets started to calm down, they headed due north. They blended in well enough with the locals to walk through a crowd, but if either of them was stopped by a soldier, they were done for. The damage to the plant was probably a lot less than the locals reckoned, Jed decided as he glanced back once or twice. The grenades had created a lot of smoke, and some loud bangs, but probably not much real damage. It could be patched up, within a few hours, he thought.

They walked until the crowds started to thin out and the noise to abate. When they found a narrow alley, they ducked down it and tried to check in with the Firm. That's when they realised the satphone was in Steve's kitbag. And now he was dead.

There was another satphone in Rob's kitbag, but that was in the river. There was no choice but to hike back, and hope he and it were still there. The walk took them another forty minutes: fortunately, the streets were empty, and by keeping their ears open for patrols, they managed to stay out of trouble.

Jed took the kitbag out of the water, and looked around for the equipment. The Iridium 9505 satphone, looking something like one of the old-style brick mobiles, weighed just two pounds and fitted neatly into the side of Rob's bag. It connected directly to the

Iridium satellite, and from there it could put you through to any phone in the world. The Firm had fitted it with a scrambler, so even if the Iraqis could intercept the signals, which was unlikely, they wouldn't be able to decipher what was being said. Jed checked his watch. It was six-thirty here in Baghdad. That made it one-thirty back in London. *Might as well wake the buggers up.*

He knelt down in front of the river wall, and switched the machine on. 'Jed Bradley, here,' he said, as soon as the phone was answered. 'Get me Laura Strangar.'

The Firm had kitted out a special hotline for its units operating inside Iraq. How many of them there might be, Jed had no idea. Maybe a dozen. Maybe only us. Either way, they weren't going to risk losing any information because nobody got around to taking the call.

'Jed, you OK?' said Laura.

Jed paused. Her voice sounded as clear and as pure as if she was lying right next to him in bed. He glanced along the river. Rob's corpse was now clearly visible through the rushes, and if they didn't cover him up again, he was going to be easy to spot. 'Steve and Rob are dead,' he said flatly. 'Matt and I are still operational.'

Another pause. He could hear the sharp intake of breath. Like most desk jockeys, Laura was uncertain how to deal with casualties in the field. 'I'm sorry,' she said quickly. 'You got inside the plant?'

'Last night,' said Jed. 'We got the pictures. Then there was a dust-up. We used a few grenades but I'm not sure how much damage we did.'

'We've already had the satellites taking a look,' said

Laura. 'We're analysing those images right now. But we need the snaps you took, and the data you retrieved.'

'Where's our pickup?'

She started to answer, then stopped. Jed could visualise her face. A trace of a smile on her lips. A flick of her hair. A slight furrow of her brow, and a tightening of her lips. 'I'm sorry, Jed, there's no pickup,' she said. 'We need you on the ground.'

'Fuck the ground,' said Jed. 'We need to get out of here.'

'And we need to see those pictures, and then we need to decide on the appropriate response.'

Appropriate response, thought Jed bitterly. Bureaucrat-ese. You could always tell when the Firm was about to screw the men on the ground because they slipped into the language of the committee room. It made it easier to tell the guys at the sharp end they were worth so little their lives could be blown away while the Ruperts sat around deciding what to do next.

'Bugger the appropriate response,' said Jed. 'We've done our job, and two of our mates have died. This craphole is teeming with soldiers, and they're all looking for us. We need to get the hell out of here.'

'Listen, Jed,' said Laura firmly. 'I'm going to give you the name of a contact in Baghdad. He's one of our men. Go to his house – there's a secure Internet connection. You can feed the pictures you took back to London. Once you've done that, then we'll arrange for you to be picked up. OK?' She paused, then added: 'And keep this one alive, please. These guys are expensive.'

211

Jed stifled his anger. He could feel his heart thumping inside his chest. Somewhere in the distance, he could hear the sound of shouting, then of a gun being fired. Sitting around in their cosy offices, they had no idea how dangerous it was out here on the ground.

'Jed . . .' she repeated.

'I'm here.'

'I know you're in danger, but don't worry, we're looking after you,' Laura said slowly.

'Spare me the bloody pep talk,' Jed spat. 'Is it an order or not?'

A silence. He could hear a sharp intake of breath. 'It's an order, Jed.'

'And a fucking stupid one. You told us we were going to be lifted out of here after we got the pictures.'

'This is a war,' she said coldly. 'The plans change all the time. Get used to it.'

He grabbed a pen, and wrote down a name and an address: Abbas Mansour. He had a house in the al-Thawra district of the city. Jed folded the phone back into his kitbag, then looked up at Matt. 'There's no pickup,' he said.

'What the fuck do you mean?' snarled Matt.

His eyes were filled with fury, and there was sweat starting to glisten on his face. Jed could hear more shouting in a nearby street, and the sound of sirens. 'We've got to upload these snaps, then await orders,' he said. 'We're meant to be picked up after they've analysed the data. But I'm not sure I believe them. Not any more.'

Jed stared back at the river. Rob's corpse was looking

up at him, but one eye had already come out of its socket, and sunk to the bottom of the Tigris. Suddenly Matt was tugging at his arm. 'You knew all along,' he said.

Jed turned to face him. 'What the hell do you mean?'

'You knew.'

'What the hell did I know?'

'You knew we weren't going to be picked up,' said Matt. 'You're a bloody Rupert, Jed. I can smell the buggers and you're one of them.'

Jed glanced nervously up towards the bridge with the lights on it. They shouldn't be making any noise, it was too dangerous. 'I didn't know any more than the rest of you,' he said, struggling to keep his anger under control.

'The fuck you didn't,' said Matt. 'Look at me straight, Jed. Two of us are already dead, and I reckon the casualty list is going to get longer before this job is finished. Tell me what this bloody mission is all about.'

I don't know any more than he does, Jed thought bitterly. *Whatever shit they were being dropped into, they were all being thrown into it together.*

'I don't know any more than you do,' he repeated.

'You're lying.'

The blow hit Jed hard on the side of the face. It smashed into the side of his jaw like a hammer. Jed had seen it coming, and had rolled with the punch, deflecting some of the force of the blow, but he could still feel the bone numbing beneath his skin. He controlled his anger, telling himself not to return the punch. *We're in enough trouble already without fighting among ourselves.*

'Cool it, you fucking madman,' said Jed.

'There's going to a reckoning soon, Jed,' said Matt. 'Two good men are dead, and it's your fault.'

'You want to go your own way?' said Jed. 'I'll just tell them we got lost.'

'And have me tried for desertion?' said Matt. 'No bloody way.'

Jed started walking. Matt was cracking under the strain of combat. It might be better to turn him loose, and try to finish the job by himself, but right now that wasn't an option. A fight on the streets would bring the soldiers down on them in a minute. He climbed back on to the street, checked the direction, then turned left. From the map in his kitbag, it was about a two-mile walk due north to the al-Thawra district, where they would meet their contact, and the only way to get there was on foot. He didn't want to risk the buses, and anyway, he didn't have a clue where any of them went: despite the millions spent by the Firm on gathering intelligence in Iraq in the last few years, they still didn't have a public transport map. Taxis were too dangerous: the drivers were all vetted by the Fedayeen, and would inform the police of anyone suspicious in their cars.

After finding a side alley, they grabbed three hours' rest, then resumed the journey at ten. It was hitting mid-morning, and the streets were thick with people once again. They walked along the side streets, making sure they weren't being followed. Matt was walking at his side, brooding and silent. Another day, thought Jed. Then we can get the hell out of here.

★   ★   ★

From the looks of his house Abbas Mansour was a wealthy man. It was a detached villa, two storeys high, built around an inner courtyard, with a row of palm trees along its front. Baghdad had plenty of traders and middlemen who had made some money despite the sanctions: Iraq was still permitted to trade oil, and wherever there was an oil industry, Jed thought, there was always a few guys living well. Most of them seemed to be in this street. It was full of posh-looking houses, with air-conditioned cars parked outside them.

Jed pressed the intercom. There was no reply, but that didn't trouble him. Laura had told him just to press the button and wait. He checked his watch. Eleven thirty-five, local time. A minute ticked by, then another one. Jed looked anxiously up and down the street. About six blocks away he could see a green jeep cruising down the street: a teenage boy in a black uniform was hanging out of the back of it, an AK-47 clutched to his hand. Matt was looking edgy at his side, shifting uncomfortably from foot to foot. 'Where's the fucker got to?' he hissed.

'Buggered if I know,' said Jed.

'There's soldiers everywhere.'

'Five minutes,' said Jed. 'Then we get the hell out of here, and head down to the coast. Fight our way back into Kuwait if we have to, and sod what the Firm wants.'

The jeep disappeared from view, and Jed breathed a sigh of relief. A truck made its way down the street, but didn't even slow down. On the other side of the road, Jed could see a woman and her baby coming out of one of the houses, then opening her car door. She glanced nervously at the two rough-looking characters, then slammed the door and locked it. Don't bother, thought Jed. *It's us that's afraid of you.*

A black Honda CR-V pulled up on the street. The door slid open. 'Get in,' the driver hissed. Jed glanced at him. About forty, with a lean, angular face, a scar on his left cheek, and the thick, black moustache that seemed to be mandatory for Iraqi men; his hands were hovering on the wheel. Alone, Jed noted. With no sign of a gun. 'Get in,' he hissed again. 'We haven't much time.'

They climbed into the back of the four-wheel drive and the car pulled away from the kerb, gradually cruising at a steady thirty miles an hour down the street. Some Arabic music was playing on the radio. The driver looked at them in his rear-view mirror. 'You Mansour?' said Jed.

The air conditioning was on, and the car was heavily scented with air-freshener. The smell hit Jed straight in the chest, and made him nauseous: it was more than twenty-four hours since he'd had anything proper to eat, and his stomach was churning. Mansour nodded. 'I'm taking a big risk.'

'So are we,' snapped Matt.

Mansour nodded again, but remained silent. Jed could smell the cheap aftershave burning off the man's skin. 'Where are we going?' he said.

'My house is being watched, so we can't go there,' said Mansour. 'I'll take you to a workshop. You'll be OK.'

Matt looked at Jed, and although he remained silent,

the question was evident in his eyes. How can we trust this man? Jed just shrugged, but at the same time fingered the knife tucked into the inside of his jacket. For a moment, he wondered if they should just turf the guy out here. The CR-V looked in good nick: it could get them down to the border in a day. No, he told himself. Get the job done. Then get home.

He glanced out of the window. There was an army truck up ahead, but no roadblocks. A police car was spinning in the opposite direction, its siren blaring. Jed tucked his head down. The city was on high alert. You could smell the fear and tension in the air, and see it in the faces of the people as they walked by.

Mansour turned the Honda into a whitewashed courtyard. They were surrounded on all sides by walls, with only one gate looking out on to the street. Killing the engine, he turned round. 'You'll be safe here,' he said.

Jed climbed from the car. Ten yards ahead of him, Mansour was opening the padlock on a door that led into a small workshop. There was a bench in one corner, with a set of lathes. Next to that, there was a desk with an old-looking Hewlett-Packard computer and a single wooden chair. The room was dark, illuminated by a single forty-watt bulb, and it smelt of metal and grease. 'We used to make machine tools in here for the local factories,' said Mansour. 'Since the sanctions started to bite, half the factories in Baghdad have closed down.' He shrugged. 'It doesn't matter. Things will be better once the Americans get here.'

'You're betraying your country,' said Matt, looking at Mansour.

The man laughed, his moustache wrinkling up on his face as he did so. 'The regime is changing,' he said. 'Everyone in Baghdad knows that. It is just a question of getting on the right side.'

'You're helping foreigners,' persisted Matt.

'Helping foreigners?' Mansour laughed again. 'I don't think President Bush, or your Tony Blair, know very much history. People have been invading Iraq for centuries, but the same people always end up in charge of the place. And I'm planning to be one of them, that's all.'

'It's not a bloody debating society,' interrupted Jed. 'We've got work to do.' He pointed at the computer. 'That piece of kit work?'

Mansour leant over the machine, powering it up. Behind them, Matt had already shut the steel doors on the workshop, and the room was absolutely quiet. Jed could hear the whirring of the computer's fan as it booted itself into life. 'We need an Internet connection,' he said.

'This connects through an ISP in Jordan, and the traffic gets routed straight through to London.'

'Is it secure?'

Mansour smiled. 'On the Internet, nothing is secure. But the chances of the Fedayeen intercepting the message are slight, and even if they do, they'll have no way of knowing where it has come from.'

Jed sat down at the desk. He had no idea what kind

of deal the Firm had cut with Mansour. At a guess, a couple of oil wells down near Basra already had his name on them for after the invasion: he didn't look like the kind of man who'd sell his life cheaply. 'Is this place safe for a few hours?' he asked.

Mansour nodded. 'It belongs to one of my companies,' he replied. 'It's been shut for six months, so there's no reason for anyone to come here. For one day, you should be OK. Any more than that is risky. Any of the neighbours could report that this building is back in use, and the secret police will come around to investigate.'

Jed took the digital camera from his kitbag, hooked out its wire and plugged it into the USB port on the computer. It took a moment for the machine to find the right software, then a few more minutes for the pictures to download. As soon as they were loaded, he fired up the Internet connection, and started putting the pictures on to an email to send to Laura. Next he plugged the memory stick into the computer to upload the data they had taken from the computers at the plant. The connection was slow – no chance of broadband out here, he thought – and it looked set to take at least an hour to complete the task. 'Any chance of something to eat?' he said, looking up at Mansour.

'I've got a few dates in the car, maybe some bread. I'll get them for you,' said Mansour. 'And there's a microwave out the back if you want coffee.'

'Thanks,' said Jed.

He looked back at the computer. Another batch of

pictures had loaded themselves on to an email and were about to send.

Mansour stood next to Jed, staring at the screen. 'Tell me,' he said softly. 'How soon do you think the invasion will be?'

Jed shrugged. 'Couple more weeks at least,' he said. 'They haven't got all the kit into Kuwait yet.'

Mansour nodded. His right hand was playing with his moustache. 'Will they attack Baghdad first? I have children. Maybe I should move them.'

Jesus, thought Jed to himself. How the hell do I know what the nutters in charge of this war are going to do? 'The plan is to punch our way up from Kuwait,' he said. 'With any luck it will all be over by the time we get to Baghdad.'

Mansour looked at him doubtfully. 'Are you sure?'

'Not really,' said Jed. 'The men on the ground are the last guys who are likely to have any idea what the hell is going on.'

Jed closed his eyes, and tried to sleep. He was stretched out in a corner of the workshop, and the last time he'd checked his watch, it was just after three in the afternoon. Mansour had brought them the dates, some day-old bread and a jar of instant coffee. It wasn't much, but Jed was grateful for anything he could get. It had taken an hour in total to send all the pictures through to Vauxhall, and by the time that was done there was nothing to do except get as much rest as they could while they were waiting for the pictures to be analysed.

With any luck, they'll be fuelling up a Black Hawk down in Kuwait right now, he'd told himself as he lay down, putting his head back on his kitbag. *Ready to lift us out of this hellhole.*

Sleep wouldn't come. He'd closed his eyes a dozen times, and slowed his breath. Usually Jed could kip anywhere: for all the hard-guy image it was, he sometimes thought, the main qualification for surviving in the Regiment. Get your head down, and you'll be OK. Not today, however. The deaths of Rob and Steve were still too fresh in his mind. He could see their faces and hear their voices in the days before they died: they were still there, alive in his mind. Two guys had died on the training courses he'd been on, and he'd had to go and talk to their parents about it afterwards. Sometime in the next few weeks, I'll have to go and talk to Rob and Steve's parents, he thought. Give them some crap about how they were brave men who believed in what they were fighting for. He'd have to talk to Rob's wife Sandra, and tell his four-year-old son Callum why his dad wouldn't be buying him that Nottingham Forest shirt for Christmas after all.

Sod it. *It's hardly surprising I can't sleep . . .*

He glanced towards the computer. A message was flashing on the screen.

Mail.

Jed clambered to his feet. Matt was still sleeping, an occasional snore rolling across from where he'd kipped down. He sat down in front of the computer, hitting the keys and looking closely at the screen. A string of meaningless letters flashed across it. Encrypted, Jed realised. Whatever they're about to tell me, they don't want anyone who might be eavesdropping on this Web connection reading it.

In his kitbag, he'd been given a USB flash key with a set of codes on it: they were one-use encrypts, applicable only to one message, so even if the Iraqis captured him, it wouldn't matter if they found the key. He plugged it into the back of the computer, waiting a moment while the program downloaded itself. Then he opened up the email again. Slowly, the message started to take shape, until the words were crisp and clear on the screen.

'Fuck,' said Jed.

He slammed his fist down hard on the table.

'Bugger, fuck,' he said again.

Like any solider, Matt could wake up at the first hint of danger. He got up from the floor, and moved swiftly across to the desk. 'What is it?' he said.

'Take a look for yourself,' said Jed, standing up and walking away from the desk.

Matt leant over the computer. Jed was watching him as he looked at the screen. The words on the email were already burnt into his mind. He didn't need to see them again. 'The mission has been extended,' it said flatly. 'The plant needs to be completely destroyed. Repeat, completely destroyed. An incoming missile strike is scheduled for 2300 hours tomorrow. Repeat, tomorrow. The missiles will need incoming guidance. Position yourself for missile guidance. Confirm this order received and understood.'

'I thought the invasion wasn't scheduled for at least a couple of weeks,' said Matt looking up. 'Bugger it, man, I though the plan was to punch our way up through Basra, not start with missile strikes on the fucking centre of Baghdad.'

Jed shrugged. He tossed two spoons of instant coffee into a stained, cracked mug, added some water and put it into the microwave. 'I don't know what the hell was in that plant we took pictures of,' he said grimly. 'But whatever the hell it was, they're starting a whole bloody war to destroy it.'

SEVENTEEN

Nick stood outside the house. It was a cold, imposing Victorian villa on Ballington Road in north Cambridge. Many of the other houses in the road had long since been split up into flats. This one was still intact. Worth at least a million, he thought. There was a Mercedes on the driveway, and the marks on the gravel suggested another car as well.

Professor Wilmington might be short on charm and honesty. *But for an academic he clearly wasn't short of money.*

Nick checked his watch. It was just after nine in the evening. He'd walked for two hours after he'd left Beston in the pub. Enough time to straighten out his thoughts. And enough time to decide what to do next.

The lights were on in the hallway, but there was no sign of life in the main room, nor on the first floor. Nick started walking again. He'd take a closer look at the house from the back. The villa was detached, one of several, each one standing in its own neatly manicured plot. He walked a hundred yards, putting a couple of houses between himself and the professor. This one was empty, he thought. The lights were out, and there were no cars in the driveway. He stepped across the gravel, and headed towards the side alley that led into the garden. The door on the alley was locked, and there was some glass across its top, but Nick had equipped himself with some strong gloves, and could scale it easily enough. He dropped down into the garden, walking alongside the fence. It was a dark night, with the moon obscured by clouds, but most of the rain had cleared and he could see well enough. There was a shed, then a wall. Reaching up, he grabbed hold of it and hoisted himself up. With one swift look he checked whether it was empty, then lowered himself into the garden below. Somewhere nearby he could hear a dog barking. Not here, he decided with relief, and he stepped quickly through the garden towards the next wall.

The puzzle had slowly taken shape in his mind. Sarah was working on something to do with cold fusion. She might even have cracked it, though that might not matter. There would be plenty of people interested if she was just getting close. The oil industry for starters. Maybe a government. Maybe some other corporation. *Hell, there was enough at stake for half the world to be looking for my daughter.*

Wilmington was the key. He had been lying to him from the start. To protect what? Or whom? Nick didn't know. *That is why I have to get into his house.*

He dropped down into the back garden of Wilmington's villa. For a moment he just crouched in the flower bed, glancing up at the house. A light was shining from the hallway, casting some flickering shadows out towards the lawn. He'd found the professor's address by calling his mate Bill Horton, and getting him to tap it up from one of his police sources, but he hadn't been able to get a phone number. It was unlisted, and would take several hours to find out. I don't have that kind of time to play with, thought Nick as he started to walk across the lawn. I'll just take my chances that he isn't home tonight. And if he is? Then I'll just beat the information out of him. *There isn't any risk I wouldn't run if it meant helping Sarah.*

Nick had only broken into a house twice before: once when he was fourteen, and some of the lads he ran around with had tried it on for a dare; and once when he was on his counterterrorism course during his early days with the Regiment. That was a quarter of a century ago now. The skills were rusty, but they were still there, and that was what mattered.

The back door led into the utility room. Glancing through, Nick could see a washing machine and freezer. He tried the door but it was locked. Next he tried the window to the utility room. Locked. He edged around the side of the house. A pair of French windows led from the sitting room on to the kitchen. Locked, with a bolt slung across the back. The professor was taking his security seriously. Nick edged towards the kitchen. There was one lamp on, but no one inside. The main window was locked, but next to it was a smaller window, half open, letting out the smells from the kitchen. Carelessness, thought Nick. That's what burglars rely on. He pushed the window down. Just enough space for a man to squeeze through. He levered himself up the side

226

of the wall, gripping on to the brick, and started to push himself through the space. His coat was snagging on its side, but there was enough space. He lowered himself to the floor. Mackerel, he thought, sniffing the air. Bloody smelly fish. That's why they left the window open.

He'd equipped himself with a six-inch stainless-steel kitchen knife, its blade polished and glinting in the pale light coming through from the hallway. He gripped the weapon in his hand as he walked softly through to the hallway. One light was on, but otherwise the house was dark. He listened carefully. No TV, no hi-fi. Just silence. So far as it was possible to tell, there was no one home.

On one side of the hallway there was a large formal sitting room, painted a dark cream with two sofas positioned around a plasma TV screen. Nothing of interest there, Nick figured. Next to that, a dining room. A half-drunk bottle of wine was standing on the table, but apart from that it was clear. Behind the dining room was a study. Nick slipped inside. It was a small room, with a long window looking out on to the garden. There was a desk in one corner, with a computer on it, and the walls were lined with bookshelves. It was dark, and Nick didn't want to switch on the lights. He took a moment to adjust his eyes to the gloom. A set of papers and notebooks were laid out on the desk. The man's personal records, thought Nick. *Maybe that's where I'll find the truth about the professor.*

He took a small torch out of his jacket pocket and leant over the desk, flicking through a black leather desktop diary. Wilmington was a man of routines.

Lectures on Mondays and Thursdays, tutorials on Tuesday afternoons, college appointments on Friday mornings. All ordinary stuff. Only one name stood out. Salek had been to see him five times in the last month. Who the hell was he exactly, Nick wondered. I'd like to know a lot more about that ugly-looking Arab.

Nick checked one of the drawers. They were piled thick with sheets of neatly tabulated paper. Equations littered most of them. They meant nothing to Nick: you had to be a trained physicist to know what any of them might mean. Next to them were some scrawled notes in spidery, pinched handwriting. Nick flicked through them, wondering if it would be safe to take them. Maybe Beston could figure out what they meant, or at least point him in the direction of someone who could. Then he paused. One of the pages was written in a different hand. He recognised it at once. A full, confident handwriting. Sarah's. The page he was holding right now was written in Sarah's hand, and he'd found it in the desk. *The desk of the guy who said he didn't follow her work . . .*

The bastard, thought Nick. Maybe Sarah really had made an important breakthrough, just the way Beston said she had. Maybe the professor was planning on stealing it and passing it off as his own work. He could feel a sudden chill in his heart, as if he had just been plunged into a pool of icy water. *Maybe the bastard murdered her so that he could take her discovery . . .*

Nick could feel his hands shake as he gripped hold of the paper. In the past week he'd grown used to the

228

idea that Sarah had disappeared. It was still possible she'd taken herself into hiding. It was possible she'd been kidnapped. But the idea that she might be dead? That hadn't occurred to him before, not even as a possibility. *And it was, in truth, too awful even to contemplate . . .*

He looked at the words, but they meant nothing to him. A series of symbols, equations and formulas. He glanced around for a photocopier, but couldn't see one. He cursed himself for not having brought a digital camera with him: he could have snapped away at the pages, then got copies made later. He riffled through the rest of the pages, then stopped. A bank statement. He held it between his hands. It was printed on Lloyds TSB paper, for an account in Wilmington's name. He glanced at it quickly. There was a balance of more statements, nearly fifty thousand pounds in the account, but larger sums had been flowing through it in the past few months. There were nearly thirty sheets of paper in total. Nick took two, and folded them into his pocket. The chances were he'd never even notice they were missing.

Glancing at his watch, he could see that it was just after ten. Don't push your luck, he told himself. The professor could be back at any minute. He walked quickly through the kitchen, riffling through the drawers of the dresser. Within seconds, he'd found what he was looking for. Everyone keeps a spare set of back-door keys somewhere around the house, and Wilmington was no exception. Never know when I might want to come back, Nick thought as he slipped the keys into his pocket. *I haven't finished with this bastard yet.*

He opened the back door, locked it behind him and slipped back up to the street. It was empty at this time of the evening. Nick glanced left and right, but could see no sign of the professor. He started walking quickly, heading back towards the centre of Cambridge. He kept on walking until he saw a McDonald's. Stopping inside, he ordered a quarter-pounder meal with a large coffee. As he sat down, he took a bite on the burger, suddenly aware that he hadn't had anything proper to eat for a day at least. His body was weak with hunger, and he paused, stirring some sugar into the coffee, knowing that he needed to compose himself, and get some food into his stomach before he tried to do anything else. Christ, man, he told himself angrily. You're bloody Regiment. *You're supposed to be able to keep fighting for days on a couple of biscuits and a bottle of water.*

The food settled in his stomach, and he could feel the sugar hitting his bloodstream. He looked down at the bank statements. In the course of two weeks in January, slightly over ninety thousand had passed through Wilmington's account. Another forty thousand had been paid out. There were no names next to any of the trans-actions, just a series of numbers from anonymous bank accounts. Nick stared at them for a minute, then fished out the mobile from his pocket. He checked the messages. There weren't any. No missed calls. No texts. Nothing. He took a sip on his coffee, then pressed dial on one of the numbers stored in the phone's memory earlier today.

'You again?' said Bill Horton as he picked up his call.

'I need some help,' said Nick. 'I wanted to see if you could trace some bank account transactions for me.'

'What are you up to, Nick?' said Horton.

'I've told you, it's personal,' said Nick. 'I just need to know who an account belongs to.'

He was well aware that Horton's firm did a lot of work for the big City banks. They all had plenty of high rollers who needed protection sometimes, and they never minded paying big money to keep their key staff safe. That meant Horton had contacts with their security offices, which also meant he could tap into the networks that allowed banks to share information with one another. If anyone could figure out who these transactions were between, and do it fast, then it was Horton.

'Please, mate . . .' said Nick.

In the Regiment, a guy never said please. You didn't say it among ex-Regiment men either. Unless you were really desperate, thought Nick. *Like I am now.*

There was just a moment's hesitation on the line. 'Email me the details,' said Horton. 'I'll get it sorted for you first thing in the morning.'

'I need it now,' pressed Nick.

'Sod it, mate,' said Horton. 'I've got to talk to some bankers, and I'm not calling them now.'

'First thing in the morning,' said Nick.

'Sorted, mate.'

Nick shut the phone, and put the last of the chips in his mouth. He drained the coffee, and stood up. A cold blast of air hit him in the face as he started walking along the street. He tracked a man who appeared to be

231

loitering outside the burger bar, wondering if he was following him. The man glanced up at him, scowled menacingly, then walked on. Just a drunk, Nick decided. He kept on walking. Cambridge was a student city, and he should be able to find an Internet café that was open all night. If he couldn't, he'd just have to make his way down to London. He had to get these bank account details to Horton before morning.

If I can find out where Wilmington's money comes from, maybe I can find out what's happened to Sarah.

EIGHTEEN

Jed looked at Mansour. He was a strong, thick-boned man, with discipline and willpower. You needed to be strong just to survive in Saddam's Iraq. To make the kind of living that Mansour was obviously making took guts and strength and brains. But this afternoon there was fear in his eyes. And rightly so, thought Jed grimly. The battle was about to rage down on the city, and there was no telling what the furnace would consume before it burnt itself out.

'We need to get back to the plant,' said Jed.

Mansour paused. 'That's up to you,' he replied.

'Too right it's up to us,' said Matt. 'Trouble is, it's up to you too. We need some transport, and we need you to help us.'

Mansour tried to smile, but there was no humour in the expression. He had the look of a man who was trying to calculate who he was most afraid of: the men in front of him, or the men who would be dealing with him if he was caught helping a pair of British soldiers. Not a pretty calculation for anyone to make, thought Jed. Still, if he didn't want to play with those odds, then he shouldn't have got into this game in the first place. 'Where do you need to go?' he said nervously.

'Across town,' said Jed. 'We've got the address.'

After getting the order from the Firm, he'd sent a message back to say they'd received it, and it would be executed tomorrow night as instructed. Both he and Matt were pissed off about it. Even though they knew what they were signing up for when they joined the Regiment, and it was too late to start complaining now, it didn't stop either of them being pissed off at the position they were being put in – and the risks they were being asked to run.

Jed had contacted the Firm to get details of RVP for the pickup. They were planning a cruise missile strike on the plant, with fighter bombers in support if necessary. People thought cruises were smart missiles the way they were written up in the press. But actually they were only smart in the way a stag party tumbling out of a lap-dancing club at three in the morning was smart. They didn't know their way home, and neither did a cruise. They were fine for taking out a village, but useless for a precision target. That's why you needed what the army referred to as 'man-in-the-loop' technology. Roughly translated, that meant some poor bugger had to risk his bollocks bringing the big angry bird home. You used a laser-target designator to pinpoint an invisible laser beam straight on to the target, and that guided the bomb straight into its path. The LTD had a range of more than a mile, so you could put a bit of distance between yourself and the big bang, but it was still rough and dangerous work. And the closer you got into the centre of a city, the rougher and more dangerous it became.

The LTD was a small piece of kit, but it needed a tripod to set it up properly. Somebody – and Jed had no idea who – had stashed weapons and materials at different points around Baghdad – as if they'd been planning this war for a while, Jed thought. The Firm had given them the address of the place where they could pick the kit up. All they had to do was get there, then head back to the plant. *And stay alive.*

'I'm not a taxi driver,' said Mansour.

'You are now, mate,' said Matt. 'Nothing wrong with doing a bit of minicabbing on the side. Comes in handy when you need a bit of extra cash.'

He shook his head. 'It's too dangerous.'

'For us as well,' said Matt.

'It's too dangerous,' repeated Mansour, ignoring the remark. 'There are roadblocks all over this city. I get found with you two, I'm a dead man.'

Matt took a menacing step towards him. 'And you're a bloody dead man if you don't.'

A bead of sweat had already started to form on Mansour's forehead. It was hot in the workshop, and Jed could feel the tension crackling between the men. 'Cut my throat if you have to, Englishman,' said Mansour. 'At least it will just be me that dies.'

'I'm bloody tempted,' said Matt, taking another step forward.

'It makes no difference,' said Mansour. 'You have no idea what it's like in this city. If the Fedayeen capture me transporting a couple of British soldiers around Baghdad, they won't just shoot me on the spot. They'll

235

torture me first. They'll round up family. They'll gang-rape my wife and my sister, in front of me, then kill them. They'll torture my children before my own eyes. They'll get my brothers, cousins, their wives, everybody, and shoot them all.' He looked first at Matt, then at Jed, the defiance gleaming in his eyes. 'So just fucking do it if you want to. Getting my throat cut here would be a blessing.'

Matt had already pulled a hunting knife from his pocket. The blade was glistening in the pale light. Jed stepped forward. 'Leave it,' he said. 'The guy's got family. He's done enough for us already.'

'You trying to get us bloody killed again, Jed?' said Matt.

Jed shook his head. 'Just trying to come out of this war without causing any more carnage than necessary.'

He looked at Mansour. 'Give us a car, and a decent map, we'll find our own way.'

'There's no car,' said Mansour.

'Get us one,' snapped Matt.

'I've done enough,' growled Mansour. 'My house is being watched. This is your war, you fight it. I can give you a map, that's all.'

Matt looked as if he was about to punch the man, but Jed moved to block him. There was no point squeezing the guy any more, he thought, we've already got all the juice we're going to get out of that one. 'Try and get your family somewhere safe, mate,' said Jed. 'I reckon this city is going to turn very nasty in the next forty-eight hours.'

With Matt at his side, he walked out of the workshop. It was just after four in the afternoon, and the sun was shining brightly on the city. The road was empty, but up in the distance you could hear the rumbling traffic of central Baghdad. Across the road, they found a blue Toyota Corolla with at least fifteen years on it, they thought. Matt had done training in nicking cars – he'd picked up tips as a kid – and broke into the bonnet to hot-wire the vehicle. Modern cars were hard to break into, because they had so many sophicticated anti-theft devices built into them, but an old wreck like this was easy. They would be able to have it started in a matter of minutes.

Jed slung his kitbag on to the back seat and fired the ignition. The engine spluttered, then roared into life.

Jed steered the car out on to the road. The pickup point was towards the north of the city, in the al-Zawiyah district, composed mostly of the residential streets, some factories and workshops, and an army barracks. Matt had a map out on his lap. 'Keep to the side roads,' he said. 'I reckon that's the best chance of staying out of trouble.'

Jed put the Toyota into third, and picked up speed. They had their AK-47s tucked down beneath their legs, and both of them knew what they had to do if they were stopped. Start shooting, and keep on shooting, until either they'd killed all the guys in front of them, or been killed themselves. There was no point in trying to bluff their way out. They didn't stand a chance. And there was no point in being taken alive. *Better to go down fighting.*

They covered one mile, then another. People were

coming out of the factories and offices, and the kids were all home from school. Some were kicking balls around the street, other were just hanging out, chatting. There weren't any proper shops, just stalls selling fruit and rice, and the occasional piece of meat. Christ, it's a miserable place, thought Jed, as he steered the Toyota through yet another street crowded with apartment blocks and rough-looking cafés. *At least the bombs can't make it much worse.*

'Shit,' he muttered under his breath.

He looked across at Matt, then straight ahead. There was a roadblock about a hundred yards up the street, with at least five soldiers manning it. Fifteen cars were backed up in a line. A couple of guys in front were honking. Jed craned his neck, trying to see what was happening. The car at the front of the queue had been stopped, and two men ordered out of it. Another man was sitting on the back seat. Three soldiers were shouting at the men, their AK-47s pointing straight at them. Suddenly a shot rattled through the crowded street. Instinctively, Jed flinched, then looked back up. The cars had all fallen silent. Up ahead, he could see that one man was slumped over the bonnet of the car, blood seeping from the open wounds on his head. The second man was cowering at his side. Another soldier was pulling the third man from the car.

'Shit,' muttered Matt. 'What the hell do we do now?'

'Hold tight,' said Jed.

'We should run for it,' said Matt. 'While we still have a chance.'

'I said, hold tight,' repeated Jed through gritted teeth.

He stretched his neck to keep an eye on the fight. Another rapid burst of gunfire split through the sky, then another. A silence had overtaken the street. None of the cars were moving. No one was running away. Nobody was saying a word, just sitting quietly, thought Jed grimly. And giving thanks to Allah it was those buggers and not them.

The captain started waving the cars through. Almost reluctantly, they started to move again. Jed's breath was shallow, and a bead of cold sweat was running down the back of his spine. Whatever those boys were doing, it probably wasn't as bad as what we're planning. *If they shot them on the spot, what the hell would they do to us?*

The Toyota drew level with the roadblock. Jed looked straight ahead, keeping his eyes on the bumper of the Renault in front of him. Don't look round, he told himself. Don't let them look into your eyes. The soldier was inspecting one of the corpses on the ground. Another was being lifted up and bundled into the back seat of the car he'd been driving just a few minutes before. They'll probably take him to the river, thought Jed. *Life is cheap in this city.*

They drove straight through. The guards were no longer stopping people. I guess they've had enough trouble for one day. He pressed his foot on the accelerator, putting as much distance as he could between himself and the roadblock. Through the rear-view mirror, he could see a woman running up to the guards, shouting and waving her arms. Already, the soldiers were aiming their AK-47s at her, and their commander was pointing his pistol into the air. Bugger, thought Jed. This city is on a knife edge. *When cruise missiles start crashing into the streets, the whole place is going to implode.*

It was another two miles to the house. The drive was slow and painful, twisting through the early-evening traffic. They saw plenty of soldiers on the streets, but no more roadblocks: most of the troops looked to be digging trenches and putting sandbags around gun emplacements. Street-to-street fighting, that's what they're planning for, thought Jed. It's going to be a hard, nasty slog when our boys start trying to take this place.

The house in al-Zawiyah seemed boarded up when they pulled the Toyota up outside. The whitewash on the walls had long since faded, and a layer of grime had attached itself to the surface. Jed got out of the car, and looked quickly up and down the street. It was a quiet district. There were a couple of restaurants and a shop opposite, but otherwise the street was overlooked mainly by five- or six-storey residential apartment blocks. A few people were drifting home, and it didn't look like they were planning to come out again until morning. They're just hunkering down in their homes, Jed thought. *Waiting for the worst.*

Matt was already pushing the front gate open. It creaked on its hinges, and a coating of dust came away. Jed followed him into the internal courtyard. It was surprisingly quiet and cool inside. He checked his watch. It was just after seven in the evening. Their guns were packed into their kitbags, concealed from view, but Jed knew he could have it ready for action within three seconds. He listened. Silence. He stood perfectly still, his eyes scanning the four walls that surrounded him. One had a doorway that led into the house, another into the garage. There were weeds growing up between the paving stones in the courtyard, and ahead of him there was a broken can once used to collect rainwater coming in from the gutters but now rusting into the wall. It didn't look like anyone lived here any more. And if they did, they were letting the place fall apart.

'British?' said a voice.

The accent was heavy, Arabic, but not like the other voices they'd heard in Baghdad. The man was clearly expecting them. Jed held his right hand ready to whip out his Browning handgun, and he knew where his grenades were. The Firm has sent them to this address, and it was meant to be a safe house, one of a series that had been set up after the first Gulf War to help support the coup that was widely expected to topple Saddam; during the last few months many of them had been reactivated to stash kit for the special forces guys who'd be swarming through the place once the war started. It should still be safe. They'd told him it was. But what the hell did they know? They were all sitting at their desks in Vauxhall, swivelling around in their shiny leather seats, with nothing worse to worry about than how much this year's pay rise might be. The house could have been compromised at any time in the last few weeks. And the Iraqis might well be staking the place out, watching and waiting for someone to turn up to collect the gear. *And then gun them down in cold blood*.

'Who's there?' Jed said warily.

'Show yourself,' growled Matt.

Silence.

It was nearly dark now, and the moon was out, sending a set of shadows flickering across the courtyard. A noise. Jed's eyes darted across the walls, but he couldn't see anything. A door was squeaking. He looked behind him. The gate on to the street was shut. Ahead of him, the door to the house was pushed open. A pale light was shining behind it. Slowly, the figure of a man stepped forward. He was dressed in long black robes, with a belt around the middle. His face was dark, but most of it was obscured by ten inches of scruffy grey beard. Some kind of mullah, thought Jed. *What kind of nutters has the Firm hooked up with in this city?*

'You are the British soldiers?' he said.

Jed nodded.

'Then come inside,' said the man.

He turned round, heading back into the house. Jed exchanged glances with Matt, then both men nodded and started to walk. In his pocket, Jed was gripping on to his knife. He looked harmless enough, but you could never be too careful. They might just be luring them into a trap. He went through the door and looked into the room. The walls were stripped and empty, like the interior of a barn. There was a smell of boiled rice, and some kind of meat stew. Lamb or goat, maybe, thought Jed. Christ, maybe even dog. Who knows? The mullah was leading them towards the back of the room. He had a single gas ring on which the food was slowly cooking, and a crate of bottled water. In the corner there was nothing but a strip of blankets, and some sheets of cardboard that were being used as a pillow.

'We're here to pick up some kit,' said Jed. 'British kit.'

The mullah nodded. 'It's all downstairs,' he said. 'I will show you in a moment.'

He spoke English fluently, but with a fraction of a second delay between each word: the manner of a man who had learnt the language many years ago and had let it grow rusty.

'Show us now,' said Matt.

The mullah glanced at him. 'Of course,' he said. 'Whatever you want.'

'What's your name?' said Jed.

The mullah shook his head. 'It doesn't matter,' he replied. 'We don't need any names here. It's better that way.'

Flicking on a torch, the mullah led the way. A thin beam of light broke through the gloom. Jed followed the mullah down into the cellar, with Matt closely behind. The cellar smelt damp, mixed with spilt fuel oil. 'Here,' said the mullah, shining the torch around.

It took Jed a moment to adjust his eyes. There were six rows of metal shelving, pre-built, and jammed towards the back of the wall. Enough kit to start a small war, thought Jed. Which was probably exactly what the guys who shipped it here were planning. He could see RPGs, machine guns, equipped with what looked like about ten thousand rounds of ammo, regular grenades and stun grenades, sniper rifles, a dozen surface-to-air missiles, and five mortars plus shells. He scanned the shelves more closely. There were six pieces of laser kit, although they would only need one. Jed took it from the shelf. It was a GLTD II, manufactured in America by Northrop Grumann. Painted military olive green, it looked something like a squat film camera, with a rifle butt sticking out of its back. It weighed just twelve pounds, and was powered by a lithium battery fuel cell. It could mark out a target at a range of up to ten kilometres, with a deviation of no more than five centimetres, and was specifically built to bring home Paveway bombs, Hellfire missiles and Copperhead munitions. Jed handed it to Matt. 'I don't know how the hell they got these here,' he said. 'But it's just what we need.'

'Anything else?' said Matt.

Jed looked at the armoury. If it came to a fight, they could use all this and more, but the risk of carrying it across town was too great. You couldn't conceal a surface-to-air missile in the back of a Toyota Corolla. He picked up a box of grenades. 'Just these,' he said. 'If anything goes wrong, we'll have another go at blowing the place ourselves.'

He followed Matt and the mullah as they went back upstairs to the single room. The mullah put the torch down on the floor, and switched it off. There was a copy of the Koran lying on the floor next to him. 'We'll be off,' said Matt.

The mullah raised a hand. 'Don't go out on the streets,' he said. 'You'll be picked up by the army in no time.'

'We've got a car,' said Matt.

The mullah looked at him sharply. 'I'm not here to help the British,' he said. 'I'm just looking after this equipment because I've been paid to. But I can tell you that after eight in the evening Saddam's Fedayeen and the Syrians stop anyone out on the streets. They take them in for torture, or they shoot them on the spot.' He chuckled to himself. 'A lot of the young men get press-ganged into the army, and I don't think you'd enjoy that.'

He nodded towards the floor. 'You can stay here for the night, and have something to eat.'

Jed hesitated, then sat down. The mullah was almost certainly right. It was too dangerous to try and get around Baghdad by night. This was as good a place as any. Matt slumped down against the wall, resting on the side of his kitbag. Glancing at him, Jed suddenly noticed how terrible he looked. His hair was matted thick with sweat and dirt. And there was a layer of grime across his face. his clothes looked shredded and worn, and his eyes were sunk deep into his face, blood-shot and tired.

The mullah handed across a helping of stew mixed with some rice. Using a plastic spoon, Jed dug into it. The smell was sweet, a mixture of raisins, dates and nuts mixed in with stringy bits of meat. Not too bad, he decided as he hungrily wolfed it down. I've had better, but I've also had a lot worse.

He took a gulp from one of the water bottles, then looked up at the mullah. 'Where are you from?' he said.

The mullah smiled up at him, and picked up his copy of the Koran. 'Iran,' he replied softly.

'Then what are you doing here?' said Jed.

The mullah shrugged. He opened the book on his lap, and started to read. '"God does not forbid you from being good to those who have not fought you in religion or driven you from your homes, or from being just towards them. God loves those who are just. God merely forbids you from taking as friends those who have fought you in religion and driven you from your homes and who supported your expulsion. Any who take them as friends are wrongdoers."' The mullah paused. 'That is the word of the Prophet.'

He looked at Jed. 'We have been enemies of Saddam for many more years than you have. We know our way around this country, and if the Americans and the British want to finish the work that we were not able to finish ourselves, then it is not up to us to question the wisdom of Allah.'

'You're a bleeding nutter,' said Matt. 'You'll have the Yanks running this craphole in a few months' time. You won't like that much.'

The mullah scratched his beard. 'Who knows who will be in charge here,' he replied. 'Invaders come and they go, and the Prophet always wins in the end, because he has the force of God on his side.'

'Yeah, well, I'll settle for the force of a cruise missile,

thanks,' said Matt, arranging his kitbag into a rough pillow and putting his head down.

'Who's going to win the war, you reckon?' said Jed.

'God,' the mullah replied. 'God wins all wars.'

'Yours or mine?' said Jed.

'They are the same,' said the mullah. 'Your God in your country, and mine in mine.' He paused. 'Why do you come here to fight? It's a long way from your home.'

'Buggered if any of the boys know,' said Jed. 'We're just following our orders.'

'Then you have your answer,' said the mullah. 'Because men who don't know what they're fighting for or why will always lose in the end.' He looked back down at the Koran. 'Get some sleep. When the war starts, you'll need all the strength you can get.'

Jed lay back, resting his head on his kitbag. The surface of the floor felt rough and uncomfortable, but he was so tired he knew sleep would come soon. He thought about Sarah, and for a moment it struck him that he was unlikely to ever see her again. Both of them had disappeared from the face of the planet. He had no idea where she was, and no way of getting hold of Nick to see if he might have found her. He was tempted to use the satellite phone to call him, but he knew it was too dangerous. Every time it was switched on, there was a risk the army or police would track the signal. His eyes felt heavier. He could already hear Matt snoring: maybe that was why he was a good soldier, despite his hot head, because he could always grab some kip. He was trying to remember the last time he saw Sarah. Two months ago, in Cambridge. A few drinks in the pub, then a pizza, then back to her flat. Nothing special. Just part of the on-off relationship they'd been carrying on for years, both of them too nervous to commit, and too bound up in their own lives to make enough space for the other person.

I should have said something more to her. I should have told her that she was the only person who ever really mattered in my life. I should have told her that I loved her. *Because I might never get the chance now.*

NINETEEN

At lunchtime, a call had come through on his mobile. Nick had already checked out of his B&B, and was eating a sandwich in a café. I've found something about that money, Horton had told him. What, Nick had asked him instantly. Horton had paused before replying. 'I can't tell you on the phone. It's too dangerous. We'll have to meet up tonight.' Then he'd given him the name of the Chelmsford pub and put the phone down.

Too dangerous.

Can't tell you on the phone.

Nick had repeated the phrases to himself a hundred times since then. *What the hell is too dangerous to talk about on the phone?*

Nick took a sip on the Coke he'd orderd, then walked over to a table. It was just after seven on a Tuesday evening, and the Ram's Head was filling up with commuters stopping off for a quick drink on their way home from work. It was tucked into one of the side streets between Chelmsford station and the high street. Local enough to be welcoming, thought Nick, but not so local that a strange face would attract any attention. Maybe that's why Bill chose the place: the guy has been playing the circuit long enough to know when to stay in the shadows, and when to come out of them.

He jostled past a couple of guys trying to get to the bar. WAR JUST DAYS AWAY, blared the headline in the *Evening Standard* that one of them was holding. Next to it there was a picture of some soldiers stationed in Kuwait. OUR BOYS GEAR UP FOR BATTLE, said the subhead running across it. IT AIN'T HALF HOT MUM, said the caption underneath. Spare us the sodding war dance, thought Nick as he turned away. None of the people writing that rubbish have any idea what it's like to actually be there. They don't know the sense of exhilaration and fear that grips the men on the eve of any battle. And they knew nothing of the remorse of the survivors for all the good men who don't come back. If they did, they wouldn't be celebrating the outbreak of any war. *Not a chance.*

Nick held on to his Coke, briefly wishing it was something stronger. For a guy who's trying to stay on the wagon, I'm spending a lot of time in pubs, he thought.

He looked down at his mobile. No messages, no texts, nothing. He was still checking his phone a dozen times a day, but Sarah hadn't been in touch, and he'd stopped calling her. He didn't expect to get a message any more. He knew she hadn't just taken off for a few days. Something had happened to her. That much was certain. The only question was whether he could find her. *Or whether it was too late.*

He looked around the pub again. No sign of Horton.

It was now ten past seven. Late, he said to himself, rolling the word around in his mind. He's Regiment. He's never late. Lateness is beaten out of the men in the first weeks of training.

'Still off the juice, I see.'

Nick looked up. Horton was standing right next to him. Somehow he hadn't seen him come in. Slowing down, he wondered to himself. Horton sat down next to him at the small table. He was wearing black jeans and a blue sweatshirt, with a brown leather jacket over it. He had a whisky and soda with a generous helping of ice. He looked at Nick. 'You sure you're not drinking?'

Nick shook his head.

'You should be.'

Nick leant forward on the table. He could smell the alcohol on Horton's lips. 'What the fuck have you found out?' he muttered.

Horton drained his glass, sinking the whisky in one gulp. He glanced around the pub, scanning the faces of the men lining the bar. 'Let's go outside.'

Nick stood and followed him out of the pub, towards the car park. He could see the strain on Horton's face. His skin was drawn tight, and his eyes were narrowing. He was studying the car park, examining the shadows, checking the thin spaces between the cars. As if he was looking for something. Or somebody.

This is a tough guy, thought Nick grimly. He's been in plenty of fights. He feeds bodies and munitions into half the world's wars. *And something has just made him very frightened.*

251

Horton leant against the bonnet of an Audi A3. He looked at Nick. 'You're mixed up in some heavy shit,' he said.

'Just give it to me straight.'

Horton glanced around the car park. He pulled out a Hamlet miniature cigar from his pocket, torching it from a greasy, oil-fuelled lighter. 'I checked that account number you gave me,' he started. 'We do a bit of work for the banks, and one of the security officers owes me a favour or two. All the banks have informal networks of information, because they all want to stay away from the dodgy customers – or at least the ones who won't pay off their overdraft in time. It took him a couple of hours, but he came back with the info. The money was paid into Wilmington's bank account from a numbered account in the Cayman Islands. That was registered in his own name. The money from that came from an account in Hong Kong. It had been through three separate accounts, but started out in a bank in Switzerland. Basic money-laundering stuff. It might fool the police, and give you some protection, but it doesn't fool the bankers. They know this game, because they invented it.' Horton relit his cigar, drew deeply on it, then blew a puff of smoke into the air. It caught on the chilly breeze, blowing past Nick's face. 'It was linked to a consortium of oil traders registered in the name of Salek al-Fayadh. We traced that back as well. Took another couple of hours. Eventually, my pal at the bank comes on to me and says I shouldn't touch that money with a bargepole. It comes out of the United Nations oil-for-food programme.'

'Meaning what?' said Nick.

'Oil for food, man,' said Horton. 'Jesus, where have you been hiding? For the past decade there have been sanctions on Iraq. They are allowed to sell a limited amount of oil through the UN to pay for food and medical supplies. It's corrupt as hell. Everyone knows the money is used by Saddam Hussein.' He took another puff on his cigar. 'Your professor is being paid by the Iraqis.'

It took a moment for the information to sink in. It was as if a bullet had just struck him: he was numbed by the information. 'Jesus,' he muttered eventually. In his mind, he was still unpacking the consequences of what Horton had just told him. If Wilmington was being paid by the Iraqis, then they would know all about the work Sarah was doing in the lab. They would know about any breakthroughs she had made.

Could she possibly have been lifted by the Iraqis?

What the hell would they want from her? The cold-fusion technology?

'They've got Sarah,' he said out loud.

Horton looked up at him. 'Your girl?'

'Someone's taken her, that's for sure. If Wilmington is working for the Iraqis then I reckon it's those bastards. I've just got to find out where.'

Horton puffed on his cigar again. In the darkness, the pale orange glow of its tip illuminated his lined, weather-beaten face. 'They're mad fuckers,' he said. 'There are a lot of bad people in the world. You and I have had to deal with more than our fair share of them.

But Saddam and his boys take everything to extremes. Nobody messes with them, and nobody should.'

'It's my daughter,' snapped Nick.

Horton nodded. The smoke was curling up around his face. Neither man needed to say anything else. They both understood that when family was at stake, all the usual calculations of risk turned into dust. You would do whatever was necessary. If it cost you life, that was just the tab you had to pick up.

He reached out with his right hand, and took hold of Nick's shoulder. 'You need help, you just ask for it,' he said.

'Thanks, but this is my battle,' said Nick, turning away. 'I'll fight it myself.'

A few lights were shining from the building, but Nick reckoned the laboratory would be empty at this time of night. From Chelmsford, he'd got the train straight back to Cambridge, then walked from the station to here. Along the way, there had been plenty of time to think.

Cold fusion would change the geography of the global energy industry completely, and nobody had more of a stake in that than Saddam Hussein. If he could control cold fusion, he would stop it ever coming on to the market, because it would destroy the oil industry overnight. But he could also hold all his enemies in the Middle East to ransom. Because the secret of cold fusion threatened to destroy all their economies.

I know why the bastards wanted to lift her. But where

would they have taken her? To Iraq? *I hope to God she's not there.*

He'd already checked the front of the lab. The night guard was on duty in the lobby, but it was just a university building, and didn't have any special security. The back door he and Jed had used a few days earlier had just a simple latchkey lock on it, and it gave way easily enough when Nick wrenched at it with a penknife. Once inside, he couldn't see anybody in the corridors. One or two of the students might be working late, but it was unlikely they would pay him much attention. One good thing about students, he thought as he walked purposefully down the hallway. Most of them were so dopey, they could be relied upon not to notice anything that was happening around them.

The door to Wilmington's office wasn't locked. Nick pushed it open, and stepped quickly inside. He left the lights turned off: there was no point in drawing attention to himself. A street lamp was casting a soft glow in through the window, enough for Nick to see by once his vision had adjusted. He glanced around the room. The same pile of papers. Same faint equations on the board. Some book open on the desk. Nick started to search the drawers. A diary, maybe? he wondered. A map, some notes, perhaps a passport with some visa stamps in it. *Anything that might contain some lead on where they have taken Sarah.*

He pulled out a yellow folder, riffling through the pages. Some interdepartmental university memos. He pushed those aside. Notes on university admissions proceedings. A grid showing next term's lecture schedule. Bugger it, thought Nick. Where does he keep the stuff that tells me what the bastard is really doing? Maybe I'm just going to have to beat it out of him. Take him hostage, and get him to speak to the bastards who've lifted Sarah. Tell them that if they don't release her in the next twenty-four hours, then the professor is a dead man. Maximum speed, and maximum aggression. That's what we learnt in the Regiment. *It worked then, and it will work now.*

He glanced at the computer. It had been left on, and as soon as he touched the mouse, the screen jumped back into life. His hands were sweaty. The tension was getting to him, he could tell that. He stared at the screen, examining the files. Using the mouse, he started to point and click. He opened up 'My Documents', clicking first on 'History'. More memos, a couple of them written today. A reference for a postgrad applying to Harvard. A note to the college about a collaborative project with Hamburg University.

Nothing, thought Nick. *Whatever the bugger's hiding, it's not here.*

Nick sat back in the chair. He scanned the shelves on the cupboard wall. Science books, mostly. A couple of histories of the Second World War, a biography of Churchill, and one of Einstein, a pictorial book about Kurdistan. Three books by the professor himself, all on particle physics, and each of them translated into both German and Japanese.

Why would a man such as this be taking money from

Iraq, he wondered. Good job, distinguished career, he had everything to lose. Maybe he needs the money. Gambling debts? *Perhaps they've got something bad on him.*

A noise.

The door was creaking.

Nick spun round in the chair. The door was ajar, a hand gripping the handle. Through the murky light, he could see a pair of shoulders. He whipped himself up from the chair, steadying himself for the fight. Wilmington was not a big man, and he was in his fifties. There won't be much punch in him, Nick told himself grimly. Knock him out cold, then take him somewhere I can deal with him slowly. *Make the bugger talk.*

Nick stood behind the door, his knuckles poised to strike the first blow. A clean blow to the windpipe, he told himself. Then another to the centre of his jaw. Put him straight out before he knows what's happened to him.

One person was entering the room. *Then another.*

Nick threw a punch. It flew into the air, then was caught in the palm of a hand. A young hand. A strong one. In the next instant, a blow smashed into his stomach. Then another one into the back of his neck. It felt as if iron rods were crashing into his bones, splintering and chewing them as they crashed into his body. A sharp pain was ripping up through his spine, and his vision was blurring. His knees buckled, and he could feel himself starting to fall to the floor. Another punch. This time it was back to the stomach, knocking the air from his lungs and numbing his ribcage. Nick had taken a fair share of punches in his time, but this was different: the pain was searing, intense, as if his nerves were being burnt up, and it was impossible for him to react quickly enough to respond. In the next instant, two men were pressing down hard on him. One man was pinning down his chest, and another was gripping his legs: they were clearly trained to subdue a man no matter how hard he might fight back. He could smell processed cheese sandwiches on their breath, and the cologne on their necks. He looked up. A woman was peering into his face. Elegant, blonde, but with eyes that were as cold as they were blue. 'My name is Laura Strangar,' she said, her tone clipped and formal. 'You're under arrest.'

'What the fuck for?'

He could feel some blood spitting from his torn lip as he spoke the words.

Laura glanced around the room. 'Is this your office?' she said sharply. 'No. Well then, breaking and entering will do for a start. I'm sure we can find a few more things to charge you with once we get you down to the office.'

TWENTY

The streets looked darker than the last time Jed had walked along them. The people were moving faster. Nobody was stopping to talk. The pavement cafés were emptied of the men who usually spent half the day sitting around talking. The shops were sold out, a few even boarded up. Everywhere you looked, the faces of the people were strained and tired. Only the children were still playing in the streets.

They're afraid, thought Jed. And right to be. *This city is about to hammered into dust.*

It was early afternoon, and Jed and Matt had just driven back across Baghdad towards the plant. The journey had been completed without incident. Jed couldn't say for certain, but there seemed to be fewer soldiers on the streets today. Maybe they'd all returned to their barracks, getting in some training before the battle kicked off. Maybe they've already started abandoning their posts. There was no way of knowing. He was just grateful to get to the right district without meeting any roadblocks.

'You think it's safe to approach the plant?' he whispered to Matt.

Matt glanced down the street, then nodded. 'So long as we don't draw any attention to ourselves.'

They walked in silence, keeping a couple of yards apart and never breaking stride. One or two men glanced in their direction, but the more time they spent in Baghdad, Jed noticed, the more they started to blend in with the locals. The skin on their faces was tanned, and lined with the grime and dust that seemed to cling to every surface of the city. Their clothes were unwashed, and their beards growing. *If we start looking much worse*, Jed thought, *they'll arrest us as tramps, not as enemy soldiers.*

'Stop,' hissed Matt.

He pointed up ahead to a roadblock. A cordon of soldiers was surrounding the plant, and temporary wooden fencing had been put up around its perimeter. There was a soldier standing about every ten yards or so, and from their purple insignia, they looked like crack troops. Special Republican Guard. Not the raw conscripts who were patrolling the rest of Baghdad. The Iraqis knew this place had been attacked by special forces two nights ago, and they knew they hadn't captured the men responsible. *If we come back, they're planning to be ready for us this time.*

Both Jed and Matt turned round, and walked purposefully but not too quickly in the other direction. The Toyota was parked half a mile away, but they didn't want to go back there. 'Where can we fix our kit?' said Jed.

'The higher up we get, the better chance we have.'

'Then we keep walking. Until we find something.'

Jed checked his watch. It was almost two o'clock. The number of people on the streets was thinning out, making him feel vulnerable. In a crowd, they could blend in. By themselves, they were more likely to stand out.

He was starting to get a sense of the layout of the area. The streets curved away from the plant, and most of the buildings were four or five storeys high: apartment blocks, with shops and cafés at the ground level, and some workshops in the basement. They needed to get up high to set up their kit. The LTD beam was invisible to the naked eye, and the Firm was pretty confident that the Iraqis didn't have any of the sophisticated kit needed to detect it electronically. So long as they could find a position, then they would just need to shoot the laser beam down into the plant at the designated moment, and the bombs would land right at the tip of the beam.

The Firm is confident of a lot of things about this country, thought Jed. *The only trouble is, most of them turn out to be wrong.*

They walked for at least half an hour, studying the layout and assessing different potential OPs. They needed a clear view of the site, but they also needed to be far enough away so as not to be injured in the blast when the cruises started to come in. At one point, Matt was convinced an old guy was following them, and wanted to slot him. Jed persuaded him to drop it: they didn't need to take the risk of starting a fight in the street. Eventually they lost him, but Matt remained convinced they'd been compromised. He was edgier than a knife, thought Jed: they'd been behind the lines for three days now, lost two of their mates and his nerves were shot to pieces. *If they didn't get picked up soon, the guy was going to lose it.*

'Here,' said Matt.

He was pointing towards an open staircase on a block of flats. The building was made of concrete, and was six storeys, slightly higher than the rest of the blocks in the area. There was a smell of boiled rice drifting down the staircase, and Jed could hear a dog barking from one of the flats. The staircase was open to the street, with layers of pale green paint peeling off the wall. Looks good enough, thought Jed. There must be at least thirty people in the block. Enough, he hoped, for one or two strangers not to attract any attention.

At the top of the stairs, a trapdoor led on to a flat roof. Jed used his knife to squeeze open the bolt, then stepped outside. It measured about two hundred feet lengthwise and a hundred feet across, with a covering of black tar, and a gentle slope leading down to the gutter channels that drained off the water. Kneeling, Jed started to crawl across its surface, approaching the edge. There was a clear view of the plant. The orb was still intact: the explosion two nights ago might have damaged its base, but the main structure had been left mostly unscathed. He peered down at the admin block. The front door had been blown away, and most of the windows had been broken, but at least half of them had been patched up already, and he could see a couple of workmen hammering away at the rest. People were coming and going. At a rough guess, he'd say there were thirty soldiers guarding the perimeter, and another twenty inside the compound: there could well be another fifty men hidden from view.

Matt crawled up to him. 'Reckon we can get a clear shot at the bugger with the LTD?' he said.

Jed examined the layout of territory again. There was a clear line of sight that led down from the rooftop on to the orb. If they put the LTD on to it, it would guide the missiles straight into the plant. They didn't have much cover. If the Iraqis had any intelligence suggesting a strike was scheduled for tonight, they'd be patrolling the place with choppers. If they were spotted, they were an easy target. But the surface of the roof was black, and they were wearing black trousers and T-shirts. Black up their faces, and they should blend into its surface. Perhaps there was a decent chance of completing the mission. *Hell, they might even escape with their lives afterwards.*

'It'll do,' said Jed.

Matt nodded. 'We'll set up the LTD right here.'

'I'll get the kit from the Toyota,' said Jed.

He felt a hand clasping his shoulder. Matt was looking at him intently, his eyes staring straight into him. 'I'll get it,' he hissed. 'You bloody wait here.'

Jed shrugged. If Matt wanted to take the risks that was fine with him. This mission was dangerous enough already. Walking through these streets with a piece of LTD kit could well get you stopped by the police. You didn't need to put yourself in the line of any more fire than was completely necessary. 'Why?' he said.

'Because I don't bloody trust you to come back,' said Matt.

Jed steadied the LTD on its tripod, then slipped behind. Together with Matt, he had mounted the device on the edge of the roof. It was lifted two metres from the ground, and facing straight at the plant.

Jed looked through the viewfinder, getting a measure of the distance to the target. It was just over a kilometre: eleven hundred and forty-five metres, according to the LTD. They were looking straight across at the orb, with nothing to disturb their view. The rangefinder on the LTD locked on to the target, and Jed flicked the button. The laser beamed out of the LTD. It was invisible to the naked eye, but to a cruise missile it was as clear as if you had a guy waving a big flag reading 'Target This Way'. Chances were the cruises would be fired from the US Navy ships parked down off the coasts of Kuwait and Saudi Arabia. They had to travel about five hundred kilometres to get here: the journey would take about fifteen minutes. They would come into the city at a low angle, with rough coordinates of the designated target already programmed into them. When they came within range, their on-board computers would lock on to the laser, and use its position to make the tiny adjustments to its trajectory necessary to bring it precisely onto the target.

'What kind of missile are they using?' said Matt, glancing at Jed.

He shrugged. The same question had occurred to

him. Anyone operating an LTD was putting themselves directly in the line of fire. He guessed they'd use Paveways or Hellfires, because that's what the LTD was designed for. Both of them were big, ugly missiles, with hardened noses that could dig deep in the target before exploding. How much punch they'd pack depended on the amount of explosive they were carrying. If you wanted to you could even equip them with a nuclear warhead. But the plant was right next to a residential area. The Americans wouldn't want to take out too many civilians, at least not on the first day. It wouldn't look good on al-Jazeera. If they had any sense, they'd be using powerful, but limited impact explosives: enough to make sure the plant was totally destroyed but without taking out too much of the surrounding area.

If the missile strayed from its course, though, it could land anywhere within a mile or two of the plant. *Right on top of us.*

'We'll be OK,' said Jed. 'We cost too much to train.'

Matt was looking at the staircase. 'How the hell are we going to get out of here once the fireworks start going off?'

'I'll hold the LTD, until the missiles have all gone home,' said Jed. 'You hold the staircase. That's our only way down. If we allow that to get blocked, we're buggered.'

Matt was already hunkering down on the surface of the roof. He'd unpacked some biscuits and a flask of water from his kitbag, and had eaten three. Jed peered out across the rooftops. Dusk had already started to fall.

It was just after eight at night. The sun was setting across the city. In the distance, he could see the turret of a mosque. Down below, five soldiers were pacing around the perimeter fence, while inside the compound the guards had started a brazier, and were brewing up some cups of sweet coffee. Next to it, they had parked a black van with blackened windows and thick steel armour around its sides.

In a few hours, Jed thought, the missiles are going to be smashing into this place. The flames will chew up everything in their path. *And we're going to be in the middle of it.*

TWENTY-ONE

Nick looked around the cell. It measured just ten feet by seven, and the walls were made of concrete, with a thin coating of standard, government-issue grey paint slapped on it. There was a steel-framed bed, a jug of water and a loo. Apart from that, nothing. He was alone. *With only his nightmares to torment him.*

He'd been in jails before, but nothing like this. Tonight he was being incarcerated in his own country. And he no longer knew who, if anyone, he could trust.

Two hours had been spent in the cell now. After picking him up in Cambridge, they had slapped a pair of handcuffs on him, then bundled him into a Land Rover Discovery they had waiting outside. They weren't regular police, he could tell that right away. From the outside, the Discovery looked like a regular vehicle, but Nick could tell its windows were made from reinforced, shatterproof glass, while there were sheets of armour lining the inside skin of the machine. You could hit it with a couple of RPG rounds, and not even burst a tyre. Whoever they were planning to transport in this thing, they were classified as bloody dangerous, Nick had thought. *A lot more dangerous than me.*

He'd been strapped to the wall for the duration of a journey that he reckoned lasted just over an hour: with the handcuffs around his wrists, and the straps pinning him back it was impossible to look at his watch. After the van shuddered to a halt, the door was thrown open, and the same blonde woman, accompanied by her two thugs, led him through a courtyard. It was an ugly, rainy evening, but Nick recognised the place at once. He'd been here several times when he was still in the Regiment, and he'd regretted it every time. It was the Vauxhall headquarters of the Firm. The security services, he thought to himself, as he was led roughly into the building. That's who picked me up. But how the hell did they know I was there? *And what do they want with me?*

He took a sip of water, and paced around the cell. He must have done a thousand circuits by now, the same questions rattling though his mind. He knew Sarah was in danger, and he reckoned the Firm knew all about it. But if they knew, why hadn't they done anything?

I'm getting old, he told himself angrily. The German guy on the hillside gave me a thrashing, the professor's friend was too strong for me, and now I've let a couple of heavies from the Firm beat me. If I was a younger man, I could have punched my way out of all those situations. *And now . . . I don't know.*

Footsteps. He could hear them in the corridor, soft at first then louder. Then the thick steel door of the cell was pushed open. Nick steadied himself. A man walked in, about six foot, no more than twenty-five, dressed in a white shirt, black trousers, no tie. 'This way,' he said.

He started to follow him down the length of the corridor. There were several other cells in the block, but they were each at least ten feet apart, with thick blocks of reinforced concrete separating each one. Making sure the prisoners don't have any way of communicating with each other, thought Nick. They were at least three storeys underground, and there were bars and grilles everywhere you looked. London had plenty of high-security police stations. But this was where they brought the really hard cases. *The men who were about to disappear off the radar screen.*

At the end of the corridor, the door to the interview room was already open. The man guided Nick inside, then closed the door behind him. He could hear it thumping shut. Laura was sitting at the desk, with a big, plasma screen television behind her. At her side was a man in his early sixties. He had silvery-white hair, thinning, and combed across his forehead. His face was pinched and lined with grooves, like a piece of old stone, but his eyes were sharp and clear. Nick recognised him at once, even though it was years since he had last laid eyes on him. David Marlow. The commanding officer of the Regiment from 1990 to 1995: the man who had sent Nick into Iraq last time around.

'Let me the hell out of here,' said Nick, looking at both of them in turn. 'I've done nothing wrong.'

Laura looked at him coldly. She was wearing a black suit, with a string of pearls around her neck, and although it was getting close to midnight, to Nick she looked as fresh as if she had woken up five minutes ago. 'I've already told you, breaking and entering,' she said.

'Bollocks,' said Nick, still standing close to the doorway. 'The professor is a mate of mine. I was just running an errand for him.'

A smile flickered across Laura's face. 'Funny,' she said. 'Somebody broke the lock into the place. Somebody has been into his house as well. We got fingerprints from both locations. Found some DNA as well. We haven't had them processed yet, but I've got a feeling we don't really need to.'

'Book me then, if you want to,' said Nick. 'What do you get for breaking and entering these days anyway? A bit of community service, and one of those little electronic tags wrapped around your big toe? Fine, I'll take my punishment. It's a fair cop. I'm guilty, case closed.' He ground his fists together. 'Now let me go. I've got things to do.'

'Like what, Nick?' said Marlow.

Nick stared at the man. He was sitting calmly at the desk, his face impassive. Nick hadn't liked him much when he was a Rupert, and he had even less time for him now he was in civilian clothes.

'That's my business.'

'I think you'll find it's our business as well.'

Nick looked at Laura. 'Has Wilmington pressed charges?'

There was a moment of hesitation on her face: a tightening of the lips and a narrowing of her eyes. It lasted just a fraction of second, but it told Nick all he needed to know. 'Then you've no reason to hold me here,' he persisted. 'Let me go.'

'We'll let you go when it's safe,' said Laura.

'I can decide when it's safe,' snapped Nick.

Slowly, Marlow stood up. He was a tall man, over six foot three, and he had grown thinner since Nick had last seen him, the way some men do when they age. He peered at Nick. 'Listen, man,' he said. 'You know bugger all about what's going on here. I suggest you stop shooting your ruddy mouth off and start listening.' He paused, his face reddening slightly. 'For once in your miserable life.'

Nick could feel the anger building within him. It was welling up in his stomach, and he tightened his fists together to try and control it. It was going to take all the willpower he possessed not to throw a punch in the next few seconds. 'My daughter's missing,' he said, his voice low and determined, all the anger buried within it. 'She discovered something.'

He hesitated, debating with himself how much to tell them. Sod it, he thought. I might as well level with them. It might be the only chance I have of getting out of this place – and finding Sarah.

'Cold fusion,' he continued. 'Don't press me for the details of the science, but I'm sure you know more about it than me. I think the Iraqis might have got hold of it, and lifted her out of the country.' He looked first at Marlow, then at Laura. 'So I haven't got time to piss around talking to you two. My daughter's in danger, and I mean to find her.'

'We do know,' said Laura.

His could feel the rage reddening his cheeks. 'What do you bloody know?' he spluttered.

'We know,' Laura repeated.

'You know my daughter's been kidnapped by Saddam Hussein?' said Nick.

'Of course,' said Laura. 'That's why we brought you here.'

Marlow glanced at Nick, a hint of a smile on his face. 'We didn't want to run the risk of you blundering around Iraq trying to find her,' he said. 'You'd just screw everything up. Like the last time.'

Laura shot Marlow an angry glance. 'Why don't you sit down, and tell us everything you know?' she said. 'I think it's time we started cooperating.'

Nick pulled up a chair. He didn't have much choice. They had taken him prisoner. And they clearly knew a lot more about Sarah than he did. If he didn't work with them, they would just throw him back into that cell and forget about him.

I'll work with them, he told himself. But I won't trust them. *Not for an instant.*

'You tell me what you know,' he said bitterly.

'That's not the way it works, and you know it,' said Laura. 'Now, you tell us what *you* know.'

Nick reached out for a glass of water. Behind the desk, the television was tuned to BBC News 24. The sound was turned down, but he could see they were reporting the build-up to the invasion of Iraq. There were reporters talking to camera from the Kuwaiti border. He looked back at Laura. 'Sarah disappeared about ten days ago.'

'You don't know the actual day?' said Marlow.

'She's a grown woman,' said Nick gruffly. 'I don't speak to her every day.'

'But you were suspicious?' said Laura.

Nick nodded. 'She'd never go more than a few days without contacting someone.'

'Your daughter drank heavily,' said Laura.

'I know,' snapped Nick.

'And took drugs.'

Nick paused. He didn't know that, but it didn't surprise him either. Sarah had a talent for getting herself into trouble. She had done ever since she was a teenager. 'She wasn't just on a bender,' said Nick. 'For starters, they never lasted that long. Next, there was money in her account.'

'A hundred thousand,' said Laura.

'You know?'

'We've been keeping tabs on Sarah for a while.'

'Because of what she was working on?'

'Precisely.' Laura's tone was clipped, businesslike, but Nick reckoned there was an emotion in there somewhere. As if she was still concealing something, and that made her uncomfortable.

'Cold fusion,' said Nick.

'It's a very important piece of science,' said Laura. 'If Sarah has made the breakthrough we think she has, and I'm not really qualified to say whether she has or hasn't, then it has global implications. It matters for the state. And we're concerned about Sarah's safety as well, of course.'

'Bollocks,' Nick snapped. 'You don't give a toss for anyone's safety except your own.'

'Watch your language, Nick,' said Marlow. 'You're not on an oil rig now.'

'I'll speak as I like,' said Nick. He looked back at Laura. He despised himself for wanting to impress her, but he did. 'Her professor has been working for the Iraqis,' he said.

'For some years, yes,' said Laura.

'So why the hell haven't you arrested him?' said Nick angrily.

'We wanted to, as soon as we were aware of the full magnitude of the situation,' she said. 'We were trailing him to find out who his handlers were. There must be senior Iraqi agents controlling him in this country, and we want to know who they are. Unfortunately, he seems to have vanished.'

'Just like Sarah . . .'

'That's why we were monitoring his office,' said Laura. 'When we saw you going in there, we had to intervene. We don't want amateurs crashing into an investigation that is being handled by us.'

Nick glared at her. 'She's in Iraq, isn't she?'

Laura paused. 'She may well be,' she said. 'Right now, we really have no idea where she might be. We're doing our best to find out.'

'She's in fucking Iraq. I know it.'

'I've already told you to watch your language,' Marlow snapped.

'My daughter's in the middle of what's about to become a bloody war zone, so I'll swear if I want to,' Nick snapped back. 'Why do the Iraqis want cold fusion,

274

anyway? They're already sitting on top of half the oil in the world.'

'Precisely,' says Laura. 'If cold fusion works, Saddam and the rest of the Arabs are back to growing dates for a living. If Saddam gets control of this technology, he can bury it. Even better, he can threaten his neighbours that he'll release it, so destroying their economies. It will give him control over all the Middle Eastern oil, which is what he has always dreamt about. And that would allow him to hold the West hostage as well.' She paused, glancing at Marlow. 'It would make him the most powerful man in the world.'

'I thought we were invading because of WMD?' said Nick.

Laura laughed, flicking away a few strands of her blonde hair with her right hand. 'That's just to bring the bearded polytechnic lecturers on the Labour back-benches on board. It's much more serious than that.'

'As serious as getting my daughter back,' said Nick.

Laura didn't respond. She was turning to the television behind the desk. News 24 had cut to live pictures from Baghdad. Marlow, perched on the edge of the desk, was also peering at the TV screen, his expression intent, focused, as if he was searching for something.

What the hell are they looking for, wondered Nick. 'Are you serious about getting my daughter back?' he said, his voice louder this time.

Laura glanced back at him. 'We have to go,' she said, getting up. 'You'll stay here. The doors will be locked, and there is no other way out of this room. Don't try to move. You'll only hurt yourself.'

'Let me the fuck out of here,' Nick growled.

He took a menacing step towards her. Marlow suddenly stood to attention, putting his body between them. He was a tall man, but he was in his sixties now: even Regiment training did you no good in a fight once you got past a certain age. Nick knew he could take him apart with a couple of blows. 'Back off,' Marlow said. 'We've got dozens of guards in here who'd be only too happy to beat the crap out of you.'

Laura had already opened the door, and Marlow moved swiftly behind her. Nick took a couple of steps forward to follow them, but in the next instant the door slammed shut. He pushed hard against it, but it had already been locked. He started pulling on the steel handle, but there was no give in it.

'You bastards,' he muttered.

Turning round, he wiped the sweat from his brow. He took a sip of the water from the desk, trying to calm himself down. His heart was thumping, and he could feel his pulse racing. What kind of brutal game have they been playing with Sarah, he asked himself. *If she gets hurt, I'll make them pay for it with their blood.*

He looked at the television. The sound was still turned down, and he couldn't see a remote to turn the volume up. On the screen, he could see a panoramic view of Baghdad at night. The city was shrouded in darkness. Then he could see one or two flashes of lights. Lightning? An explosion? No, Nick realised, with a sudden chill to his spine. I know what that light looks like. I'm familiar with the sudden, violent thunderball that splits open the sky. I've seen it before.

A cruise missile.

Suddenly, the lights were popping up over the screen like a firework display. The city, as displayed on the TV screen, was bathed in an ugly mixture of blue, orange and white. A terrifying storm was engulfing the place, turning what were once streets and roads into a raging inferno of smoke and fire.

On the screen, underneath the picture, Nick could read the rolling headline news. 'Shock and Awe attack starts on Baghdad,' it read. 'Allies launch massive missile strikes.'

Christ, thought Nick.

He wiped away a fresh layer of sweat that had formed on his brow.

The war has started already.

And Sarah is right there, somewhere in the middle of it.

TWENTY-TWO

Jed lay perfectly still. He'd already checked his watch a dozen times, and there was no point in checking it again. The time for waiting had passed. The war would start in the next few seconds.

Looking down, he could see movement. A black van was pulling up at the plant. Inside the courtyard, the door to the admin building was open, and he could see several figures running back and forth.

Jesus, he thought. *Do they know something?*

He listened intently. For the past three hours, he'd just been lying here, listening to the sounds of the city. It was quiet. Baghdad was already in a state of high alert. All the lights had been turned out, as a blackout as well as a curfew had been imposed. The people were inside their houses, keeping their heads down, hoping for the best. Only a few ventured outside, and then they risked being rounded up by the police and soldiers. Twice, he had seen people shot on the streets below, as the army rushed forwards, building up its defences. Most of the time, however, the city was virtually silent, with just the low background noise of a couple of million people trying to keep out of harm's way.

Now, he could hear something different.

At first, it was a low, growling sound, like a blocked drain.

Then an audible buzz, like a washing machine.

And now, a whooshing sound, as the air was sucked out of the sky.

The sound of an incoming cruise missile.

He leant in, checking the LTD. The laser was in position. Its beam was locked onto the main orb within the compound, providing perfect guidance for the incoming strike.

He could see the cruise flying overhead now, and started counting down the seconds in his head. The missile was long and thin, like a cigar, but it moved so fast through the air, all Jed could see was a flash of hot metal slicing through the night sky.

Five, four . . .

Something was moving in the compound. The van had been loaded. The gates had been opened. It was driving away . . .

'What the fuck's happening down there?' muttered Jed.

'They're scarpering,' said Matt. 'Sodding chicken ragheads. They're buggering off just as things turn interesting.'

Three, two . . .

The van was skidding into the street, its lights flashing, and even a kilometre away Jed could hear its horn blaring.

One . . .

Jed steeled himself, taking a sharp intake of breath. *Impact*.

The missile collided with the plant, crashing into its target with pinpoint accuracy. There was a momentary stillness in the air, as the hardened tip of the missile forged its deadly path into the metal skin of the plant. It drilled into the building, cutting a channel through it. Jed held his breath. In the next fraction of a second, its explosives detonated. How much power had been packed into the missile, Jed had no way of knowing, but from the sudden gust of wind that rustled past his ears as the missile ignited, he guessed it was at least a couple of hundred pounds of explosives. A flash of lightning suddenly struck up into the air, and he could smell the burning of metal, wood, oil and flesh. A wave of heat rolled out from the plant, hitting him straight in the face, as if the whole city had just been put into the microwave.

A chorus of strangled screams started to rise up from the plant: the pitiful, anguished moaning of bodies that were already burnt beyond survival. Flames were licking up around the centre, and a huge, thick cloud of black smoke was billowing above it. Jed could see the soldiers on the perimeter rushing into action. Men were shouting, running in different directions, but the strike had already destroyed their command and control. No one had any idea what to do. Glancing sideways, he could see the black van screeching down the side road that led out of the city, its lights flashing and its siren screaming.

It had escaped, unscathed.

Whatever the hell it was.

Jed could suddenly hear the noise again.

Another approaching missile.

He looked up into the sky. There were missiles coming in from all directions. The city was full of noise and light, as if you were trapped in the middle of an electronic thunderstorm. From up here, they had a grandstand view of the mayhem. There were flashes and explosions everywhere. Jed looked to his right. A missile was striking the centre of the Republican Palace compound, closely followed by another one. Two huge explosions rocked the ground, crashing into Jed's eardrums. Great walls of fire were shooting up into the sky. He looked to his left. A missile had struck one of the bridges, slicing it clean in half, sending a river of flame licking down into the streets on either side. Another had crashed straight into the Tigris, sending jets of water high into the air, then creating a fifteen-foot wave that was hurtling down the riverbed.

'Jesus, they're taking down the whole sodding city,' gasped Jed.

'Nice of them to fucking tell us,' said Matt. 'Seeing as we're in the fucking middle of it.'

Instinctively, Jed ducked, as a missile flew in low over his head. It was maybe fifty feet above him but, looking up, he could see its thick steel hide whizzing past. Within seconds it had crashed into the plant. A deafening roar rolled out through the building, shattering windows and making the building shake. People were flooding out into the streets, shouting and crying. Too frightened to stay inside, thought Jed. *This is what it must have been like during the worse nights of the Blitz.*

'There's soldiers on the bloody stairs,' shouted Matt.

Jed spun round. Matt was peering down the stairwell that led down into the interior of the building. 'That old guy who was following us earlier, he's bloody come to get us,' he said. Sweat was pouring off his face, and his voice was ragged. His AK-47 had already been whipped out of his kitbag. He was jabbing the tip of his gun down into the stairwell, and had already loosened off a couple of rounds of fire. About five miles to the left, another missile had crashed into the city, sending an electric firestorm shooting up into the sky and briefly making it as bright as the middle of the day. Down below, soldiers were streaming away from the burning plant, shouting and firing their guns to clear the streets. Up above, Jed felt certain he could hear the sound of more oncoming missiles. 'Get me a bloody grenade,' shouted Matt.

The sweat was streaming down the side of his face, mixing with the blackening on his skin. His eyes were bloodshot and tense, glinting with a murderous anger.

Jed threw open his kitbag, and ran towards the stairs, passing Matt two grenades. 'They're fucking looking for us,' said Matt.

He ripped the pin from the stun grenade, and tossed it down the stairs. Jed listened to it rattling across the concrete as it fell, then the burst of noise as it exploded. Both men paused for a second, while the smell of thick, acrid smoke started to drift back up the stairs. Matt ripped the pin on the second grenade and tossed it down. Within seconds, they heard the blast and the muffled screams of the men below.

'I'm going down,' said Matt. 'You count for one minute, then follow my arse.'

Jed flinched as another missile crashed into the city. How far away it was he couldn't tell. Two miles, maybe three. The rolling sound of explosions was rocking the night, and the sky was now completely lit up by fires and explosions. Down below, the Iraqi Army was wildly shooting up into the sky, trying to hit the incoming missiles. Poor sods, thought Jed grimly. *They might as well be using pea-shooters for all the good they are doing.*

'It's too bloody dangerous,' shouted Jed.

'It's my fucking skin,' shouted Matt. 'I'll decide when to risk it.'

Jed grabbed his arm. It was suicide for him to go down there by himself. The army could be crawling all over the staircase. They were outgunned. 'It's bloody madness,' he shouted. 'We can defend this position.'

'Let go of my fucking arm,' growled Matt.

'You've no bloody idea what's down there.'

'I said let the fuck go,' shouted Matt, shrugging him aside. 'Steve and Rob are already dead because you keep fucking up. I'm not going down as well.'

He ripped himself free, and disappeared down the staircase. His AK-47 was held out in front of him, and he was already ripping loose, firing off round after round. Thick clouds of yellow smoke were billowing up the stairs from the grenades. Another missile was streaking through the sky, and in the next second the building shook as the ground three miles away was shattered by another incoming strike.

Jed heard a scream. Matt, he thought instantly. There was a volley of gunfire, then more shouting. 'Fuck it,' he muttered. 'Here goes.'

With his AK-47 in front of him, Jed plunged into the smoke. He was holding his breath, but his eyes were already wet and stinging from the smoke. He was tearing down the stairs, his feet crashing into the concrete. Another scream. A woman this time. Or maybe a child. It was impossible to tell amid the noise. He pressed on, down one flight of stairs, then another. Suddenly a movement caught his eye. Jed narrowed his eyes, focusing hard through the billowing smoke. A hand. With a gun in it. Jed didn't think the man had seen him yet, but he might well have heard him. Gripping on to the AK-47, Jed slammed his finger hard into the trigger. The bullets rattled from the barrel of the gun, smashing into the man's body like a storm of lethal hailstones. He turned, looking up at Jed, but the blood was already seeping from his open wounds. In the next instant he'd collapsed. Jed skipped over his body. The smoke was thinning out as he went down another level. A woman was cowering in the doorway, her body rigid with fear. Jed crashed down one more level. A body was lying crumpled in front of him. Jed looked down. A black sweatshirt, and a couple of days' growth of beard.

Matt.

You mad bugger, thought Jed grimly.

He knelt down, but it only took a moment to realise he was dead. He must have taken at least three or four bullets straight to his head, smashing open his skull. Half his brain was smeared across the damp concrete.

There was just one more flight of stairs. Jed loosed off a burst of gunfire, but the stairs had been cleared already. The smoke from the grenades was clearing, and he could hear nothing except the wailing of a baby inside one of the apartments and the sobs of the mother as she tried to calm it. We should fight our bloody wars in the desert, thought Jed, as he ran down the last flight of stairs. *Not in here, the centre of a city, among ordinary people.*

With a sharp intake of breath, Jed filled his lungs as soon as he hit the street. He had to get away from here, find somewhere he could hide until the missile strike was done with and he could check in with the Firm to arrange his pickup. There was sweat pouring off his face and back, his gun hanging from his chest. The streets had descended into panic. A few people turned to look at him, unsure whether he was a soldier or not, but most were running in all directions, shouting, pushing and jostling one another. Jed could see the fear in the faces, but also glimpses of defiance. They were steeling themselves for a long fight. Up ahead, a huge ball of fire was still leaping out of the plant, illuminating the night sky like a bonfire. A couple of miles to the right, more fires were raging. You could feel the whole city getting hotter and hotter by the minute. Just then, the ground shook, and the echo of an explosion started to rumble through the streets. Another missile strike. Jesus, Jed thought. What the hell is our strategy here? Just to keep bombing the bloody place until it's completely flattened?

Does anyone know what kind of hell this place is being turned into?

Got to get away, he told himself. Three of us are dead already, and in the next few minutes I could well make it four out of four.

About a hundred yards away, Jed could see an army truck. A dozen soldiers were shouting orders, sometimes firing their guns over the heads of the anxious crowd. But even the troops seemed to be too nervous to climb down from their vehicles.

He slung his AK-47 into his kitbag, and started running down the street. Just keep moving until you see somewhere, he told himself. The bulk of the crowd was heading east, trying to get out of the city. Maybe they have friends or family in the villages there, he thought. Maybe they're just going anywhere to get away from the missiles. He saw a small boy, maybe six or seven, crying, looking for the parents who had lost him in the rush. Jed pushed on. The soldiers had moved away. A couple of cars were trying to force their way down the street. One of them hit Jed in the thigh, and he cried out as the pain rippled through his leg, then stifled the noise. As he looked up, the driver was already leaning out of his window shouting at him. For a brief second, he seemed to realise Jed might be a foreigner, but then he moved on, interested only in saving his own skin.

Jed ran another hundred yards, then turned left into a quieter street. Another missile had hit the city, maybe three or four miles away, and the sky was filled with sparks. He paused. No way anyone's getting out of this hellhole, he told himself. *The only thing is to hunker down and wait for it to end.*

A sewer. Jed had tucked into a small alley squeezed between two apartment buildings. He could smell burning not very far away, but neither of the buildings were alight. Not yet anyway. There were three manhole covers right beneath his feet, arranged in a neat circle. He knelt down and ripped open the first one. The smell wasn't as bad as he might have expected: a mixture of rotting fruit, bad eggs and diesel fuel. He lowered himself down slowly. It was dark inside, and impossible to tell how far a drop it might be, but Jed could hear the rushing water below, and judged it couldn't be more than a few feet. He let go, his body collapsing through the air.

The fall lasted only a fraction of a second. His feet hit the freezing water first, then he rolled his body on to its side, to deflect the impact on his legs. In the next moment, he could feel the water rushing around his side, and over his head. He clamped his mouth tight, and closed his eyes. Kicking his legs down, he found his footing, stopped himself from being dragged along by the water, then stood up. He opened his eyes. The water was flowing around him, but only came up to his waist. Two yards away, he could see a ledge running along the side of water.

The tunnel was about ten feet across, and eight or

nine feet high. Walking towards its side, he pulled himself up, and sat down. His clothes were wet through, and something sticky had attached itself to his hair and the beard that was growing on his chin. His hands felt clammy and hot, and his stomach was heaving. He closed his eyes, getting his breath back under control. Up above, he could hear the explosions of another pair of missiles striking the city, and even below the manholes, the noise of people running through the streets filtered through. Reaching into his kitbag, he took out a bottle of water, uncapped it, and swilled the water around his mouth to clean it out. Next he took out a packet of biscuits, eating three of them in quick succession. Get as much sugar into your bloodstream as you can, he told himself. You're going to have to find some energy from somewhere.

Time to phone home, he thought. He walked through the putrid, icy water until he found a manhole cover, then edged it aside. He needed to hold the satphone to the open street to pick up a signal, but he knew as he was doing so he was creating an electronic splash that could be picked up by the enemy. Hold your breath and take the risk, he told himself. You don't have any choice.

At least this bloody mission is over now, he thought. There can't be anything more we can do in this godforsaken city. With the punishment it's taking tonight, there may not be much of Baghdad left by the morning.

He glimpsed a flash of light and heard the thunderous echo of another missile strike as he punched out the number. One ring, then another. 'Get me Laura,' he snapped as soon as the phone was answered. 'Right now.'

One second passed, then two. He could hear shouting above him, about a hundred yards away. Then a round of gunfire.

'Laura here,' she said. Her voice was breathless, clipped, like a woman waiting for the results of a cancer test. 'What happened?'

'Didn't you get satellites to take some pictures?'

'Of course,' she snapped. 'But it's not the same as having a man on the ground.'

'It's a fuck-up,' said Jed tersely.

A pause. He could sense her lips tightening over the phone. *That wasn't what she wanted to hear.*

'The other three guys are dead,' he continued. 'Matt about an hour ago.'

'The missile didn't hit the plant?'

'They hit it all right. We guided them home just like you asked us to, and it cost Matt his life. But there was a van that drove out of the place just before the missiles came in. I reckon that whatever you were trying to hit was inside.'

Jed paused. Another round of gunfire was rattling through the street and it sounded like at least one person had been shot.

'The plant was destroyed?'

'Wiped out,' said Jed. 'Two missiles slammed straight into it. I reckon even the cockroaches aren't going to walk out of that place.'

'You've done your job then,' said Laura. 'We'll pick you up tomorrow night. Twenty-three hundred hours. The same spot where you were dropped down.' She paused, and then her voice softened. 'I'm sorry about the rest of the guys, Jed. I didn't realise it was going to get so rough in there.'

'It's fucking World War Three in this place,' snapped Jed. 'I need to be picked up tonight. I'm not going to survive twenty-four hours in this craphole.'

'Those are the orders, Jed.'

He gripped the bulky satphone tight into his fist. 'Then fucking change them,' he growled.

'Too dangerous, Jed. Nothing can fly into that city tonight.'

Bugger, thought Jed. Can't argue with that. *Even if a chopper could pick me up, we'd be dodging our way through cruise missiles.*

'Tomorrow night. Twenty-three hundred hours,' said Laura. 'Good luck.'

The phone went dead. Jed had been about to speak, but the words had stalled on his lips. Now she killed the call, and it was too dangerous to try again: satellite phones created a splash out, and you had to limit yourself to no more than a few moments of talking. He took another hit of the water, and stuffed another biscuit into his mouth. Through the open manhole cover, he could see the flash of another missile strike. The noise and the screams would follow within a few seconds.

Jed sat on the ledge, and looked at the sewage flowing below. He buried his face in his hands, and could feel the exhaustion in every muscle of his body. Christ, man, he thought. *You really are in the shit now.*

TWENTY-THREE

The room felt cold and empty, and although Nick was a man used to spending time by himself, he had never felt as alone as he did right now. The television was still switched on, but after two hours Nick had tired of watching the lights flashing over Baghdad. Nobody knew what was going on, and the way he felt right now, it didn't make any difference any more anyway.

First her mother died. Then her. *And it's all my fault . . .*

Sarah was dead, he felt certain of it. They had lifted her into Iraq, there could be no doubt of that any longer. The Firm didn't have any idea where she was now. Even if they did, they wouldn't have a clue what to do about it.

The words repeated themselves in his mind, caught in an endless loop. *I've lost her, I've lost her, I've lost her . . .*

The British are now at war with Iraq. We're bombing the hell out of the place. The Iraqis will be questioning Sarah about what she knows. But once they've got what they need, they'll show her no mercy. They'll break her, then they'll dispose of her. Hell, that's what they did to me.

Nick slammed his fist down hard on the table. It shook and wobbled. He could feel a shot of pain where the bone had collided with the wood. 'Fuck it,' he muttered. He was desperate for a drink: there wasn't even any water left in this room, and his throat was parched. *Once I get out of this pisshole, I'm going to go straight to the nearest pub and get completely smashed. Then I'm going to find myself somewhere to crash, and as soon as I wake up, I'm going back to the pub to get pissed again. There's nothing to keep myself sober for now.*

How many hours had he been sitting here? He had lost count. Three, maybe four. He had no idea of the time. It could be two or three in the morning for all he knew. It made no difference. They could keep him here for a day, two days, a month even, but they had to let him out eventually. Nick stood up, pacing around the room. *As soon as I get out of here, between the drinking, I'm going to rip that professor apart with my bare hands. I don't care if they send me down for killing the bugger. There's nothing worth living for anyway.*

A noise. He turned round. The door had already been opened. Laura walked in, with Marlow a few paces behind her. She looked strained, tired. There were lines around her eyes, and her make-up had faded.

'We're going to make you a deal,' she said, looking sharply at Nick.

Nick looked straight back. 'Piss off,' he spat. 'There's nothing you can do for me any more.'

Marlow stepped up close to him. 'I've already told you to watch your damned language, man.'

Chris Ryan

Nick turned away, his expression sullen. Just swallow your pride, he warned himself. Take as much of their crap as you have to so you can get out of this place.

'As it happens, there might be quite a lot that we can do for you,' said Laura archly. She sat down behind the desk, glancing at the TV screen. 'Take a seat.'

'I'll stand,' snapped Nick.

'She said, take a seat,' said Marlow.

He sighed, then sat down. 'Do you have any idea whether Sarah is alive or dead?'

'That's what we need to discuss.'

Nick could feel his pulse racing. *Maybe there was hope after all?*

Laura picked up a remote control from inside the desk. She pointed it towards the TV and flicked a button. The news channel disappeared from the screen, and was replaced by a grainy piece of black-and-white footage. Nick recognised it at once, even though it was clear the technology had advanced a lot since he'd last seen a set of pictures like these. A satellite image, he told himself. *And at a rough guess, I'd say the bird was pointing at Iraq.*

'This is a research plant in the suburbs of Baghdad,' said Laura. 'From what we know, this is where we think Sarah was taken —'

'You bloody knew where she was,' interrupted Nick.

Laura glared at him. 'Like I said, we *think* she was there.'

She flicked the remote again. Another series of images flashed on to the screen, showing various shots of the compound. They were black and white again, and there

293

293

were some small clouds obscuring the view, but Nick could clearly make out a chemical plant with a large spherical orb at its centre, and next to that an admin block surrounded by military vehicles. 'We ordered a missile strike for earlier this evening –'

'You did what?' snapped Nick.

'Let her finish,' said Marlow.

Nick tried to control his anger. Every instinct in his body told him to reach out and break her neck with his bare hands, but he knew he had to contain himself. *That's not going to do me any good. Or Sarah.*

'Listen, I know this is going to be tough for you to hear, but it's important, so I'm just going to carry on,' said Laura. 'We believe Sarah was in that plant, and we believe she was about to give them important scientific information. Information, remember, which could make Saddam Hussein the most powerful man in the Middle East. We can't allow that to happen. So we arranged for a missile strike to take out the plant. So as not to cause too much suspicion in the rest of the world, or among the Iraqis, we disguised the strike by launching a more general attack on Baghdad. The media are calling it "Shock and Awe" because that's the briefing they're getting. They think it's an attempt to kill Saddam Hussein. But it's not that at all. We're well aware that Saddam almost certainly isn't in Baghdad, and if he is, he's buried so deep in a bunker that a cruise missile isn't going to find him. We were just trying to destroy the plant where Sarah was being held prisoner.'

'And kill my daughter –'

294

'This is war, Nick,' said Marlow. 'You're a soldier, you know that individual lives don't count.'

'Sarah's not a soldier,' said Nick.

Marlow shrugged. 'Lots of people lose their children in wartime,' he said. 'You've seen that plenty of times. Their families take the news with dignity and pride because they know it's for the good of their country.'

'Or the good of some intelligence agency.'

'Drop it,' said Laura. 'You two can debate the ethics of war on your own bloody time. It doesn't matter right now, because there is a good chance that if she was in the compound Sarah survived.'

Nick looked at her closely. For the first time in hours, days, he could feel a few fragile embers of hope sparking to life within him. 'Alive . . . ?'

Laura nodded.

'What kind of missiles did you use?'

'Paveways,' said Laura.

'How many pounds?'

'Two thousand.'

Nick flinched. He'd seen a 2,000-pound Paveway land on a building during the first Iraq War, and if you hadn't been told otherwise, you'd have thought it was a nuclear strike. 'Nothing can survive that,' he said flatly. 'Don't even think about it.'

Laura turned towards the screen. She clicked on the remote control, bringing up another grainy black-and-white image. With two more clicks of the remote, she enlarged the image. It was starting to take shape before Nick's eyes. A road. He could see that clearly. And the roof of a van. He looked towards the plant. It was undamaged. That picture was taken before the missile strike, he realised. *The van was escaping.*

'This picture was taken from the satellite one minute before the missile strike,' said Laura.

She glanced at Nick, then flicked the remote control once more. Another picture flashed on to the screen. Enlarged twice over, the image started to take shape. The van was another two hundred yards down the road. And behind it, there was a huge fireball exploding out of the plant.

'And this picture was taken thirty seconds after the strike.' She turned back to at Nick. 'As you can see, the van escaped unhurt. We think Sarah may have been inside it.'

Nick paused for a moment. A hundred different thoughts were raging inside his head, and he needed a few seconds to straighten them out. 'You think she was in that van? Or you *know* . . . ?'

A fraction of a second passed before Laura replied. 'We *think*. . .' she said slowly. 'All the intelligence coming out of Iraq is pretty shaky now. But they were clearly taking something valuable out of that plant in the few minutes before the missile strike. We reckon Sarah was the most valuable thing they had in there.' She shrugged. 'So it figures she may well have been in the van.'

'It's just a small van,' said Marlow. 'But from the look of the picture it has some kind of armour plating on it. It's not big enough to carry any kind of serious industrial kit, so that means . . .'

Nick leant forward on the desk. His breathing was slow and measured. 'Then you have to get her out,' he said. 'If there's a chance she's still alive, you have to go and get her.'

'Exactly,' said Laura. She hesitated, looking first at Marlow, then back at Nick. 'In fact, we'd like you to do it.'

Nick didn't reply. He'd expected a dozen different forms of betrayal from the Firm, but he hadn't expected that.

'If she's alive, and somewhere in Iraq, then we have to find her,' Laura continued. 'So we have a proposition for you. We'll drop you into Iraq, and give you all the kit and backup you need. You find her for us, and bring her out.'

'You've got a whole army out there, just waiting on the Kuwait border,' said Nick suspiciously. 'Why me?'

Marlow perched himself on the edge of the desk, and looked down at Nick. 'If Sarah is inside that van, and the war has already started, then I reckon there's just one place they will take her.'

'Where?'

Even as he asked the question, Nick sensed he already knew the answer.

'Into the cells underneath the Republican Palace.' A frown creased up Marlow's forehead before he continued. 'There is only one man who has been there and come out alive,' he continued. 'That's you. And that makes you the best man for the job. You're the only guy who knows his way around the place.'

'It's my daughter,' said Nick. 'If she's there, you don't need to ask me twice.'

Marlow rested a hand on his shoulder. 'Just try and get it right this time, old boy,' he said, a thin smile spreading across his lips as he spoke. 'It would be a shame if your daughter had to die the same way some of your mates did the last time around. And all because you weren't able to take a bit of a beating . . .'

His voice trailed off, but Nick could already feel the anger welling up inside him. Nobody really knew what had happened to him in Iraq, but Marlow had a better idea of the truth than most people. 'I'll be fine,' he snapped. 'Just give me the kit, and I'll get her back.' He looked at Laura. 'I'm getting her back for myself,' he said. 'Not for you. And I'm on my own payroll. I'm not working for the Firm again, and I'm not signing back on for the Regiment.'

'We've got some transport going out to Kuwait tonight,' said Laura. 'There are planes shuttling out there all the time. We'll get you to RAF Northolt, and take you out there. Then we'll drop you into Iraq tomorrow night.'

Nick stood up. 'I'm ready to go.' he said.

TWENTY-FOUR

Jed looked out across the open road. He could smell the diesel in the air, and see the embers of tracer fire streaked across the night sky. About a mile ahead of him, a column of tanks was rolling down the highway. He could hear the thunderous noise of their heavy tracks creaking across the tarmac.

Nobody in their right mind is going to stay in this city over the next few days.

The tanks were mostly T-55s – big, ugly Russian-designed machines that had first been manufactured as a replacement for the World War II T-34s. They had later been manufactured in their tens of thousands by the Czechs and the Chinese, and sold to regimes around the world. There was nothing elegant about the design, but there didn't need to be. The T-55 was a brutal killing machine. Weighting thirty-six tonnes, it could still move at almost forty miles an hour when it was revved up to full speed, and its main 100mm D-10 rifle gun could loose off enough firepower to take out a small village. The Americans like to joke about the Iraqi kit, thought Jed, and it was true that it wasn't a match for their own armour. *But the T-55*

*was still going to kill anything that came within five hundred
yards of it.*

Jed shut the door on the blue Toyota, and started to
drive. It was at least seven miles to RVP, and he didn't
reckon his chances of getting across the city on foot
were more than fifty-fifty. They weren't much higher in
the car, but at least he'd save himself some boot leather.
He'd spent the night curled up in the sewers, then spent
most of the day there as well. There was no point in
trying to get anywhere: he just had to kill time until he
was lifted out of the country, and he was safer underground than anywhere else. When dusk fell, he emerged
from a manhole cover, and slipped silently through the
streets to retrieve the Toyota. It was three blocks away,
a distance of five hundred yards from his hiding place.
Miraculously, the car was where he had left it the
previous day, but you could see the devastation from the
first wave of allied attacks all around. Smoke was still
rising from smouldering fires, and the population was
cowed and afraid, with hardly anyone on the streets. At
the road junctions, soldiers were digging gun emplacements and throwing up barricades.

He fired the ignition, and started to drive. His route
would take him out of the city the same way they'd
come in. He'd take Highway 8 out to the south of the
city, switch on to Highway 1, then drop down off the
road into the patch of wasteland where the chopper was
coming in. Be a nice simple run on a quiet Sunday afternoon, Jed thought as he kicked the Toyota up into third
gear. On day two of a war, it would be a drive into hell.

It was just after seven at night. He had four hours to make the pickup. Plenty, he told himself. *So long as the buggers don't start shooting at me.* A mile or so behind him, the plant was still spitting thick clouds of black smoke up into the air, but the Iraqis no longer seemed to be trying to put the fires out. Too many of the bloody things, thought Jed. *And not long before the next wave of missile strikes begins.*

Dusk had already fallen, and as he drove up the slip route on to Highway 8, the road was virtually clear. There was one truck further up the road, but whether it was civilian or military Jed couldn't tell. *We should try sending a few cruise missiles along the M4*, thought Jed. *At least it would help clear the traffic.*

Keeping to the slow lane, Jed pumped the accelerator. The Toyota's engine roared, spluttered, but the power picked up, pushing the speed to over fifty miles an hour. *The sooner I get there the better*, he told himself. Glancing up, he checked the night sky. *No sign of incoming missiles, but that didn't mean they wouldn't come later. We might be planning to bomb our way to victory, just the way we did against the Serbs*, he thought. *And even if we aren't, they're bound to send in a few cruises tonight. Bringing a chopper down in hostile territory is dangerous at the best of times. By sending in some incoming missile fire, you could distract and confuse the Iraqis enough to allow the chopper to slip through. It doesn't matter whether they hit their targets last night*, Jed thought. *These poor buggers are going to see some more missiles tonight anyway.*

At least I'll be getting my head down safely in a barracks in Kuwait tonight. It shouldn't take more than an hour and a half for a Black Hawk to fly down to the border. It'll be just after midnight local time when we touch down at the base. Time to get a shower and some decent grub, maybe a beer if I can find one. I can give Nick a call and see if there's any sign of Sarah. Then I'll just have to wait and see where they send me next – and start thinking about what I'll say to Matt, Rob and Steve's families.

He glanced in the mirror. It was another mile to the junction with Highway 1, and then another two miles to the pickup point. A jeep was following him in the nearside lane, about five hundred yards back. 'Shit,' Jed muttered. It was impossible to tell whether it was following him, or just using the road. He gunned the accelerator, coaxing the Toyota up to sixty. Another glance in the mirror. The jeep was picking up speed as well. Jed couldn't tell what make it was, but even the Russian-made vehicles had big diesel engines that were capable of up to eighty miles an hour. Jed had no idea how fast the Toyota would go if you really pushed it. More than a hundred when it was new, but this machine was a wreck, patched together with pirated parts. It was a miracle it went at all.

He pressed harder on the accelerator, taking it past seventy. Behind, the jeep was still gaining. It was maybe three hundred yards behind him now. Then two hundred. The jeep pulled out into the outer lane. It was still accelerating. Jed slammed his foot down on to the floor. Got to outrun them, he told himself. There's a curfew in this city, and they are shooting people on sight. They certainly aren't going to stop and ask me what they hell I'm doing out on the road at this time of night. *And if they do, they won't like the answers.*

The engine on the Toyota roared, then lost power. Jed took his foot off the juice, then tried it again. The rev counter was swinging around wildly, but although the engine was turning, the power wasn't getting through to the wheels. His speed was dropping back to sixty, then fifty. The jeep was closing fast in the outside lane. Jed checked the mirror. The driver was flashing him with his lights. Pull over, that's what he's telling me. *No bloody way, mate.*

He took his foot off the accelerator again, then pressed it even harder. This time a surge of power came up from the engine, taking him back up to sixty. Jed reckoned it was less than half a mile now to the junction. Maybe he could lose them there. Somewhere down in the city, he could hear the sound of gunfire. Anti-aircraft fire was sporadically lighting up the night sky but, so far, he could neither hear any aircraft nor see any missiles. The jeep was pulling up alongside him now. Jed glanced towards the side. The driver was leaning towards the passenger-side window, signalling for him to pull over to the hard shoulder. Jed shrugged, ignoring him. Play stupid, he told himself. Pretend you are just a fright-ened commuter trying to get home before the bombs start falling again. Maybe they'll take pity on you.

The jeep pulled ahead of him, cutting into the lane,

and slowing down. 'Bugger,' muttered Jed. He swerved the Toyota into the outer lane, and gunned the accelerator, but the engine was over-revving and the power wasn't coming through. He could smell burning rubber from the engine.

Right ahead of him, he could see a soldier leaning out of the back of the truck. He was holding an AK-47 in his hand, and pointing it straight at the Toyota. 'Fuck,' said Jed. He swerved the car out into the far lane, the tyres screeching against the tarmac as he did so. The marksman fired once, then twice. Jed felt the impact of one bullet hitting the bonnet of the car, another slashing into the tyre. The Toyota skidded across the road. Jed gripped the wheel, trying to bring it back under control. The car was losing power fast – glancing down, Jed could see the speedometer dropping below forty, then thirty. Another round of gunfire exploded from the back of the jeep. Jed could see a couple of rounds pinging off the surface of the road. Then there was a crash, as the windscreen exploded. He could feel tiny shards of glass colliding with his face, and instinctively his hands flew up to stop anything slicing his eyes. The car skidded wildly. His hands shot out to grab hold of the wheel again, and as he opened his eyes, he could see through the cracked and broken windscreen that he was heading straight into the crash barrier on the side of the road. He yanked hard on the wheel, the muscles straining in his shoulder as he struggled hard to straighten the car up. With his foot, he slammed hard on the brake. His hand shot down to grab hold of the handbrake, pulling it hard upwards. The car screeched, the tyres melting on the surface of the road, as it struggled to get a grip. Its speed was slowing, dropping through thirty, towards twenty miles an hour. Jed pulled harder on the hand-brake.

Too bloody late, he told himself. *Ready yourself for a bruising, man.*

Looking ahead, the jeep was accelerating away from him. The sniper loosened off another few rounds from his AK-47, but his aim was poor, and the bullets were just digging into the surface of the tarmac. Jed's own gun was in his kitbag on the passenger seat, and he knew there was no point in trying to grab it and fire back. There was no time.

In the next instant, the side of the Toyota collided with the crash barrier. The machine shuddered and shook, and the air was suddenly filled with the ugly noise of metal smashing against metal. Sparks were flying everywhere, spitting up into the air. Jed felt the force of the collision first in his spine, as he was thrown back deep into the car seat. The crash barrier was ripping the right-hand side of the car to pieces: the door had come off and so had half the front bonnet. Jed could feel himself being thrown violently forward. He gripped the wheel to try and stop himself, but the force of the impact was too strong, and his head was thrown against the wheel, then into the broken window. He could feel a piece of glass snagging on to his jaw, ripping into the flesh. A trickle of warm blood started to flow down his neck.

As the car came to a halt, Jed lay still for a moment. 'Fucking craphole of a country,' he muttered, as he climbed out of the car.

He looked anxiously up the road. The jeep had long since disappeared into the distance, and for the moment the highway was empty. The buggers are just enforcing their curfew by shooting at anyone who happens to be on the road, he thought. They don't care who they are, and can't even be bothered to check whether they're dead or not. What kind of an army is that? *One on the edge of desperation* . . .

The Toyota was finished. Half the engine had been crushed in the collision, and the glass from the wind-screen had skidded across the road, along with one wheel. Jed reached inside for his bag, and pulled out a first-aid kit. He splashed some alcohol onto the wound in his cheek, wincing as the raw spirit stung every nerve in his face. He stretched out a strip of plaster, and used it to patch himself up.

Beneath the highway there was a patch of wasteland, with big concrete pylons supporting the road dug deep into it. In the distance, Jed could hear the rumble of a military convoy. Whether it was tanks or trucks it was impossible to say. Makes no difference, he told himself. I've met enough of those buggers for one day.

With his kitbag on his shoulder, Jed hopped across the barrier and climbed down on to the open ground. It was dark now, and there was a layer of clouds black-ening the sky, but the occasional burst of anti-aircraft fire provided sporadic bursts of illumination. Jed started walking across the scrubland. Two more miles to go, he told himself. I don't want to miss that chopper. It's the last train home. *If I'm not on it, I'm a dead man.*

Nick looked down on the countryside unfolding below him. The Black Hawk had been flying low for an hour now, making its way upcountry from Kuwait. It was twisting close to the ground, flying beneath the radar – a technique Nick recognised from the last time he'd been dropped into the country. Hovering low to the ground, he could see the blackened-out villages and townships that covered the road from Basra up to Baghdad, and although the pilot was keeping well away from the main road, off in the distance he could see the lights from the military convoys taking up their positions for the coming battle.

'Christ,' he muttered. 'I swore I'd never come back to this bloody hellhole.'

Nick had been travelling non-stop for almost twenty-four hours now. From the Firm's office in Vauxhall, he had been led out to an unmarked van that had driven him to RAF Northolt on the M40 heading out of London. A military transport jet had already been fuelled and was ready to go. There could have been a hundred men on board, but Nick wasn't counting. Marlow came with him for the seven-hour flight to Kuwait. He grabbed a couple of hours' sleep on the plane, but had been woken up by some heavy turbulence over the Mediterranean.

By the time they touched down, there had just been

time for a wash, some food and then a briefing with the local commanders who had a better assessment of the situation on the ground, before he was bundled into the Black Hawk for take-off. The commanders didn't know much, as it turned out. A massive missile strike had been launched against Baghdad the night before, but how much damage had been done to the city, to the military infrastructure or to Saddam's command and control systems, it was still unclear. 'You mean nobody's got a sodding clue?' Nick had said to the young American staffer showing him the satellite images of central Baghdad. The man had stiffened, then relaxed. 'That's a pretty accurate summary,' he had replied.

Nothing changes, thought Nick grimly. They sit behind their desks, firing off missiles, then they send in some guys like me to find out what happens. *The computers might get smarter, but the people behind them are as thick as ever.*

'Ready for touchdown in two minutes,' said the pilot into the headphones Nick had on his head.

He glanced at the door of the Black Hawk. The chopper hit the ground hard, and the pilot was shouting in his ears to get out of the machine. Nick's stomach was heaving: he'd never liked choppers much, and staying close to the ground meant the Black Hawk swayed around like a boat on rough seas. There were two pilots, plus one soldier in the back, but otherwise Nick was alone. They had kitted him out with basic survival tools: medical supplies, an AK-47, a pistol, a dozen grenades, a hunting knife, some food and a satphone. They had also given him a couple of Iraqi Army uniforms taken from the deserters already streaming across the frontier: they might be the best way of travelling through Iraq. Otherwise, it was up to him. Go in there, and get her out, those were the instructions. How you do it is up to you.

Well, I hate to admit it, but the buggers are right about one thing. *If anyone can get Sarah out of there, it's me.*

Nick unstrapped the seat belt, throwing his kitbag over his shoulder. The soldier opened the door, and a sudden blast of hot air ripped through the machine.

'Go! Go!' shouted the soldier.

Nick pushed himself forward. The air was rushing through the open door. He gripped the metal frame of the Black Hawk, and glanced down. The swirling blades of the machine had kicked up a cloud of dust, blasting it up into the air. It spat into his face. For a moment, Nick's mind flashed back more than a decade, to the day he was released from an Iraqi jail and put on a chopper to lift him out of the country. He could remember taking one last look, and promising himself that whatever else might happen he would never again set foot in this brutal wreck of a country. Bugger it, he muttered as he pushed himself away from the door into the open air. Promises are there to be broken. Soldiering is the one thing in my life I was actually good at, whatever they say about me. *Here goes.*

He hit the ground with a thud. His legs smashed into the sand, and he immediately rolled his body to take the impact. The dust was flying everywhere. He could hear the roar of the throttle being opened up on the Black Hawk, and the hurricane raging around him intensified as the pilot put maximum power into the machine's blades. Looking up, Nick could see the Black Hawk accelerating into the air. I'm on my own now, he thought.

Nick reached out for his kitbag, grabbed hold of it and started to pick himself up from the ground. He'd taken a couple of bruises to the ribs, but the landing hadn't been too bad. The chopper had brought him down in a patch of wasteland, within a hollow surrounded by a series of ridges. In the distance, he could see the highway curving down towards central Baghdad. And in front of him, he could see a man running towards him.

Jed.

'Where the fuck's that chopper going?' Jed was shouting. 'Where the fuck's it going?'

Nick shrugged. 'Home.'

Jed stood with his mouth open, following the arc of the chopper as it soared up in to the sky, and disappeared towards the south. Then he turned towards Nick. 'What the fuck are you doing here?' he spat, his tone angry.

'Giving you your orders, mate,' said Nick.

'You're not a bloody officer. You're not even in the army.'

'Don't need to be, son.'

'You can fuck off, then.'

Nick put a hand out on Jed's shoulder, but it was instantly pushed away. 'Listen,' he said. 'A Black Hawk has just dropped me down here. The Iraqis may have the stupidest excuse for an army that's ever been assembled, but even those clowns can spot an enemy helicopter hovering a couple of miles outside their capital city.' He paused, then started walking towards a ridge that ran through the wasteland and up to the concrete girders of the highway. 'Now we can stand around here chatting all day and wait for a truckload of sodding ragheads to come along and start shooting us, or we can get our arses into gear and start moving out of here.'

'They said they were picking me up to take me home,' said Jed.

Nick laughed. 'Why, you homesick for your mum?' he said. 'So they lied to you. Get used to it.'

Jed hesitated. It took a moment, but it was starting to sink in. Laura hadn't told him to meet the chopper here because they were planning to pick him up. It was because they wanted him to hook up with Nick. But why the hell did they want the old bastard back in Iraq? He was useless enough in Britain.

'So just what are you doing here exactly?'

'Looking for Sarah,' said Nick flatly.

Jed stopped in his tracks. 'Sarah?'

'Is there a bloody echo around here?' said Nick.

Jed remained rooted to the spot. The Black Hawk had long since disappeared above the clouds, and the scrubland had fallen completely silent. 'Sarah's in Iraq?'

Nick nodded. 'So I'm told,' he replied gruffly. He

311

turned round, and started marching towards the ridge again. 'Like I said, if we don't get our arses out of here, the Iraqis are going to be serving our balls up for Saddam Hussein's breakfast. Now, how the fuck do we get out of here? And how the hell do we get into Baghdad?'

Jed shook his head. 'Christ,' he muttered. 'What the hell did I do to deserve this?'

'Search me,' said Nick. 'Now, which way to Baghdad? Or do I have to hail a bloody taxi?'

Jed jerked his hand to the east. 'Big dirty-looking place in that direction,' he said. 'Keep walking, and if you get lost, just follow a missile. You'll find it OK.'

Nick turned round to look at him. 'So, are you coming?' he said.

TWENTY-FIVE

Jed crouched down by the side of the concrete pylon. About fifty feet above him, he could hear the heavy rumble of a tank moving across the tarmac surface of the road. He glanced at Nick. 'You reckon we rest?' he asked.

Nick shook his head. 'While it's night, we keep walking.'

Jed checked his watch. It was just after two. They had been walking for more than an hour already, going first through open wasteland, then snaking alongside Highway 8 which ran up towards the Tigris and then into the centre of the city. When the road dipped down so it was level with the ground, they moved out five hundred yards to make sure they were out of range of the headlamps of any vehicles moving along it. Where the highway was raised above the road on pylons, they moved underneath it, keeping within the shadows of the concrete. Occasionally they heard the roar of a passing vehicle above them. At other times, the rattle of anti-aircraft fire. They counted six missile strikes on the city as they walked, each one marked by a brilliant electric flash as it exploded. But it was quiet compared with last night.

'I don't suppose you brought any grub with you,' said Jed.

'Some biscuits,' said Nick. 'A few chocolate bars and some of the Yank MREs.'

'No chance of a bacon sarnie, then,' said Jed.

'In your dreams, mate,' said Nick.

Jed shrugged. He already had some biscuits and some water in his kitbag. He stopped to take a swig from his bottle, then started moving again. This part of the journey was easy enough. Getting into the centre would be a lot more difficult. And finding Sarah and getting her out again might be virtually impossible.

I've watched three men die there already. I wouldn't be surprised to watch a couple more.

Along the way, Nick had explained what had happened, at least so far as he knew. Sarah had been lifted into Iraq, and was being held captive here. Jed was furious when he learnt that the missile strike he'd directed into the plant had really been designed to kill the woman he loved. Even by the standards of the Firm, that seemed a shocking decision. The only consolation he could find was that she had escaped: if he hadn't spotted the van moving out of the plant, the Firm would have assumed she was dead, and Sarah would be rotting inside some Iraqi jail, with no hope of escape. At least this way, they'd sent somebody to get her out again.

'Why the hell did they send you, then?' said Jed.

'I'm her dad, and I know this country,' said Nick. 'God knows when the ground troops might make their way up to Baghdad. They might be cruel bastards over in Vauxhall, but they aren't stupid. They want Sarah back, and you and I are the best two men to find her.' He paused, looking across at Jed. 'Well, one of us is anyway.'

'Right,' said Jed gruffly.

They were approaching the inner circle of the city now. Jed checked his watch. Three fifteen. He reckoned they had another couple of hours before the sun started to rise, and the city started to come to life. There was a strict curfew, and if an army patrol saw them, they would certainly be shot on sight, but if they stuck to the side streets, moved through the shadows, and kept well away from any moving vehicles, they had a chance. Much of the army looked to have been moved to the outskirts of the city already, working on its defences, and some of the troops would have already headed south to meet the expected invasion, so there were fewer men left to patrol Baghdad. That would work to their advantage. *They just had to make sure they were cautious every step of the way.*

Keeping at least five yards apart, they carried on walking. A couple of times as they made their way through the industrial suburbs they heard military vehicles approaching, but by ducking into alleyways they managed to avoid being noticed. Two fires were raging where missiles had struck near the centre of the city, and the orange glow of the flames fanned out across the town, but apart from that, there seemed to be a strict blackout in force. All the windows were shuttered and the lights switched off. It was harder to find your way, particularly on the narrow side streets, but it also gave them more cover. In the darkness, two men in black clothes who didn't want to be seen could get hidden easily enough.

By four in the morning, they had hit the banks of the Tigris. Jed knelt down by the water and dipped his fingers into the fast-flowing water. It felt colder than he remembered it, and dirtier as well; at least one bridge had been taken out in the missile strikes the previous night, filling the water with swirling debris that was still floating past more than twenty-four hours later. They were about a mile downstream from where they had attempted the crossing last time: Jed could still vividly remember the look of agony on Rob's face as they left him.

'It's a decade since I was last here and it still looks like crap,' said Nick.

'One of our boys died here,' said Jed.

'How?' asked Nick gruffly.

'We were trying to get across in a boat,' said Jed. 'We were spotted from the bridge and came under heavy fire. Rob was wounded and there was nothing we could do for the poor sod.'

'A boat,' spluttered Nick. 'Christ, what's the matter with you boys? Afraid of getting your hair wet, are you?'

'What the hell are we meant to do?' said Jed. 'Swim across?'

Nick was already stripping off his shirt, and taking off his heavy boots. He knelt down, packing both items into his kitbag, then slung it over his back and started walking across the pebbles that led down into the water.

Fuck, thought Jed. He's serious about swimming this thing. 'Listen,' he hissed. 'I've been in this bastard of a river once already. The currents are stronger than you can imagine.'

Nick turned to look at him. The water was already up to his waist, and already swirling around him. 'My daughter's on the other side of that river somewhere, and I'm the only bugger who's likely to help her,' he said, the grim resolve evident in the tone of his voice. 'There isn't a boat, and even if there was, it would be a lot easier to spot than a man swimming alone. The bridges are going to be guarded. That means the only way across is to swim, and if I sink to the bottom, well, at least I'll have tried.' He paused, turning round and wading deeper into the river. 'But if you're afraid, then you just stay right there.'

Sod it, thought Jed. The old bugger is even crazier than I thought. 'Let's do it properly,' he muttered. He stripped off his shirt, and tucked his boots into his kitbag. The bags needed as much buoyancy as possible to help keep them afloat. They strapped the rifles on to the top of the bags then slung a rope between them to keep them together. That way, they wouldn't lose each other in the river.

Jed scanned the surface of the river, but it looked quiet enough. They were at least a mile from any of the bridges, and although there were some boats moored about three hundred yards upstream, they looked as if they were empty. It was, he judged, about five hundred yards across the river at this point, but from what he

317

knew of it, the swell and currents would be dangerous, taking them a long way downstream before they managed to hit the safety of the opposite shore.

Nick had already plunged into the water, kicking forward with a series of powerful strokes. Jed followed in his wake. The water felt freezing cold against his skin, and his feet were sinking deep into the mud and slime of the riverbed. He was determined to stay on his feet for as long as possible: he was a strong swimmer, but it was a good distance across and he needed to conserve his strength. As the water swirled up around his neck, Jed kicked up with his feet and started to swim, using all the muscles in his shoulders and legs to propel himself swiftly along. Nick was close by, holding on to his kitbag and making solid progress. The swimming was easy enough, Jed found. The swells were helping to keep him afloat, while the current was no major obstacle. *Not yet, anyway.*

Within minutes he had covered the first hundred yards, then two hundred. He was close to the centre of the river now. A burst of anti-aircraft fire exploded from one of the gun emplacements staggered along the bank of the Tigris, briefly filling the sky with showers of green and yellow light, but when that died down the river was shrouded in darkness. A sudden wave was kicked up by a distant explosion, hitting Jed in the side with the force of a hammer. His grip loosened on the rope, and he could feel himself being carried away from it.

'Nick,' he shouted.

Nothing.

As he recovered, Jed started swimming again. He suddenly realised he could no longer see the shoreline he had swum from, nor the one he was swimming towards. He could see Nick, just, still ploughing ahead of him, maybe twenty-five yards away, but otherwise nothing. He was completely surrounded by water. There was no way of knowing how far he had come, or how far he still had to swim. The current was picking up strength. All rivers have their own streams and flow, Jed reminded himself. On the Tigris, the strong currents were all on the north side of the river. The water was pushing harder into him now, and the strokes were becoming more difficult. He was pulling his arms through the water, but like a boxer whose blood was up, the river was now fighting back. For every five yards he moved forward, he was being dragged another yard downstream. The debris from the missile strikes had been caught up in the stronger currents and was swirling past him. A chunk of wood caught Jed in the ribs, pushing him off balance. A sheet of plastic snagged on to his legs, and had to be kicked away. His hands were catching on rubbish as he tried to push himself further forwards, and on the surface of the Tigris there was a thickening layer of foam and dirt.

Jed could feel himself tiring. His muscles were aching, and his breath was starting to shorten. Looking ahead, he'd lost sight of Nick. The old man had been some yards ahead, but he must have been dragged downstream. Or under. It was impossible to tell. He took a deep breath, and put his head down, trying to swim underwater for a few yards, avoiding the debris. As he burst back up to the surface, he could feel the thick foam sticking to his hair, as if he had been dipped in slime. Taking a lungful of air, he looked around. The water was pitch black. Nothing. Not even a glimpse of the shore. 'Nick,' he hissed. 'Where the fuck are you, man?'

Jed paused, waiting for the reply, and sensing this was way beyond him. He could feel the water closing around him, and for a moment he felt cold with fear. 'Where the fuck are you?' he repeated, risking raising his voice.

Silence.

He kicked his legs hard into the water to propel himself forward. A twitch. Jed could feel it in the back of his thigh. 'Bugger,' he muttered. He'd had cramp before, and knew how to recognise its first signs. He could make another hundred yards, but not much more. He looked ahead, peering into the darkness. He'd lost track of how far he'd come, and how far he still had to go. There were no lights visible from either shore, no matter how hard he looked. Maybe the debris has knocked me off course, Jed told himself grimly. *Fuck it, I might even be swimming the wrong direction by now.*

Reaching out, Jed grabbed at a large object floating by. He needed something to keep himself afloat, so he could use all his strength to kick back with his legs and propel himself forward. He gripped it with both hands, steadied himself, then pushed out. The cramp in his leg was starting to ache, the pain creeping up into his back, but he still had movement. Ignore it, he told himself. Succumb to the pain, and you're a dead man.

Jed looked at the object he was clinging on to. A glassy eye was staring back at him, cold and sad and dead. Shit, he thought. I'm holding on to one of the corpses the Iraqis have tossed into the river. The body was bloated, the stomach and lungs waterlogged and swollen, allowing it to float easily on the surface of the river. His hands were gripping the man's stomach. The skin was peeling away, and the body smelt of a vile mixture of decomposing eggs and rotten meat. It was slimy to the touch, and the single eye looking back at him was already starting to loosen from its socket. The smell was making Jed's stomach heave, but he had to hold on tight to the body, his nose just a few inches away from the decomposing intestines.

He kicked furiously with his legs to push himself forward. In the next instant, a burst of anti-aircraft fire lit up the sky. Through the hazy blue light thrown up by the guns Jed could see a shape. It was like a thin, wavy line looming up out of the darkness. A shoreline.

Land.

It was eighty yards away, he judged. One more heave, and I can make it.

'Jed,' shouted Nick.

Jed's head spun round. The older man was thirty yards downstream, clutching on to what looked like a piece of a sentry hut that must have been blown off the destroyed bridge.

'Meet me by the riverbank,' he yelled.

A furious light suddenly illuminated the city, as if a bulb had been turned on in a dark room. Jed realised a missile had just struck. Maybe two miles downstream. You saw the light first, then waited a few seconds for the sound of rolling thunder to reach you. Jed kicked. Sixty yards to go. The noise of the missile strike suddenly hit the river, followed by a wave that rolled along its surface. The water rolled up over the corpse, and over Jed's head, briefly submerging him. As he came to the surface again, he took a deep breath. He'd swallowed some of the water that was seeping out of the corpse, and his stomach was heaving. He kicked once again. Thirty more yards now, he told himself. That's all.

A fire was burning a couple of miles downstream. It was impossible to say from here what the missile had struck, but whatever it was, it had set off some impressive fireworks. An oil depot maybe, thought Jed. Or a munitions dump. Sparks and flames were leaping up into the sky, spreading a dull orange glow across the city, and Jed could already hear the sound of sirens as fire trucks rushed towards it.

Ten more yards. Jed pushed the corpse away, and dug his arms into the water to move himself forward. Seven yards . . . Six.

He thrust his legs down, looking for the ground. It felt sticky and muddy, but he was grateful to have anything he could stand up in. Wading, Jed completed the last few yards of the journey, throwing himself down on the pebbled shoreline. For a moment, he just lay on the ground, exhausted and frozen, breathing deeply as he tried to recover his breath.

'What the hell are we hanging around for?' said Nick, standing over him. 'A bus?'

Jed slowly picked himself up: every muscle in his body was aching and frozen. Reaching into his kitbag, he took out some water, swilling it around his mouth and spitting it out to clean the river from his mouth.

'Christ, man, don't waste water,' said Nick. 'Maybe we'll see if they've got a nice hotel you can check into.'

Jed looked up. Nick looked in as bad shape as he did. His hair was covered with a thick layer of greasy foam, and his veins were blue and bulging out of his skin. There were some cuts and splinters to his hands, where he had been hanging on to the wood, and which could well turn septic if he didn't clean them up properly. He had no top, and no shoes, and water was still dripping from his trousers: even the clothes in the kitbag would be wet through.

'We've got an hour of darkness left,' Nick persisted. 'Let's move while we still can.'

Jed pulled his top back on, and slipped his boots on to his feet. Nick was already scrambling along the river-bank. There was a six-foot embankment that led directly on to the road running alongside the south bank of the Tigris. So far as Jed could see, there was no traffic, but two miles away he could see the flames rising up from the missile strike. Nick was already moving his hands along the slippery, wet walls of the embankment, looking for grips he could use to climb over it. 'Where the hell are you going now?' snapped Jed.

'To find Sarah,' said Nick grimly, not even looking round.

'Then get a fucking grip, man,' hissed Jed. 'You're running around like a bloody madman.'

'Maximum speed, maximum aggression, that's the Regiment way of doing things,' said Nick.

He turned away from the wall. Removing his kitbag from his back, he took out his boots and started to pull them on to his wet feet. He looked up at Jed. 'But maybe the Regiment's gone soft,' he said quietly. 'Maybe that's not the way things work any more.'

'There's plenty of bloody aggression,' said Jed. 'Just maybe a bit more brains as well. We need to think about what we're doing.'

'I'm in charge of this mission,' said Nick.

'Nobody's in sodding charge.'

'I'm twice your age, and I've got twice your balls as well.'

'You nearly got us both bloody killed trying to swim across that river,' growled Jed. 'Now you're about to charge into the centre of Baghdad half naked, just asking to get yourself shot. That's not bloody helping anyone, is it?'

Nick pulled his T-shirt over his head. Water from the river was still dripping from his chest. 'I'm in charge, and I say we get in there and start searching for Sarah.' He put his kitbag over his shoulder, and started hauling himself up the side of the embankment. 'Or we die trying.'

Jed dug his fingers angrily into a crevice in the wall. The skin scraped against the rock, and he could see some blood smearing against the side of his hand. He winced at the pain, then dug his fingers in harder, kicked his right foot into the wall and started to climb. Bugger it, he muttered under his breath. Unless the old sod calms down, he's going to get both of us killed before dawn. *And who's going to help Sarah once we're both dead?*

TWENTY-SIX

The presidential compound was clearly visible even from half a mile away. Jed stood at the side of the street, and glanced up at the building. Like an architectural oasis, it nestled into the banks of the Tigris, surrounded by tall palm trees and lush grasses. The main complex was surrounded by high, ornately carved colonnades, while inside there was a network of buildings and underground bunkers. At the centre, the huge green dome of the Republican Palace rose up into the sky, its polished surface glistening in the morning sun. Next to it, the high towers of the Palace of Peace and the Palace of Flowers, two massive administration blocks that housed the planners and staff officers of Saddam's regime.

Despite more than a hundred cruise missiles crashing into the city, the thing, although damaged is still standing, thought Jed. *And so is the bugger inside.*

He was standing next to Nick on the corner of a busy street. They had walked this morning from the Tigris, taking the two miles from where they had come ashore up to the edge of the presidential compound with extreme care. They kept to the backstreets, and walked separately to avoid drawing any more attention to themselves than they had to. The streets were in chaos. Glass had been shattered out of the shop windows, and was now lying in splinters all over the roads. Schools had been closed, and so had most of the offices and factories: only the military admin blocks were open. A few fires were still smouldering, and they passed dozens of damaged and burnt-out buildings. The fire service was concentrating on a handful of major missile strikes, while the rest were left to burn themselves out, or were brought under control by neighbours armed with nothing more than buckets of water. Most people were still hiding in their houses, but a few had started to drift out on to the streets, gawping like tourists at the slow destruction of their city.

'We're going in,' said Nick, nodding up towards the compound.

Jed laughed. 'You're a bloody madman.' Sod the Iraqis, he thought. The next man he was going to be taking out was Nick. 'You're just planning to knock on the door, say you're from Britain and ask to have a look around, are you?' he said.

Nick didn't answer. He was looking up and down the street. There were a few cars driving along, and a couple of shopkeepers were trying to reopen their businesses, even though there wasn't much to sell. On the other side of the street, a woman was shouting at passers-by, asking them if they had seen her husband. 'We'll find a way in,' he said. He turned to Jed. 'All I know is the Firm reckons Sarah's been taken into that compound, and if we want to find her, that's where we have to go. If you've got any better ideas, I'm listening.'

327

They started walking. In the rest of the city, law and order had been abandoned since the missile strikes began, but the presidential compound was still under close protection. There was a thick concrete and barbed-wire barrier two hundred yards out from the main ten-foot wall of the compound, and surrounding that was a circular cordon of army trucks, each one filled with a dozen or more troops. Some of them must be pretty badly shaken up by now, Jed reckoned, but none of them showed any signs of abandoning their positions. To get through, you'd need a fully equipped battalion, Jed thought. And even then, you'd have a nasty fight on your hands.

They walked the circumference of the compound, a distance of a mile and half in total. They kept a couple of side streets away to stop the troops paying any attention to them, but it was clear that there was no easy way through. There were no breaks in the line. And the Iraqis were building new defences all the time: at three different points, they saw sandbags and gun emplacements being dug into position for the defence of the city's inner ring. For all their bluster and bravado, it seemed to Jed that the Iraqi high command didn't rate their chances of holding the south of the country very highly. They might not even hold the outer ring of Baghdad for very long. But here at the compound, they'd make their last stand. *And it would almost certainly be a bloody one.*

Jed looked at Nick. 'Did you learn any Arabic during your last time here?'

Nick nodded, his expression grim. 'A few essential

phrases,' he said. '"Stop frying my balls, mate" and "Go easy with the thumbscrews, old fruit".' He smiled. 'That kind of thing.'

They were standing on one of the streets running away from the compound, about three hundred yards back from its first defensive perimeter. A few people had glanced in their direction, but Jed was surprised by how easily they could pass through the streets. Since the war started, the whole city was so wired up, tense and edgy, nobody appeared to be paying any attention to anything but themselves. So long as they kept their heads down, they should be OK.

The trouble was, that wasn't going to get them inside. *It wasn't going to help Sarah.*

'They're letting guys in and out,' said Jed, nodding towards the compound.

He'd been watching as they paced the outer ring of the compound. There could be ten thousand or more troops inside, a couple of battalions at least, and there was a constant stream of men pouring through the three main entrances. It was a working military and administrative headquarters, not a sealed camp. 'If they think you're Iraqi, they'll let you in.'

'The Firm's kitted us out with some uniforms,' said Nick. 'We're going in as soldiers – Iraqi soldiers, that is.' A sly grin spread out over his lips. 'We've just signed up for the Iraqi Army, mate,' he said. 'The pay's crap, the food is shit and none of the kit works. I reckon a couple of blokes like us will fit right in.'

★   ★   ★

The uniform was a poor fit, but that didn't matter to Jed. He pulled the camouflaged green trousers up around his waist, and tightened a notch on the cheap plastic belt to hold them in position. The tunic was just as baggy, made for a man with a much larger build, and the fabric was a cheap polyester that felt clammy and scratchy against the skin: at night, it wouldn't keep you warm, and in the heat of a battle you'd be sweating like a pig. Same with any army, thought Jed. You can always save a few quid or dinar by scrimping on the kit for the guys who do the actual fighting.

'You look like crap,' said Nick, a grin flashing up on his face.

They were hiding down a side street, in the store-room of an abandoned engineering workshop. They had walked back to within half a mile of the presidential compound and hunted around three of the back alleys before they found this workshop. The door had been blown out by a missile that had landed about five hundred yards away, and the owner must have abandoned the place in the fires and chaos that followed. As they stepped inside, you could still smell the axle oil and the cigarette smoke from the mechanics who worked here, but there was no sign of any of them this evening. Like everyone else, they had either fled to relatives in another part of the country, or hunkered down in their homes. *What was the point in coming into work when you didn't even know if the country would still be around in a few days' time?*

'I mean you *really* look like crap,' Nick continued.

'You've a filthy beard on you, and your hair looks like Cherie bloody Blair's on a bad day. Even by the standards of the Iraqi Army, you're a mess.' He reached into his kitbag, and tossed over a disposable razor, a bar of soap and a pair of scissors. 'Smarten yourself up, mate.'

The beard on Jed's face had a week of growth on it, and had turned into an ugly mess of hair. Nick attacked it with the razor, giving Jed a small cut on the side of his cheek: he claimed it was a slip of the hand, but it felt deliberate to Jed. A moustache was left behind. 'You look just like Saddam, mate,' said Nick when he'd finished.

'Leave it out,' said Jed.

There was a mirror in the workshop's loo, and he used that to sort his hair out, clipping it back into shape with the scissors. By the time he was done, he looked and felt a lot better. 'Aftershave,' said Nick, handing across a bottle containing a pale-looking yellow liquid. The top was still on it, but just holding it in his hand, Jed caught a whiff of a pungently scented mixture of dried fruit and disinfectant. 'I bought this for us at the market.'

Jed looked at him suspiciously. 'Why do you give a fuck what I smell like?' he said. 'We're going on a mission, not a date.'

'Iraqi bath,' said Nick, nodding towards the aftershave. 'Everyone knows the ragheads only wash in leap years. They put this stuff on to cover up the pong. You might look like an Iraqi soldier, but *smell* is the most sensitive of all the senses. You never heard that expression "smell a rat?" Well, you walk into that compound and you

331

don't smell like an Iraqi bugger, they're going to nick you right away.'

Experience, thought Jed. He might be a difficult old sod, but he's been here before. *There aren't many tricks to this trade that he hasn't learnt by now.*

He took the top off the bottle, poured a liberal dose of the aftershave on to his hands, and rubbed it into his face and neck. The stink was horrible. If we do find Sarah tonight, thought Jed, she'll probably tell me to bugger off home. *Who'd want to go out with a bloke who smelt of this stuff?*

'You scrub up lovely,' said Nick. 'Now, let's go.'

It was night by the time they stepped out into the alley. The curfew was tightly controlled, and the streets were empty. They probably don't need to tell people any more, thought Jed. Nobody's going to go out when the city is coming under sustained missile strikes.

It was a half-mile walk to their target. Of the three checkpoints where troops were going in and out of the presidential compound, they had chosen the one to the east as their point of entry. It was taking the most traffic: at least a couple of trucks a minute, several jeeps and dozens of men on foot patrols. It was the point where the guards were likely to be too busy to make many checks.

'You do realise the presidential compound has come under the most sustained missile attack of the whole bloody city,' said Jed, as they stepped on to the street leading down to the entrance. 'And I don't suppose our pals back at the Firm are organised enough to stop the missile attacks for a few hours while we're in there.'

332

'Stop bloody whingeing,' said Nick, with a shake of the head. 'You want a note from your mum saying you're not up for this one, then you go and get one.'

From the corner of his eye, Jed could see a Fedayeen officer walking on the other side of the street, the black tunic that marked out the most feared of Saddam's internal troops flapping in the early-evening breeze. The man looked at them suspiciously. Jed looked at the ground, and kept on walking. Too dangerous to say anything in English around here, he told himself. *One word and we're dead.*

Two trucks and a dozen men were standing in line at the back of the compound. Jed could feel his heart thumping inside his chest. A bead of sweat was forming on his forehead. He wiped it clean with the back of his hand. He glanced at Nick. The old guy looked calm enough, but it was only too easy to imagine how his guts were churning up inside. He'd been taken in here, and tortured to within an inch of his life. *It wasn't a place any man would want to come back to.*

The entrance was guarded by barbed wire, and two armoured vehicles. There were six guards, each one with an AK-47 slung over his neck, checking the papers. Three more guys to go, Jed noted. The man heading through the entrance had just been given a going-over by the guards, been asked a long series of questions, and looked nervous as he gave his replies. Overstayed his leave, maybe, thought Jed. The next two guys were waved through with only a cursory glance at their papers. Nick and Jed stepped forward. The guard barked at them in

Arabic. Without a moment's hesitation, they both thrust forward the papers they'd been supplied with by the Firm. Unquestioning, sullen obedience, thought Jed. *That is the attitude drilled into soldiers the world over.*

The guard looked away, barking at the next soldier. Jed stepped quickly through the carved gates and into the inner courtyard. We're through, he thought. Nick was already walking quickly away, putting as much distance as he could between himself and the guards. On the inside, the presidential compound was a mini-city. The entrance led on to a huge square dominated by a fifty-foot statue of Saddam Hussein. On one side, there was the huge green-domed palace itself, its façade dominated by a huge marble-and-stone staircase that would not have looked out of place in Versailles. It was protected by a ring of troops. Next to that were two barracks buildings that housed the regime's most elite and feared troops, the Special Republican Guard, and the Syrian mercenaries who had streamed across the border. Then there were the two big admin blocks, the Palace of Flowers and the Palace of Peace, where the brutal henchmen, bureaucrats and torturers of Saddam's government administered the country. Both looked badly damaged by the missile strikes of the past two nights. Windows had been shattered, craters dug up in the road, and some of the unfortunately named Palace of Peace had been blown clean away, so that the top floors now had gaping holes in their walls exposing them to the night air. Even so, on the lower floors Jed could see lights burning, and some of the desks seemed to be occupied. People were afraid of the bombs, but they were even more afraid of the torturers who would set upon them and their families if they failed to show up for work.

As he looked around, Jed noticed a dozen different Saddams looking down at him from the gaudy murals painted on to the walls: Saddam on his horse; Saddam reviewing his troops; Saddam holding a gun; Saddam lecturing a crowd of workers. Everywhere you looked, the same thick, black moustache, and the same brooding, dark, vengeful eyes looked back down on you.

A siren.

Jed spun round.

A wah-wah sound was blasting from speakers positioned every few yards. In the same instant, Jed could feel a collective fear grip hold of the compound. There were troops swilling through the main courtyard, trucks and jeeps honking their way towards their shelters. Men were shouting wildly. If there was any plan or drill, it had been abandoned. People were taking cover wherever they could.

'Into the palace,' hissed Nick.

He was running already. Jed followed close on his heels. The main entrance to the palace was only thirty yards ahead of them. The sirens were still blaring, and although you couldn't yet hear the hiss of any incoming cruise missile, it could only be a few seconds away. All around the compound, the anti-aircraft guns were in full blast, loosing off a deadly chatter of fire into the night sky. Theoretically, it was possible to explode a Tomahawk in the air, but the chances of getting a direct hit that penetrated and exploded its payload were minimal. *The idiots were firing into thin air.*

Nick had reached the steps of the palace. He was running up the stairs. Jed followed swiftly in his wake. There were guards across the entrance, but during an air-raid alert security seemed to have been abandoned. Hundreds of men were crowding into the main hallway. Somewhere in the distance, the sound of gunfire was rattling against the walls of the palace. A man screamed, then the gun fell silent.

'Downstairs,' hissed Nick. 'That's where the dungeons are.'

All around them, men were heaving and shouting. Nick was pointing to a staircase. As they descended one flight, Jed could suddenly hear the explosion of the incoming missile. A blast of heat ripped through the air first, as if you had just stepped into a microwave. Then you could feel a rush of air. Next, the building shook, as if it was a toy castle that a child had just picked up. The walls vibrated, and the floor seemed to shift. Jed could feel himself losing his grip, and he snapped his fists around the railing that ran down the staircase to steady himself. The sound of thunder ripped through the building, one huge blast followed by a smaller series of secondary blasts. Then, for a second, the bangs ceased and the sirens fell silent. An eerie quiet gripped the compound. Nothing was moving. Even the dust seemed to have been suspended in the air. Then you could hear the screams and cries of the men who were being burnt alive in the fireball that followed the explosion. The sirens started up again, and the sound of orders being barked by officers could be heard ricocheting through the buildings above them.

'Keep going down,' hissed Nick.

They descended through another flight, then another. As you dropped down into the depths of the compound, the corridors became darker, and the concrete on the walls thicker – you could feel the damp creeping through them.

'Where the fuck are we going?' hissed Jed as both men paused to catch their breath.

The stairway was lit by a strip of bulbs, but half of them had fused during the missile strikes of the past few days. The light was dim and unsteady. So far as Jed could see, the staircase went down another four or five flights, with a door every other flight.

'Like I said, to the dungeons.'

'How the hell do we know where they are?'

Nick looked at him. His brow was furrowed, and his eyes were suddenly ablaze with anger. 'Listen, boy,' he said. 'When a man's been to hell, he doesn't forget the way.'

Jed fell silent. Nick was already barrelling down another staircase, rushing like a man possessed by demons. Too much noise, thought Jed as he followed in his trail. *We're making too much bloody noise.* 'Keep it quiet,' he hissed.

'We haven't got any time to lose,' snapped Nick.

'And the fucking racket you're making, Saddam can probably hear us himself.'

Nick carried on, his boots clattering against the concrete. The echoes were bouncing off the walls, assaulting Jed's ears.

'*Qif*,' shouted a voice behind them.

Jed knew that word, and he knew he didn't want to hear it. *Stop.*

He spun round.

At the doorway, he saw a man looking straight at them. He was a wearing an olive-green uniform, with the purple shoulder insignia of the Special Republican Guard.

In his hand, there was a Russian-made MP412 handgun, with a distinctive snub-nosed silver barrel.

And he was aiming it straight at Nick's head.

TWENTY-SEVEN

Jed paused, holding himself perfectly still, his right hand gripping the railing. The SRG officer was standing with his legs slightly apart, and with both his hands firmly holding the gun. On his face, there was a look of resolute concentration.

Jed glanced at Nick. His body was immobile, but Jed could tell what he was thinking. Shall I rush the bugger before he has a chance to shoot? That was the Regiment drill. Make your move quickly, before your opponent has a chance to steady themselves.

Don't do it, thought Jed. The guy is good. I can tell that just from the way he holds himself. *As soon as you move, he is going to put two bullets through your forehead.*

'*Qif*,' the man repeated. His voice was louder this time. Nick didn't move.

The officer rattled out another phrase in Arabic, but it meant nothing to Jed, and he was pretty sure that Nick was as clueless as he was.

His finger jutted forward on the gun.

An Iraqi soldier who doesn't speak Arabic, thought Jed. *You don't exactly need to be Muhammad bloody Holmes to figure out that something fishy is going on.*

He could see Nick's shoulder muscles twitching, the stance of a man about to move. And he could see the officer steadying his finger on the trigger of his gun, and narrowing his eyes to make sure his aim was true.

The old bugger is not going to make it.

Reaching down into his boot, Jed slipped out a hunting knife. They had guns but it was too dangerous to start shooting in here: it would bring the entire Iraqi Army down on them. The blade was just six inches long, but strong and razor-sharp. He twisted it into the palm of his hand. Taking a deep breath, he took a mental calculation of the distance between him and the officer, and the flight and spin the knife would need to reach its target. Then, with a sudden movement, the knife flew from his hand. It arced through the air, travelling for just a fraction of a second, before hitting the officer in the side of the head. Jed had meant to slice open his throat, but his aim wasn't good enough. The blow momentarily stunned the Iraqi, and in the next instant, Nick lunged at him, knocking him to the ground. Jed followed swiftly, pressing himself down on the man's chest, and ramming his left hand over his mouth to stop him from crying out. Nick was holding on to his legs, but the man was wriggling around like a fish out of water. 'Stab the fucker,' Nick hissed.

Jed picked up the knife from the floor, and carved it deep into the man's chest. He could feel him heaving, and blood spurted out of his mouth. Jed took the knife out, then stabbed again, then again, each time the man coughed up more blood, and his teeth bit on Jed's left hand in agony. It took five plunges of the knife before the life was finally drained out of him.

'You were in trouble,' said Jed, pulling his bloodstained knife out of the man's body.

'I'd have been OK,' growled Nick.

Jed angrily put the knife back into his boot. 'He'd have bloody shot you.'

Nick shrugged. 'He didn't look that good to me. I reckon I could have taken him before he got the bullet out.'

He bent down, picking up the officer's handgun, and tucking it into the pocket of his trousers. 'And you should have cut the guy's throat, you tosser, not buggered around stabbing his chest,' he said. 'Let's get the hell out of here, before they find the sod's body.'

They had two more flights to descend. Jed noticed that Nick was moving more slowly now, careful not to make any more noise than was strictly necessary. He might not admit it, Jed thought, but he knew he'd made a mistake, and one that could have easily cost both their lives.

At the bottom of the staircase, there was a fire door, leading on to a corridor that stretched for about twenty yards. Jed had lost track of how deep underground they might be by now. At least seven flights of stairs, which meant a hundred feet or more. No wonder the cruise missiles weren't making any difference, he thought. Against a bunker this deep, and this well protected, even a fully loaded Paveway had all the impact of a light sprinkling of drizzle.

'We're going in,' said Nick. 'This is the heart of the place.'

Jed felt certain he could detect a note of hesitancy in the man's voice as he pushed aside the door. This is where the dark memories are all buried, he thought. Stepping back into these corridors is like stepping voluntarily back into a nightmare after you've already awoken. His voice, usually strong and robust, was touched with uncertainty and doubt.

'You go first,' said Nick suddenly.

'You okay?' said Jed.

'My eyes, maybe,' said Nick. 'It's . . . it's dark in there.' He paused. 'Just get a bloody move on.'

Christ, thought Jed. That's the first time I've heard the old bugger admit he's not as young as he used to be.

He stepped through the door, and started walking along the corridor. The walls were built from thick slabs of concrete, and there was a series of metal tubes running alongside them. Every few yards, there was a bulb, throwing off a pale light, but since half of them were broken it remained dim and murky. There were no windows, of course, and no doors, apart from a single exit at the end of the twenty-yard stretch. Some kind of ventilation shaft, or service tunnel, Jed reckoned as he walked carefully along its length. The command and control centre and the interrogation rooms will be somewhere else.

Somewhere above him, Jed could hear the sound of another missile strike. Even though they were so deep underground, they could suddenly feel the earth vibrating beneath them. Dust from the walls filled the air, and then a muffled thunderclap rattled through the atmosphere. Another few days, there isn't going to be much left of this place, thought Jed. *We have to get Sarah out while we still can.*

The door at the end of the twenty-yard corridor was shut, but not bolted. Jed slid it ajar, just wide enough to see what was on the other side. He looked back towards Nick. 'Some kind of a junction,' he said. 'There are three different corridors leading off it. Two guards, both with their backs to us.'

Nick took his own knife out of his boot, and gestured towards Jed's. The blade was glimmering in the pale light.

Jed reached out and touched his arm. 'No,' he said, with quiet determination. 'We can't kill all the fuckers in this place. We've got uniforms, let's try and walk past them.'

Nick nodded. 'The corridor to the right,' he said. 'Make it look like you know where you're going.'

It's the army, right, and they're all the same, thought Jed. *Walk quickly, and look important, and they'll assume you're an officer and be too scared to stop you.*

He pushed the door firmly open. The knife was held in his pocket, ready to be whipped out within a second. The junction was better lit, with a series of neon tubes on the ceiling, but the walls were the same drab concrete. The two guards, both men in the twenties, clean-shaven and with clear, brown eyes, were wearing the uniform of the Fedayeen. Both were standing to attention, on either side of the central corridor. Jed walked swiftly, his boots clipping against the concrete floor. He glanced once at the guard closest to him, making sure there was nothing in his eyes: neither fear, nor suspicion, nor interest, just the indifferent look of a soldier going about his business. The guard didn't smile or look back. Relieved, Jed walked on towards the right corridor. Nick was following close behind. Made it, he thought. This time at least.

'You OK,' Jed hissed, glancing at Nick.

He could see the fear etched into the man's face: his eyes were flipping around, and there were beads of cold sweat running down the side of his face.

'I'm fine,' he muttered

'No, you're not,' Jed said.

'I just fucking told you, I'm OK,' Nick growled.

The corridor stretched for fifty yards in front of them. They could tell they were drawing closer to the centre of the operation because the walls were now painted a pale green, and someone had taken the trouble to replace the light bulbs. As he reached the end, Jed pushed his way decisively through another fire door. This one led into a room, from which five corridors led in different directions. Don't hesitate, Jed told himself. That would suggest you aren't familiar with the place. *That you don't belong here.*

He walked along the third corridor. A series of offices led off it, most of them with the doors open. Men were walking from one to another. There was a nervous round of tense chatter, punctuated by the occasional laugh then fits of swearing. In one room, Jed caught sight of someone he could have sworn was Saddam Hussein. This is the hub, thought Jed with a sharp intake of breath. They're directing the whole bloody war from right here on this corridor. *And I'm at the centre of it.*

On screens he glimpsed through the office doors, he could see satellite TV pictures captured from around the world: CNN, Fox News, BBC News 24 and al-Jazeera were all flashed up on different screens. From what he could see, the ground invasion of Basra had already begun. British and American troops had punched their way through the coastal defences, and were on the road to Baghdad. Perhaps we should just wait right here, thought Jed. *We could get a kettle on and have a nice brew waiting for the boys when they make it through to Baghdad.*

An officer of the Special Republican Guard pushed Jed from where he was blocking the corridor. '*Koos*,' he barked. Jed didn't know a lot of Arabic, but he knew when a guy was calling him a cunt, and he could feel the anger swelling up inside his chest. Cool it, he told himself. *You can't get in a fight here.*

He nodded apologetically, and kept on walking. They went past three more offices, each time glancing through to the TV screens. From what they could read of the news bars scrolling along the bottom of the screens, the allies were making good progress, but the Iraqis were expected to put up a stout defence of the heartlands closer to Baghdad. In the rooms, Jed could see staff officers poring over maps, no doubt debating how they would deploy their resources. They'd have a good laugh if they knew a couple of British guys were standing right here, he thought. And when they stopped laughing, they'd rip us limb from limb.

Jed looked round suddenly. A heated argument had just broken out among a group of officers. One of the junior staffers was getting a right monstering: his face, Jed noticed, was the mixture of resentment and fear familiar to soldiers being bollocked everywhere.

'Keep going,' muttered Nick, his voice barely registering above a whisper.

They were still walking towards the end of the corridor, trying to find a way to the dungeons. In his mind, Nick could see a picture of Marlow, his old commander's face sneering at him across a desk. 'Don't fuck it up this time, old boy,' he was saying.

Nick's expression snapped. Suddenly, he was brisk and purposeful. They were approaching the end of the corridor. There were two more guards standing to attention, both with AK-47s held rigidly to their chests. They paid no attention as Nick and Jed moved quickly past them. They came out into another junction, this time with three corridors leading off it. One seemed to be a ventilation shaft, another led to a canteen. They could see a few officers eating, and drinking small cups of coffee. Their expressions were tense and nervous, and the mood among them was brittle. Nobody was laughing, as they would be in the British Army. Nobody was smiling, or even talking if they could avoid it. They were just keeping their heads down, getting on with their work, and hoping to survive.

The third corridor led towards what looked like a staircase. Nick headed for it, gesturing to Jed to follow him. From what he remembered of the place – and he'd done his best over the years to erase every last shred of the memory – the dungeons were two levels below the command and control complex. *They had to keep going down if they were to have a chance of finding Sarah.*

Another clap of thunder reverberated though the corridor. The ground shook, and the walls vibrated around them. Another missile strike, thought Jed. A big bastard this time. From the noise, it could have been a direct hit on the presidential compound. The men around them were looking up anxiously. They were probably safe down here, seven levels below the ground, but it was impossible to say what kind of hell was raging on the ground above them.

Ignore it, he told himself. This isn't the time to think about how you're going to get out of here.

Pushing through the door, he could see a staircase. Half the bulbs were out, leaving little light to steer yourself by. 'Down here,' hissed Nick.

'You sure?'

'I've bloody been here before,' snapped Nick.

They dropped down one flight, then another. Up above, Jed could hear the sound of a siren blasting through the corridors. He could hear feet running along the corridors, followed by the racket of orders being barked. He knew the Americans had been working hard on bunker-busting bombs: cruise missiles with reinforced tips that could drill through layer after layer of concrete and armour. Had they made something that could get down this deep?

'Keep going,' hissed Nick. 'We're almost there.'

Jed pressed on. As they went deeper underground, the sound of the sirens above started to fade. A doorway loomed ahead of them. Nick pushed it aside, stepping through, and Jed followed closely behind. It led into a room, at the front of which was a set of strong steel bars, with a small doorway cut into them. Two guards snapped to attention. One of them barked at Nick in Arabic. He stepped forward, taking his knife from his pocket in a flash. The man was starting to unhook his AK-47 from his chest, but it was too late. Nick had already crashed into his side, knocking him off balance. His knife was gripped hard in his hand. With a sudden brutal movement, he had stabbed it into the side of the man's neck, and was twisting the blade around. The skin was being cut open, and the blood started to seep on to the floor. A cry of pain erupted from his lips.

The second guard was advancing on Jed. Jed had already drawn his knife, and the blade was glinting in the dull light. The soldier could see it was too late to use his gun: in the time it took him to take aim and fire, Jed would have already sliced him open. 'Come on, you bastard,' said Jed.

With steel in his eyes, the man gripped his rifle by the wooden butt, and swung it through the air. The blow caught Jed on the side of his ribcage, knocking the wind out of his lungs, and for a moment he was struggling to breathe. A malicious smile started to spread across his opponent's lips. He sensed that he'd hurt Jed, and that gave him the advantage. Jed steadied himself, and gripped the knife tighter in his hand. He slashed out at the man, and his knife cut through the nylon fabric of his tunic, but Jed could tell he was only cutting through cloth, not skin. At his side, he could see Nick stabbing hard at the guard he was fighting, hacking into his neck. Jed threw himself forward, stabbing the knife into the soldier's ribcage. He could feel the blade digging into the flesh, and a howl of pain burst from the man's lips. Jed twisted the blade, searching for an artery he could sever. Got to finish the buggers off, he told himself.

The soldier was strong, and his eyes were burning with the hatred of a man who's just been wounded. *Koos, koos, koos,* he was repeating, the words spitting from his lips, and the saliva spitting on to Jed's face. He pulled back suddenly, so that the knife was ripped out of Jed's hand, and was left sticking in the man's ribcage. With a roar, he thrust himself forward, landing on top of Jed. Both men crashed hard on to the floor, the soldier lying on top of Jed. Blood was seeping from the wound, dripping down Jed's side. With his fists, the man was pummelling him with blows, hitting the side of his head again and again and again. Jed could feel himself starting to grow dizzy. His vision was misting up, and his senses were groggy, like a boxer in the twelfth round of a hard fight. He was heaving upwards with his arms and legs, trying to push the man away, but the weight was too much for him. The blows were raining down hard, and Jed started scrambling for the knife still sticking in the ribcage. Twist that, he thought, and I can get the initiative again.

With his right hand, he gripped the man's chest,

trying to hold him close to his body so that he couldn't hit so hard. With his left hand he reached for the handle of the knife. He couldn't see it, but he could feel it. With a sudden movement, he gripped the handle, then tugged it free. The man screamed as the knife cut through his bleeding flesh. In the same instant, he ripped free of Jed's embrace, swinging his right arm out, and knocking the blade clean out of Jed's hand. It smashed against the wall, and fell to the ground with a crash. 'Bugger,' muttered Jed.

The man was thrusting his knee down into Jed's chest, pinning him down. With his hands crossed together, he started to press down savagely on Jed's throat, slowly cutting off the air supply. Jed could feel himself starting to weaken. The blows were still pummelling against the side of his face. Sharp knuckles were digging into his skin, cutting into the veins, and he could feel blood streaming from a cut in his forehead. *Koos, koos, koos,* spat the soldier, the sweat pouring from his face and dripping down on to Jed's skin.

Then he screamed. His mouth opened, and a howl erupted from deep within his gut. His back arched up, and his eyes were bulging from their sockets. Jed struggled to regain his focus. The soldier had already started to loosen his grip, and a trickle of blood was choking out of his lips. Jed could see now that Nick was standing behind him. He had just ripped the man backwards by the neck. He thrust him on to the floor, punching him savagely in the head and neck. 'Sit on his chest,' Nick snapped.

Jed pulled himself swiftly up from the floor. He rolled himself on top of the guard, pressing his knees down on his chest, while Nick folded the palms of his hands around his neck. He started to squeeze, while Jed's pressing force on his chest emptied his lungs, making him easier to strangle. Nick might be getting on, Jed thought, but he still knows how to handle himself in a fight. The man's eyes were already starting to close. He struggled to see what was happening to him, but it was already too late. The life was ebbing away from him. Within another few seconds he was dead.

Jed climbed off the corpse in disgust. Standing up, he was still dizzy and dripping with blood. That was close, he told himself. *Bloody close.*

'You looked like you were fucked to me,' said Nick, a grim smile on his lips.

'I'd have been fine,' said Jed tersely.

'Well, just thought I'd save time, mate –'

'Drop it,' snapped Jed.

He picked up a set of keys, which had fallen from the grip of one of the guards. There were a dozen of them, enough to throw open the dungeons. They were smeared with blood, and felt slimy to the touch. He thrust the largest key into the door set within the steel bars, and started to turn. The doors creaked. Somewhere inside, he could hear a man groaning quietly to himself: the low, agonised sound of a creature that has long since given up hope.

'You go first, mate,' said Nick standing at his side.

TWENTY-EIGHT

Jed walked steadily into the corridor. It was much wider than any of the other passages they had passed through, and there was only a light bulb every ten yards, making the light murky and dim. Immediately in front of him there was an array of equipment arranged neatly on the shelves of a steel-framed unit: tubes and wires, fuse boxes and tongs. On one shelf there was a set of surgical instruments, most of them stained with blood. On another, there were the thick straps of leather used to tie electrical circuits on to a man's skin. On a third was a series of thumbscrews and presses designed to break the bones on a hand or a foot one by one to draw out the maximum levels of pain.

Jesus, thought Jed. That's the kit they use to torture the poor bastards who get thrown in here. This is where Nick was taken. *No wonder he's such a miserable old bastard.*

'You OK?' he said, looking round.

'Just fine,' Nick muttered.

'Coming back in here, I mean –'

'We're here to find Sarah, and we haven't much time before they discover we just cut up a couple of their boys.'

Jed looked back along the corridor. The smell was terrible. He'd grown used to trench-in-the-ground latrines for a thousand men or more when he'd been serving in the Balkans, and as a boy he'd visited an abattoir a couple of times. But this was a hundred times worse: a vile mixture of excrement and blood, mixed in with fear, sweat and rotten food. As he took a breath of the air, Jed could feel himself gagging. Such food as was left in his stomach was swirling around inside him, and for a minute he thought he might throw up. Not that it would make any difference to the cleanliness of this place, he thought grimly. *It might even improve it.*

He started walking. The light was just good enough to see by. The corridor stretched for about a hundred yards, driven deep into the ground. Every ten yards, it broke off, with a small passageway leading to a group of six cells. 'You take the left, I'll take the right,' hissed Jed.

Moving into the block of cells, he adjusted his eyes to the pale light. Checking his watch, he could see that it was well past midnight now. The prisoners might be awake, they might be asleep. It wouldn't make much difference anyway, he thought. *The poor bastards probably don't even know what planet they are on after a couple of weeks in this place.*

The first two cells were empty. Glancing inside, Jed could see some straw littered across the back of the cell, and a bucket that was used as a latrine. The walls were made from rough stone, and you could see scratches in the mortar where one of the inmates had been trying

353

to claw his way out. No point, mate, thought Jed. *There isn't anywhere to go.*

He moved quickly on. The third cell in the block had a man in it. He was lying on the straw at the back of his cell, but it was impossible to tell anything more about him. There was a terrible smell of pus and vomit rolling out of the tiny space, and he looked to have one leg missing. In the next, two men, sleeping on either sides of the cell, with just a yard or two of space between them. Both had long, matted black hair, and beards that grew for several inches from the face. Neither looked at him. It was hard to tell if they were even still alive.

'See anything?' Jed hissed as he hooked up with Nick again in the main corridor.

Nick shook his head. 'Just a few Iraqi buggers.'

'Keep looking,' said Jed.

He checked the next block of cells. Two of them were empty, but the other four had men in them: in one, six guys were cramped together in a space so tiny they hardly even had room to lie down. One man was sitting up, his battered frame wedged up close to the iron bars. He looked up briefly at Jed, with scared and lonely eyes, like a stray dog foraging for some food. '*Min fadlik,*' he was muttering. '*Min fadlik.*'

Please, Jed realised. That's what he's saying.

Sorry, mate . . . nothing can help you now.

As he walked on, a few more men tried to speak to him. Some begged, some swore at him, and a couple just rattled on the iron bars that kept them caged in. Jed couldn't think that he had ever seen men in a worse state. They looked ridden with disease, and many had missing limbs. Some were wasting away, reduced to little more than skeletons. You could see the ribs, some of them broken, sticking out of the chests. They were dressed in nothing more than rags: what had once been trousers and T-shirts that might not have been changed for years, all of them caked in dried blood and sweat. A couple of men were completely naked, their bodies covered in scabs, boils and scars.

'How can anyone live in this hellhole?' said Jed, back in the corridor again.

'I survived here for three months,' said Nick, his voice touched with sorrow. 'A man can bear anything, so long as he has the will to cling on to life.'

Jed took another turning. The same dismal row of cells, each one with a fresh collection of victims. One man was moaning horribly, and clutching his stomach. Another was begging for water. Jed just walked past, his heart stiffening all the time. No time to help the poor buggers. I've just got to find Sarah and get out of here.

If there's any chance of her surviving in this place . . .

'Shit,' muttered Nick.

Jed walked swiftly to where he was standing on the other side of the corridor.

'Steve, mate, is that you?' said Nick.

He was looking into the cage, his hands gripping hold of its bars. Jed glanced inside. There was just one man inside, a guy who could have been in his sixties. His hair was grey and matted, long down the sides, but balding on top. He had about six inches of greying, messy beard hanging off his face. He was slumped at the back of the cell, his head bowed down. At his side, there were a few scraps of stale food, and a spilt bucket of slops.

'Steve, mate,' hissed Nick.

Slowly the man looked up. His eyes were tired and bloodshot, devoid of any expression except for a quiet despair. And blue. Jed looked closer. It took a moment before it struck him. The man had blue eyes. He wasn't an Arab. *He was . . . he might even be an Englishman.*

'You know this guy?' said Jed.

'Steve Hatstone, that's him, I'm sure of it,' said Nick, speaking hurriedly.

'Who the hell's he?'

'He was behind the lines in the last dust-up in this craphole. We were together in these bloody cells, but his mission was so sensitive, the British always denied his part in it. Because of that, the Iraqis wouldn't negotiate his release in the prisoner exchange after the war.'

Jed glanced across at the pitiful creature. He'd heard of Hatstone, because he was one of the handful of Regiment men who'd vanished during the last Iraq War. He was presumed killed in action. Yet now he was looking right at him. *Or what was left of the poor sod.*

'I can't believe the bugger is still alive,' Nick said.

The man was looking up at the two people peering into his cells, but there was nothing in his eyes: no interest, no hope, no sign of life; just a blank, resigned indifference. 'You English, mate?' said Jed. 'Because if you are, maybe we can help you.'

The blue eyes stared up at him. His lips started to move, and he mumbled something in Arabic. Jed leant forward, but it was impossible to hear anything he was saying. Even if you could catch the words, the language meant nothing to him. Christ, thought Jed. The guy has been here so long, he's forgotten who he is. *He's even forgotten how to speak English.*

'Steve,' hissed Nick, his tone louder this time. 'Steve, mate, it's me, Nick.'

The man looked at him, his expression bored. Then he turned away.

Jed reached out and grabbed hold of Nick's arm. 'Leave it,' he said tersely. 'There's nothing we can do for the poor sod.'

'He's my mate,' snapped Nick.

'*Was* your mate. We're here to find Sarah, remember.'

'Then where the hell is she?'

Nick put his pistol down on the ground. He was fumbling with the keys, trying to find one that would open the cage and let Hatstone free. We might not be able to do anything for him, he reflected grimly, but we can't leave him caged up here like an animal. He was one of us once. I knew his wife and kids.

Suddenly, Hatstone darted forward, flicking his hand through the bars. The speed and agility of the man caught both Nick and Jed by surprise: he moved with the swiftness and stealth of a snake. Nick's pistol was already in his hand, his finger poised on the trigger. Jed pulled out his own gun, pointing it straight at him.

Hatstone looked at him and smiled, revealing a mouth

with only one stubby tooth left in it. Then he turned the gun around, putting it against his own head. He squeezed the trigger. The bullet blew through his brain, and in the next instant he fell sideways, crashing against the floor.

'Christ,' said Nick, burying his face in his hand.

Jed picked up the gun, and put it back in Nick's pocket. 'Don't even think about it,' he said softly. 'We'll see worse things before this war is over, I reckon.'

Jed looked around. They were almost at the end of the cell block and he reckoned they didn't have much time left. It was twenty minutes since they had killed the two guards, and you had to reckon they had some system of changing the guards. At any moment, fresh soldiers were going to arrive, and then they were done for. He walked swiftly through the remaining rooms, glancing into the cells, but all he could see were men, broken and battered, most of whom looked as if they had been here for years. 'Sarah,' he said.

He was surprised at the echo of his own voice, the words rattling back at him as they bounced back through the cages. 'Sarah, where the hell are you?'

'She's gone,' said a voice.

Jed snapped to attention. It was coming from about twenty yards back.

'If you're looking for her, she's gone already,' the voice continued.

Jed started to run. His feet were hammering along the corridor. He reached the turning, and looked around wildly. All the cells were dark, and he could see nothing

Chris Ryan

except for a few frightened eyes staring back at him.

'Who the hell is that?' he snapped into the darkness. 'Who spoke?'

'Here,' came back the voice.

Jed looked into a cell. The man was standing close up to him, his hands gripping on to the bars.

Wilmington.

'What the fuck are you doing here?' said Nick.

Jed turned round. Nick was standing right behind him, staring into the cell. His face was sweaty and tense, like a man who was nearing the end of a marathon run. He was looking straight at Wilmington, and the professor was staring right back at him.

'What the fuck are you doing here?' Nick said again, his voice louder this time.

Wilmington's eyes were narrow and tight, focusing intently on Nick: the expression of a man weighing his own chances of survival. 'I might ask you the same question,' he said eventually, pronouncing the words with deliberate slowness.

Nick took a step closer, so that he was leaning into the bars of the cage. 'I'm looking for my bloody daughter,' said Nick. 'And I don't want to hear any bollocks from you about how you don't know where she is.'

The professor nodded. 'Let me out,' he said, speaking with quiet determination. 'I can take you to her.'

Jed eyed him suspiciously. He had the set of keys in his pocket they had taken from the two guards. They could open the doors to any cell if they wanted to. But, he thought, I'm not in the mood to negotiate. *If Sarah's not here, we need to know where she is.*

He held the keys in his hand, just a few inches away from Wilmington. 'Don't play games,' he said. 'Tell us where she is, or you can rot in here.'

'Let me out,' repeated Wilmington. His voice was calm and determined: he was speaking with the tone of a man who had made up his mind and was not about to change it.

Jed glanced at Nick. 'We break his balls here, or we do it later.'

'Later,' said Nick. 'Hang around here, the buggers are going to find us.'

After several attempts, Jed slipped the right key into the lock, and turned it. Wilmington flung the door open, grasping for his freedom the way a starving dog will grasp for food. Jed grabbed him by the arm, and started to hustle his way quickly back towards the entrance. So far as he could see, there was no other exit. Makes no difference, he thought grimly. *Usually, the only way out of here is in a coffin.*

Two men were moaning desperately as he approached the doorway. He could hear gasps for help, and a rattling of chains. One man was beginning to scream. They were making enough noise now to wake some of the other prisoners, and the few whose spirit had not yet been completely broken were desperate to find any way to escape they could.

Jed closed his ears, shutting out the pleas echoing up from deep within the cells. You found your own way in here, boys, he thought. *You can find your own way out as well.*

The lights were brighter as they stepped back into the guards' room. Nick had already rushed ahead of them, and was kneeling down on the floor, stripping the uniform off one of the two dead guards. He handed the olive-green trousers and tunic up to Wilmington. 'Here,' he snapped. 'Get your kit off and get these on instead.'

Blood was still smeared across the uniform. 'I'm not a soldier.'

Nick shot up to Wilmington, ripping the torn and stained T-shirt he was wearing off his chest. 'You try and walk out of here, and a soldier is exactly what you want to look like. If they see a civilian, they're going to bloody shoot him.'

'It's got blood on it,' said Wilmington.

Nick leant closer into Wilmington face. 'I've got one message for you,' he said. 'You do every single thing I say, and you do it immediately, and we're going to rub along just fine. But you give me any aggro, pal, I'm going to take great pleasure in slicing your balls off and stuffing them down your throat.'

Jed noticed the professor turning visibly paler. You're on our territory now, mate. You're going to have to get used to our way of talking. *And our way of doing things.*

'Just do what he says,' said Jed to Wilmington.

In a moment, Wilmington had pulled the tunic over his chest and the army trousers up to his waist. They were a lousy fit: the professor was running to middle-

361

aged flab, and his stomach was bulging out of the trousers of the young man they'd been taken from. It makes no difference, Jed thought. Most of the Iraqi Army seemed to be running around in uniforms that didn't fit: one more wouldn't make any difference.

'Now move it,' snapped Nick.

All three men started to run up the stairs. Nick led the way, while Jed brought up the rear, pushing Wilmington forward. He was in no shape for strenuous physical exercise, and from the looks of him, he probably hadn't eaten for the last few days. Just keep going, Jed thought. We can patch you up when we get you to safety. *That's if we haven't killed you first.*

At the top of the stairs, they pushed through the door that led back into the main corridors occupied by the staff officers and military planners. 'Just keep completely quiet,' Jed hissed into Wilmington's ear. 'Walk like you belong here, and we'll be OK. One false move, and I'll kill you so quickly, you won't even have time to ask sodding Muhammad for forgiveness.'

Nick was already walking briskly along the corridor. The atmosphere had changed for the worse in the last hour, Jed decided. The air was crackling with tension. You could smell the anger of the commanders. Somewhere in the distance, he could hear the blaring of air-raid sirens. It was a vicious, squawking sound, like a duck being strangled, that assaulted your ears and senses. Jed tried to shut it out of his mind, as he pushed on. The corridors were crowded with soldiers, all trying to figure out what was going on. From the looks of confusion and anger on their faces, Jed figured they had no idea whether they were safe down here or not. *Just like us.*

Nick had already pushed his way through the door that led to the main staircase, and Jed bundled Wilmington ahead of him, making sure he kept a tight grip on the professor's arm. As he hurried up the staircase, he could see Nick pause. He'd turned round, and was holding up an arm. Stop. That's what's he's telling me. *Something's wrong.*

They were one flight up, with six more to go before they hit ground level. Nick was standing on the turning of the bleak, dark staircase. During the missile strike, even more of the bulbs had popped: with no more than one in five lit, it was impossible to see anything more than a few yards ahead. Jed took five more steps, bringing him closer to where Nick was standing. He could see two corpses lying on the ground up ahead: the two men they had killed on their way down. They were lying in a bloody, messy heap. Above them, a Fedayeen officer was kneeling, examining the wounds that had felled them.

The officer barked something at Nick. What he was saying, Jed had no idea. *But it didn't sound friendly . . .*

Wilmington replied in Arabic, his voice grovelling. For a moment, the officer looked to be taken in. Maybe he'll let us pass, thought Jed hopefully. Then he turned aggressive. He was pointing at Nick and Jed and shouting.

Nick nodded, then glanced at Jed. 'Cover me,' he hissed.

With a swift movement, Nick grabbed the AK-47 from his kitbag. It was a slow and cumbersome movement, getting the gun out of the bag, and fixing it into a position in your arms where you could start firing. Even the best-trained soldiers couldn't do that in less than three seconds, Jed thought. And there was no way of knowing when Nick had last been trained. The guy could be as rusty as a vintage Jag.

The officer was already reaching down to his gun. It was tucked into a leather holster, concealed at the side of his baggy tunic. What make it was, Jed couldn't tell at this distance. It makes no difference, he thought. At five yards, it would be accurate enough. *Saddam might be a dumb sod, but he knew enough to kit out his bodyguards with decent shooters.*

Jed thrust Wilmington aside, flicked his knife out of his pocket, and let rip a massive roar of anger from his lungs as he lunged at the soldier. There was fifteen feet between them, and, as he well knew, there was little chance of closing that distance and stabbing the knife into the man's chest before he was shot. Even as he threw himself forward, Jed was sweating, aware he might have just taken the risk that would end his life.

The soldier's eyes flickered towards Jed, then back to Nick. Mistake, pal, thought Jed. You can't make up your mind who to shoot first. His hand was shaking slightly, as he flipped from target to target. Then a shot loosened off from the pistol, crashing into the wall between them. In the same instant, Nick had brought the AK-47 tight into his chest. His finger had slammed into its trigger. The neat, methodical chatter of the machine gun suddenly filled the staircase. You could see the bullets screeching into the man's body, perforating his chest. He staggered back, clutching his side. Nick was maintaining a steady rate of fire, laying a stream of lead into the body reeling away from him. With an ugly crash, he tumbled to the ground, blood spurting out of him.

'You killed him,' muttered Wilmington, his voice choking with fear.

'What do you think we are?' growled Jed. 'The Women's Institute? Of course we killed the fucker.'

'You started this whole bloody thing, mate,' snapped Nick. 'Now bloody move.'

His voice was raw and angry. It didn't matter how experienced a soldier you were, thought Jed. In the seconds after killing a man, your head was a weird mixture of elation and regret. The danger and adrenalin left you wired, and tense, struggling to think straight. Nick had been within a microsecond of dying. It could take him hours to calm down from that. *Some men never did*.

Jed knew that the sound of the fight could have alerted more guards to their escape. There was no time to lose. He shoved Wilmington from the back, pushing him up the next flight of stairs. As they got closer to the surface, they could hear the wail of sirens, and the sound of anti-aircraft guns. Maybe machine guns as well. It was impossible to tell from this distance. There is no way of knowing what kind of hell we'll be running into when we break out on to the surface, thought Jed. There could be more air strikes. There could be a parachute raid. *Hell, they might have decided to nuke the place and get this war over and done with in a couple of days.*

Wilmington was starting to freeze up. The fear was starting to take hold of him. Bloody civilians, thought Jed, as he gave the man another sharp push to get him up the stairs. As soon as the fireworks start up, their blood turns cold, they're paralysed, they can hardly move. They're worse than useless, they're a liability.

'Move your sodding arse, mate,' he hissed into Wilmington's ear. 'Otherwise, we'll just leave you here, and you can find out how they treat guys who break out of their jails.'

Nick was already standing by the door that led back into the hallway of the Republican Palace. There was sweat streaming down his face, and his eyes looked bloodshot and worn. His breath was short. Behind the flimsy door, the sound of explosions and screams could be clearly heard. 'Ready?' said Nick.

Jed nodded. 'Make a run for it,' he said.

'It's bloody chaos out there already, I reckon,' said Nick. 'Three blokes should be able to get through.'

'Go, then,' snapped Jed, gripping Wilmington tightly by the arm.

Nick pushed the door open, and bundled himself through. Jed followed swiftly in his wake. A blast of hot air hit him straight in the face as he stepped into the ornately decorated hallway of the palace. He glanced sideways. A fire was raging close to the staircase: giant flames were spitting and leaping into the air, crackling with sparks and sending out huge plumes of noxious black smoke. A missile strike, thought Jed. One of the bombs must have struck right here, taking down a chunk of the palace. The noise rippled out from the explosion with a series of murderous claps, shaking the dust loose from every wall of the building.

'This craphole palace is all made of plastic and foam,' shouted Nick. 'The fumes will kill you if you let them.'

Jed pushed his way along the hallway. Teams of men were rushing towards the flames with buckets and hoses, but the heat was driving them back. There were great waves of hot air swirling through the building: drapes and items of furniture were spontaneously combusting as the searing temperatures consumed them. Jed kept moving, ignoring the sweat trickling out of every pore of his skin. Eventually, they made it to the stairway that led down into the central courtyard. As they did so, Jed paused, taking a lungful of air, drawing it down deeply. It tasted putrid, vile, filled with soot and charred plastic. Looking out, Jed could see at least three huge fires burning in different parts of the compound. The missiles had struck at least three locations, leaving chunks blown out of buildings, and scattering the ground with great piles of burning, smoking fuel. There were dozens of corpses strewn like crushed confetti across the court-yard, and everywhere your ears were assaulted by the screams and moans of wounded men.

'Incoming strike,' snapped Nick. 'Run for your bloody lives.'

Jed looked up. You couldn't see it yet, but Nick was

right. The night air was buzzing with the squealing, hissing sound of an incoming cruise missile. The sirens had already started to blast, and the few soldiers left trying to put out the flames licking up around the edges of the main palace building were already running for cover.

'Move it,' hissed Jed, as he bundled Wilmington forward.

He could see the fear etched into the man's face as all three of them started to run. Jed was pushing himself as hard as he could, hurling himself down the stairway and across the hard concrete of the courtyard. It was two hundred yards or so to the perimeter wall, and the exit that would take them back on to the street. The sirens were getting louder, blasting into Jed's eardrums. He ran harder, and harder, aware that Wilmington was becoming short of breath. A hundred yards. He could hear the hissing sound of the missile coming closer and closer: something like an incoming jet, but much lower, and faster. 'Move it,' he snapped, turning round to yell at Wilmington as he sensed him falling further and further behind.

'I can't,' screamed Wilmington.

The man was doubled over in pain, clutching his stomach. Jed took two strides back, glancing anxiously around him, but he quickly realised he didn't have to worry about anyone hearing him speaking in English. The courtyard was already empty – all the soldiers had taken cover. The buggers know what's coming, thought Jed. It's only us madmen left out here.

'Move, you fucker,' he screamed at Wilmington. 'We're all going to bloody die.'

'I can't.' Wilmington was panting. His face was red and strained, like a man about to have a heart attack. 'I can't, I tell you,' he repeated.

Jed bent down. He grabbed Wilmington, and with one swift movement hoisted him up on to his shoulders. The man weighed at least twelve stone. Ignore the pain, Jed told himself as he felt the load pressing down into his shoulder blade. He started to jog, pushing himself to move as fast as possible. A hundred yards, then fifty. He could see the exit drawing closer to him: an empty, abandoned guard post getting tantalisingly nearer by the second.

I can make it, he told himself, repeating the phrase over and over. *Maybe . . .*

The explosion struck two, maybe three hundred yards behind him. Jed wasn't looking. You could feel the heat on your back first, as the air burnt all around you. Then you could feel the ground rumble and shake beneath your feet as the missile dug like a scalpel into the ground, cutting and splitting it open. Then you could hear the first deafening roar as the hundreds of pounds of high explosives packed into its tip exploded in a fraction of a second.

Jed pushed himself on, running desperately towards the exit. Whether Wilmington was conscious or not it was impossible to say: he was silent, and had the weight and stillness of a corpse. Nick was already through to the other side, flinging aside the flimsy wooden barrier the guards had left behind. Jed ran out on to the street, following Nick as he rushed round the first corner leading away from the palace. As he reached the spot, Jed collapsed to the ground, tossing the professor down behind him. Blood and sweat was streaming down the side of his face, and every muscle in his body felt like it had been punched.

'Bugger it,' said Nick, sitting at his side and trying to get some air back into his lungs. 'Last time I promised I was never going back into that hellhole. But this time I really mean it.'

TWENTY-NINE

Nick threw a bucket of water into Wilmington's face. 'Welcome back to the land of the living,' he said, looking down into Wilmington's scared and frightened eyes. 'Now, if you want to stay in it for more than another minute, I have a simple piece of advice for you. Tell us what we want to fucking know, and tell us right now.'

'Where am I?' said Wilmington, looking around desperately.

He was lying on the floor of the workshop where Nick and Jed had hidden earlier. By the time they had made their way out of the Republican Palace, Wilmington had already been unconscious, and there had been no choice but to carry the guy the few hundred yards back to their hiding place. The ferocity of the attacks on the city meant the streets were empty. Even the cockroaches were leaving, Jed had reflected as they'd hurried through the shattered, dark streets. The workshop was still empty – no chance of anyone clocking in tonight. With Wilmington still out cold, they took some biscuits and water from their kitbags, then took it in turns to get some kip. No point trying to do any more tonight, Jed told himself as he shut his eyes. *We're lucky enough just to be alive.*

'Where am I?' Wilmington repeated.

'The cemetery, mate,' snapped Jed. 'Or one step away from it, anyway.'

There was a wild, frightened look in his eye, like a whipped dog. Jed leant forward, gripping him by the scruff of his torn shirt. The water was still dripping from his matted, dirty hair, and soot was still clinging to his skin, making his face almost black. I don't know what they did to you in there, mate, thought Jed, but it doesn't look like you enjoyed it much. *And you aren't about to enjoy what happens next either.*

'Are . . . are we still in Baghdad?' said Wilmington.

Jed nodded. 'For now.'

'Where's Sarah?' said Nick, kneeling down so that his eyes were level with Wilmington's.

'I need some water,' said Wilmington, his tone hoarse and dry. 'And something to eat. I've had nothing for days.'

Jed reached across for a couple of biscuits and a bottle of water. 'You going to talk?' he said, holding the food in front of him. Wilmington nodded. His eyes were fixed on the biscuits. Jed handed them over. He stuffed the first one into his mouth, but his lips were so dry it just crumbled into dust. He took the water, swigging it back, then scooped up the crumbs, forcing them down his dry throat.

'Where's Sarah?' Nick repeated.

Wilmington glanced from one man to the next. 'Tikrit,' he said flatly.

'What the fuck is she doing there?' said Nick.

'They took her yesterday,' said Wilmington. 'We'd spent two days down in the cells of the palace. The guards came in yesterday morning and took Sarah away.'

'Did they say where she was going?' said Nick.

Wilmington shook his head.

'Then how the hell do you know?'

'The main scientific research laboratory for the whole of Iraq is in Tikrit,' said Wilmington. 'It's the heartland of Saddam's regime.'

'Why are they shunting her around?' said Nick.

'They need her to produce a successful cold-fusion experiment,' said Wilmington. 'That's what this is all about. After the original plant was hit, and this place came under attack, they had to take her somewhere she could finish her work.'

'The war's already started,' said Jed. 'What difference does it make to them now?'

Wilmington took a sip from his bottle of water. 'With a successful cold-fusion system, Saddam can blackmail all the countries in the Arab world to stop supporting the Americans and the British. You'd be thrown out of Saudi Arabia and Kuwait in an instant.'

He paused, stuffing another biscuit hungrily into his mouth. 'It's their one chance of saving themselves,' said Wilmington coldly. 'And they aren't about to let it slip through their fingers now.'

After leaving the hiding place, the three of them walked for twenty minutes, until Jed spotted an ancient Renault

21. Jed ran up to the car, his gun drawn, and pointed it straight at the driver, telling him to piss off. He didn't need any more persuading. The three of them climbed into the vehicle, then drove it straight out of town. They had changed out of the army uniforms into their civilian clothes so they didn't look like deserting soliders. Highway 1 snaked out of the city, heading due north, following the path of the Tigris, first to Tikrit then on towards Mosul. It was like the M1 on a bank holiday afternoon, Jed thought as they hit the road. Only a hundred times worse. By the time they had got their hands on the car, and got out of the city, it was already after three in the afternoon. It was two hundred miles to Tikrit, and the Renault wasn't going to get above fifty or sixty miles an hour at best. That's if you could work up that kind of speed. Half of Baghdad appeared to be trying to get as far north of the city as possible. Saddam's regime might be pumping out propaganda about how they were winning the war, but nobody believed it. Baghdad was coming under nightly missile attack, and everybody expected the Americans to be assaulting the city from the ground in weeks if not days. They were getting as far away as possible. The car had three-quarters of a tank of petrol in it, but Jed was prepared to take another car if they ran out: there was no way you were going find a petrol station open in this place.

Police and army checks were cursory. So far as Jed could see, law and order had broken down completely. The police had fled, and the army – or that section of it that hadn't already deserted – had been sent south to meet the invaders. The roads were swarming with cars, all of them piled high with people and possessions. Dozens of vehicles were breaking down, filling one whole lane of the three-lane highway. On the rest, progress was sluggish. Sometimes you could pick up some speed, but then a car would lose power, and everyone would brake as the driver pushed it stutteringly into the slow lane. Waiting for what, wondered Jed, as he looked at the succession of miserable, desperate families in their broken-down vehicles. The AA isn't going to come for you here. *The best you can hope for is that you are still alive when the Red Cross comes along to clear up the mess left by the soldiers.*

As the drive progressed, they learnt something of Wilmington's story. He'd been born in Kurdistan in northern Iraq in the early 1950s, but his father had smuggled him out of the country, across the border into Turkey, and then into Britain when he was seven. He could remember almost nothing of Kurdistan, except that some of his family was still there: his mother had died a year before his father made his escape, but there was a sister who had been left with his aunt, and six cousins from his mother's side of the family as well. It wasn't until he was sixteen that his father had even talked about the rest of his family that had been left behind. On arriving in Britain penniless, his father had applied for political asylum, and moved to Nottingham. He got a job as a librarian, and had stayed there ever since. The two of them lived very simply, and his father never remarried. The family name was changed, and Wilmington went to Cambridge, then to Harvard, before returning to Cambridge six years ago as Professor of Physics.

'So what happened then?' said Jed. 'How the hell did you get mixed up with the Iraqis again?'

'In physics, the first thing we learn is that time is relative,' said Wilmington. 'It's just one more dimension we pass though.'

'What in the name of Christ does that mean?' said Nick.

Wilmington was driving the car, and Jed was sitting in the front seat next to him. Nick had insisted the professor should drive. Any guards glancing towards the car would look at the driver first, and should they ask any questions then Wilmington would be able to answer in Arabic. He was a rubbish driver, Jed noted: hesitant, nervous, then bullying, with nothing in between. That didn't matter. Out on this road, there was no space to pick up enough speed to do yourself any damage. And all the other Iraqis were just as bad at driving their clapped-out bangers as Wilmington was.

'Eventually they caught up with me,' said Wilmington.

'Who?' said Jed.

'Saddam's men,' said Wilmington. You could still hear the shudder of fear in his voice as he mentioned the words. 'They first came to see me about two years ago. Salek came first –'

'The guy in your office,' said Jed.

'The same,' said Wilmington.

On the side of the road, Jed could see two men fighting next to a broken-down van. A woman was trying to pull them apart, but was pushed roughly away. Fumes from the vehicles backing up along the highway were heavy in the air, and somewhere up in the sky Jed felt certain he could hear the drone of approaching bombers. He glanced back towards Wilmington. 'Go on,' he muttered.

'He started offering me money for research, for myself, anything I wanted. I didn't know who he was at first, but I found out pretty quickly. He's a Kurd as well, but a bad one. The Kurds hate Saddam. He gassed our people back in the eighties, and has slaughtered hundreds of thousands of us to keep us in our place. Salek didn't care about any of that. He just cared about the money he was being paid to do the regime's dirty work.'

'So why the hell did you take it?' said Nick.

'My family.'

'You don't trade one family for another,' said Nick.

Wilmington turned round to look at him, taking his eyes off the road. 'Really?' he said. 'And have you ever been in the position where you had to make that choice?'

'Keep your eyes on the bloody road,' snapped Jed. The Renault drew dangerously close to a truck that had braked ahead of it. A man was climbing out of it, and all around horns were starting to blast as the traffic ground to yet another halt.

'Just tell us what happened,' said Jed.

'That first visit, I turned down their money, said I

377

wasn't interested,' said Wilmington, his voice strained and croaky as he stuttered through the words. 'I'm a scientist, I can live simply, and I'm perfectly well paid by the university. Salek came back. He's a mercenary, basically. He started out in the army, and he was one of the few Kurds who was willing to work with Saddam. He helped suppress his own people, then he became one of Saddam's fixers, trading in oil and arms around the world. He came to me and said they had taken my sister prisoner. My cousins as well, and their children. They were going to be tortured to death unless I cooperated with them.'

Wilmington paused, steering the Renault out into an open stretch of road. 'I didn't have any choice,' he said slowly. 'I had to do what they said.'

'You should have gone to the police,' said Nick. 'Or the intelligence services. They could have helped you.'

Wilmington shook his head. 'What are they going to do?' he said, his tone touched with anger. 'They can protect me in Cambridge – if they believe me, that is. They can't protect my family in Iraq.'

'So you told them about Sarah?' said Jed.

'Like I said, I had no choice,' said Wilmington. 'They started off by wanting weapons research. Saddam was desperate to build a nuclear bomb, and his men thought I might be able to help them. Then they got wind of the work we were doing on cold fusion in the laboratory. They realised how important it was, and they wanted it. Once Sarah made her breakthrough, Salek was all over me. He wanted Sarah in Iraq, and he wanted her work.'

Jed glanced round. He could see the dark waves of anger cross Nick's face. 'You took her out of the country?' he said.

'Salek arranged it all,' said Wilmington. 'We took her to what was supposed to be a meeting, then she was put in a van and driven to a private airfield in Norfolk. She was smuggled on to a plane that was registered to a Saudi businessman, and it was given permission to take off by air-traffic control – customs checks at those tiny airports are pretty light. The plane landed in Jordan and she was brought into Iraq by car. Then she was taken to the research facility to complete her work. I was brought out for a day. She knew what she was being made to do, and she was very angry about it. But at the same time there was nothing she could do. If she didn't work with them, they would kill her.'

'So what the hell was she doing in the cells?' said Nick.

Wilmington sighed. You could see the strain in the man's eyes, and hear it in his voice. He's tired, thought Jed. And afraid. That's a bad combination. A man like that could lose hope. And then he'd be no use to us at all.

'She'd been working in the facility in Baghdad for two weeks without being able to replicate the experimental work she'd done in Cambridge. I was back at my house. Six days ago, Salek came for me and brought me over here. He insisted that she needed help. I had no choice. When I got here, she seemed nervous, afraid. I tried to reassure her. I told her that all she needed to do was give the Iraqis the experiment, let them see it, and have the proof that it worked, and she was free to leave the country. She was reluctant, didn't seem to believe me. So they took both of us off to the palace. They guessed that there was going to be a strike on the plant, and they didn't want Sarah to be killed: we escaped just seconds before the missile came in. They kept us there for thirty-six hours. At first I thought we were going to be roughed up. They wouldn't hesitate to torture us if they thought it would give them the results they need more quickly. But I think they just threw us in the cells because it was the safest place they could think of while the city was under attack.'

'Then the bastards took her?' said Nick.

Wilmington nodded. 'Yesterday, a couple of soldiers came into the cells and led her away. I shouted at them to tell me what was happening, but they paid no attention. I think that's why they left me there, because I was no more use to them, and because I was objecting to what was happening to Sarah.' He paused, slamming his fist on to the horn as a truck slowed up ahead of them. 'But she's in Tikrit, I'm certain of it. The finest scientific facility in Iraq is here, and if she is anywhere, this is where the Iraqis will bring her. I just hope she's all right.'

'I thought you said the Iraqis need her alive,' said Nick. He was leaning forward, his mouth just a fraction of an inch from Wilmington's ear. 'They need her to complete the experiment.'

'So long as they think she's cooperating and making

progress, she'll be OK,' said Wilmington. 'But these are desperate times. The war has already started, and may only last a few days. If she can't give them what they want . . .' He paused, then shrugged. 'Well, they may dispose of her.'

'Then we better get a bloody move on,' Nick snapped.

It was dark now, and Jed could see they were approaching the outskirts of Tikrit. He checked his watch. Ten thirty, local time. It had taken more than seven hours to cover just two hundred miles. 'Be careful,' said Wilmington, as the road sign ahead of them declared they were just ten kilometres from the city. 'It won't be like Baghdad. Up here, everyone is a Saddam loyalist. They'll fight for the regime until the bitter end. The police and army will still be functioning. If they catch us, we're all dead men.'

'It's not death that bothers us,' said Nick. 'It's failure. Keep bloody driving.'

Jed glanced at Wilmington. He could see the sweat forming on his forehead, and he could see how clammy and sticky his hands were on the wheel of the car. The Renault was edging forward in heavy traffic. Two kilometres from the town centre, Wilmington dropped down on to a slip road, then swung right. They were now driving through a residential area, with neat rows of houses on either side of the street. Compared to Baghdad, it struck Jed as relatively calm and ordered. There was no sign of the missile strikes that had been raining down on the capital. You couldn't hear the drone of the fighters or bombers in the night sky. There were even a few people out and about. Close to the main highway, you could see the first wave of refugees from the south starting to build themselves makeshift camps, but once you got into the heart of Tikrit, you could easily forget this was a country at war at all. There's still life in these people, thought Jed. *It's not over yet.*

'You know where you're going?' said Jed.

Wilmington nodded.

In the back seat, Nick had pulled out his knife. He was leaning forward, flashing the sharpened blade in front of Wilmington's throat. 'Just don't try anything clever,' he said. 'You try leading us into a trap, we'll kill you.'

Jed then jammed his pistol into Wilmington's thigh: he could feel it all right, but no one outside the car would see it. 'One false move and I'll blow your balls off,' he snarled.

Wilmington slowed down the Renault as he approached some wasteland outside the city. They had passed two military convoys on their journey through the city, but neither of them had paid them much attention. They had moved through the residential area into a set of streets dominated by workshops, admin blocks, and then, as they drove out of the city through the remote wasteland, a forbidding concrete building with a thick wall of barbed wire all around it. There were no street lights, and as the Renault pulled up, the building was shrouded in darkness. A few lights were escaping from the third and fourth floors of the six-storey building, but otherwise there wasn't even a moon to guide you. 'Here,' said Wilmington. 'The main Iraqi weapons lab. If Saddam really does have any weapons of mass destruction, that's where they are.'

Jed climbed out of the car. His limbs were stiff from the drive, and he could feel the cold night air chilling his skin. He looked at the pale light shining down on the barbed wire. Could she be in there, he wondered. In all honesty, Jed had no idea. For the first time, he was starting to wonder if Sarah might be dead. No, he told himself, pushing the thought out of his mind. Don't even think that.

'You've been in there?' he hissed.

Wilmington nodded.

'How do we get in?'

Wilmington stared at Jed like he was mad. 'It's the main weapons lab for the whole country,' he said. 'You'll never get in there.'

'We're going in,' said Nick, putting a hand firmly on Wilmington's shoulder. 'And you're coming with us.'

THIRTY

It was past midnight now. Nick and Jed were crouched behind a wall, a couple of hundred yards away from the laboratory building. The lab was set in its own patch of wasteland, at least half a mile from the rest of the city, with one main road leading up to it, and a couple of smaller roads leading from its side and back into the town. Wilmington was a hundred yards behind them, dumped with the rest of their kit, apart from the AK-47s and the grenades. The building was heavily fortified, with the wall of barbed wire, and what looked like at least a couple of dozen soldiers. It was impossible to tell how many from the outside. They had waited for two hours before they saw one man go into the building, watching as his papers were thoroughly checked. There was no chance of going through the front entrance without being captured, even if they were disguised as Iraqis. If they were going to get inside, they would have to fight their way in. After walking through the streets on the perimeter of the building for almost half an hour, they spotted the resting tank crew. 'That's how we get in,' said Nick instantly. 'Nobody stops a T-55 and asks for its papers. You could park one of these buggers in Oxford Street and not even get a ticket.'

The tank crew was clustered by the side of their vehicle, half a mile from the lab. One man was squatting on the ground beside it, brewing himself up a cup of sticky coffee on a gas burner. Another was cleaning his AK-47. The third was having a kip, his body stretched out on the ground, close to the thick, black treads of the Russian-built T-55.

'Reckon you can take them?' whispered Nick.

Jed nodded. 'Sitting ducks,' he said.

Nick grabbed his shoulder. 'There are no sitting ducks, Jed,' he growled. 'I've been in more fights than you have, and I can tell you, the most dangerous enemy any soldier ever faces is his own overconfidence. Any man with a gun in his hand can kill you.'

'I can take them,' hissed Jed angrily.

'OK, OK,' said Nick. 'Just wait until they're drowsy, ready to kip. That's when they'll be at their most vulnerable.'

Jed nodded grimly and bit his lip.

Nick shrugged. 'Not that I give a toss whether you get killed or not,' he said. 'I just might need some help in breaking Sarah out.'

As he focused on the three soldiers, Jed could see one of them switch off the gas burner, and drink the last of his coffee. He got up, and walked behind the tank for a piss. Nick looked at Jed. 'OK,' he said. 'Let's take them.'

The plan was simple, as old as warfare itself: charge them, guns blazing. There were no buildings close by, so no one should hear the attack, and if they went in hard enough they could finish them before they could radio for help. It was two against three, but one of them was asleep, and none of them was expecting an attack. As far as they knew they were several hundred miles from the front, and no doubt glad of it. *The odds were with the attackers.*

Jed started running, his feet hitting the ground hard. He was closing swiftly on his target, the AK-47 jutting from his chest like a sword. He remained silent, except for the tread of his boots on the tarmac. Four hundred yards, he judged. Three hundred and fifty. At two hundred yards, he'd open up with the machine gun. *With any luck, the buggers will all be dead before we get within a hundred yards of them.*

His pulse was beating hard, and he could feel his heart thumping inside his chest. As he kept moving, he could hear the sound of his boots echoing off the wall in the distance. Ahead, he could see the soldier who'd been drinking coffee look up towards him. He could see the expression on the man's face. At first interested, as if he was wondering why a man was running at him. Then afraid.

Two hundred and fifty yards, Jed told himself. *Fifty more . . .*

The man had jumped to his feet. He was shouting something, first towards Jed, then towards his two mates. Ten yards to his right, he could see Nick also running in the direction of the tank, his AK-47 thrust in front of him. He wasn't keeping pace, Jed noted. Second by second, he was falling a fraction behind.

I'm the sod who's going to have to take the brunt of this attack.

A second passed, then another. Two hundred and twenty yards . . .

The soldier was reaching for his gun. Jed slammed his finger hard into the trigger of the AK–47. The gun exploded into a rapid burst of fire, the bullets screeching through the empty night air. As he looked ahead, Jed knew he'd fired too soon. The bullets were pinging off the skin of the tank, or smashing uselessly into the tarmac. But he'd bought himself a few more fractions of a second, while the man looked up and tried to understand what was happening.

'Get the bugger behind the tank,' Jed snapped at Nick.

He could see him veering off towards the right. He moved steadily forward, his breath shortening as he'd pushed himself as fast as he could. Two hundred yards, a hundred and ninety . . .

The man was reaching down for his own gun. It was in his hands now. His fingers were grasping for the trigger, but his hands were shaking. The fear has already gripped him, thought Jed. His training's forgotten. *The poor sod no longer knows how to fight.*

Jed kept firing, ripping a lethal blast of bullets in the direction of his opponent. The bullets were smashing into the ground, but then he could hear the satisfyingly gentle sound of steel ripping into flesh. The man spun round as one bullet after another smashed into him. One had taken out a chunk of his chest, another had ripped open his face. Another set of bullets shredded his lungs, and in the next instant he had slumped to the ground, blood oozing from a dozen different holes in his body.

A hundred yards, Jed noted with grim satisfaction. *On target . . .*

The guy sleeping was now alert. He'd leapt to his feet, and was scrabbling around for his gun. Jed had changed direction, veering slightly to the left as he closed in on the tank. The AK-47 was spraying bullets in the direction of the second man. Seventy-five yards, noted Jed. Fifty . . . then you'll be dead. The soldier already knew he wasn't going to get to his gun in time. With the desperate will to live of a man who knew he was already done for, he was trying to bury himself underneath the heavy tracks of the T-55. Jed pointed the AK-47 right at him, letting off a rapid burst of fire. The bullets smashed into his legs as he tried to get himself beneath the protective skin of the tank. He was howling in agony as the metal shredded the arteries, and within seconds it was clear he was already numbed with pain and shock, unable to move another muscle. Jed arrived by the tank, panting and exhausted, with sweat seeping from every pore of his skin. He looked down at the man. Poor bastard, he thought grimly. The blood was oozing out of him, but he wasn't yet dead. Jed knelt down and, placing the gun into the side of his neck, fired one bullet. The soldier was dead.

As Jed walked swiftly around the tank, he saw Nick standing next to the third soldier. The guy hadn't even had time to finish taking a piss. He was standing, immobilised by fear, holding on to his dick. '*Min fadlik*,' he kept saying, the words trembling on his lips. '*Min fadlik.*'

Please, thought Jed. I'm getting used to that phrase. *The guy is begging for his life.*

'What's keeping you?' said Jed roughly.

'What shall I do with him?' said Nick tersely.

Jed shrugged. 'Kill the bugger,' he said.

He looked at the man. He was tall, over six foot, and no more than twenty-one or twenty-two. His black hair was slicked down over his head, and though his brown eyes were strong and determined, you could tell how scared he was. 'We could just tie him up,' said Nick.

Jed glanced at him. It's been a while, he thought. Nick hasn't been in the forces for a decade. He's forgotten that callous brutality is the first trick of our trade. 'I said, kill him.'

Nick was turning his AK-47 towards the man. '*Min fadlik,*' he repeated, his voice starting to break into a sob. Nick's finger was hovering on the trigger. 'We're not sodding murderers,' he growled. 'At least we weren't in my day.'

'Want me to do it?' said Jed, turning his own gun on the man.

Nick paused. 'Yes, you do it,' he said.

The soldier was glancing anxiously from man to man. His eyes were swivelling like a frightened dog. Sod it, thought Jed. Put the bastard out of his misery. He squeezed the trigger hard on the AK-47, holding the gun rock steady as a rapid burst of fire exploded from its barrel. The bullet ripped through the man's chest, shredding his lungs and heart in a fraction of a second. The blood spilt from him, and some words were about to form on his lips, but the air had already emptied out of him, and he was unable to speak. As his legs crumpled beneath him, he crashed into an ugly mess on the ground.

Jed folded the gun behind his back. A surge of anger and aggression was raging through him, and he took a deep, hard breath of the night air to try and calm himself. He looked at Nick. He'd already put away his gun, and was heading for the tank. 'Let's go,' he said tersely. 'We've got work to do.'

With one powerful movement of his forearms, Nick hoisted himself up on to the platform of the T-55. The tank had been painted desert sand, natural camouflage for its most natural arena. There was some evidence of rust around the tracks, but to Nick it looked in pretty good shape. The Russians had built thousands of T-55s during the 1950s and 60s, then passed the designs on to the Chinese. It was the most common tank in the world, the Ford Mondeo of military vehicles: it wasn't the best in the world, and didn't pretend to be, but it was cheap and reliable, and it could punch a deadly hole in just about any opponent it came up against.

Nick pulled back the turret, and glanced inside. Empty. He was about to drop down into the cockpit when he could feel Jed tugging at his shoulder. 'You fucking bottled it,' he snapped.

Spinning round, Nick looked straight at the younger man. His face was red with anger. 'I what . . . ?'

'You bloody bottled it back there, Nick,' said Jed. He was staring into Nick's eyes. 'You were meant to drop the bastard but you couldn't do it.'

'I'd have been fine,' said Nick. 'I was just about to shoot him.'

'You bloody froze, mate. You couldn't do it.'

'I didn't have any bloody ammo left in my gun, you tosser. I didn't bottle anything, never have done.' He started to lever himself down into the cockpit, but Jed was still tugging at the shoulder of his military tunic. 'Let go,' he snapped.

'What happened to you in Iraq last time?'

'None of your bloody business.'

'It is my business, because I'm stuck with you right now. And if I'm stuck with a bloke who bottles a fight I need to know.' He leant close into Nick's face, and his voice dropped to no more than a whisper. 'Did you bottle it last time round, Nick? Is that what happened? Did you let your mates down?

'I don't let anyone down,' Nick shouted, his face hot with anger. 'It's a fucking lie, I tell you. *A lie.*'

Leave it, thought Jed. I've seen enough to draw my own conclusions, and I don't believe that bollocks about being out of ammo. Nick isn't a man you can rely on. When you're in the last ditch, he's not going to be there for you. *When this mission turns rough, I'm going to have to look after myself.*

The interior of the tank was cramped, even with only two men inside it, although it was designed for four. There was space for a driver, a navigator and two gunners, one at the front and back. The Iraqis had re-inforced the basic design with an extra layer of armour designed to provide some protection against the anti-tank missiles the machine could now expect to face, and that extra thick metal skin had reduced the interior space even more. Nick was already firing up the massive diesel engine, and as the machine started to roll into life, Jed could feel the metal frame start to vibrate beneath him. 'You can drive this bugger?' said Jed.

Nick grimaced. 'You young bastards don't know anything,' he said. 'I joined the army when we still had a Cold War. Learning how to drive a Soviet tank was one of the first things we did.' He smiled to himself at the memory. 'We had proper enemies in those days. Not just the bloody ragheads.'

He kick-started the accelerator, and slowly the machine started to rumble into life. There was the sound of metal scratching against metal as the wheels turned, pulling it across the tarmac. It shook violently as Nick searched around for the right gear, shuddering as it lurched forwards. 'Christ,' said Jed. 'I've been in mini-cabs where the drivers had more idea what they were bloody doing.'

'Just leave it,' said Nick.

The tank was rolling towards the entrance to the admin building. They stopped to pick up Wilmington, and although the scientist was clearly terrified, he was more frightened of being left by himself than getting inside the tank. Then they advanced onwards. Jed had done training in tanks, but he'd never liked them. You felt trapped inside them, and even if you looked through the viewfinders, you never really had any idea what was happening around you. He preferred to be in the thick of the battle, where he could see and smell what was happening, and where you still had some chance of reacting fast enough to save your life.

Looking through the thin viewing strip, he could see the building looming up fast. It was only a couple of hundred yards away from them now. The first strip of barbed wire wasn't going to provide any opposition to a T-55. Nick drove the tank straight up to it, and in the next instant you could feel the weight of the machine crushing it. The enormous bulk of the T-55 rolled across the wire like it was cotton wool, then accelerated towards the secondary layer of ditches, wire and sentry posts that provided the building with its main protection. As soon as they crushed the first layer of wire, Jed could hear soldiers shouting, and then the sound of gunfire. How many men were out there, he couldn't yet tell. Perhaps two dozen. Whatever number it was, he reflected grimly, they hadn't expected one of their own tanks to come after them.

Slamming his foot down hard on the accelerator, Nick took the T-55 up a gear. It rolled violently into a ditch, then started to climb its way out. You could hear the metal screeching all around you as it punched its way through the barbed wire. The T-55 was equipped with two machine guns, as well its main artillery piece: a coaxial gun on its main turret, and a smaller anti-aircraft gun on its side. Both could be operated from the driver's cockpit. Through the viewfinder, Jed could see three Iraqi soldiers rushing towards them, their guns blazing. He turned the machine gun on them and rattled off a quick burst of fire. The tank fired high-calibre bullets that completely shredded people: limbs and heads were strewn over the ground. It's like mowing the lawn, he thought grimly. From somewhere, he could hear more firing, a machine gun from the racket it was making. The bullets were smashing into the side of the T-55, but bouncing harmlessly away.

It was hot and sweaty within the cramped confines of the T-55. Looking ahead, Jed could see they just had one more set of barriers to break through, then they could punch their way into the main building. 'I'm going to shell the bastard,' muttered Nick. 'Hold tight.'

'What about Sarah?' shouted Jed, straining to make his voice heard above the noise of the tank.

'I'll take out the entrance, that's all. If she's there, they won't be holding her by the bloody door.'

Slamming his hand down hard on the controls, Nick fired a shell from the tank's main artillery cannon. There was a brief silence while the hulking piece of metal whizzed through the air, then a terrifying explosion as it smashed into the security barrier and tore into the main entrance to the building. Without pausing for a second, Nick slammed his fist down hard again, firing another shell straight into the same space. Up ahead, a fireball erupted into the sky. He could hear the cries and screams of wounded, dying men, as the shell cut deep into the ground, then exploded upwards, destroying everything around it. Dust and smoke were filling the air, but as it gradually began to clear, Jed could see that the barrier had been completely destroyed. A dozen corpses were lying mutilated across the ground, and half the front wall of the building had been blown away. The T-55 might be an antique, thought Jed, but that didn't mean it couldn't destroy a building in a couple of minutes.

'Any more of the bastards?' grunted Nick.

Jed looked around. The tank was still rolling forwards so that it was within yards of the main entrance. The smoke from the two shells was gradually clearing, and so far as Jed could see, the guards had all been killed. Touching the brakes, Nick brought the tank to a juddering halt. In the back, Wilmington was squatting immobilised, too terrified even to move. 'You think it's safe to get out?' said Jed.

Nick shrugged. 'There's only one way to find out,' he said roughly. 'Stick your head out, and see if it gets shot off.'

Jed paused. 'I don't suppose you're volunteering.'

'Somebody's got to drive the tank,' said Nick. 'You go.'

Jed readied his AK-47. He flipped open the turret of the T-55, and put the barrel of his gun out first. Were there any snipers out there waiting to have a shot at him? He waited, counting up to five. Nothing. With one swift movement, he hauled himself out of the tank, and jumped down to the ground, keeping his finger poised on the trigger of his AK-47 as he did so. There was blood spilt across the ground: from a quick glance, he reckoned at least a dozen men had been killed by the two shells. He checked the bodies one by one, making sure each man was dead before he moved on: there was nothing more dangerous than a badly wounded soldier who suddenly recovered enough strength to lob a grenade at you. Only two of them were still alive, but neither seemed to be conscious. Jed finished them off with a quick double tap to the head. Sorry, boys, he thought grimly, as he delivered the bullets. No time to call in the Red Cross. *You'd do the same if you were in my boots.*

'Clear,' he shouted towards the tank.

Nick was hauling a clearly terrified Wilmington out of the tank. He jumped down to the ground, shoving the professor out in front of him. Jed glanced quickly down the street, checking there were no reinforcements on the way, then stepped through into what remained of the lobby. Plaster and dust were strewn everywhere from where the shells had taken out the front wall. Shards of metal and severed wires were sticking out of the broken wall, and somewhere Jed could hear the sound of gushing water where a pipe had been burst open.

'What are we looking for?' Nick said to Wilmington.

For a moment, he remained silent. Then his lips started to move, but he was trembling too badly for the words to form on his lips.

'I said, what the hell are we looking for?' Nick repeated, louder this time, leaning close into the professor's face.

'Second floor,' said Wilmington. 'Last time I was here, that's where all the main weapons research was being done.'

The shattered lobby had three lifts, but they were all broken: the power lines had all been severed when the shells struck. Through a back door there was a service staircase that ran up the back of the building. Jed started to run, with Nick bringing Wilmington along behind. His finger was poised on the trigger of his AK-47: anyone who came to see what was happening was going to be shot on sight.

On the second floor, he stopped. The lights were working up here: they must be on a different electrical circuit, Jed figured. He checked his watch. It was just after two in the morning. 'Why here?' he said, to Wilmington.

'This is the most sensitive part of Saddam's weapons research network. This is where all the most intense work on trying to create nuclear and biological weapons is done.'

'I thought he already had stockpiles of them,' said Nick.

'So Tony Blair keeps telling everyone,' said Wilmington with a shrug.

Jed steadied himself, held his gun in front of him, then kicked the door open and stepped into the brightly lit corridor. Nothing. So far as he could see, there was nobody around. The main room had two dozen computer terminals arranged on workbenches. Along the back wall there was a set of sensitive measuring equipment, and behind that a sealed room that looked something like an operating theatre. Jed started to march through the room. 'Sarah,' he shouted. 'Sarah.'

Nothing.

Just silence.

'Where the hell are you?' shouted Nick behind him.

Nothing.

You could hear the quiet electronic hum of the computer terminals that were glowing on the desk, and down below you could hear the gushing of water from the burst pipes. *But you couldn't hear anything that sounded like a person.*

'I thought you said she'd be here,' Nick shouted, turning towards Wilmington.

'I thought . . . I thought . . .' he stuttered.

'Where the bloody hell is she?' Nick roared.

'This was the most obvious place to bring her.' Wilmington's words were suddenly garbled and rushed.

Nick was jabbing the barrel of his AK-47 into Wilmington's stomach. 'I should just finish you off now,' he shouted.

Jed put his hand on his shoulder. 'Not yet,' he said quietly.

'He's fucking lied to us from the beginning. He's the reason Sarah ever came to this hellhole. I haven't met many men who deserved to die, but this arsehole is right at the top of the list.'

Wilmington was backing away. 'No . . . no . . .' he mumbled.

'Quick,' Jed said suddenly. 'I can hear something.'

All three stood stock-still. Jed looked towards the far end of the room. A cough, he was certain of it. He started walking. It was silent again now, but that meant nothing: just that the bastard was trying to keep his throat clear. He glanced along the last row of workbenches. Nothing. The next row. Nothing. Then on the third, he saw what he was looking for. A shoe.

'Gotcha,' he said.

The man was cowering in a tight ball beneath the desk. He was wearing a white overall, and thick glasses, and even though he didn't look any more than thirty-five, most of his hair was already gone. 'Come out, you bastard,' said Jed, tapping the man's ankle with the tip of his AK-47.

The man didn't move.

'I said, come out, you bastard. Unless you want your foot shot off.'

Slowly, the man emerged. He looked nervously at Jed, then Nick, then across at Wilmington. His eyes were tired and wary. 'We're looking for a woman,' said Jed. 'A white woman.' The man looked blank.

Wilmington stepped forward, repeating the question in Arabic. Slowly, the man understood. He nodded, the way an animal does when it has earned itself a reward. 'Sarah,' he said. He started speaking quickly to Wilmington in Arabic. 'Well?' said Nick, looking towards Wilmington.

'She was here,' he replied. 'Until yesterday –'

'Where the fuck is she now, then?' snapped Jed.

'Gone,' said the man, the terror written on to his face. 'She's gone.'

'Why the hell should we believe him?' said Nick roughly. 'I say we put a bullet into his thigh, then ask him again.'

'There should be pictures,' said Wilmington. 'Everything in this lab is filmed.'

'Where?' said Nick.

'This way,' said Wilmington.

Jed kept his gun trained on both men as they led the way forward. They walked to the end of the laboratory, through a set of fire doors, then up one flight of stairs. The room they were led into was dominated by a set of television screens, with two swivel chairs in front of them, both empty. The security guards had long since abandoned their positions. The Iraqi was saying something in Arabic, and leaning into the controls. On the screen in front of him, Jed could see the minutes and the hours ticking backwards, as the tapes in the machine were rewound. Suddenly, he could see her quite clearly. The film was black-and-white and grainy, and the back lighting in the laboratory was so intense, it gave anyone in the room a robotic quality. But there could be no question who he was looking at in the centre of the picture.

'Christ, that's her,' he muttered, his voice no more than a whisper.

Sarah was not a conventionally beautiful woman. Her figure was nothing special, and her face was pretty rather than stunning. Her nose was long and thin, her eyes large and her face shaped like an almond, yet she had a kind of beauty that Jed felt was all her own. It shone

400

out of her, even when she looked at her worst, as she did in the pictures in front of him. Her brown hair fell over the side of her face, and looked as if it had been neither washed nor combed for a week. She was dressed in a blue sweatshirt, with some Arabic writing on it, and a pair of jeans that looked too big for her. But she had a look of concentration on her face that Jed recognised instantly. That was what Sarah was all about, he thought: the ability to put all of herself into every moment she lived. *Even here . . .*

Nick was at his side, staring at the image. In the video, Sarah was standing at one of the workbenches, using the measuring equipment. It was impossible to tell from this angle what she was doing. You could only just see her face. But at least she was alive, Jed told himself. *When this was filmed, anyway?*

'This was filmed at four. What time was she taken away again?' said Nick.

Wilmington spoke to the Iraqi, then looked back at Nick. 'Around five yesterday afternoon,' he said. 'Sarah was here for less than a day. They were going to keep her for longer to try and produce the laboratory evidence that would show the world cold fusion worked. But they decided it was too dangerous here. The Americans know this place, and it's a prime target for a missile strike.'

Jed kept watching the film. You could see Sarah working patiently, methodically, but it was impossible on the grainy film to read any of the motives for what she was doing. Was she really going to hand over her discovery to the Iraqis? To let Saddam use it for his own ends. If it was a choice between that and her own life, she might.

He could see a man coming into view. He was standing next to Sarah, with his back to the camera. Then the man turned round. 'That's the fucker who was in your office,' said Nick, jabbing his thumb against the screen.

Salek.

Jed and Wilmington stared at the screen as well. They could see Salek leading her away, holding on to her arm. Suddenly Sarah glanced up at the camera. It was unlikely she knew it was there – the camera was discreetly tucked into the corner of the laboratory – but she seemed to be looking straight up at them. You could see the fear in her eyes. Her expression was hollow, like a child separated from its parents. Her shoulders were sagging, and there was a look of defeat about her, as if she no longer knew how much more she could take. Sarah never looked like that, thought Jed bitterly. *There was always fight in her.*

Sarah and Salek had gone from the screen. You could still see the tape, and you could see the other scientists sitting at their benches. But Sarah had already disappeared from view.

'He's taken her,' said Wilmington.

'I can bloody see that,' snapped Nick. 'Where?'

Wilmington backed away. 'Where?' repeated Nick.

'I don't know,' said Wilmington.

The stutter was back in his voice, Jed noted. He's afraid. *And so he should be . . .*

402

Nick was advancing on the man, his face red with anger. 'I'm tired of your bloody games,' he growled.

'I told you she was here,' said Wilmington, struggling to get the words out. 'She *was* here. You've seen it with your own eyes . . .'

He gestured towards the bank of screens on the wall. Several of them showed what was happening on the perimeter of the laboratory right now.

Jed was already studying them. Something had caught his eye in the far right-hand corner. A grainy, slow-moving shape. 'Look,' he said, pointing at the image.

Nick stared at the screen. He could see the vehicle moving slowly down the main road that led up to the building. One vehicle, with a second following straight behind.

A tank.

'Bugger it,' he muttered. 'It's coming straight at us.'

THIRTY-ONE

Nick and Jed rushed out of the security room, taking Wilmington with them, but leaving the other scientist behind: it made no difference who he spoke to, since the Iraqis already knew they were there. As they ran through the broken hallway, they could already hear the rumble of the tanks as they advanced on the building. Only one thought was on Jed's mind: move as fast as you can.

'You stay right there,' he muttered to Wilmington, then climbed up on to the tank, following Nick down into the cockpit. A rapid burst of gunfire raked through the night sky. Jed realised they'd been spotted, and the gunners in the tanks were trying to take them down before they even got into the vehicle. 'This is fucking madness,' he said. 'They've seen us already.'

Nick turned round. 'You go home to your mum if you want to, I'm staying right here.'

He already had his hands on the controls of the main gun. The T-55 was nothing like a modern British or American tank. There were no sophisticated, electronic controls. You couldn't use laser-targeting, and there wasn't a computer to take care of the tank while you concentrated on the fighting. None of that video-game warfare, thought Jed grimly. You had to take down your enemy the old-fashioned way. *By pointing your gun straight at him, and hoping you were a better shot than he was.*

'He's in range,' Nick shouted.

The main artillery gun was swivelling fast into position. A shell was already loaded, but whether it was armour-piercing, and what kind of protection their opponent had, Jed had no idea. We're flying sodding blind, he thought. Looking through the sights, he lined up the shot straight into the guts of the first tank. It was six hundred yards away now, well within range. 'Take the turret,' said Nick. 'That's the weakest point in the T-55.'

Nick had grabbed hold of the gears, kicked the engine into life, and the tank was starting to roll forwards. Every T-55 had a distinctive semicircular turret that covered the top of the tank, and housed its main gun. Jed started lowering the artillery cannon, trying to line it up close to the turret.

Furiously, he was trying to remember his anti-tank training. You had to bring the shell in at exactly the right angle, and at the right velocity, to stand any chance of piercing the tank's armour. On a T-55, that meant bringing the shell right into the turret, at an angle of less than forty-five degrees, so the shell could slice open the top of the machine like a tin can, and blow up whatever was inside. Get it wrong, and your shell would bounce harmlessly off the tank's thick metal skin. Christ, thought Jed as he swivelled the gun into place, trying to make the calculations in his head. Men train for years as tank gunners. *Neither of us have any sodding idea what we're doing.*

The pair of tanks were advancing down the road with menacing resilience. Jed could see the burnished, sandy-coloured metal of the armour emerging through the dark night air, the long artillery gun pointing straight at them. Any minute now, he thought grimly, they are going to start firing at us.

'We can take them,' Nick muttered.

'You're bloody crazy,' Jed snapped. 'We should get the hell out of here while we still can.'

'Fire,' Nick shouted. 'Bloody fire, you tosser.'

Jed slammed his fist hard on the firing mechanism. You could feel the skin of the T-55 shudder as the shell's explosives charged up, then exploded with terrifying power up through the main cannon. Jed steeled himself, watching as the shell started to arc in the air. Only a fraction of a second passed before it hit. Jed strained into the viewfinder, getting as close a look as possible. The shell winged the side of the first tank. It burst open, sending a cloud of fire and smoke up into the air. Flames were spilling out across the pavement, but the T-55 was still rolling forwards. Its side was battered, and the right side track was smouldering, but it was still operable. And it was about to retaliate.

'You're a fucking crap shot,' muttered Nick. 'Try again.'

The T-55 started to automatically load another shell, but even though Jed didn't know much about Russian tanks, he knew that one of the key weaknesses of the T-55 was the forty-five seconds it took to reload its cannons. As the shell started to winch itself into position, Jed could see the cannon on the first tank swinging towards them.

It was levering gently upwards as the tank rolled forward. The machine was only five hundred yards from them. Shit, muttered Jed to himself, as he tried to get his own gun lined up with the moving target. That guy knows what he's doing. *Which is more than can be said for us.*

As he heard the explosion of the shell leaving the cannon, Jed winced. There was no time to follow the arc of the missile, or to plan your reaction. The shell had already travelled through the air, and impacted with the turret of their T-55. The top armour of the tank took the main force of the blow, knocking the cannon clean away, and the explosion ripped off a sheet of metal armour. The cramped, poky interior of the tank was filled with fire and smoke. Jed could feel an intense heat searing the surface of his skin, and the air was thick with black fumes. He could already smell diesel pouring from the machine's fuel tank. We've only got seconds, he thought desperately. *Then this bugger is going to blow.*

Through the black smoke, he could no longer see Nick. His right hand shot up, and he clamped it down on the twisted surface of the tank's armour. It scalded the skin on the palm of his hand, but he had no choice. He had to lever himself out of the tank. His eyes were streaming with tears from the stinging smoke, but he ignored the pain, and with one effort pulled himself upwards. He rolled his body across the burning surface of the tank, knowing that if he moved fast enough, the flames wouldn't have time to ignite his clothes. With a desperate thud he landed on the ground. 'Nick, Nick,' he shouted. 'Where the hell are you, you old fucker?'

'Watch your language, boy,' Nick snapped.

He emerged from the thick clouds of smoke swirling around the tank. His face was black and sweaty, and there was a trickle of blood down the side of his chest where he had taken a flesh wound to the shoulder. 'That was a fucking stupid idea,' shouted Jed.

Nick shrugged. He knelt down and picked up the kitbag he had left next to Wilmington, and slung it across his back. 'Maybe,' he muttered sourly. 'But if you'd taken the trouble to learn how to shoot straight before you signed up for the army, perhaps we wouldn't be up to our bollocks in shit right now.' He paused, hauling the shaking professor up off the ground. 'In the meantime, I suggest you run like hell. The next shell is coming straight for us.'

Jed started running. It was late and dark, he reminded himself. That always gives a man a chance. His feet were pounding hard against the tarmac surface of the road, and with the kitbag on his back, his breath was short and angry. He skirted around the edge of the tank, towards the side road leading away from the building. It was impossible to see exactly where he was going, or what might be lying ahead of him. The lane twisted past a couple of warehouses, then ran through some empty scrubland, before taking you towards the centre of Tikrit. Just keep running, Jed told himself. *Stay on your feet and you still have a chance of staying alive until dawn.*

A huge roar struck through the night air, followed by a flash of brilliant white light. The shell must have struck the ground twenty or thirty yards behind him, Jed reckoned. But still the force of the impact was deadly.

The ground started to quiver and shake, and in the next instant a huge pile of mud and smoke was thrown up into the air. The blast shattered your eardrums, and the air was filled with noxious fumes. Jed could feel himself being thrown forward by the wave of hot air radiating from where the shell had impacted. The flames spitting out from the crater ignited the diesel spilling from the T-55, and with a sudden deafening roar the tank exploded, sending a fireball rippling up into the sky. The explosion was followed by a wave of secondary blasts, like a series of bubbles popping, as the shells inside the tank were detonated one by one.

Jed threw himself to the ground. As the tank went up in smoke, shrapnel was spitting through the air: tiny shards of razor-sharp metal were flying everywhere, each one with the power to slice your arm off.

'Fuck it,' screamed Nick.

Jed looked round. Nick was lying on the ground, ten yards to his right, with Wilmington next to him. Blood was seeping from Nick's left leg. He had rolled to his side, clutching his lower calf, his mouth locked in a grimace as he tried to control the pain. Jed was about to move, but he could already hear the roar of another shell exploding from the cannon of the advancing tank. Within a fraction of a second, it had struck the ground, digging up the mud, sending a cloud of dust and fire screaming up into the sky. Jed lay as close to the ground as he could as another hailstorm of metal and concrete swirled around him: he had learnt enough about surviving an attack by shelling to know that it was the shrapnel that shredded you. He could feel a couple of pieces of broken concrete striking him in the back as he lay there. It was worse than being thumped by Mike Tyson, but he ignored the pain, holding himself perfectly still. Survive, he told himself through gritted teeth. *That's the only thing that counts.*

Within seconds, the hailstorm had subsided. Jed glanced anxiously at Nick. He was still lying on his side. Jed picked up his kitbag and started to run towards him. He could hear the rumble of the tanks approaching the main building, but for the moment he guessed the shelling had stopped. The tank commanders probably reckoned they were still inside the T-55 and weren't going to waste any more valuable ammunition on a couple of corpses. They would just be moving in close to make certain they were dead.

'Get me a rag,' he shouted to Wilmington as he helped Nick to his feet.

Wilmington looked confused. 'Where . . . ?'

'From your sodding shirt,' Jed shouted. He grabbed hold of Wilmington's shoulder and, with one swift movement, ripped the arm straight off his shirt. Turning back to Nick, he squeezed tight just above the shrapnel wound. A shard of metal had cut its way into his calf, lodging itself deep in the flesh. Jed had seen a few wounds in his time, and this was a nasty one: if they couldn't find a doctor to cut that shrapnel out, Nick was in trouble. When he was satisfied the bleeding was staunched, he wrapped the torn shirt tight into the leg, pulled hard, then slipped it into a knot. He could feel

Nick shuddering as the pain ripped through him, but his lips remained silent. Say what you like about the old guy, thought Jed, he knew how to roll with a punch.

'You OK?' he said.

Nick glanced back towards where the tanks were advancing on the shattered, broken T-55. They were within twenty yards of it now. It would take them a few minutes to inspect the carnage, and to realise there weren't any corpses inside. 'Let's move,' he snapped. 'We haven't much time.'

'You run on that leg, you bloody lose it, mate,' said Jed.

Nick looked at him, a glint of steel shimmering in his eye. 'There isn't any kind of punishment I can't take if I need to,' he growled. 'Now, let's get the hell out of here.'

The track led towards the heart of the city: they had to get as far away from the lab as possible, then they needed to check in with the Firm, then find a vehicle. The road wound through the scrubland, then dipped into a built-up maze of small shops, apartment buildings and workshops. Jed kept running, keeping his eyes tight on the road for police or soldiers. Nothing. It was almost four in the morning now, and the streets were empty. His breath was short, and his back was still stinging from where the shrapnel had hit him, but he was starting to feel confident they had outrun the tanks. Maybe the commanders assumed they were already dead. Maybe they didn't care: they just wanted to get back for a kip at their barracks. *Either way, they're not giving chase.*

411

He paused, bending over to try and regain his breath. Wilmington and Nick were following him close behind. To his left, there was a square filled with cafés and shops, all of them closed at this time of night. To his right, a small alleyway that twisted between two factory buildings. Somewhere in the distance, Jed could hear the sound of trucks. Dawn was approaching. Soon it would be light. *They had to find somewhere to hide before then.*

'Here,' he hissed.

Together the three of them started to walk down the alley. There were some bins overflowing with rubbish, and an open sewer from one of the factories taking industrial waste out towards the river. The alley reeked of garbage and chemicals, and Jed could suddenly feel the exhaustion washing over him. He tossed his kitbag on the ground, and sat down. At his side Nick and Wilmington did the same. For a minute, none of them spoke. They were just trying to get their strength back. Sweat was dripping down their faces. From Nick's bandage, some blood was starting to seep out of the edges. 'What the fuck do we do now?' said Jed eventually.

'Phone home,' said Nick, his tone firm and decisive. 'They got us into this shit, they can get us out of it as well. They must have a line on where we can find Sarah.'

Jed paused for a moment. He looked up towards the sky. Some heavy black clouds were rolling overhead, obscuring the moon and stars. There was a light breeze in the air, and he could feel the cold biting into his skin: in the winter, Iraq had a harsh climate, with temperatures dropping below zero every night. He'd taken some light burns to the skin on his arms as the tank exploded, and it tingled as the air touched it. Like sunburn, he thought grimly, except a hundred times worse. Like everything in this hellhole of a country.

'OK,' he said. 'Let's check in, and tell them everything's fucked.'

Nick fished the satphone from Jed's kitbag, and tossed it across to him. Checking first that it had located a signal, Jed punched in the number. There was delay of almost a minute, as the phone connected with the satellite, then searched for the right connection. 'Laura, is that you?' he said as soon as the phone was answered.

'Christ, Jed, where are you?' said Laura.

He could feel the tension in her voice, even at a distance of three thousand miles. 'Margate,' he said. 'Thought we'd catch some sea air.' He paused, waiting to see if she would react, but she remained rock silent. 'We're in sodding Iraq,' he continued. 'Where do you think we are?'

'You've found Sarah?'

Even though he knew she couldn't see him, Jed found himself shaking his head. 'She's vanished,' he said bitterly. 'We've just blown up the research lab in Tikrit. We found some video footage of her working there, but they took her away yesterday.'

'Who's "they"?'

'A guy called Salek.'

'He's on our files,' said Laura. 'He's one of the main go-betweens for Saddam's attempts to buy WMD around the world. Missile launchers, plutonium, nerve gases, the works. If there's a market for it, and it's nasty enough, then Salek has been trying to buy it for his bosses.'

'Well, now he's got Sarah.' Jed paused. 'So where the hell would *he* take her?'

He listened intently to the line, but for a moment he could just hear the crackle and fizz of the satellite signal fading in and out. The Firm must have some leads on where he might take her, he told himself. *They must . . .*

'We don't know, Jed,' she said. 'I'm sorry.'

'You must bloody know,' said Jed, he tone turning harsh.

'We don't.'

'I thought this country was crawling with your agents.'

A dry laugh could be heard down the line. 'If only . . .' Then she snapped to attention. 'You'll just have to keep looking.'

'I know that,' said Jed, his tone exasperated. 'But where?'

'You're soldiers, use force if you have to,' Laura snapped. 'She has to be found. If Sarah delivers the secret of cold fusion, there's still a chance Saddam could use it to negotiate a ceasefire, to buy his own passage out of Iraq. We can't allow that to happen.'

'And I'm telling you, we need some help,' Jed snapped back.

Another pause.

414

'Well, if you think you and Nick can't handle it . . .' said Laura coldly.

'Qaladiza,' said Wilmington.

Jed turned round, looking first at Nick, then at the professor. 'What did you say?'

'He's taken her to Qaladiza,' Wilmington repeated.

'Where the hell's that?'

'It's in Kurdistan,' said Wilmington. 'Salek comes from Kurdistan. It's his home town. I'm ashamed to say it, but he is one of my own people.'

Nick was looking closely at Wilmington. 'Are you sure?'

Wilmington nodded. 'The Iraqi told me. Salek said it was too dangerous in Iraq, he was taking her to Qaladiza. It's the last place in this country he reckons he can hide her safely. And if Saddam does fall in the next few days, then Salek will take her across the border into Iran, and sell the cold-fusion technology to them.'

Jed put the receiver back to his ear. 'She's in Kurdistan,' he said flatly.

'Then we're coming to get her,' said Laura. 'I'll meet you on the border.'

For a second, Jed was too surprised to say anything. 'You'll do what?'

'I'll meet you on the border. In twenty-four hours. I can be there by then.'

'We're the soldiers, we can take care of it.'

'Kurdistan is friendly territory,' said Laura. 'The Firm needs to be there to pick her up. This is our operation, remember.'

415

'It's too sodding dangerous.'

'It's also an order,' said Laura archly. 'We'll rendezvous tomorrow night. Just make sure you're there. We need to get Sarah, and as soon as possible. We can't leave anything to chance any more.'

The phone call was over. Jed looked across to Nick and Wilmington. 'We're meeting her in twenty-four hours,' he said. 'Up by the border.'

Nick started to stand. 'Then we'd better get moving,' he said.

Jed packed the satphone back into his kitbag, then he put his hand on Nick's shoulder, and pushed him back down to the ground. 'First we deal with that leg,' he said.

'It's fine,' Nick growled.

'I tell you, you walk any more on it, you're going to lose it,' said Jed. 'We've got to get the shrapnel out.'

'We haven't got time.'

Nick was trying to stand again, but Jed held him down, looking straight into his eyes. They were blood-shot and worn: the eyes of a man who was ignoring the terrible battering his body had taken in the past few hours. 'Are you scared?'

'I'm only scared of one thing,' Nick snapped. 'And that's losing my daughter.'

He lay down on the ground, and ripped aside the rough bandage Jed had made earlier. The calf where the shrapnel had gone in was now caked with dried blood. The bleeding had been staunched, but the flesh was still open where the shard of metal had ripped into it. From his bag, Jed took out a knife, the same one he had used to kill the Iraqi soldiers the day before. In the medical kit, there was a bottle of alcohol, and Jed rubbed some into the knife to disinfect it. He'd never operated on a wounded man before, but he'd seen the videos and he knew what to do. In theory anyway, he thought grimly. *But I wouldn't want to be the bloke I was practising on.*

'Want some morphine?' said Jed.

There was a single vial in the medical bag: most soldiers carried one with them, if only to ease the pain of dying if the wounds they had taken were fatal. If he needed it, Jed could jab it into him.

'It'll just slow me down,' said Nick. 'A man with morphine in him needs time to rest, and that's what I don't have.'

'So does a man with a wound,' said Jed.

Nick glanced towards Wilmington. 'Just give me something to bite on.'

Wilmington unhooked his belt and handed it across to Nick. He folded the strip of leather into his fists, and pulled it down tight between his teeth. The belt tasted of sweat, and he could smell the blood on it. Doesn't matter, he told himself grimly. It will stop me from screaming. That's all that counts.

He nodded at Jed.

'Hold his shoulders,' said Jed to Wilmington.

The professor grabbed hold of Nick's shoulders. He gripped him tight, pulling him down on to the ground. His back was arched, and the tension was buzzing through him, but he remained still. Jed looked down at the wound, a fleshy, bloody mess, then with one swift movement, stabbed the knife down into the calf. Nick grunted as the pain ripped up into his spine, but said nothing. Jed twisted the knife around, looking for the remains of the shrapnel. The knife hit something. A bone? No, not deep enough for that. He flicked it upwards, cutting through the flesh with savage intensity. Again, Nick bucked upwards, and for a moment the knife vibrated in Jed's hands, cutting through yet more flesh. Some blood squirted out. Found something, thought Jed, as the knife struck the shrapnel. He pulled up again, bringing a tiny shard of jagged, lethal metal that looked as if it had once been part of a tank to the surface. Nick was starting to whimper, and there were tears streaming down his face. Above him, Wilmington was leaning down harder, using all his strength to keep him pinned to the ground.

'Almost there, mate,' muttered Jed.

Jed twisted the knife into the raw flesh, then turned it again, The shard of metal fell out and, using the tip of the blade, Jed swiped it on to the ground. Picking up the bottle of alcohol, Jed pressed hard on the leg, then splashed the cold liquid on to the open wound. Suddenly, Nick's back arched upwards, and a howl of pain erupted from his mouth. Jed held on to the leg, poured more alcohol into the wound, then reached for the rag they had used as a bandage. He wrapped it around the calf and pulled tight, using all his strength to staunch the bleeding. Nick had fallen silent again now, but he was still shaking. 'Done,' he said, looking at Nick.

'Jesus, I could use a fucking drink,' Nick spat, taking the belt out of his mouth. Tears were oozing from his eyes, as he tried to master the pain stinging up from his leg.

'You should try and rest it,' said Jed, putting a hand on his shoulder.

'I should probably have a couple of dolly-bird nurses mopping my brow as well, and a nice stack of DVDs to watch at the bottom of my bed,' said Nick roughly. 'But those are the breaks, so let's get a sodding move on.'

Slowly, he stood up. He was keeping as much weight as possible off the wounded leg, and was using Jed's shoulder to help him walk. Every step he took on it was doing terrible damage to the blood vessels and nerves in the leg, Jed noted.

Jed helped him struggle towards the main street. He was hobbling, but there was a look of fierce determination in his eyes. The sun was starting to rise, with the first pale rays of the dawn shimmering through the clouds. Somewhere in the distance, Jed could hear a bird singing: the first cheerful sound he'd heard since he landed in this hellish country, he thought. 'I don't care what they say,' said Jed, helping Nick out on to the street. 'You've got guts.'

'We'll see about that in the next twenty-four hours,' said Nick gruffly. 'A father who can't save his own daughter doesn't have any guts worth having.'

THIRTY-TWO

Jed and Nick were positioned behind a low wall of rocks, just outside the dusty Kurdish town of Bashiqa, about thirty miles east of Mosul. It was part of the no-man's-land between Iraq and the autonomous Kurdish region that had been formed a decade ago after the British and Americans started the no-fly zone that effectively kept Saddam's forces out of the area. They had been on the go for the last twenty-four hours, and the sweat and blood was starting to cake to the skins of all three of them. In Tikrit, they had forced Wilmington to buy them a car from a local: a beaten-up Honda Civic that cost six ounces of gold, but which seemed reliable. From there, they had driven along the back roads that led up towards Mosul: a distance of no more than couple of hundred kilometres on the map, but which took a good part of a day when you were trying to steer clear of both soldiers and bandits.

As they drove, they could see the signs everywhere of a country where civilisation was fast starting to unravel. The roads were thronged with people desperate to get away from the front lines of the war, as well as bandits and robbers and deserting soldiers. Twice their car was stopped by hijackers, but a quick burst of gunfire from the AK-47s soon settled the argument: there were more than enough defenceless victims for the robbers to want to get into a fight with anyone who looked as if they knew how to use a machine gun. As they made their way across the border into the Kurdish district, they had called into London with their position, and had been given the coordinates of the drop-off point. Laura would meet them at 1 a.m. precisely, they had been told. They should make their own way to the rendezvous point, and lay up there.

They were two miles from the village, on a stretch of empty, barren countryside: the nearest farmhouse was at least a mile away, so, Jed reckoned, it was unlikely anyone had heard them.

Laura stepped away from the jeep, and scanned the horizon. The headlamps were beaming out of the vehicle: it was just after one and, with heavy cloud cover, the valley was cloaked in darkness. She had just arrived at the RVP overland, after flying into Turkey a few hours earlier. She had four burly-looking men with her, protection for her journey, and some extra help for lifting Sarah out of whatever hiding place Salek had taken her away to. The wind was swirling through the valley, pushing her hair up across her face. 'This is no place for a bloke,' said Nick. 'And it's certainly no place for a bird.'

'You haven't met her,' said Jed.

'I haven't?' said Nick. 'That's the bitch that sent me into this hellhole.'

Laura was striding towards them, dressed in black

jeans, a sweatshirt and a black leather jacket, with a small kitbag slung over her back. She stopped a few feet from where Nick, Jed and Wilmington had stationed themselves. 'Have you managed to get a car?' she said to Jed. 'I don't think we should waste any time.'

Jed walked her over to the Civic. They had parked it a hundred yards away, in a dip in the ground, about twenty yards off the dirt road that led up to the RVP. 'You smell like crap,' she said, dropping her kitbag on to the back seat of the car. 'What the hell happened to you?'

'It's been a rough few days,' said Jed.

Laura nodded. 'Well, you've done well to get this far.'

Suddenly Jed grabbed her by the arm. 'Why didn't you tell me Sarah was in that lab in Baghdad?' he snapped. 'I'd never have sent that missile strike in there if I'd known it was aimed at killing her.'

Laura shook her arm free. 'That's why I didn't tell you.'

'Sod it,' said Jed, the anger pulsing through him. 'I'd have gone in there myself if I'd known Sarah was there.'

'And got yourself bloody killed,' said Laura. 'That wouldn't have done anyone any good.' She climbed into the back seat of the Civic. 'Let's move. We haven't got much time. The jeep has got some extra men in it, and it's going to lead the way. Just follow.'

They took turns to drive. There was no main road that led up to Qaladiza. The map showed it was in the far north of the country, near the Turkish border. Kurdistan straddled three countries: Turkey, Iraq and

Syria, but the most lawless chunk of the nation was the Iraqi section. There were few proper roads, and not many towns; the people were either farmers or drug dealers. Qaladiza nestled in a valley close to the Zagros Mountains that ran along the Turkish border, and then down into Iran: wild, rugged bandit country which even Saddam's violent henchmen hadn't managed to subdue. On the map, it was about 150 miles away. In the dark of the night, and with no decent roads, it could easily be dawn before they got there.

They drove mostly in silence. Jed took the wheel first, and with four of them plus kitbags in the Civic, it was a tight squeeze. Nick sat next to him, with Laura and Wilmington in the back. The roads were a mixture of dirt tracks and the occasional few miles of tarmac, but the Civic was in good enough shape to make it through. There were plenty of bumps, and a couple of times Jed felt certain they were about to break the suspension, but by keeping the speed down to thirty miles an hour, he managed to avoid too much damage to the vehicle. He'd have liked to have gone faster, but push the car too hard and the bumps and potholes would crack it apart. Then we'd bloody well have to walk the last fifty miles. *And I'm not sure we'd make it.*

Thirty miles into the journey, there was a sudden and terrifying explosion. The Civic juddered to a halt. A hundred yards ahead of them, the jeep had turned into a raging fireball. Flames and shards of burnt metal were flying everywhere. Nick and Jed immediately took cover, whipping their AK-47s out of their kitbags, readying themselves for a fight. Gradually the fireball subsided. On inspection, it turned out the jeep had run over a landmine, killing the four men inside instantly. The country is littered with them, Wilmington explained. It's just the way things are in Kurdistan. Neverthess, they had to press on with their journey. They told Wilmington to keep as close as he could to the mud tracks on the rough road. So long as they only drove where they knew other vehicles had travelled they had more chance of avoiding the landmines.

The country changed shape as you approached the Zagros Mountains. The roads started to twist steeply uphill, and it became much more lush and green. There were some wild flowers dotting the hillsides, blooming at the first approach of spring, and a faint smell of honey filled the air. Over in the distance, they could see snow covering some of the mountain tops, but along the valley paths they were driving through, the thaw had already started. There were villages along the way, but the streets were all empty at this time of night. Compared with Baghdad and Tikrit, it was peaceful up here. The fighting was a long way away. And this was the one part of Iraq that welcomed the British and Americans into the country. They would bring them their freedom.

As dawn broke, Jed, back in the driving seat, slowed down the car. Laura had a fresh supply of biscuits and chocolate bars in her kitbag which she handed round. Jed munched on the biscuits gratefully, and wolfed down the chocolate. He could feel the burst of sugar hitting his bloodstream, and reviving him. It had been at least twenty-four hours now since he'd slept, and days since he'd had a proper kip. The dirt, exhaustion and tension were eating into him: another day, maybe two, that was all Jed reckoned he was good for before he collapsed from exhaustion. You can only push your body so far, he warned himself. Cross the line, and it's damaged for ever. And nobody is going to give you a new one.

'I don't suppose you've brought anything we can brew up,' he said, finishing off the chocolate, and turning round to look at Laura.

'Keep your eyes peeled for a Starbucks,' she said. 'If we see one, the lattes are on me.'

'How much further?' he said to Nick.

Nick finished his own chocolate and studied the map. 'Another ten miles,' he said. 'Not far.'

'And the road is OK,' said Wilmington.

'You know it?' asked Jed.

'Some of my family comes from near here,' said Wilmington. 'This is my country.'

'And you can sodding keep it,' said Nick.

Jed pushed his foot down on the accelerator, and steered the Civic along the road. There was one more steep mountain to twist through before they dropped down into the final valley. At times the road squeezed down to no more than a track that looked as if it was designed for a donkey rather than a car. Even a small vehicle like the Civic was struggling to squeeze through, and at one point Jed could feel the tyres struggling to keep their grip on the gravel as they turned through yet another sharp corner. Down below, there was a drop of at least a thousand feet, and Jed could feel his pulse racing as he tried to keep the car on the road. The first rays of the morning sun were shooting through the clouds as he turned the final corner, and took the Civic up into third gear for the final, straight road that led down towards the village. The valley was bathed in a dusty orange light, catching on the petals of the wild flowers and the water of the streams that were gushing down from the snow melting in the mountains.

Maybe this morning we'll actually find Sarah, he thought. *There has to be at least one dawn that isn't false.*

By the time Jed pulled the car to a stop in the centre of the village, it was already seven thirty. Qaladiza was little more than a single street of houses, built along the banks of a river. Maybe fifty houses in all, Jed reckoned, most of them looking as if they belonged to farmers who spread out through the valley to cultivate their land. There was a small mosque, and what looked like a schoolroom next to it, and that was about it. Jed climbed out of the car, looking around him as Nick and Wilmington did the same. Some men were herding their goats out towards the pasture, and they looked suspiciously at the car and its occupants. After a minute or so, they stopped the animals and started to talk among themselves. In the next instant, the village sprung to life. Men were emerging from the houses. Jed had his kitbag on his back, and he knew precisely where his AK-47 was, where his stun grenades were and what he would do if this turned into a fight. He could see twenty to thirty men, ranging in age from twenty to fifty, lining

the sides of the street. They were rough-looking characters, with dark brown eyes and thick black hair, and
skin that was as beaten and craggy as the landscape they
were living in. 'I thought you said the Kurds were on
our side,' said Jed, glancing towards Wilmington. 'Bloody
say something to them.'

One man was advancing towards the car. He looked
about fifty, and had a long grey beard that covered his
face. He was wearing a thick sheepskin jacket, and his
hands were covered in scars and bruises. The imam,
thought Jed. Or some kind of tribal elder. He pushed
Wilmington forward. The professor began to speak,
slowly and softly at first, but with his voice gathering
in strength and confidence, and the Kurd was listening
to him intently. He looked suspiciously at Nick and Jed,
then he noticed Laura sitting in the car, and his face
clouded with anger. The other village men – all the
women and children stayed inside – advanced closer, so
that they formed a circle that completely enclosed the
intruders. Wilmington talked some more, starting to
gesticulate with his arms, and slowly the mood light-
ened. The man started to nod enthusiastically, and a smile
was breaking on to his lips. 'He says it's OK,' said
Wilmington, turning to Nick and Jed.

'Ask him if he knows where Sarah is,' said Jed.

'He says to have breakfast with him, and he'll tell us
what he knows.'

Laura climbed out of the car, and they walked across
the muddy dirt track. The man was leading them towards
the back of the mosque, and at least a dozen of the

villagers were following behind them. In the distance, Jed could hear the sound of goats and sheep braying, and could smell the fresh tea being brewed. A full English would be a treat, he thought: sausages, bacon, eggs, fried bread, some beans, and a big hot mug of PG Tips. Not much chance of that in this hellhole. We'll probably get a couple of boiled goat's eyes for breakfast. *If we're lucky*.

'Can we trust them?' Laura hissed, looking around nervously as they approached the mosque.

Jed glanced back at the steady line of men that was blocking their way back to the car. 'I'm more worried about whether I can trust *you* than the local ragheads.'

Behind the mosque, there was a simple, one-storey dwelling. It was made out of wood, with a straw roof. Tied up next to it was a donkey, and at its side, a pile of straw and firewood. The man led them inside. The building was just one room, with a fire in the corner, filling it with a sweet, sticky smoke. He pointed towards a table with a bench on either side of it. An elderly woman started to lay out some plates. She poured hot, sweet tea into their cups, and put down a series of wooden platters: pitta bread, black olives, tomatoes, white cheese, a jar of honey, and some deep-fried soujouk, a type of sausage made out of ground meats and spices. Jed waited a moment. It was days since he'd had anything proper to eat, and he knew that if he tucked in too quickly he would just make himself ill. He took a hit of the tea, letting the sugar fill his veins, then filled some pitta bread with sausage and cheese, taking a deep bite. Slowly, he could feel the food feeding some strength back into his muscles. Eat while you can, he told himself, as he packed another pitta. *Any meal out here could be your last.*

Wilmington and the man were talking quietly to each other in Kurdish, while Nick and Jed fell on their food. Laura hardly touched hers. Eventually, Wilmington turned to them. 'Salek was here,' he said. 'He had a young woman with him, and she answers to Sarah's description.'

Jed could see Nick stop chewing. He was holding his pitta bread in his hand, all interest lost in the food. 'Was she OK?'

Wilmington nodded. 'Tired, stressed, but not harmed.'

'And where the hell is she now?'

'Still with Salek,' said Wilmington. 'He's known in these parts, and has enough money and connections to buy himself a safe passage through the mountains. He was taking her towards Khailyhameh.'

'Where the hell's that?' said Nick.

'A village, about forty miles from here, right up in the corner of the Zagros Mountains, where Iraq, Iran and Turkey all meet.'

'Why?' said Nick. 'I don't get it.'

'He wants to hide her,' said Laura. 'Sarah is the only bargaining chip Salek has left now. He needs to take her to the most remote part of the country he can find. Salek's looking after himself now, and he knows Sarah is valuable property. As Wilmington says, if the Iraqis are done for, he can just take her over the border to Iran.'

Nick put down his food. 'Then let's move,' he said.

'If that's where she is, that's where we're going as well.'

Wilmington exchanged a few words in Kurdish with the man, then turned back to Nick. 'Khailyhameh is a bad place,' he said, with fear in his eyes. 'It is part of Halabja valley, which saw some of the heaviest fighting during the Iran–Iraq War. Much of the society around there was destroyed. It was where Saddam used chemical gases against the Kurds who remained. These days, it is controlled by Ansar al-Islam, a radical Islamic group with links to al-Qaeda. They hate all Westerners. It isn't safe for anyone to go there.'

'And Sarah's there?' said Nick.

Wilmington nodded.

'Then she's in danger, and we're going to get her.' He looked straight at Wilmington. 'And you can risk dying there, or you can die right here. It's your choice.'

The late-afternoon sun was streaming through the valley. Jed steered the car along what was nothing more than a mud track. From the village to Halabja might have only been forty miles, but there was no proper road, and the Civic wasn't built to drive across country. Along the way they'd had to stop a dozen times as the car had to be pushed through some thick mud. Once, they'd had to clear away a tree that had fallen across the track. It might have been quicker to walk, thought Jed. It would certainly have been faster on horseback.

Along the way, you could see the remnants of old battles everywhere. More than fifteen years might have passed since the end of the Iran–Iraq War, but there were still burnt-out husks of old tanks, abandoned trenches and empty trucks. They went through three ghost villages, the buildings still intact, but crumbling as the stones and mortar slowly turned back into dust: all the people had been wiped out in Saddam's gas attacks. You could smell the destruction all around you, thought Jed, as he powered the car towards their destination. What must Sarah have felt as she was taken through these villages? That she was leaving all civilisation behind her. *And all hope with it.*

When they reached the village, Jed climbed out of the car. A dozen men were walking towards them, talking among themselves. They were rough-looking characters, with thick black beards, and AK-47s slung around their leather and sheepskin coats. Jed scanned their faces, looking to see who was the village elder, but none of the men looked to be more than twenty-five. Christ, who's in charge here? *Maybe no one.*

Nick and Laura also climbed out of the car. The three of them stood next to the Civic, looking straight at the men walking towards them. Jed steadied himself. Show no fear, he told himself. Make sure they know you're not afraid, and you'll have earned their respect. *That's at least one battle won.*

'Get out, Professor,' barked Jed. 'Your mates are here.'

Wilmington started to climb out of the Civic. His face was drenched with sweat, and the fear was evident in his eyes. A few days' growth of beard had collected on his face, and there were scratches and cuts on his skin. His clothes had been reduced to rags, and exhaustion had turned his skin and eyes to a grey, soggy pulp. His hands were shaking, and his voice was fractured. 'Move it,' Jed snapped.

In front of him, one man stood out from the pack. He was holding his finger tight on the trigger of his AK-47 and there was a pair of long, curved hunting knives hanging from the belt around his waist. His beard was long and scraggy, and he was so thin he was little more than a skeleton with bit of muscle hanging off it. Jed hadn't met many men he wanted to kill the first moment he saw them, but this was one of them.

The sun was beginning to shade into the mountains, sending beams of pale orange light down into the valley. As Jed glanced around the village, all he could see were six single-storey houses. There was no sign of electricity, and just a well at the end of the single dirt street for water.

The man in front of the pack barked something in Kurdish. It was a rough, harsh dialect, different from Arabic or Turkish. He was pointing at Wilmington, and waving his gun at the same time.

'He wants to speak to me,' said Wilmington nervously.

'Then bloody speak to him,' said Jed, pushing him forward.

Wilmington staggered across the ten yards of scuffed ground that separated the dozen men from the Civic. One of the men grabbed his hands, yanking them hard behind his back. Wilmington cried out in pain.

'Bloody leave him alone,' Jed snapped.

The leader took a step forward. He was pointing his gun straight at Jed, and his finger was hovering menacingly on the trigger. Jed glanced into the car. His own kitbag was lying on the back seat, with his gun inside it. Out of reach. *Even if they could take on all twelve of the bastards, they could never get to their guns in time.*

'Quiet, Jed,' said Nick firmly. 'Let Wilmington speak to them. He knows their language. If he tells them we're British, maybe they'll start to cooperate.'

'Right,' said Jed. 'Or maybe they'll get their frying pans out to put our balls in.'

The man was leading Wilmington towards a tree that lay behind the main road. It was still early in the year, but the first buds of fresh blossom could just be detected on its branches. The men were talking quickly in Kurdish, and Wilmington was shouting at them. As they pushed him, his expression was turning wilder and wilder. Eventually they thrust him against the tree trunk. Suddenly, five men were standing in a semicircle around him, their guns raised straight in front of their eyes.

'What the hell is happening?' said Jed.

'Buggered if I know,' said Nick.

One man had pulled out a rope, and had already tied Wilmington's hands behind his back. The knot was tight and cutting into his skin: his wrists were starting to bleed heavily where the bark and the rope were slicing the flesh open. He was shaking, and there were tears streaming down his face. He was shouting at the men in the Kurdish, yet Jed found it impossible to decipher a word. You don't need to translate, he told himself grimly. He's pleading desperately for his life. *That sounds the same in any language.*

'Stop them,' shouted Wilmington desperately.

His eyes were swivelling between Jed and Nick. 'Please, please,' he stuttered. 'Stop them . . .'

'What the fuck are you doing?' shouted Jed, heading for the tree.

One of the men took a pace forward, thumping the barrel of his AK-47 in Jed's chest. He could feel the metal slamming into his muscles, and could see the man's finger hovering on the trigger. 'Leave it,' snapped Nick.

'They're going to shoot the bastard,' said Jed.

'He brought Sarah here,' said Nick. 'He was going to pay for that one day.'

The barrel of the gun was still jabbing into Jed's chest. He looked into the eyes of the gunman, just inches from his own face, and he could see the fury rising inside him, but also the fear. He looked no more than eighteen. No training, and no discipline, he realised. Just a teenager with a machine gun.

'Leave it, Jed,' said Laura. 'We can't help him now.'

For a brief second, the valley was silent. Wilmington had stopped screaming. His legs had buckled, and there was urine running down his trousers. He was falling to the ground, held up only by the knot securing him to the tree trunk. The leader barked a single command, triggering a rapid burst of fire from the five gunmen positioned around the tree. A hundred bullets ripped simultaneously through Wilmington's body, puncturing it in a dozen different places. His lungs collapsed, and his head fell to one side, virtually sliced clean from his neck, held in place only by a thin twist of muscle.

Christ, thought Jed. *No matter what he might have done, no man deserves to die like that.*

The leader turned to face them. There was a jagged smile on his face. 'That's what we do to collaborators,' he said, speaking in a rough, broken English.

'You speak English,' said Jed.

'Of course,' said the man angrily. 'What do you think we are? Savages?'

He walked towards the Civic, while the boy with his AK-47 jabbed into Jed's chest started to back away. There was a sparkle in his eyes, Jed noted: the look of a man who enjoyed giving the orders to kill. 'He said you were British,' he said, looking towards Nick.

'We are,' replied Nick.

His face was calm and impassive, like a piece of rock.

He nodded. 'Then we have no quarrel with you,' he said. 'So long as you understand our rules. My name is Rezo. We are the law around here. Only us. You do what we ask, and you don't cause any trouble.'

'You killed our guide,' said Nick.

Rezo shrugged. 'He was a collaborator.'

'I thought you said we weren't your enemies,' said Nick.

'Kurds should never work with Iraqis,' said Rezo. 'It offends our pride. The punishment for that is death. But we have no quarrel with you because you are British.' He stood back, resting the tip of his gun on the ground. 'Now, what are you doing here?'

'We're looking for someone,' said Nick. 'A man named Salek. He should have passed through here with a young girl. A British girl . . .'

Rezo nodded. 'He passed through here last night.'

Jed glanced across at Nick. As their eyes met, both men were thinking the same thing. *We're getting closer.*

'By himself?' said Nick. 'Or with a girl.'

'With the Iraqis,' said Rezo. 'About twelve of them. Special Republican Guard, I think.' He spat on the ground. 'We hate them.'

'What was he doing here?'

Again Rezo shrugged. 'I don't know,' he said. 'Salek is a Kurd but he had Iraqi soldiers with him. They gassed our people, they tortured us, they slaughtered our wives and children.'

'Where are they?'

'Up in the mountains, I believe,' said Rezo. 'Where the caves are.'

'The caves?' said Nick.

'A network of passages cut into the mountains,' said Rezo. 'Some of them are natural, some of the them are man-made. Anyone can disappear up there.'

'We need to get in,' said Nick. 'We need to find him.'

Rezo chuckled, scratching his beard as he did so. As he looked at the man, Jed felt sure he could see lice moving around inside the thick layer of matted hair on his cheeks. 'Then I wish you luck, British man,' he said.

Nick shook his head. 'We need help,' he said. 'There's twelve trained soldiers up there and only three of us.' He looked straight at Rezo. 'We'd like you to help us.'

Rezo laughed again, louder this time. He turned around to the other men, barked a few words in Kurdish, then all of them laughed at the same time.

'We'll pay you,' said Nick.

Jed remained silent, waiting for the response. Better to let Nick do the talking, he told himself. This Rezo guy seems to prefer talking to an older man.

'How much is my life worth, you think?' said Rezo.

Nick remained impassive. 'We have gold and dollars,' he said. 'We'll pay you what we can.'

'How much?' Rezo repeated.

Nick was already running the calculations in his head. Both he and Jed had another couple of hundred dollars in bills in their kitbags, and ten ounces of gold. They would need something to get out of here. 'Two hundred dollars, and five ounces of gold,' said Nick.

Rezo stepped closer. He was standing just a few inches from Nick, looking straight into the man's eyes. 'You just give me everything you have,' he said.

'We need some money to get out of here,' said Nick firmly.

'Everything,' Rezo repeated. 'Or else we can't help you.'

Nick glanced at Jed, but neither man needed to speak. They had come this far: there was no way they could turn back now, not without Sarah.

He looked back to Rezo and nodded. 'Four hundred dollars, and ten ounces of gold, that's all we have,' he said.

'I have ten ounces, and a thousand dollars,' said Laura.

Already Rezo was barking some instructions to his men. There was a few minutes' conversation, before he turned back to Nick. 'Five men will come with us,' he said. 'I will lead them.'

'Then let's go,' said Nick.

'No,' said Rezo firmly. 'The mountains are impassable at night. We march at dawn.'

THIRTY-THREE

Jed peered into the darkness. The moon was starting to fade into the clouds, and on the horizon the first glimmers of the dawn were starting to break through the mountains, but the valley was still shrouded in a thick, menacing darkness. He could smell the dew rolling off the hillsides, and the scent of the wild juniper bushes that filled the area.

Some men could sleep before a battle. He'd known guys in the Regiment who could grab some kip knowing that they might never wake up again. Yet he was finding it harder all the time. He could shut his eyes, but as tired as he was, he couldn't quite reach out and catch hold of sleep. It kept dancing away from him, like a leaf caught on the breeze.

'It gets harder as you get older,' said Nick.

Jed was surprised to find the old guy standing right next to him. From somewhere, he'd managed to find some sweet tea, and had brewed up a couple of cups. He handed one to Jed. 'I read once that even infantry soldiers at the Somme thought they were going to be OK. Somehow they figured they'd get through, that there wasn't a bullet with their number on it. Even though the poor bastards didn't have a chance.'

Jed took a sip of the tea. It tasted hot and sticky, nothing like the way he'd usually make a brew, but it was better than nothing.

'They were just teenagers, you see, and they thought nothing could ever happen to them. Then, as you get older, and you see more men around you dying, you realise there isn't rhyme or reason to a battle. Some guys get a bullet, and some don't, and none of it makes any sense. That's when you figure out it might be you next time around. And that's when it gets harder to sleep.'

'You think I'm losing my nerve.'

Nick shook his head. 'Just wising up,' he said. 'Realising that there is nothing special about you, and no reason why you should live to see another dawn.'

'Is that what happened to you?' asked Jed, sitting down. 'After you came back from Iraq last time.'

Nick sat down next to Jed. They had spent a few hours trying to sleep on a pile of straw in one of the abandoned houses in the village. It might once have been the home of a whole family, and maybe a couple of goats as well, but you could still see the craters all around it where the shells had hit the village, and it was more than a decade since anyone had lived here. The place smelt of damp, and crumbling cement. Right now, they were sitting on what would have once been the front step, but was now just a slab of stone. 'Is that why you started drinking?' Jed persisted.

Nick thought for a moment, sipping on his tea. 'I

was shaken up pretty bad when I came back,' he said. 'They'd kept me in the cells for months, they'd tortured me, squeezed the life out of me until I thought there was nothing left. They sent me to the Regiment shrinks when I got back, but it was worse than bloody useless. Confront your demons, and all that therapy bollocks. It's no good when you can't sleep for months on end. There was only one place I could look my demons in the eye, and that was at the bottom of a whisky bottle.'

He scratched the thick, greying stubble that was growing on his chin. 'I went on some missions, but the spirit was all beaten out of me. The Regiment could tell, they felt sorry for me, and they shuffled me off into some cushy jobs, but I wasn't interested. It was time for me to get out and do something different.'

'Did you let your mates down?' said Jed.

Nick hesitated. 'That's what they think,' he said.

'Who?'

'Marlow and some of the other Ruperts. They think I cracked under torture.'

'Did you?'

Nick shrugged. 'After I was captured, two of our patrol were intercepted by the Iraqis,' he said. 'There were four men on each, and they were all killed. The Ruperts reckon I gave the Iraqis enough information for them to track our boys down.'

Jed hesitated. A couple of cocks were starting to crow in the distance as the light crept down further into the valley. 'And did you?'

Nick shook his head. 'I would have broken if I could,'

he said. 'No man can hold up under torture, it doesn't matter what they tell you. That's why armies operate on a need-to-know basis. I didn't know anything worth telling them. Those patrols copped it because the Ruperts fucked it up the way they always do. Dropped them down in the wrong place, with the wrong kit. They just don't like admitting it, so they put the word around that I'd talked after I'd been captured. The story went out that I'd told the Iraqis Steve Hatstone's location. It was bollocks, but a lot of people still believed it. It gave them a nice handy excuse for their own incompetence.'

'So you didn't let anyone down?'

Nick shook his head. 'I didn't say that,' he replied. 'I let Mary down. And I let Sarah down as well.'

'What *really* happened to her mother?'

Nick sighed, as if the memory was still painful for him. 'I've never told anyone.'

'Well, you might well be dead by lunchtime,' said Jed. 'So if you don't tell someone now, you might never get another chance.'

'We'd set up this ski school out in the French Alps, and we'd been there for about a year,' said Nick. 'It wasn't going very well. I was still drinking, I just couldn't shake it. I was meant to be doing the teaching while Mary looked after the books, but nobody wants a ski instructor who can't even stand up straight. We got a few clients, but they didn't last long, and there certainly wasn't any word of mouth. We had a bit of cash saved up but it was slowly draining away, and there was nothing coming in. We were rowing all the time. Mary was pissed off with me for not pulling myself together, and I couldn't blame her.' He paused, looking up into the sunlight that was starting to fill up the valley. 'One afternoon I was meant to be meeting some Austrian tour company that was interested in booking a series of military ski courses. It could have been a big contract for us. I completely forgot about the meeting. When they called to see where the hell I was, I was already in one of the bars having a couple of pints. When Mary found me, she went crazy, started shouting at me, I shouted back, then she drove off in her car.' Nick stopped again, taking another sip of his tea, as if he needed something to fortify himself for the next sentence. 'That's when she had her car crash. The next time I saw her she was lying in a morgue. If it hadn't been for that row, she wouldn't have died. It was my fault.'

'You don't know that,' said Jed.

Nick shrugged. 'Sure, people have car crashes all the time. I've tried to tell myself that a million times. I've never managed to convince myself, though. Not for a second.'

'You blame yourself . . .'

Nick laughed. 'If I could find some other bastard to blame, I would. I just can't seem to find anyone. It was my fault, as surely as if I'd killed her myself. I let her down. And I let Sarah down as well. She was just a kid, and she needed her mum. After that, the ski school closed down. We came back to England, and I was still drinking heavily. I just couldn't get any kind of handle on myself. Eventually, Sarah was taken into care. That's what finally got me to sober up. It gave me enough of a shock to pull myself together. I stopped drinking and found myself some work. In time, they let me take Sarah back again. She was damaged by it, though. She never quite trusted me to look after her again, not the way a girl should be able to trust her dad to take care of her.'

'A lot of dads are useless,' said Jed.

'Like yours?'

'A thief, and he wasn't even any bloody good at it,' said Jed. 'My mum couldn't cope either. That's how I ended up in care, and that's how I met Sarah. The rest you know.'

'So how'd you end up in the army, then?'

Jed shrugged. 'Buggered if I know,' he said briskly. 'Trying to prove something, I suppose. That I could take the punishment, not like my dad.'

'Trying to prove it to me?' said Nick. 'That you were good enough for Sarah?'

Jed remained silent. *It might be true, but I'm not going to bloody well tell him.*

Nick stood up. 'It won't work, you know,' he said sourly. 'A soldier wasn't good enough to be her dad, and no soldier is ever going to be good enough to be her husband either. We all let our women down in the end. That's just the way things are.'

'Not necessarily,' said Jed.

'Right,' said Nick. 'I've seen the way you and Laura look at each other.'

Jed fell silent. Before he could reply, Nick was on his feet and heading purposefully towards the mountains.

Rezo was up, and was finishing his breakfast. Laura had slept in the next hut, and had already washed herself down. She was walking towards Jed.

'You've done really well so far,' she said. 'There might well be an MC in this for you. Maybe even a VC.'

'You can stuff the medals,' Jed replied sourly. Nick's remark was still stinging his eyes, and he was regretting ever having allowed himself to get close to Laura. 'I just want to get Sarah back.'

'Yes, well, I'm doing my best to help you,' said Laura sharply.

'Then let's go,' said Jed, turning to walk away.

Five of Rezo's men were lined up, ready for the mission: they were introduced as Darwen, Mezdar, Camer, Neroz and Joro. Doesn't make much difference what they're called, thought Jed. None of them can speak English. We're not about to become mates, even if we do stay alive through the next few hours.

'You ready?' said Rezo.

Nick nodded. He'd already hoisted his kitbag up on to his back, and readied his AK-47. 'We're good to go,' he said.

They started to walk up the narrow twisting path that turned steeply into the mountains rising up from the side of the valley. It was still early in the morning, the ground was wet with dew, and there was a cold breeze blowing in from the east. Jed had been on plenty of marches before, a few of them even into the face of gunfire, but this one felt different. They had no idea what kind of enemy they might face, how strong he might be, or what resources he might have. All they knew was that Sarah was up there somewhere, and they had to find her. *If she was still alive.*

'Can't we call into Hereford for some air cover?' said Jed to Laura.

'We lost four guys last night,' said Laura. 'They aren't going to send us any more. There isn't an unlimited supply.'

'They think we're coming in with the heavy stuff, the chances are they'll kill Sarah,' said Nick. 'To have a chance of getting her, we have to get up so close we can smell their aftershave. Then catch them off guard.'

Jed looked up ahead. Rezo was leading the way, with the five Kurds following close behind in single file. They were like mountain goats: thin and wiry, they glided across the rocks and stones the way skaters move across the ice. This is their territory, he reflected. The trouble is, it's Salek's territory as well. *We're fighting on foreign soil. Their soil.*

After two hours' walking, they stopped. Rezo handed out some dried pitta bread and dates, and they drank from a mountain stream. The water tasted pure and fresh, melted from the snow, which, as they climbed higher and higher, was drawing closer all the time. 'How far to the caves?' said Jed, spitting out a date stone and looking towards Rezo.

'Another hour,' he replied.

He pointed to the east. They were already two thousand feet above the floor of the valley, tucked into a flat shelf of rocky ground that stretched for a half-mile in front of them. Then the mountains started to rise in a series of steep ridges, before soaring up into the snow-covered peaks just beyond them. Where the steps started, Rezo explained, they would find the caves: a long, dark set of interlocking tunnels and spaces carved into the rock over hundreds of centuries.

They started walking again. It was getting chillier as they rose higher into the mountains, and even though Jed could feel himself starting to perspire from the climb, it was a cold sweat that was running down his spine. Nick was starting to slow down. Jed could tell that the wound in his leg was too bad for him to attempt a long mountain trek like this. For a brief moment, he considered telling him that he should wait for them back down in the village, that he was just going to slow down the march, and they'd have more chance of finding Sarah without him. But there was no point. You could no more keep a raging bull tethered to a matchstick than you could keep the old guy out of a fight to save his daughter. If they couldn't find her, it would ruin what was left of him. *There is only so much punishment one man can take, and he's reached his limit.*

'You going to make it?' he said, looking at Nick, and the way he was dragging the wounded leg behind him.

'I'll be fine.'

Jed noticed that his teeth were gritted, and there was sweat pouring off his face. As he glanced down, he could see fresh blood seeping from the wound, and staining the outside of his trousers.

It was just after ten in the morning by the time they

closed in on the entrance to the caves. The ground was rocky and barren, covered in a dusting of hard frost. The wild flowers and grasses of the valley couldn't grow up here. Rezo called them to a halt, and pointed to a slit opening up in the rock in front of them. 'Right there,' he said. 'That's where the cave network starts.'

Jed looked into it. You could see the way the thick slabs of granite opened up, and a few feet of the tunnel were visible, but after that it was completely dark. They were equipped with AK-47s, and they still had some stun grenades in their kitbags, about a dozen in total. 'How many men do you reckon are in there?' said Jed.

'A dozen,' he said firmly. 'We counted them as they went past. We like to know how many Iraqi bastards are on our land.' He paused for a moment, exchanging a few words with his men in Kurdish. 'They will have built their defences by now. The Republican Guard have fought in these tunnels before and they know their way around.'

'We draw them out,' said Nick. 'Fight the bastards in the open. That's our best chance.'

Jed glanced at Nick. 'A diversion?'

Nick nodded. Scanning the area, he could see two cuts in the rock: one here, and another four hundred yards to their right, across a strip of barren rock. There was clear open ground between the two entrances. About twenty yards back from the second entrance there was a group of rocks, about ten feet high: natural cover for men contemplating an assault. He nodded towards Rezo. 'You take your men over there, then lay down some heavy machine-gun fire, and a few grenades. Make plenty of noise, but make sure you're well dug in behind the rocks. Jed and I will stay right here. When the bastards come out to see what all the fuss is, we'll open up. Let them have it right where they deserve it. In the back.'

Rezo nodded. A few more words were exchanged in Kurdish, then he looked back at Nick. 'How many grenades do you have?'

'A dozen.'

'Then let us have six.'

Nick took the grenades from his kitbag, and handed them over. Rezo led his men across the four hundred yards to the second entrance. As they started to move carefully up to the open rock, Jed scanned the entrance to the caves. The opening was six feet high and twenty feet wide: you could drive a whole brigade into this mountain if you wanted to. There was no sign of any men, but that didn't mean there weren't any listening to them. An attack could come any minute. You had to be prepared.

'Step back behind those rocks,' said Nick to Laura.

'I'm staying right here,' she said defiantly.

'You ever been in a firefight?'

Laura remained silent.

'Just as I thought,' said Nick. 'You can do office warfare, but let me tell you, the real thing is different.'

'I'll be fine,' hissed Laura.

Nick knelt down. He pushed his hand into the ground, bringing up a lump of cold moss with a few bits of earth attached to it. Below that, there was just rock. 'There's nowhere up here to build a bloody grave,' he snarled. 'So unless you want the local rats chewing up your corpse, I suggest you move back.'

Slowly, Laura started to move away. She positioned herself behind a circular clump of rocks, looking out over the scene of the impending battle. Jed lay down on the cold ground, keeping his body as flat as possible. Nick was kneeling down next to him, tying a rough bandage around his wounded leg as he did so. He was finding it difficult to move. Specks of blood were dripping out into the moss where his wound had opened up, and from the strain on his face, Jed could tell he was burning up from the pain running through him. 'You cover this entrance closer to us, I'll fire on the men who go after Rezo and his mates,' he hissed.

Jed nodded. He put the AK-47 into position, checked that the thirty-round magazine was slotted into place, and that he had a spare lying right next to him. Both he and Nick pulled some moss up around their faces and guns to obscure their position. Unless you were walking right into them, they shouldn't be visible. 'Ready,' he said firmly.

Nick looked up towards where Rezo had taken up position. He was dug in behind a set of rocks, guns lined up in a row. With his right hand, Nick gave him a salute, and Rezo nodded in reply. There was a moment of silence in the mountains. Somewhere in the distance, Jed could hear some birds fluttering down the slopes, and he could feel the breeze whistling across the barren rock. In the next instant, his ears were exploding to the raucous sound of gunfire. A barrage of heavy fire was spitting against the far entrance to the cave. Bullets were raging furiously into the air, cutting into the rock, hurling splinters everywhere. As they ricocheted, they were striking the ground, then flying upwards. The noise was echoing in a thousand different directions, so that if you closed your eyes, it seemed you were surrounded by guns. Jed looked into the hurricane, keeping himself steady on the ground, tracking the volleys of fire. One grenade was thrown into the air, then another. They crashed near the entrance to the caves, throwing up thick clouds of smoke that swirled through the air. That should grab their attention, thought Jed grimly. *If it doesn't, there is nobody there.*

A silence. The initial volley of fire died away, and the mountains were suddenly eerily quiet. Jed looked towards the entrance closest to him. The soldiers inside would know they were under attack by now, and they would know they had to respond. The issue was, how? And how long would they wait? Unless they were planning to throw their lives away, they wouldn't attempt a frontal assault. They would slip out of the other entrance, then try and attack them from the flank. Unless there was some other way out of the caves, thought Jed. *Unless they could mount a surprise of their own.*

'Get ready,' said Nick.

A figure emerged from the tunnel. It was no more than a shadow at first. Some kind of animal, Jed wondered as he tracked its movements. No, he could see more clearly now. A man. He was wearing a green military tunic, marked with the purple insignia of the Special Republican Guard. In his hands, there was an AK-47. He was emerging slowly into the sunlight, inching forward suspiciously, his eyes peering around the corner to see if he could see where the assault was coming from. He let off a few rounds of gunfire, but the bullets struck the stony ground harmlessly. 'Hold it steady,' said Nick. 'Let more of them come out.'

Jed lay tight into the ground, as still and as calm as the rock on which he was lying. The man edged forward again, so that he was now outside the tunnel. He was looking towards the far entrance, and he could see Rezo's men in their position four hundred yards away. A hundred yards to his left, he hadn't noticed Nick and Jed. 'Give it another minute.' Nick's voice was no more than a whisper.

The soldier shouted something back into the tunnel. He tucked himself into the side of the rock, so that he was out of range of Rezo's men. A minute passed. Jed kept his finger hovering on the trigger of his AK-47. Another man was standing on the side of the rock, then another. Within a few seconds, Jed could see six of them, grouped in a tight unit. They were moving out slowly, making sure they kept themselves under cover as they planned their assault on Rezo's position. 'Three seconds . . .' whispered Nick.

Jed took aim. One man was clearly in sight of his gun, two others near by. The AK-47 was not a sniper's weapon: it laid down a barrage of fire that could destroy anything it encountered, but it was impossible to target with pinpoint accuracy. Both men silently counted down the three seconds. In the next instant, their guns leapt into life, as bullets rattled out through the air. There was a delay of just a fraction of a second before the first shards of lethal metal tore into their victims. The man in Jed's sights spun round as a dozen different bullets cut open his chest. As he fell to the ground, Jed moved his gun just a fraction of a millimetre, directing his fire at two more men. The bullets lashed into them: one man was hit in the face, another had his back peppered with bullets as he tried to turn and run back into the caves.

In less than five seconds it was all over. Not so much a firefight as a slaughterhouse, thought Jed grimly.

He took his finger off the trigger. Once again, the mountainside was silent. As Nick did the same, Jed looked up to check how much damage they had done. Six men were lying flat on the ground. Picking himself up, he ran quickly across to the corpses. All of them were dead, apart from one man, who was lying on his side, moaning. Without hesitating for a second, Jed dropped his gun to the man's head. *A double tap, and he was finished.*

'Good work,' said Nick, approaching where Jed was standing.

He was trying to run, but it was clear that his leg was hurting too much.

They moved swiftly towards where Rezo and his men were stationed. All of them were unharmed. 'Six down,' said Jed to Rezo.

He nodded. 'Six left,' he said. 'At least.'

'They won't come out that way again,' said Nick.

Rezo shook his head. 'We'll have to squeeze the others out,' he said. 'You wait here.'

Jed grabbed hold of his arm. 'We'll come with you,' he said.

Rezo shook him loose. 'We know these caves,' he snapped. 'It's our territory.'

He signalled towards two men, exchanging a few brief words with them. Then they started advancing on the cave they had just attacked. 'What the hell are they doing?' said Jed.

'Drawing out the enemy again,' said Rezo. 'The only way to beat them is to make them come to us.'

Sounds like suicide to me, thought Jed. He lay up behind the rock, and waited. Two of the men who remained were smoking, filling the air with the smell of heavy Turkish tobacco. The sun was shining down into their faces, making it difficult to see anything. He kept his eyes peeled on the entrance to the cave. Suddenly he heard a rapid burst of gunfire. There was an explosion of noise rattling out of the tunnel, like a car backfiring, followed by flashes of white light.

'What the fuck's happening?' said Nick.

'We're luring them out,' said Rezo.

'My daughter's in there, man,' Nick snapped. 'The point is to rescue her, not stage a bloody bloodbath.'

Jed was readying himself, holding his AK-47 steady, using the last fraction of a second to decide whether to rush the place. If Sarah was in there, they had to get in, get hold of her and get her out, before these nutters blew the whole place back to hell. In the next instant, one of Rezo's two men started to emerge out of the cave. He was facing into the tunnel, firing off round after round from his gun. You could hear screams everywhere. The man was wounded in two places, his leg and his chest, and blood was dripping out of him. He stayed steady on his feet until a burst of fire lashed through him, knocking him several feet sideways, his body split in two. Five Iraqis rushed forwards, their guns blazing furiously. A hail of bullets descended on their position. Jed dropped to the ground, holding his gun in front of him, but it was impossible even to look at what was happening without risking getting your head blown off.

'Christ, these blokes don't really do tactics, do they?' Jed muttered towards Nick.

'And I thought our lot were aggressive,' Nick grunted.

At the side, Rezo was shouting furiously. One of the men had tossed aside his cigarette, and was running down the side of the mountain. That left two more. One looked steady enough, the other was shaking like a leaf. The Iraqis were crouching in the entrance to the cave, using the rock formations for cover, but still crawling stealthily towards them, in a line of at least six men, with the AK-47s blazing out a murderous hail of bullets.

'Throw in the fucking grenades,' shouted Jed.

Nobody moved.

Rezo had grabbed one of his men by the shoulders, the more nervous of the two, and was shaking him by the shoulders. He threw the boy forward, so that he was exposed, standing straight in front of the advancing Iraqis. He stood stock-still for a second, opening up a burst of gunfire that took down two men, before he himself was sliced open, and tumbled down dead on to the ground.

Jed glanced through the rocks. Four Iraqis left, a hundred yards from them, still advancing. He picked up two of the stun grenades, and hurled them in quick succession up into the air. As they crashed into the ground, huge clouds of smoke rose up into the air, swirling around the advancing men. He could hear choking, then more wild bursts of gunfire, the bullets spraying higher and higher into the air.

'Fucking move out,' he shouted at Rezo.

Both men started running in tight formation, with Nick and the last of Rezo's men following close behind. The remaining Iraqis were already retreating back towards the cave: they were taking casualties, and they knew they'd be safer back there. Up ahead, there was nothing but a cloud of smoke. Jed held his gun steady, spraying a steady stream of fire into the smoke. It was impossible to see anything he could lock his gun on to, but he had a fairly good idea where the opposition was: keep on laying down a barrage of fire into that space and you should hit something, he told himself. He heard one scream, then another. One corpse was lying bleeding on the ground, his gun lying abandoned on the ground at his side. Not good enough. There are still two or three of the bastards left.

Enough to kill us all.

The bullets were still spitting out from their assailants. At his side, he could see Rezo falling to the ground, clutching his chest. Jed surged forward, jamming his finger hard on the trigger of the AK-47, keeping up his rate of fire. Behind him, from the corner of his eye, he could see Nick tumbling to the ground. 'Christ,' he muttered. 'The fuckers are taking us apart.'

'Take the right,' he shouted at the only one of Rezo's men who was still fighting.

He veered off to the left, hoping to complete a pincer movement that would take down the last two or three Iraqis.

'Take the bloody right,' he shouted, louder this time.

It was useless. The boy couldn't hear him. He was charging forward, a roar of anger erupting from his lips, spraying bullets from his gun. The rate of fire was terrifying. One man fell, then a hailstorm of bullets whipped into the boy, shredding him into pieces.

Just me, thought Jed grimly. *Alone.*

He steadied himself, still running towards the side of their attackers. A gust of wind was blowing from the side of the mountain, pushing the smoke from the stun grenade high into the air. Slowly it began to clear. Through the fog, Jed could see two men still standing. One was coughing violently, doubled up in pain: his lungs hadn't been strong enough to hold his breath any longer, and he was already drawing in the noxious fumes from the stun grenade. The other was standing still, his gun gripped tightly in his fists, a malevolent, dangerous grimace on his face. Jed steadied himself, put the AK-47 into position and let off a volley of fire. The man already coughing on the fumes was hit by one bullet in the side of his stomach. His mouth opened, letting in a lungful of fumes. Another bullet struck him in the chest, splitting him open. He collapsed in a pool of blood on the ground.

The second man turned to face Jed. He was standing upright, his gun still gripped in his fists, looking straight at Jed. There was no more than thirty yards separating the two men, and Jed could see the desperation in his eyes: he'd looked at men who wanted him dead before, but not with the desire and hunger that this guy had to finish him off.

Without thinking, he jabbed the barrel of the AK-47 in the direction of the one Iraqi left standing. He slammed his finger down hard on the trigger. One bullet spat out of the gun, missed its target, then the gun fell silent. The magazine was empty.

A smile was spreading across the man's lips. He started walking a few paces forward, putting himself in a position where he couldn't miss.

Christ, thought Jed. This is it. *The bullet with my name on it is looking straight at me.*

Only twenty yards separated them now. Jed briefly wondered if he should turn and run. No, he told himself. You still have a knife in your pocket, and that means you still have a chance. Better to take a bullet in the front than the back.

A rattle of gunfire. The man crumpled right in front

of him. A bullet had pierced him clean through the forehead, killing him instantly. Before the man even knew what had hit him, he'd fallen dead on the ground.

Jed looked round. Laura was standing straight behind him, a Beretta 92 compact pistol in her hand. She walked slowly up towards where Jed was standing, a bead of perspiration dripping down her face.

'A firefight doesn't look so bad,' she said softly. 'Not once you get used to the noise.'

Jed started to smile. 'You're not a bad shot,' he said.

'Better than you, I reckon,' Laura replied.

'Maybe we'll find out,' said Jed.

Taking a fresh magazine from his kitbag, he jammed it into his AK-47, then ran across to where Nick had fallen. He was starting to pick himself up off the ground. Jed checked him for signs of wounds, but he looked OK. He'd stumbled, and his wounded leg had collapsed beneath him, taking him out of the fight. 'Are they dead?' he said.

Jed surveyed the carnage laid out all around them. There were a dozen Iraqi corpses; and four of Rezo's men, plus Rezo himself, were all dead. One man had fled down the mountainside. The air was thick with the smell of blood and smoke. 'They're all gone,' he replied.

'Sarah must be in there somewhere,' said Nick.

Laura nodded, looking towards the entrance to the tunnel. 'There might be more guards,' she said.

'I'm going in,' said Nick.

Jed shook his head. 'I'm going,' he snapped.

Nick was levering himself up. Blood was still seeping

from the wounded leg, and he was grimacing from the pain. 'I'm going,' he said firmly.

'We need one guy to assess the situation in there,' said Jed. 'We all go, we all might get shot, and that's no bloody use to anyone.'

'Then I'm going,' repeated Nick.

He started to shove Jed aside, but Jed pushed back. 'Your leg is too badly bloody hurt,' he said.

'She's my daughter,' shouted Nick.

'Calm it,' snapped Laura. 'Jed should go. We'll wait here.'

Jed started to walk away, but as he did so, Nick tugged on his shirt. He looked round. A fist suddenly landed in his face, crashing into the side of his jaw. 'Leave it, you old bastard,' he shouted.

Nick punched again, the blow this time landing on the top of Jed's neck. His punch was solid, like a piece of metal slapping into your skin. Jed could feel the pain rippling down into his spine and his legs. The anger was boiling inside him. 'You've pushed your luck once too often, grandad,' he snarled. 'I can turn one cheek, mate, but two? That's bloody pushing it.'

Already Nick's fist was raised again, ready to smash into Jed's ribs. Jed swerved, avoiding the blow. 'I'm getting my daughter,' he snapped. 'I'm fucking sick of everyone getting in the way.'

Jed kicked out with his leg. His boot caught Nick on the side of his ribs, knocking him off balance. With his right hand clenched into a fist, Jed drove a punch straight into Nick's stomach. The anger within him was coiled up into the blow, exploding with brutal force into his opponent. *I've been wanting to lay a blow on that old sod for years,* thought Jed sternly as he drew his fist back again. *Feels good to finally have the chance.*

Nick wobbled, then crashed to the floor. The wound on his leg had opened further, and blood was smeared across the bandage and seeping on to the rock. 'Sarah needs the best man for the job,' he said. 'That's not you, and never bloody has been.'

He started to pull himself up from the ground, a murderous look raging through his eyes. From his shoe, he'd whipped out a flick knife. The blade sprang open, nestling in the palm of his hand. One jab, then another. Jed jumped away, avoiding the knife. Nick was standing on both feet, even though the wounded leg was shaking and bleeding badly. He started to edge forward.

Laura stepped in front of Nick, pointing her Beretta straight at him. 'I've already shot one man today,' she said calmly. 'You want to join the list?'

Nick started to prepare another jab of the knife at Jed. Laura thrust the gun another inch forward. 'I mean it,' she snapped.

'Drop the knife, Nick,' said Jed.

A moment passed. Nick tossed the knife to the ground, the blade smashing into the rough mountain stone. 'Go,' he said sourly. 'And make sure you bring her out OK.'

'I'll need a handgun,' he said, glancing at Laura. She nodded, giving him the Beretta, which Jed tucked it into the palm of his hand. 'If I'm not back in twenty minutes, assume I'm dead. Get on to Hereford, and tell them to send some reinforcements.'

He started walking. It was just twenty yards to the entrance to the caves. As he stepped over the pile of Iraqi corpses, he felt certain he could see one of the men move. No, just the wind, he told himself, as he looked into the dead man's eyes. He kept walking. As he headed into the tunnel, he could feel the rock surrounding him. The air was completely still, but somewhere up ahead, there was a faint scratching noise. As he looked ahead, he could see nothing. Only darkness.

THIRTY-FOUR

There was a flashlight nestling in Jed's pocket, but he didn't want to use it. Switch on a light, and you might as well put a big target round your neck, with the words 'Shoot me' written on it, he thought. The darkness might be the only thing keeping me alive. *You just have to get used to it, that's all.*

He kept walking. From the entrance of the caves, he reckoned he'd covered about a hundred yards by now. The rock felt damp to the touch, and cold. There were bits of moss growing along the ground, but as you went further into the interior of the mountain, the rock became completely bare. Somewhere in the distance, he felt certain he could hear water. A stream maybe. He was using his hands to creep along the wall of the tunnel, feeling his way forward. The rock was jagged and twisted and there were already a couple of cuts on the palms of his hands. Where the hell are you, Sarah? Say something. *Let me know where you are.*

How many Iraqis might still be inside, Jed had no sure way of knowing. Rezo had said *around* a dozen Special Republican Guard troops had passed through the valley on their way up to the mountains. Twelve of them were dead, but there could be one or two men left inside. *The only way to find out was to go in and face them.*

A hundred yards turned into two hundred, then three. Jed started to have an idea why Salek had come here. The interior of the mountain was a natural hiding place. You couldn't raid or storm it. It was too dark, and there were too many hidden crevices. If you defended it well enough, you could stay here for ever. With the right kit, and enough guts, one man could hold out against a battalion.

Any light from the entrance had completely faded now. For the first hundred yards, a few flickerings of sunlight had bounced down among the rocks, but as the tunnel twisted around, it had disappeared. Jed was edging forward painfully slowly, keeping his hands on the wall. Twice he stumbled, once as his foot dipped into a pool of stagnant water, the second as he kicked into a ridge of rock that rose up out of nowhere and caught him on the side. Both times, he had to bite his lip to stop himself swearing. Give yourself away and you're a dead man, he warned himself. Silence is your only friend in here.

As he recovered his balance, he pressed on. Each yard was a struggle, a battle against fear and distance. Never liked the dark, he thought. Too much like death. *You spend enough time staring that in the face in this line of work.*

Up ahead, Jed could see something. A light. He squinted through the darkness, and edged forward another dozen yards. The light was clearer now. He could see a guard, standing by himself. He'd propped up a powerful flashlight by his side which was throwing out an arc of light that stretched for fifty yards. As Jed inched along, careful to keep himself in the shadows, he could see that the tunnel opened up into a wide, broad cave. The stone was a dense, grey granite, streaked with black and purple traces. At points, it was no more than ten feet high, but at others it vaulted up to fifty feet or more. Right at the back, there was a stream running along its edge, a remnant of the underground river that must have cut the tunnels and caves into the mountain. Jed steadied himself, keeping his body pressed tight to the wall where the tunnel opened out into the cave. As he looked around, he couldn't see any sign of either Salek or Sarah, but he could see that behind the guard, there was another tunnel. And through that, another light was shining.

He took the Beretta from his pocket, and held it in the palm of his hand. He knew the gun was certainly capable of an accurate shot across the fifty yards that separated him from the man. One movement, however, and he would alert the man to his presence. An AK-47 was nestling in his ribcage. His finger was on the trigger. He looked fit and alert: no risk of this guy grabbing some kip while he was meant to be on duty. He knew a dozen of his mates had gone out to see what the trouble was, and he knew they hadn't come back. He was expecting trouble. As soon as Jed showed himself, the guy would start spraying the cave with bullets. The AK-47 might not be a precision weapon, but with that much lead flying through the cave, some of it was bound to hit the target.

One shot. That's all I'll get. *Miss it and I'll join the fossils in this cave.*

With one sudden movement, Jed leapt away from the

wall and started running. His right hand was straight out in front of him. Forty yards. The soldier looked up, saw the gun and took a second to react. Thirty yards. Jed levelled the pistol, looking through its sights and placing it so the bullet would strike just a fraction of an inch above the man's nose. Twenty yards. The soldier started to raise his own AK–47, his finger ready to slam down on the trigger.

Fifteen yards.

I can't miss from this distance.

Jed squeezed his finger tightly on to the trigger of the Beretta.

One shot.

Then another.

The bullet smashed into the man's face. He rolled back, shaking. The second bullet blew into his skull, splitting it open. He collapsed to the floor, dead.

Jed ran towards the back tunnel. He could hear movement. There was light from the soldier's torch, and he could see into the tunnel, and the cave beyond. People moving. Two, maybe three. Jed ran through the entrance to the tunnel, looking straight ahead of him. It stretched for thirty yards, with the stream running through it. He pushed on, his legs hammering against the rocky surface of the ground. He could hear voices, then a shout: the noise echoed through the stone, so that within seconds it sounded like a hundred voices were surrounding him.

As he reached the end of the tunnel, Jed glanced through the cave that confronted him. It was much smaller than the last one, just thirty feet in length and twenty wide, and there was a single torch in the corner, spreading a pale light over the grey rock. Right ahead of him, he could see a man, shrouded in a thick, green overcoat, starting to run into another tunnel. Salek, he thought. *It has to be.*

'Stop,' he shouted. 'Stop, you bastard, or I'll blow your bloody brains out.'

There was a woman at his side. About five foot six, dressed in a burka, which covered her face. Sarah, Jed told himself. It *must* be. The bastard has made her dress like a local. The man was starting to shove her towards the tunnel that led out of the cave. The woman tried to turn, but the man slapped her forward.

'Sarah,' shouted Jed. 'Sarah, it's me.'

He was standing still now, holding the Beretta in his outstretched hand. He pointed it straight ahead, but it was impossible to get a clean shot on the man's back without risking putting a bullet into the woman. 'Move aside, you bastard,' said Jed.

At his side he heard a noise. A soldier was lunging towards him, just a few feet away, the blade in his hand glinting in the pale light from the torch. How the hell did I miss you, Jed asked himself. He moved swiftly to the left, dodging the man's blow. He looked older than the rest of the soldiers. At least forty, with a few inches of fat around his waist, but his eyes were strong, and his expression determined. Jed spun round on his ankles, raising the Beretta straight in front of him, positioning the gun for a clean shot. He fired once, then again. One bullet pinged into the rock. The second blasted into the man's shoulder, punching a hole through the muscle and flesh. Blood was starting to stain his shirt, but there was plenty of fight in him yet. He roared, his lungs stretching with anger, and lunged forward with the knife again. Jed backed away, stumbling across rock, trying to keep his balance and stay out of range of the knife, and yet avoid turning his back on his attacker. Jed fired the Beretta twice more. One bullet went nowhere, but the other struck the man in the chest. Still he kept coming. Jed stepped back another yard, then another. The soldier made one last desperate lunge. The wounds were taking him apart, and he was coughing blood, choking on it as it foamed up in his mouth, but he still had enough momentum to carry himself forward. Jed stumbled, crashing to the floor, and in the next instant, the soldier was falling on top of him. The man was heavy, like a hod of bricks smashing down. His breath was stale, and there was blood dripping from his mouth. The impact knocked the Beretta from Jed's hand, sending it skidding across the wet rock towards the gushing stream.

Jed grunted, then heaved upwards. With one movement, he'd turned the man off him, so he was lying flat out on his back. He managed to retrieve his gun and hovered over the soldier. His eyes had closed, and although he was still just breathing, it was clear the fight was out of him. You'll be dead in a couple of minutes, mate, thought Jed grimly. No point in finishing you off. *It's a waste of a good bullet.*

As Jed glanced back up towards the tunnel, he could see the man and woman had escaped. 'Fuck it,' he muttered. 'They've gone.'

Moving fast, he grabbed the torch from the ground, and shone it into the tunnel down which they had disappeared. It stretched for a hundred yards, narrowing at one point to just a few feet, before twisting round a corner. There was no way of telling where it led.

One way to find out, Jed thought. *Throw yourself into it.*

He started running. The tunnel sloped uphill, stretching a hundred yards into the distance, and the stream was gushing down through the rock. He slowed to squeeze himself through the narrow passage, wading through two feet of water to do so. As he reached the corner, he darted around it, looking into another stretch of tunnel. Still no sign of them. The climb was getting steeper, and he had to use the rock to get a grip as he pushed ahead.

Where the hell are they, he asked himself as he flung himself up yet another turning.

Daylight.

About two hundred yards ahead, he could see a narrow crack in the rock. Sunlight was streaming through it, with a light that seemed sudden and dazzling after being incarcerated inside the mountain for the last ten minutes.

But still no sign of Salek. Or the woman.

Jed threw himself harder forward. Fifty yards passed, then another fifty. He was getting closer. As he drew up to the light, he gripped on to the side of the rock, and pulled himself up and out of the tunnel. The stream was coming into the mountain through this opening, and he had to move through the rushing water. His clothes were soaked, and his hair was matted and slicked against his head. It was bitterly cold and the icy water he'd just emerged from was still biting into his skin. But he was back on the mountainside. Looking around, he could see an expanse of rugged, grassy rock, with a waterfall where the stream originated about three hundred yards away. To his left, he could see Nick and Laura. To his right, maybe five hundred yards away, he could see Salek, dragging Sarah after him, running over the rough terrain.

He glanced back towards Nick and Laura, not sure how far his voice would carry against the stiff wind that was blowing down from the mountain. 'This way,' he yelled.

Turning, he started to run. The ground was heavy, and wet with dew, and his muscles felt punched and sore. But he was making good progress. Salek and Sarah were racing up the side of the mountain, but Jed could tell he was closing on them. Three hundred yards separated them now, he calculated. *Soon it will be two . . .*

'Sarah,' he yelled again.

The man glanced round, and Jed could see him clearly. He gripped on to the Beretta, but it was impossible to take a shot from this distance, and not risk hitting the woman he was still clinging on to.

What the hell is he running towards, Jed asked himself. *What's up there?*

Salek was moving up a steep incline, towards a formation of huge circular stones. Some kind of hiding place? Jed pushed himself harder. He was using his hands to grip the ground, to help lever himself upwards, but the cuts on his palms meant the dust and the gravel were starting to sting him. Salek disappeared briefly from view, vanishing into the thicket of stones. As Jed pulled himself up level with the rocks, he looked around wildly for any sign of them. Nothing. He listened. The wind was still blowing, rustling the tall grasses growing between the stones, but he could hear nothing else. No movement. No breathing. *Where the hell were they?*

The stones formed a rough semicircle. Some were as high as thirty feet tall, others just ten, but each one was at least six feet wide. There must be at least twenty of them, Jed reckoned. And each one big enough for a man to hide behind.

He started walking. The stones were twisted into strange, ugly shapes, some like animals, others like trees. A few seemed to be looking straight at you. Jed turned round. He felt certain he'd heard a noise behind him. An animal? No, it was louder than that. A person. From behind the rock to his right. He gripped the Beretta tight into his hand, and broke into a run. As he approached the rock, he paused, leaning close into it, edging around its circumference. His finger was hovering nervously on the trigger of the gun. He could see a shadow moving across the ground, just five feet away from him. They were there, Jed felt certain of it. He looked at the shape of the shadow on the ground. Was it the man, or the woman? It was impossible to tell from here. *I'll just have to take my chances.*

Holding tightly on to the Beretta, he leapt away from

the rock. Salek was standing just a few feet from him. The woman had fled, and was hiding behind another rock twenty yards away. Jed looked into the man's eyes: they were cold and vengeful, the eyes of a murderer. Already he was moving, starting to turn and run the moment he saw Jed. A pistol was in his right hand, poised to fire. Jabbing the Beretta forward, Jed fired once, then again. The bullets rattled out of the gun. One struck against the rock, the other crashed into the side of Salek's chest. He rocked back on his heels, but although the wound was a bad one, he was staying on his feet.

Sod this gun, thought Jed. *I couldn't hit a pigeon in Trafalgar Square with this piece of crap.*

Salek's hand was still raised, his gun level and pointing straight ahead of him. Jed swerved, making himself a harder target to aim at as he readied the Beretta for another shot. In the next instant, he could hear the explosion as the bullet exploded through the air. He knew even in the fraction of a second after the trigger was squeezed that Salek's aim had been a good one. He could see the angle of the gun as it was fired, and even as he swerved backwards there was still no more than twenty yards separating the two men. Salek wasn't going to miss from there. *Not with an aim that was as true as that one.*

As time appeared to slow down, Jed steeled himself. He had taken a bullet once before, in his calf, and he knew that the pain didn't come at once. First the body numbed up, and you could feel nothing. It was as if you'd been jabbed by an anaesthetic. The nerves froze up. Almost immediately, the bleeding would start, and slowly, as the shock started to subside, you would start to feel again. *Then the pain would rage through you like a fire.*

The bullet smashed into his shoulder. Jed could feel the flesh being ripped open, and he realised with a tremor of cold fear that it had missed his heart by just a couple of inches. The shard of hot metal brushed against the bone of his shoulder blade, and then he could feel it punching a hole through his back and tearing out of his body. The impact of the blow knocked him to the ground, and as he fell the Beretta was knocked clean from his hand.

For a moment, Jed's eyes closed. His head was starting to spin in shock and consciousness was ebbing away from him. He'd crashed nastily to the ground, catching his spine on the rock, and every muscle in his back was screaming with pain. He could hear feet, running, shouts. Snap out it, he told himself. You're not bloody dead yet. *While there's life in you, there's still fight, man.*

His eyes snapped suddenly open. Salek was running towards him, the gun in his hand pointing straight at Jed. He fired once, but the bullet smashed into the ground a couple of feet from where Jed was lying on the ground. Desperately, Jed rolled over, reaching out for the Beretta. Just a few feet, he told himself. *With a gun in your hand, you're still in this game.*

Salek was now just ten yards from Jed. There was blood seeping from his chest, but he was strong enough to take the punishment and keep going. He closed down the distance separating the two men before Jed could summon up enough strength to grab the gun. With a sudden stamp, Salek slammed his foot down on Jed's wrist. 'Good of you to come all this way,' said Salek. 'I was planning to kill you back in England. This has saved me the trouble of a trip.'

The gun was five feet from Jed's face. It was a Viper Jaws pistol, with a sleek black handle and a polished steel barrel: the Viper was a Jordanian gun, designed by the American Widley Moore who created the legendary Widley pistol. It doesn't make any difference what pistol it is, thought Jed grimly. *Every bullet is the same when it's blasted its way into your skull.*

A shot rang out, its explosive noise echoing through the mountainside. Salek staggered backwards. A bullet had landed in his right shoulder, just a few inches from the existing wound. The impact of the blow had chewed up the flesh and bone: his arm was dangling from his shoulders by just a narrow thread of bleeding muscle, and if you looked closely, you could see right through to the bone.

'Zarba,' he cried. 'Zarba.'

He was swaying, struggling to hold his balance. His foot had been taken off Jed's wrist, but he was still holding on to his gun, switching it from his right to his left hand.

As Jed glanced around, he could see Nick running towards him. He was thirty yards away and limping badly, but he was closing in on them fast, his own Browning handgun gripped in his right hand. How he'd managed to hit Salek at a distance of almost fifty yards while he was running, Jed couldn't tell. Either it was a lucky shot. *Or else he was bloody good.*

As Nick covered the last few yards separating them, Jed rolled around, pushing himself the final few inches he needed to reach his own gun. His hand shot out, grabbing hold of the Beretta. Salek was looking at him, then back up towards Nick. There was a trickle of blood running down from his mouth, and his eyes were starting to glaze over. His left hand started to rise upwards, with the Viper still nestling in his palm. He was desperately trying to steady himself and to get some sort of an aim on Nick. He fired off one bullet, than another. Nick was swerving as he ran, making himself a harder target to pin down.

One bullet smashed uselessly into the ground. But the second winged his leg, just above the knee, ripping out a chunk of flesh like a snake taking a bite of its victim. Nick roared in agony, but kept moving, suppressing the pain, finding the reserves of strength within himself. He fired the gun, once, twice, then three times, the bullets punching through the air, hitting Salek in the chest, the neck and groin. In the same instant, Jed steadied his grip on his own Beretta, straightened his arm and squeezed the trigger hard. The first bullet missed, but he'd already adjusted his aim, and the second struck Salek in the left shoulder. The force of the impact knocked the Viper from his hand. Jed fired again, then again. Leave nothing to chance, he told himself. *Kill him once, then kill him again, just to make sure the bastard doesn't ever crawl back out of hell.*

Salek slumped to the ground, a torn and mangled corpse. His head crashed against the stone, splitting open, and as he closed his eyes, his breath had already stopped.

Nick glanced down at Jed. 'You OK?' he muttered.

Jed started to lever himself from the ground. The pain in his shoulder was murderous, like having a knife continuously twisted into his raw flesh. 'I've been better,' he said.

'We've all been bloody better, mate,' he snapped. 'Where's Sarah?'

Jed looked towards the next set of stones. The last time he'd seen her, she had been twenty or so yards away, hiding out of sight. During the fight with Salek, he'd lost track of her. If she had any sense, she'd have kept her head down, and stayed well clear of the bullets.

'Over there,' he said, nodding towards the stone.

He stumbled as he got to his feet. Nick grabbed hold of his arm, helping him to steady himself. His head was spinning, and his legs were weak: it was hard to keep his eyes open for more than a few seconds at a time. The Beretta fell from his grip, and used his hand to try and staunch the bleeding from his shoulder, but he was losing blood badly. He reckoned he'd lost at least a pint. Maybe two. That was enough to make a man lose consciousness. Another couple of pints and he'd be dead.

'You sure you're OK?' said Nick.

'I'm bloody fine,' said Jed.

They started walking. Jed pointed towards the thick rock, twisted like a giant tree stump, where he had last seen the women in the black burka. It was twenty yards, but both of them were so badly wounded, it was heavy going covering the distance. Nick was limping badly on his wounded leg, and there was fresh bleeding where he had taken the second bullet. They were inching forwards, propping each other up, but Jed could tell there wasn't much fight left in them. Their number was about to be called. Let's just hope we can find Sarah first.

'Sarah,' Nick shouted. 'Sarah.'

No answer.

Only silence.

Jed pushed himself forwards, fighting to control the pain. Just another ten yards. He took a deep breath, trying to get as much oxygen into his lungs as possible. The wind was blowing down harder from the mountain now, whipping around his body. He was starting to shiver: with less blood in his veins, he had less to protect him from the cold. There were patches of ice and snow covering the rock, and Jed was taking each step carefully, grimly aware that one slip in his current condition could well prove fatal. Stay upright, and you'll stay alive, he told himself, through gritted teeth. *For long enough anyway.*

He approached the rock. It was at least fifteen feet tall, and a dozen wide: a huge, ugly slab of granite that twisted and curled in on itself. Nick let go of him, and started to walk to the left. Jed rested one arm on the rock, using it to help hold himself up, and walked slowly to the right.

The woman was standing stock-still behind it. She was dressed completely in black, with a burka covering her face. It was as if she'd been frozen in ice. Petrified, thought Jed. She's so scared, her muscles have seized up. 'Sarah,' he whispered quietly, his words carried on the gusts of wind blowing up behind him. 'It's OK, it's us.'

Nothing.

She remained silent.

'Sarah,' said Nick from the other side.

Nothing.

Nick's expression changed. 'Sarah?' he repeated. His voice was rougher this time.

The woman started to flinch.

Nick reached out, and lifted the burka away from her face.

She was about thirty, with dark, delicate skin, and round eyes that appeared smudged with tears. Her skin was dark and flawless, her hands smooth. She looked up at the two men, with tears in her eyes. Her lips were trembling, and her hands were shaking with fear.

'Who the hell are you?' Nick snarled.

She shook her head, baffled, with the look of a woman who hadn't even understood the question.

'Who are you?'

His voice was louder, more aggressive this time. He reached out for her shoulder, shaking her. She drew away, leaning against the stone, and started to say something in Arabic. The words tumbled out of her, accompanied by tears streaming down her face. 'Leave it,' snapped Jed. 'It's not bloody her, is it?'

'Then where the hell is she?'

Nick looked straight into the woman's eyes. 'Where is she?' he shouted. 'Where's my daughter?'

478

THIRTY-FIVE

Jed could feel his head spinning. He was clutching the side of the rock to stop himself from tipping over, and his left hand was trying to keep a grip on his shoulder to stop it from bleeding too much. No matter how much he tried, he could neither focus nor concentrate. He could hear Nick shouting at the woman, but the sound was fading in and out. Only one thought kept repeating in his mind, like a tape stuck in a loop: Sarah's not here, Sarah's not here.

We've come all this way, risked everything, and we still haven't found her.

Behind him, Laura was running up the mountainside, approaching the circle of rocks. She arrived panting, her face covered in sweat and dust. 'It looks like a butcher's shop down there,' she said. 'What the hell's happening?'

'There's no sign of Sarah,' said Nick, pointing towards the terrified Iraqi woman.

Jed noticed the hint of despair that had crept into his voice.

'This is the woman Salek was protecting,' he said pointing towards the woman. 'And now the bastard is dead, so we can't even ask him where she is.' He ground his fists together. 'We've bloody blown it.'

Laura stepped up to the woman, gripping hold of her shoulders, and shaking her violently. 'You speak English?' she snapped.

The woman cried, and mumbled something in Arabic.

'The Englishwoman,' said Laura. 'Where is the Englishwoman?'

She shook her head, scrunching her hands into her tear-smudged eyes. '*Ibna*,' she whispered, tears streaming down her cheeks. '*Ibna*.'

'It's his daughter,' said Jed, recognising the word from his Arabic lessons with the Regiment.

'This is bloody useless,' said Laura. 'We're getting nowhere.'

'It's finished,' said Nick. 'We've bloody failed.'

'She must be here somewhere,' said Laura angrily. 'She was with Salek. I *know* she was.'

Nick spread his hands out wide. 'Do you bloody see her then . . . ?'

Jed slid down the rock. He needed to sit, to try and preserve his strength. His eyes closed, trying to rest for a brief second. If we are going to find Sarah now, we'll need all the strength we possess, he thought. *Maybe more.*

'We can't get any backup out here,' said Laura. 'You guys will have to beat the information out of the bitch.'

Nick waved a hand at her. 'She doesn't bloody know anything,' he said. 'And we're soldiers, not sodding gangsters.'

He turned away, his face reddening with anger. Laura

was saying something, her voice hoarse and raw, but although Jed was listening to her, he was watching Nick. He was just looking at the mountain ahead of them, not as a soldier might, studying it for hiding places and defensive positions, but looking instead at the shape of it, the way a geographer might. There was a strangely detached expression on his face, as if he was trying to figure out the answer to a riddle.

But what is it? Jed asked himself. *What the hell has he seen?*

He cast his eyes up towards the mountains. From where they were sitting, the next peak seemed to soar above them, rising another hundred feet or so into the air. There were some low-lying clouds, and the ground was covered with snow. There was a dip on the left-hand side of the mountain, where the rock seemed to fade into the cloud to create a shape like a crescent. But beyond that, Jed could see nothing. Just a barren empty stretch of rock, capped by a dusting of pure white snow.

'She's up there,' said Nick suddenly, pointing towards the dip in the mountain. 'Right there.'

'Where?' said Jed.

'Right there,' said Nick, pointing towards the crescent.

'What makes you think that?' said Laura.

Nick paused. His expression was calm and determined. 'She's my daughter, I just know,' he replied.

Jed started to pull himself up from the ground. He could feel the strain in his legs, and his spine was creaking as he tried to move. 'I'm coming with you,' he said.

Nick looked at him. 'You can't move,' he said. 'You've taken a bad wound, mate. Rest it, and there's a chance the doctors will get that lead out of your shoulder and patch you up.'

'I'm coming,' Jed snapped.

If Sarah was up there, he was determined to find her. *I can't lose her now . . .*

Nick knelt down, gritting his teeth to control the pain in his own wounded leg. 'Leave it,' he said quietly. 'I'll go.'

'You're in no better state than me,' said Jed.

'Listen, there are moments when even the best of men walk away from a fight, and moments when they walk straight into one,' said Nick. 'When you get to my age, you realise that. If you get to my age . . .'

He turned round, struggling to power himself forward. His wounded leg was hurting badly, and each step was visibly agonising.

Jed tried to stand, determined to follow him. But his head was too dizzy, his eyes were closing, and it was impossible to focus. As his eyes shut, he could see Laura taking out a satellite phone and starting to press its buttons.

Nick looked up towards the dip into the mountain. It was only another hundred yards or so. He could clearly see an opening that must lead into another network of caves. Up here, there was at least a foot of snow covering the ground: hard, thick snow that had settled on these mountains last autumn and was turning into blocks of solid ice now that spring was almost here.

As he glanced back, he could see flecks of crimson spreading out across the pristine white surface of the ground. My own blood, he thought grimly. I must have lost at least a pint of it climbing up here. *And I'll shed the other seven if I need to.*

Laura was about twenty yards behind him. Even without any wounds, she was still finding the going harder than he was. In the Regiment, Nick had led several courses in snow and mountain fighting, and he'd done a year in the Alps as a ski instructor before the business fell apart. He knew more than most men about how you ploughed your way across heavy snow: Laura was just an amateur. *If she thinks you can just walk up this mountain, she has a lot to learn.*

Nick turned round and gritted his teeth. The pain ripping through him was excruciating. Every step required a new effort of will: each one sent a fresh bolt of pain jabbing up through him, as if he was walking across burning-hot coals. He could feel his leg turning rotten as he pressed on. He'd found a broken branch from one of the few trees that managed to grow this high up, and had turned that into a rough staff, using it to take some of the weight off his leg as he dragged himself painfully forwards. But you didn't need to know much about medicine to know that putting this kind of pressure on a leg that had taken as much punishment as this one had was precisely the wrong thing to be doing. Jed was right. He was only making it worse. The chances of saving the leg now were less than zero.

Fifty yards. He could see the entrance more clearly

now. The side of the mountain suddenly opened up, revealing a cave at least thirty feet long. Ice and snow were hanging over its roof, spitting down in a row of frozen spears. Inside, however, it looked like it provided some shelter from the weather. The resemblance was uncanny, thought Nick, summoning up the willpower to crunch his leg down into the snow again. His mind was drifting back more than ten years, to when he'd been walking through the Alps with Sarah, to when they'd had an argument, she'd tried to run away from him, and he'd pointed out the slopes of Les Houches to her. I told her somewhere just like this was a good place to hide. If she's anywhere on these mountains, she's right here. *I just know it.*

He stood at the entrance to the cave, peering into the darkness. The wind was blowing hard, kicking up a dusting of snow that partially obscured his vision. The cold was cutting into his skin, biting away at his shattered nerves as if he was being sliced open by a knife. 'Sarah,' he said. 'Sarah.'

His lungs were so short of air, it was painful just to speak. As he parted his lips, it felt as if part of his neck was being ripped out of him. The sound of his voice echoed around the cave, then gradually faded away, until it was replaced by silence.

Nick listened and waited.

Nothing.

'Silver girl,' he said.

Silence.

'Silver girl,' he repeated, louder this time.

484

'Dad.'

Nick's head shot up so sharply it was as if a bullet had struck it. He was looking straight into the cave. The voice was faint and weak, like a wounded animal, but he was certain he had heard it accurately. Maybe twenty yards, maybe thirty, from the right-hand side of the cave. It sounded as if something was muffling the voice, but it just about carried on the wind.

'Dad,' she repeated, the voice stronger this time. 'Is that you?'

If Nick could have run he would have, but the wound in his leg made it impossible. Using his staff, he dragged himself forwards, ignoring the pain searing through him. He took a torch from his kitbag, and shone it around the cave. It was no more than twelve feet high, with frozen ice on the ceiling, and shards of rock sticking out in every direction. Off to the right, there was a heap of boulders that appeared to have tumbled out of the mountain in a rockslide. That was where the voice was coming from, he felt certain of it. Holding the torch in one hand, and the staff in the other, Nick closed down the distance. 'Are you OK?' he shouted through the darkness, listening as his own voice echoed through the cave.

Of course not, he told himself. *Nobody would be up here if they were OK.*

Resting his staff on the first boulder, Nick looked behind the pile of tumbled rocks. As soon as they laid eyes on one another, Sarah smiled and started to lever herself up. She looked thin, Nick noted, desperately thin, like a skeleton that had come back to life. Her eyes were bloodshot, and she was wearing just some battered jeans, and a T-shirt. Her skin was frozen blue, and her veins were visible through her skin. None of that matters now, Nick told himself, the relief flooding through him. She's alive. She's OK. *We've made it.*

He knelt down, scooping her up into his chest, and cradling her the way he had when she was a baby. There were tears streaming down her face, and her body was shaking from the cold. 'I'm . . . I'm thirsty,' she said, her voice fractured.

Nick cradled her in his arms. 'Of course you are,' he said. 'Everything's going to be OK now.'

He reached into his kitbag, and took out a packet of biscuits, some dates and a bottle of water. Sarah took the water, and splashed it into her mouth, gulping down on it. How long it had been since she'd had anything to drink Nick couldn't say, but she looked badly dehydrated and the cold would have only made that worse. He cautioned her to sip slowly: too much water could damage you when you'd had nothing to drink for a long time. Next, she took one of the biscuits, stuffing it into her mouth. Her lips were still so dry and cold, and she choked before she managed to swallow any of the food.

In his arms, she was still shivering, and her face was still smudged with tears. 'It's fine,' said Nick, holding her close to his chest. 'Dad's here now. It's just fine.'

Slowly Sarah started to draw away from him. Her head lifted from his chest, and she was looking straight past him. Her eyes were locked right above his shoulder. And the look of fear had returned.

'What the fuck is she doing here?' said Sarah.

Nick turned round. Laura was standing right behind him. The Beretta was held steady in her hand. And it was pointed straight at Sarah.

'I said, what the fuck is she doing here?' Sarah's voice was louder this time.

'I would have thought that was obvious,' said Laura. 'I've come to get you.'

487

THIRTY-SIX

For a moment Nick remained perfectly still, as if he were one of the shards of ice hanging from the sides of the cave. Laura was standing five feet behind him, with the Beretta rock steady in her hand: she was far enough away that Nick couldn't reach out and strike the gun out of her hand, but close enough that she couldn't possibly miss Sarah's head if she fired the gun.

'Move away,' she said coldly, glancing towards Nick. 'And give me your gun.'

He started to rise up. The wound in his leg was still bleeding, sending droplets of blood on to the icy stone. Reluctantly, he took out his own revolver, and handed it across. Laura motioned with the gun for him to step away from the boulder. He walked slowly, measuring each pace. Behind him, Laura had motioned to Sarah to stand up. All three of them were standing close to the entrance to the mountain.

'Did you find it?' said Laura.

She had her back to the mountain, and the light was streaming in behind her. Sarah was standing six feet away from her, and Nick five further on. Both of them were looking out on the open mountain, where a rising gale was blowing up flurries of snow. Just wait until you can make your move, Nick cautioned himself. You can kill her then. *You haven't come all this way just to see Sarah shot now.*

The Beretta was still pointed straight at his daughter's head.

'You sent me into hell,' she snapped.

The anger and venom were evident in her voice. Nick looked first at his daughter, than at Laura. It was obvious that the two women knew each other, might even have worked together. 'What the hell is going on here?' he said.

Both women ignored him.

'I've already asked you once,' said Laura. 'Did you find it?'

'That science is for everyone,' said Sarah.

Laura gave a curt shake of her head. 'The Firm is about to take possession of it,' she said.

'Nobody can own that science,' said Sarah.

She was standing her ground, but her hands were shaking. Laura walked towards her, one careful pace after another, still pointing the gun. She stood by Sarah's side. Suddenly, her left hand snapped upwards, grabbing Sarah's hair and yanking it back. In the same moment, she stabbed the Beretta into the side of Sarah's face, so that its barrel was aiming straight into her ear. Nick started to move, taking one step forward, then another. His eyes locked on to Laura's, and he could feel the venom in her expression. 'Back off,' she said. 'Or this bullet goes straight into your daughter's brain.'

Nick stopped. He was five paces away from Sarah, but

he didn't dare take another step. Laura's finger was hovering on the trigger. He could smell how nervous she was. One sudden movement and she was going to kill Sarah. He felt certain of it. A sense of dread wrapped around his heart as he realised how slender was the thread on which his daughter's life was hanging. Don't mess this up, he warned himself. *Just for once, don't mess this up.*

'What's happening here?' he said, his voice firm and insistent.

'She set me up,' said Sarah. She was struggling to speak, with her head still wrenched backwards.

'Is that true?' he said to Laura.

'A month ago, it became clear that the Iraqis were close to cracking a working technology for nuclear fusion,' said Laura. She was pronouncing the words clearly and slowly, and yet Nick could hear the fear on her lips. 'Jed brought us some pictures back from the plant that showed they were creating a working reactor. We knew we couldn't let that happen. It would de-stabilise all the plans for the invasion. So we worked out a way of stopping it. We already knew that Sarah was working on fusion technology, because we keep tabs on all the science going on around the country that might have political or economic significance. We knew that Wilmington was already working with the Iraqis. Indeed, a lot of the information that allowed them to construct their lab had come from him. So we paid Sarah a hundred thousand pounds to cooperate with us.'

'The money in her account came from Iraq,' Nick muttered.

Laura shook her head. There was a bead of sweat dripping off her forehead, but her expression was still icy. 'We arranged for it to pass through those bank accounts, so that it looked that way. The Firm doesn't want to be seen to be handing out a hundred thousand to just anyone.' She paused, relaxing her grip on Sarah's hair, but keeping the Beretta tight to her head. 'In return, Sarah agreed to act as if she had cracked the secret of nuclear fusion. Wilmington would tell the Iraqis, we felt certain of that. They would lift her out of the country, and take her to their labs. That way she would find out what they were working on. Afterwards, it became clear they were closer than they imagined: they had about 90 per cent of the puzzle solved, and Sarah would give them the last 10 per cent. So the lab had to be hit, taken out.'

Laura hesitated, as if even she was embarrassed by the duplicity of the conspiracy within which Sarah had been ensnared. Outside, Nick could see that the storm blowing down the side of the mountain was getting worse: howling gusts of wind were sending drifts of snow swirling up around the entrance to the cave. Behind Laura, there was just a twisted wall of white. We're about as cut off from civilisation as it is possible to get, Nick thought grimly. And rightly so. *Civilisation has long since abandoned us.*

'But Sarah escaped from the lab before it was hit, and we could only assume that the Iraqis were desperate to keep hold of her, because putting together what they knew with what she knew meant they would finally have the technology they wanted,' continued Laura. 'So we sent Nick and Jed into the country as the two men most likely to find her. I must say that part of the operation worked rather well.'

'You never said you'd send me into Iraq,' said Sarah.

Laura smiled briefly. 'Of course not,' she said. 'If I had done, you'd never have played along.' She tapped the barrel of the Beretta against the side of Sarah's head. 'We are all called upon to make sacrifices for our country sometimes, as your father could probably tell you.'

'You lied from the start.'

'What did you think this was, the Girl Guides?' Laura shrugged. 'Now, have you and the Iraqis finally cracked the technology of nuclear fusion?'

A look of defiance descended upon Sarah's face. Nick recognised it at once. He had seen it more times than he cared to remember when she was a teenager. Her eyes would narrow and her jaw would harden, and you knew at once you had more chance of squeezing orange juice from a brick than getting her to change her mind.

'I wouldn't tell you even if I had,' said Sarah, the disgust dripping out of every vowel in the sentence.

'We had a deal,' said Laura. Once again, she tapped the barrel of her gun against the side of Sarah's head. Each time she did it, Nick could feel a stab in his heart. He wanted to run out and rescue her, but he had to will himself to hold back.

'Now tell me,' Laura snapped.

'Fuck off,' Sarah snapped back.

Easy, girl, Nick thought through gritted teeth. *Easy* . . .

Laura glanced at Nick. 'Tell her to be sensible,' she snarled. 'Tell her to talk to me.'

Nick remained silent.

'Tell her to talk to me.' Laura's voice was echoing around the cave, louder even than the noise of the storm howling outside.

Nick didn't move. He was hardly even breathing. On Laura's face, he could see the anxiety mounting. She could threaten them all she liked. But could she break them? *That was a difficult call to make.*

'You've failed your country once before, Nick,' said Laura. 'Don't do it again. Tell her to tell me everything she knows. She'll listen to you.'

She's talking too quickly, thought Nick. And too much. That's always the sign of somebody who is getting nervous. He knelt down, and picked up a shard of rock from the ground. It was just over a foot long, shaped like a knife, with a serrated edge and a sharp, deadly tip where it had been sliced away from the side of the mountain. A caveman would know how to use this to split open a skull, he decided grimly. *And so do I.*

'Stay quiet,' he said to Sarah. His voice was quiet and determined. 'I'll deal with her.'

Nick took one pace forward. The rock was in his right hand, his fingers curled around its base. 'You kill her, and I'll break open your head with this rock in the same instant,' he said, looking at Laura. 'Trust me, it will be a slow and painful death.'

Laura looked at him, at first nervously, but then with growing confidence. Nick could detect the condescension

493

flashing across her lips as they curled into a smile. 'And your daughter will still be dead. And it'll be your fault – just like her mother's death.'

The words stung, but Nick brushed the insult aside. 'Really,' he said. 'That's some gamble you're taking.'

The smile on her lips vanished. With her fingers twitching Laura yanked harder on Sarah's hair, and moved the Beretta down a fraction of an inch, so that it was pressed into the side of her cheek, pointing upwards. A bullet fired from there, Nick judged, was going to travel right through the centre of the skull and lodge itself in the brain. Nobody could survive a shot like that. Nobody.

That's some gamble I'm taking as well, he thought grimly, gripping his fist so tight on the rock in his hand he suspected it was about to pierce his skin.

'I'll do it,' said Laura. 'I'm giving you five seconds to get her talking. Or else she's dead.'

'One . . .'

Nick took another pace forward, leaving just three yards between him and the spot where both women were standing.

'Two . . .'

Nick paused, judging the speed and trajectory he would need to travel to knock the gun from her hand with the stone before she fired. *If only I wasn't bloody wounded . . .*

'Three . . .'

'Dad,' Sarah shouted.

There was a thread of fear in her voice that Nick had never heard before, not even when she was a little girl. It was the voice of a woman who realised she was about to die.

'Four . . .'

Nick hovered menacingly three yards away, the rock poised in his hand. There is nothing worse than your child dying before you do, he thought. I couldn't live with that. *I won't* . . .

'OK, you talk right now, or I'll fucking execute you,' Laura snarled.

'Hold it right there,' said Jed.

Nick glanced up. Through the swirls of snow, Jed had suddenly emerged. His hair and clothes were dusted with snow and ice, and there was still blood dripping from his wounded shoulder. The wind was blowing around him, and the skin on his face and his hands looked ragged and blue. He was standing right in the entrance to the cave, just ten yards behind where Laura was holding on to Sarah.

'Let her go,' said Jed.

In his hand was Salek's Viper. It was held out in front of him, pointing straight at Laura's head. Yet, Nick noted, it was in his left hand. His right hand was too badly damaged from the punishment his shoulder had taken to hold a gun straight. But Jed is right-handed, Nick reminded himself. Not many men can shoot equally well with both hands.

Laura glanced round. She was still holding on to Sarah's hair, and the Beretta was still nestling in her cheek. 'Get out of here,' she said. 'This is nothing to do with you.'

'Let her go,' Jed repeated.

'You'll face a court martial,' Laura snapped.

'I said, let her go.' Jed's voice was clear, almost monotonous and drained of emotion, as if it was a robot speaking.

'Tell her to talk to me, Jed.' Her voice was becoming anxious. 'Then we can all get out here.'

'You want to talk to her?' said Jed, glancing towards Sarah.

'I'm not telling her anything,' said Sarah.

Jed looked back at Laura. 'I've got a clear shot from here,' he said slowly. 'If you don't let her go right now, then I'll shoot you. Your choice.'

'And I'll shoot her,' Laura snapped, yanking harder on Sarah's hair.

Jed glanced towards Nick. 'I can drop her from here,' he said. 'Want me to squeeze the trigger?'

Nick looked at the distance between them. He'd spent half his life judging the trajectory of bullets, but this calculation was impossible. Whether the bullet would take Laura down before she had a chance to fire her own gun it was impossible to say from here. You had to be standing behind the gun. *You had to be the man squeezing the trigger.*

'You good enough?' he growled.

'Dad, he's good enough,' said Sarah.

'You good enough?' Nick repeated, looking straight at Jed.

There was a moment's hesitation, just long enough for Jed to target the Viper perfectly in line with the top of Laura's skull, but not long enough for any flickers of doubt to start clouding his vision.

Jed gave a curt nod of his head.

'You've trained with a Viper?' said Nick.

Jed shook his head.

'You've trained to shoot with your left hand?'

Jed shook his head again.

'But you still reckon you're good enough?'

Jed nodded.

'Then drop her,' snapped Nick.

Summoning all his concentration, Jed positioned the sights on the Viper with the back of Laura's head. He knew he had to hit the medulla oblongata, a tiny portion of the brain about the size of an egg that rested right on top of the spinal cord and controlled the central nervous system. Sever that, and the victim would no longer be able to control movement of any of their limbs, even if they were still alive. It was protected by a thick layer of bone, one of the toughest in the whole body, but it could still be penetrated by a bullet that came in with precisely the right force and velocity. Just eight yards, he told himself, as he felt a drop of cold sweat slither down the back of his spine. *You can't miss. You really can't miss . . .*

The bullet exploded from the barrel of the Viper. It crashed into Laura's spine, ripping through the flesh and up into the brain. In the same instant, Nick flung himself forwards. It was too late for him to do anything. The bullet had already proved true. Laura had lost control of her body the moment the bullet struck, and the Beretta had already dropped from her hand, crashing down on to the hard stone.

Sarah flung herself into her approaching father's arms. He caught her and cradled her to his chest, as Laura fell to the ground behind her. 'It's OK,' he said, holding her close to him. 'It's all over now.'

Jed closed the yards that now separated him from the spot where Laura had fallen. Even though he was still weak and half frozen from crawling up the mountain, he could feel the relief flooding through him. *If I live to a hundred, I never want to have to take another shot like that.*

He bent down. Laura's eyes were still open, and there was still breath on her lips. Her heart was still beating, but with her central nervous system out she wouldn't last more than a few minutes. Put her out of her misery, Jed told himself grimly. Leaning closer just a fraction of an inch, he squeezed on the trigger of the Viper. Two bullets smashed through the front of her skull, her head turned to one side and a trickle of blood seeped out of the corner of her mouth.

Nick looked at Jed. 'I can't believe you never trained to shoot left-handed,' he said. 'Bloody waste of space the Regiment these days, doesn't teach a guy anything.' Then he broke into a smile.

'Maybe I got lucky,' said Jed.

Nick shook his head. 'Men get lucky in the bookie's, and sometimes in a nightclub,' he said. 'But there's no such thing as a lucky shot. You've either got what it takes or you haven't.'

He let go of Sarah and she looked at Jed and smiled. Instinctively she fell into his arms, and for a moment Jed just rested on her shoulder. He could feel her warmth, and smell her familiar smell. His eyes closed. The pain in his shoulder was still burning, and as the numbness of the wound started to wear off, he could feel the hole burning his flesh every time he moved. None of that matters, he told himself. The pain will fade in time. So long as I'm in her arms.

'Christ, you're bleeding,' said Sarah. 'We've got to get you out of here.'

'I'll be fine,' said Jed through gritted teeth.

The three of them started to walk from the cave. The wind was still howling off the mountainside, and snow flurries were kicking up through the air. Looking down, Jed could see the weather had cleared down in the valley, but they had an hour's hard walking through the snow before they got there.

'Where in the name of Christ do we go now?' said Sarah.

'Just bear east,' said Nick. 'It a long walk, and we're in no state for it, I'll admit that, but if we keep heading east we'll hit Turkey. We'll be safe there.'

'Bollocks,' snapped Jed. 'We could be across into Syria in two days. We head west.'

'Syria?' said Nick. 'I'm not setting foot in that hell-hole. They'll throw us straight into their dungeons.'

'And we'll die trying to get into Turkey,' said Jed.

Sarah raised her hands. 'Guys, just stop arguing,' she said. '*Please . . .*'

EPILOGUE

3 December 2003.
Jed glanced nervously up at Nick. A lot of guys might feel a bit edgy about the father of the bride's speech, he thought, as he took another sip on his glass of wine. *But probably not as nervous as I do. There's no way of telling what the old sod might say.*

'May I just begin by thanking you all for being here today, the caterers for laying on such a magnificent spread, and particularly Jed's mother Debbie for helping out so much on all the preparations,' Nick began.

Nick looked uncomfortable in the morning suit he'd hired for the occasion. He'd already had a couple of glasses of wine, and although he might have been famous for holding his drink in his day, he'd kept himself on the wagon so long you could no longer be sure he knew how to handle his alcohol. He was standing slightly uneasily, no doubt partly the result of the false leg he'd had fitted: after walking for so long on the badly wounded thigh, the doctors had had no choice but to amputate it when they'd finally made their way back to an American military base in Turkey. He'd known all along he was going to lose the leg, Jed had realised at the time, and not complained once: that alone was a testament to the strength of the guy.

'As I watched Sarah standing there, saying "I do", I noticed the easy and calm way she pronounced the words, and I thought, that's the first time she's ever agreed with anything a man said to her . . . and it'll probably be the last as well.'

Jed joined in the ripple of laughter running around the room. He glanced at Sarah, watched her looking lovingly up at her father, and smiled. It was good to see her looking so happy. Since their return from Iraq, she'd been resting for a few months, getting her health and strength back, and would be going back to Cambridge in the new year to start her work again. And he'd be starting a new job in the City: he'd resigned from the Regiment, and found that a combination of an engineering degree from Cambridge and a couple of years in the SAS were a good enough CV to land him a job in banking. At least he'd be earning proper money, and he wouldn't have anybody shooting at him. There was still some damage to the shoulder bone where he'd taken the bullet, but the doctors said he should make a full recovery. I'm lucky even to be here today, he thought. *We all are.*

'One thing I always told Sarah as a little girl was never marry a soldier,' said Nick. 'They drink too much, they don't make enough money, and they don't come home to their families very often. Sometimes ever . . .'

He paused to take a sip on his glass of wine, and looked around the room. There were about a hundred people there, some family, some mutual friends they had grown up with around the area, and a few of Jed's mates from the Regiment. 'She ignored me, of course, just like she ignored pretty much everything I've ever advised her on. Sarah has always known her own mind. She decides what she wants, and then she goes out and gets it. Nothing is ever allowed to stand in her way, as I think Jed will probably discover during the course of what I hope will be a long and happy life together.

'But if she was going to marry a soldier, I couldn't have asked for her to marry a better one than Jed. As some of you know, I've been there and I've seen him in action. He's brave, determined, fearless . . . and he's going to have to be all of those things to put up with Sarah's driving.

'I couldn't have asked for a better son-in-law,' he continued. 'Ladies and gentlemen, raise your glasses to Jed and Sarah.'

Christ, thought Jed. I've got away with that speech. *There's just the best man's speech to get through now.*

The car pulled away from the driveway of the hotel, and started heading back towards the main road. Jed had booked a suite for them at the Ston Easton Park hotel, and from there they were getting a flight from Bristol to Malaga in the morning for their honeymoon. Two weeks of relaxation. Sarah leant back into Jed's shoulder, a peaceful, and only slightly inebriated, smile on her face.

Jed kissed her lightly on the lips. 'You're looking good, Mrs Bradley,' he said.

'We'll have no fucking around in this car, please, you

bloody rat-faced nancy boy,' snarled a voice from the front seat.

Jed looked up from the back seat, startled. Jim Muir, the government's chief spin doctor who he argued with at the Firm, was sitting on the front passenger seat, looking straight back at him. Glancing into the mirror, he could see that the hired Bentley wasn't being driven by the chauffeur who'd been supplied by the rental firm, but by David Wragg, the deputy director of the Firm, and the man who had first sent Jed into Iraq. Looking ahead, he could see an unmarked Audi slowing down a few yards in front of them. Right behind, there was a Land Rover Discovery with at least four plain-clothes officers sitting in its front and back seats.

They've sandwiched us in, Jed thought. *There's no bloody escape . . .*

'Thought I'd forgotten about you two, did you?' said Muir. 'Well, let me tell you something, the government is like an elephant, and not just because we have fat, ugly, grey arses. We *never* forget.'

'How the hell did you get into this car?' Jed snapped, leaning forward.

'We're the Firm,' said Wragg, glancing back from the driver's seat. 'We can get anywhere.'

'And we can do anything we want, to anyone, anytime,' said Muir. 'You get my meaning . . .?'

'Don't threaten me,' said Jed.

'I'll threaten anyone I fucking well please, nancy boy.'

Jed leant back in the seat, looking ahead. The car was already heading across country. It was just after eleven at night, and there wasn't any traffic around. Muir was right. They could do anything they want. *And they probably would . . .*

'Who are they, Jed?' said Sarah.

Her voice sounded fragile, nervous. In the nine months since they'd been back from Iraq, they'd talked about the consequences of what they'd learnt in that country. Jed had always supposed there would be a reckoning one day, but as the months passed by, and as he was allowed to quietly leave the Regiment and look for new work, he was starting to wonder if it hadn't all drifted into the history books.

But your past always catches up with you, he thought. *Just ask Nick . . .*

'We're very bad people,' said Muir, looking straight at Sarah. 'And we're not about to go away.'

'It's the Firm,' said Jed. 'And the Scottish arsehole . . . well, he's the government, I suppose.'

'What do you want?' said Sarah to Muir.

'Nobody knows why we really invaded Iraq,' said Muir. 'And we intend to keep it that way.'

'You mean the secret of nuclear fusion.'

Muir nodded. 'Once he had you, Saddam had it, and we couldn't have allowed that. It would have made him too powerful. It would have destroyed the global oil industry. There were big forces at stake –'

'There still are,' Jed interrupted.

Muir shook his head. 'I'm not generally a man who makes deals, but I've got an offer for you,' he said. 'We don't like this technology –'

'It could change the world economy,' Sarah interrupted.

'Yeah, well, we like the world economy just the way it is, thank you very much,' said Muir. 'And we plan to keep it just the way it is, with the same people in charge. So, we'll make you an offer. You just go back to studying atoms or whatever it is you do in the lab, nancy boy here can make some money in the City, and shag you senseless every night, and everybody's going to be happy. But if we hear anything more about nuclear fusion, there's going to be an accident. And nobody will ever hear from you again.'

Wragg pulled the car to a sudden halt. 'It's the best deal you're going to get,' he said. 'Jim wanted us to kill you right now.'

'The bloody bed-wetters at the Firm talked me out of it . . .'

'I —'

Sarah was about to speak, but Jed had already grabbed hold of her hand. 'It's fine,' he said, his voice low and determined. 'We just want to get on with our lives. You'll never hear a thing about fusion again.' He paused. 'But I have made notes of all the science technology needed to build a cold-fusion reactor, and if I ever hear from you bastards again, then they'll be released to the world.'

Muir started climbing out of the car. Wragg was already walking down the side of the road towards the Audi that had pulled up in front of them. 'You're an evil bastard,' said Sarah, as Muir stepped out on to the dark road.

Muir shook his head ruefully. 'You want to watch the lip on that one, nancy boy,' he said, glancing at Jed. 'I might shag her if it was dark enough, but I wouldn't marry the cow. Couldn't stand the arguing . . .'

'Watch it,' muttered Jed.

He'd already slammed the door on the Bentley.

'How the fuck are we going to get to our hotel now?' Jed yelled out of the window.

Muir looked back at them. 'Ask the muffin,' he said, nodding towards Sarah. 'She's the bloody rocket scientist in the family.'

Sarah climbed over to the front seat of the car. The keys were still in the ignition. She fired up the engine, and the car purred into action. Glancing at Jed in the rear-view mirror, a smile started to flicker across her face. 'You know what,' she said. 'There's no technology. I wasn't even close to cracking nuclear fusion. And neither were the Iraqis.'